Also by Janet Frame

The Adaptable Man

JANET FRAME

A THE ADAPTABLE MAN

GEORGE BRAZILLER · *New York*

For information address the publisher:
George Braziller, Inc.
60 Madison Avenue
New York, NY 10010

Library of Congress Catalog Card Number: 65-19327
ISBN: 0-8076-1285-5

First paperback reprint edition, 1992

Printed in the United States of America

ACKNOWLEDGEMENTS

p. 144, from Stephen Spender, *Collected Poems 1928-1953*, "I think Continually of Those," copyright 1934 and renewed 1961 by Stephen Spender. Reprinted by permission of the publisher, Random House, Inc.

p. 145, from *The Collected Poems of Wilfred Owen*, "Exposure," copyright © 1963 by Chatto & Windus Ltd. Reprinted by permission of the publisher, New Directions, New York.

pp. 145-6, from Thom Gunn, *My Sad Captain*, © 1961 by Thom Gunn. Reprinted by permission of the publisher, The University of Chicago Press.

To R. H. C.

The Adaptable Man

PROLOGUE

A contemporary ingredient in the caldron world of the witch-novelist is a pilot's thumb. Yet the old mixture remains: entrails, toads got from beneath a stone, fashionable racial scapegoats (Shakespeare has "blaspheming Jews," "nose of Turk," "Tartar's lips"), souls and bodies strangled at birth; murderers, adulterers. Mix, and bring forth a prophecy.

The Heath is a lonely place. It's damp and cold; witches get rheumatism. Trees are crippled and will not, cannot walk. The journey to Dunsinane is more like a Whitsun traffic jam than the progress of a united army of trees and men.

Witches still have a tough constitution; there's a kind of unselfishness, detachment in their devilish cooking. They can't eat it themselves. What do they eat? Maybe they feed on each other. Life on a heath with thunder and lightning, mixing a caldron of uneatables for others to observe, admire, shrink from, is not much fun. But who wants fun?

The idea was to have a basin inverted on his head and his hair cut to the shape of it. Skill and money were not needed. Then the idea grew that it was more convenient to leave the basin on his head. Stray thoughts were trimmed along with stray hair; brain-vines, tentacles of thought, were not encouraged to wander. Then, in the interests of human economy, the head of adaptable man became a basin of uniform shape—a basin, a crash helmet. Safe at last; no more thought-cuts. Yet:

> *Oh why do I get that enclosed feeling*
> *Oh Why Oh why,*
> *I want to break out*
> *from my crash helmet, my crash helmet,*
> *to see it from the sky.*
>
> *I've a lonely uncut thought*
> *my crash helmet may become*

3

a light-filled tomb
a cathedral dome
of sparkling glass and porous two-way stone.

Therefore his mind again took individual shape. Man has a noble skull, fine bridges of bone. Light throbs in his head; signals, messages, pending outgoing received; now a terrible exposure of skin, like blue stained glass to the sky; the blows of accidental images and prayers.

Not much fun. But who wants fun?

The thought that he is not a migrating bird might make a man mad. Human beings have little to impel them from century to century. They fix a makeshift sun in the sky, and its flame burns or does not burn, but in its fierce or fading light they make their intention movements, retreats, advances, trying to release the buried memory of their destination. When the season, *their* season, is near, they journey alone or in twos and threes or in millions, all in different directions, colliding, confused, distracting one another with promises and dreams and false memories; cleaning the vegetation from the time in which they move, preying upon each other, leaving the scattered bones of the dead upon the exhausted years which so painfully put forth the new growth that is cultivated as history, uprooted, examined, preserved. Mass movements, migrations in time have been made by man pursuing or fleeing from an idea. He settles around the chosen idea. He breeds there. This everlasting movement back and forth in time without the stability and guidance of a visible world, recognized seasons, shared sun, is enough to make a man mad with the thought that he is not a migratory bird.

Trying to fly through the unlit centuries is not much fun. But who wants fun?

I, the Reverend Aisley Maude, late Vicar of St. Cuthbert's, sufferer from quiescent tuberculosis, widower, embarrassed by personal photography during which I woke one morning, made my usual morning adjustment to God, with my Christian faith set strongly behind me, and my human limitation protecting me from too obliterating a vision, only to find that the picture was blurred, that God had moved, that the steadfast landmark, feature of all my maps, routes, views, references, had become an unidentifiable shadow. Now, if you are photographing an ancient monument of stone, and the stone moves and the photograph is blurred, perhaps it is wise to tell no one. The stone may be unwilling or unable to confirm or deny your story. People may insist that it was you who moved and spoiled the picture—especially if your camera is the old-fashioned type where you need the sun powerfully behind you, yet you must still curl your palm jealously around your tiny private view in order to reduce the obliterating effect of the same sun's light. A cynic might have said that neither God nor I had moved; that what I needed was a new camera; that I had lived for too long using an obsolete instrument to capture my view of God, that I might undertake little research to discover if the formerly accepted mark (soul-mark, mind-mark) were indeed *God*. It might also have been suggested that the true shape of the famous stone monument resembled not so much an overwhelming mountain as a small, flat, round stone beneath which men, as insects, were imprisoned and suppressed; that this sudden movement of the stone might explain why my first feeling of shock was followed by an extraordinary sense of lightness, freedom; and that later, when I perceived, as insects and men may, the immensity of space and sky uncovered, I felt a sense of loneliness, of changed destination, of confusion in the face of so much exposed time racing unexplained, unharnessed, as wind and cloud; finally I was overcome by a desire to return beneath the stone.

I longed once more to set up the obsolete camera before the moss-covered monument of my Christian faith.

I, Reverend Aisley Maude, suddenly fashionable, but inwardly out of fashion, journeying the path of St. Cuthbert from the upstairs room of Clematis Cottage, Little Burgelstatham, where I cough and convalesce . . .

I, I, I . . .

I, Russell Maude, dentist, stamp-collector.

I, Alwyn Maude, university student, budding novelist opening swiftly under the influence of More-Grow Rich-Feed applied to my roots of experience.

I, Greta Maude, housewife, former nurse, cultivating the garden of Clematis Cottage, following the dictates of Maplestone's Chart, warring against green tip, petal fall, leaf miner; millipedes, peach-leaf curl, botrytis, gall mite, mealy bug, thrips, wasps, cutworm, carrot fly, leaf hoppers, clubroot, rats, mice, voles; my enemies catalogued, my defense provided in puffer-packs.

I, Jenny Sparling, university student, spending part of my night and day with Alwyn Maude, lightly loving him, but carrying a packet of salt not yet made into tears to capture him before he flies away or is caged and dies.

I, Vic Baldry, farmer, returned from my honeymoon in Australia, wearing my digger's hat, singing "Waltzing Matilda," dreaming of the Blue Mountains of Burke and Wills and the Desert.

I, Muriel Baldry, second wife to my second husband, trying to live in a vast quiet house, lighting my dreams with thoughts of the Venini chandelier in the attic, unused.

I, Ruby Unwin, farmer's widow, dreaming of my childhood in Stamford and Rutland.

I, Lex Unwin, milkman, needing plaster for my back, iodine for the slight wounds and scratches of daily encounters.

I, Dot Unwin, milkman's wife, needing a new dress to wear at my niece's wedding.

I, Bert Whattling, pensioner, gardener, member of the British Legion, breeder and seller of rabbits, geese, needing my native place to stand in.

I, Nelly, an old mongrel bitch with twisted back legs, heavy shoulders, a snarl for strangers.

I, Botti Julio, Italian farm worker, coming to Little Burgelstatham for six weeks to help with the black-currant harvest . . .

I, I, I, I, I, I. . . .

I, I, I, I, I, I. . . .

I, the earth, fairly submissive, my seasons arranged beforehand;

lifeless but hopeful of the overflowing conceit and concern of man which spill life and feeling into my shell. Man insists that I weep, groan, vomit, laugh; man reminds me that living is not much fun. But who wants fun?

I, I, I, I, I. . . .

PART ONE

These photographs are underexposed.
Please will you intensify them.

1 Little Burgelstatham is in that part of East Suffolk which provokes little comment from the traveler when his train stops briefly, and will soon not stop at all, at the clay-colored veranda-petticoated little station with its prize-winning beds of wallflowers and rock plants, and its stationmaster, shirt-sleeved, high-stooled in his office, surrounded by bicycles taken under his care and protection for the day while their owners travel north in the train to Tydd, the largest town within seven miles, owning a Woolworth's, two ironmongers, several seed shops, auction mart, a museum, a park, a square containing a statue of a maid who dared to say no to Charles the Second, emphasizing her refusal with the present to him of a poisoned boiled rotten egg.

How rural, how flat, how green, the travelers say, looking at Little Burgelstatham; but few stop here. They smile smugly through the window at the summer posters, *Clacton for You This Year*, while the diesel train gathers speed. (Diesel trains are so *clean*. Travel used to be a process which changed you into a human trace element. You arrived with soot clinging to your clothes and body or lodged in your eyes, so that your vision was never again the same; but now it's all so *clean*, and what a relief, for *traces* suggest possible guilt and discovery, and the human race is enough burdened with guilt to want to persist in suffering it on railway trains.) So the diesel train with its two-note cry rushes north to Norwich, and the gates across the line are closed once more and the stationmaster returns to the company of the bicycles.

Were you a traveler, you might think, There's nothing of interest in Little Burgelstatham except the cool promise of a leafy summer, and that is shared by every county. Yet if you are imaginative and curious enough, you will learn that Little Burgelstatham is in that part of Great Britain where the place-names are more memories than names—memories of water-well and ocean, of worship, government by *Things*. Ought one to be afraid, surrounded by a world-mass of *Things*, to learn the derivation of our enjoyment, menace, and master, how the *Thing* was the judicial and legislative assembly of the Scandinavian nations, how it met on an island, a promontory, was derived in its name from the Old Norse *tinga*, "to speak," and its etymological brother "to think." Discuss, judge, think, speak. You may wish you had stopped at Little Burgelstatham had you known you were surrounded by the preserved earliest dreams and activities of the human mind.

Say the names, then, to yourself.

Little Burgelstatham (a *burgel* was originally a burial place of the heathen). Tydd. Lakenthorpe. Murston. Segham. Colsea. Withigford. Say the names again and again, and soon there's no weetbox-colored railway station with bicycles in custody for the day, and an old man opening and shutting the railway gates to let the green clean train pass; there's no village store where postal orders lie beside giant free offers and round-necked vests and sou'westers, socks, biscuit; there's no Clematis Cottage where the Reverend Aisley Maude will stay in the upstairs room of his brother's home, listening through the night to the lovemaking of his nephew Alwyn and the guest Jenny Sparling, staring from the window to the garden where his brother's wife Greta wages war against thrip, leaf curl, and black fly; there's no decaying old farmhouse where Mrs. Ruby Unwin lives alone receiving each morning on his milk-round her dear son Lex and his wife Dot; nor is there the White House Farm where Vic Baldry dreams of Australia, and his wife Muriel dreams of the dust-covered Venini chandelier, legacy from an unknown relative, and of the day when main electricity is brought to the farm and the chandelier is hung in the sitting room; there's no black-currant farm where Reuben and Beatrice Sapley await the arrival of the Italian worker Botti Julio, whose contract was signed during their visit to Andorra; there's no church, no Approved School at Withigford, no dental rooms at Murston where Russell Maude pounds away at his National Health mortar; there's no library at Murston, no bank, post office, no people.

Little Burgelstatham. Tydd. Lakenthorpe. Murston. Segham.

Colsea. Withigford. Nothing but a dream of earliest praise, of sea-flooded inlets, lakes, marshes, sedge, willows, and those birds, half-hidden, which walk tall camouflaged as reeds, and sound, morning and evening, their lonely cries; water, birds, and now and again the soft rustle and wash and splash of the men, the South-folk, guiding their boats through the inland seas.

2 For five weeks there had been no rain. The earth was crumbled and dry, light-brown. Even at a depth of twelve inches or more there was no dark, soft, damp soil to provide moisture for the new crops. The leaves of the vegetables withered. Flocks of thirsty pigeons, blackbirds, sparrows swooped to pick the budding shoots of peas, beans, lettuces. From very early morning until late at night shots from the mechanical carbide bird-scarers rang from every farm. And in the center of almost every field of wheat, barley, sugar beet, in the apple and black-currant orchards, in the domestic gardens the grotesque race that is born each year in the countryside in spring and dies in autumn yet is never buried, now increased and flourished: a man-made shape of men from shabby tramps to surrealistic figures whose arms were wings of crimson aluminum foil, who turned lightly crackling in a wind-driven dance; men without bodies, with only crimson one-dimensional faces; one eye, one ear; whirling faster and faster to satisfy their deprived senses; men who glittered, whose flat bodies cracked like whips as they danced. The heads of some were bowed in prayer or snatched sleep; others leaned forward, straining to escape from their own spine—a stick cut from a hazel-hedge, a bamboo stake ridged with hollow vertebrae where the wind moaned its nervous message that was yet not interpreted or understood in the flat brainless crimson heads rolling and slapping idiot-like in the air. Birds, for whose peril and benefit the race had been bred—blackbirds, crows, pigeons—timid in the early spring and summer days, now perched unafraid on the arms of this outlandishly dressed ineffectual race who had no life but the wind's life.

At night, however, the scarecrows became more human; they seemed like banished people. They moved suddenly, rousing fear. They seemed to stalk with the cloud-shadows across the moonlit wheat. They crackled like thriving flames, as if they devoured their own poor dry skeletons. It is they who were watching, the night Botti Julio came to Little Burgelstatham, and walked alone, slowly, along the road toward Withigford and Bernard Sapley's farm. The few people who met him frowned and raised their eyebrows. The scarecrows crackled at him, in sparkling snickershot. He never saw the black-currant farm, for in the morning he was found and taken, dead, from the pond at the end of the lane.

3   He knew there was nothing to be afraid of. For years since he worked for the anti-Fascist Party in Italy and was imprisoned in the concentration camp in France, he had been a stateless person with no country wanting to own him, with an expired identity card kissed so repeatedly by so many thick oval dark-blue stamps that in the end his name had been almost obliterated by this regular official compulsory brand of attentive loving, the effect of which was not unlike that of human love, where identities are kissed almost to nothingness, yet return again and again for reassurance of their separate being. Now, after the qualifying three years in Andorra, Botti Julio had been granted citizenship. He had acted as guide in the mountains to Señor Sapley and his wife. He had been promised (and signed the papers for) summer work in England on the black-currant farm, and in the weeks of waiting, his friend Juan had been playing English-language records to him, to help him. Life was full of anticipated delights; there was nothing to be afraid of.

"El Botti," Juan said, "you will soon speak wonderful B.B.C. English."

Already Botti Julio could repeat and remember so many phrases and sentences. My tailor is rich. My tailor is not rich. I have my identity papers. I have been a worker in the vineyards and the mountains. I am Italian, a citizen of Andorra. I agree to work for three months on the fruit farm in England. I am expecting important news. Do I need to report to the local police station? I am single with black hair. I am forty years of age. I was born in Milan. Could you please weigh this chicken for me? I want a plain blue tie and a colored handkerchief to match. The telephone is out of order. I beg to inform you that my electric meter is not working. I want a lounge suit. I would like to take the children to the circus. These photographs are underexposed; please could you intensify them? A brace of partridges and two rabbits. The boxers are skipping in the gymnasium to strengthen

16

their legs. What time is it? It is foggy. What a pleasant surprise to see you! Wet paint. Danger. Stick no bills. Vacant. I was a prisoner of war. I am wounded, see I am bleeding, can you send for help?

Yet Botti envied Juan because Juan was emigrating to Canada, and when he found work there he would be sending for his wife and four *crios*, and they would live in the city where they spoke French; but Canada was cold, and Botti hated the cold, and in three months working on a fruit farm in England he might marry an English woman, he might be given permission to stay forever in England where, though the rain and the fog might be something to complain of, at least if you couldn't find work they *paid* you, and when you were wounded and your wounds were bleeding, and you asked someone in the street, "Can you send for help?" they did so at once. Also, Botti had heard that many Italians lived in England, therefore he would not be lonely, and when he tired of saying My tailor is rich, my tailor is not rich, and those other strange phrases which described the life and habits of an Englishman, he would go to his own countrymen, speak in swift Italian, drink wine, sit in the sun, wear smart clothes—a striped suit and two-toned shoes—buy a blue and white racing bicycle, a fast car, sleep with women, finding words other than my tailor is rich, my tailor is not rich, a brace of partridges and two pheasants, the telephone is out of order, I would like to take the children to the circus.

The mountains were covered with snow, and the somber pine trees on the slopes were burdened with it, and the blue and white violets growing along the mountain paths had no scent in the freezing air, and though it was time for the sheep to be driven home from France they were nowhere to be seen; the snowdrifts in the passes were still too deep. Sometimes, in a sudden war urge of spring weather, giant boulders, loosened from patches of melting snow, came crashing down the mountainsides, and at night the flooding river foamed and roared, washing high against the walls of the gray stone houses lining its banks. The interior of the house where Botti lived with Juan and Lola and the four *crios* was dimly lit, and sometimes, listening in the half-dark to the roar

of the avalanche and the water, Botti grew afraid, not of the
boulders or of the river or of the snow, but of the strangeness
of a nation inhabited by tailors, by so many people in Sunday
suits walking up and down the streets of London, with even their
heads stitched up so tightly that not a thought could get in of the
Andorran night, the river, the avalanche, Botti, Juan, Lola, the
four *crios*, the house, the rickety stairs to the third floor, the little
yellow heaps of cat-mess and child-mess in the corner on each
landing; Botti's room, his bicycle which he polished each day
while the *crios* watched, asking questions which Botti answered,
mischievously, in his new language: "The boxers are skipping in
the gymnasium to strengthen their legs. A brace of partridges and
two rabbits . . ." At such times Botti suddenly grew so afraid of
his journey to England that he almost canceled it; always,
though, morning came, there was a nasty taste in his mouth, the
children were slapped and crying, the *pesetas* in his pocket had
dwindled during the night, and he sat glumly eating his bread and
milk, longing for the train and the boat to take him to England.

"What is England like, El Botti?"

"It's a kind place, and I think it might be warm, like Italy.
There's plenty of food and money and work. You go out in the
sun and pick fruit and save many *pesetas*."

"Do people like us live in England? Do they speak like us?"

"They live just as we live, but they have more tailors, rich and
poor tailors, and they spend much time visiting their tailors for
pleasure, the way your mama goes to the films every Sunday
night while Papa waits on the tables in the tourist hotel. The
English have many tailors, many doctors, and their electric
meters do not always work, and sometimes," Botti said recklessly,
enjoying the puzzled frown of Xavier, Juan, Mella, "sometimes
their photographs are underexposed and must be intensified."

Botti was a hero. He sat laughing and talking in the café. His
friends envied him and wondered why Señor Sapley had chosen
Botti instead of them. The day Botti left Andorra he was given a
grand farewell. He sat in the bus, watching the snowplow clearing the path. The woman sitting next to him had a little dog
tucked under her fur coat; it wriggled and whined and seemed
like part of her breast, and Botti smiled, wanting to grab it. He

showed his white teeth. Hee hee. He spread his hands on his bony knees and looked at the two crusted sores, side by side, on his left wrist.

"You must be found medically fit," Señor Sapley had said. "Otherwise you won't be allowed entry. They try to keep out foreign workers who may be a burden on the state."

And when Botti, looking at him, had frowned, not thinking, as Señor Sapley supposed, Why, what does he mean, how can people decide whether they will be ill or mad, how can they prevent their grandfather from murdering someone when it happened fifty years ago? but thinking, I know all that, I know how countries decide whether or not they will give you an identity card and citizenship. When I left the concentration camp I saw those who were old and mad and sick left behind, but I didn't feel sorry for them, I know how the world works, I'm cunning, I'm forty, I'm still young, there's still hope for me, I can breathe in and breathe out counting to twenty-three and more, if I choose. Then Señor Sapley had said, "Countries must have some protection from undesirable immigrants, and Great Britain is no exception. It's compulsory for you to have a medical examination. Then everything will be arranged."

In spite of the two sores on his left wrist, and his past sickness in the concentration camp, and his white white skin, Botti had been found fit, yet he could not help envying Juan his muscular body and brown skin and the perfect B.B.C. English.

"I'll visit you in England, Botti."

My tailor is rich, my tailor is not rich. I have been wounded, see I am bleeding, will you help me? These photographs are underexposed, will you intensify them?

He traveled a day and a night and another day, but his train was not the train he had been expected to travel by, and no one met him at the station.

"Señor Sapley," he explained to the stationmaster, who showed him the way to White House Farm at the end of Murston Lane. And then—well, only the scarecrows saw what happened to Botti Julio.

You might think now that his story has been stamped out,

eradicated; you might think that the world would seal itself
against Botti Julio or you might hope it would be so, but it's no
use, there's no escape, the gash is there, the foreign invasion of
people you never knew or whose language you could never
speak; you'll have to lie in bed tossing and turning, obsessed with
night, snow, mountains, avalanches, a surging river, the four
crios, the mangy cat, and the daily pile of yellow mess on the
dimly lit landings of the tenement. And should the gash in your
world be wider than at first you imagined, you'll need to extend
your dreaming to those who, unlike Botti Julio, had no chance of
reaching the new land, who were denied entry because they were
old or mad or diseased, who stayed behind in the camps, hating
the visitors and the free food and the stink of helpless ingratitude
which grew more pervasive day by day, year by year, from the
distantly excreted so closely dropped results of the world's epi-
demic of concern and kindness.

Therefore we place Botti Julio here; see—here, now, a ghost in
our story; and we return to Little Burgelstatham, East Suffolk,
and the Reverend Aisley Maude who coughs and convalesces.

4 Aisley had never been a fashionable clergyman. While his wife Katherine had been
alive (she had woken on the fifth of May
three years ago, said "I feel dizzy, I feel faint," and then died) she
had made some attempt to persuade Aisley into a "contemporary" clerical mold—to appear on television or speak over the
radio in the morning program *Banish Thy Care*, to give controversial interviews to reporters (*Parson with Model-Type Wife
Agrees the Only Thing for It Is to Get with It, Heartbeat or
Drumbeat, God Is Listening*), to become drama critic of a Sunday newspaper, captain a soccer team, compose a modern liturgy
for electric guitar. There had also been continual pressure from
Diocesan councils to make the Church "move with the times," to
give religion an appeal, a "voice" in modern life. Aisley had been
preoccupied in wondering, Move with the times—which times?
to take any form of action. He was a shy man. Even had he cared
for many public appearances the Mothers' Union, street missions,
church meetings, socials, christenings, marriages, burials, sermons, prayers, left little time for him to plan the required campaign (did God require it?) to move the Church with the
times.

And there was always God; one had to give time to Him . . .

The final stigma of unfashionableness had fallen upon Aisley's
own body when he had lately suffered from tuberculosis.

"But, Aisley," Greta had written in her invitation to stay at
Clematis Cottage, "no one these days suflers from t.b. You're
out of touch, Aisley."

It was true, he felt. He had been out of touch with everything
and everyone around him. He was out of touch with modern
diseases (it should have been *Vicar Suffers from Strange New
Disease*), with the church and its congregation, and with God.
Not in that order, at least not invariably. God once had the
power of weaving in and out of precedence, at times clumsily
marshaling Himself behind the Bishop. Often, however, it was

the Mothers' Union who led the way ("Why should we pray more often? We enjoy our get-togethers. How do you know we're not praying while we're knitting? You're not a parent yourself, Reverend Maude. How could you understand?")

Aisley supposed that he was not by nature a fashionable man, that he would have been at home in any age but the one in which he was forced to live. When he set out for Little Burgelstatham he was careful to pack his book of Anglo-Saxon poetry.

Liverpool Street Station like the sooty skeleton of a dinosaur with people, trains, refreshments, conveniences sheltered beneath its bones; the slums; the back kitchens, coal-houses, humped rusted corrugated sheds; incredibly, at the foot of each garden (pestered and bullied into fertility by some slight green speech or motion), the tortoise waking out of sealed darkness; it's May; the caution of waking from a prolonged habitual dream; slums; more slums; gardens; lettuces; a matchbox factory illuminated with a giant *Safety Match*—selective, privileged, controlled fire; more factories; then sky, fields of mustard, flowers; greenhouses; the first thatched cottages, some derelict fingers of dark poked through their town eyes, the thatch rotting, riddled with bird and rat holes, the gardens overgrown; then fields of barley growing this way and that under the cuffing of the changeable East Anglian wind; maize; staunch green wheat packed into compulsory brotherhood, each stalk unable to turn or look back without the consent of its neighbor; the field restless, sighing, unable to resist the one-way pressure of growth and the directive persuasion of the overseeing wind.

Inside the railway compartment the movable seat arms thrust down in defense against human intrusion, the peevish near-panic working of the British Railways sum described as three divided by four leaving the remainder whole, four being equal to three in the powerful holiday stress of bodies, or three being equal to four when one passenger is dead or out of sight.

Aisley had long ago formed the habit of constructing sermons from his surroundings. Not being a countryman with the opportunity to search the stones and running brooks for his material, he had been used to the study of streets, buildings, public transport. As soon as he entered the compartment he had read the British Railways equivalent of *Wayside Pulpit Thought for the Week—Opening beyond this Arrow Creates a Draft. Do Not Lean Out of Window*—and the unembarrassed acknowledgment of virility in the cramped end room where the cold ran cold and the hot ran cold and the floor held a pool of water stained with tobacco from a floating cigarette butt: *Gentlemen Lift the Seat.* At the moment he did not care to think of sermons. Since the morning movement of God, Aisley had suffered alternate mental weariness and energetic optimism which it was safe to attribute publicly to his tuberculosis. Privately, he knew that he was less concerned with the shifting blurred picture of God than with the constant pressure to "move with the times."

Times do not exist, he told himself. Only *Time* can be acknowledged. I can see Time as a huge slowly journeying animal emerging from each century as from an ocean, shaking the year-drops and weeds from its armor, lumbering toward the eternal coast, through ravines of rock which tear and crush even the last persistent limpets of moment, and the traces of weed-entanglement, even those one or two sea-flowers so beautiful in color that no man could ever describe them; see how the petals are crushed and torn; nothing remains but the beast itself. It is the beast alone which must contain God; they ask me to enclose Him in an already dying sea-flower, an imprisoned limpet from which the shell will be torn and the naked body crushed to death. I've put my confidence in the beast, the tiny brain and eyes which in the end will think and see both God and Man, will be both God and Man."

The train was approaching Ipswich. Aisley closed his eyes to shut out the drearily distributed sheets of gray water which were, he supposed, the finished statement of the Orwell river. The train stopped. Aisley twitched his shoulders and jerked his eyes open. The man and woman who had been sitting opposite him lowered their newspapers and were staring at him with the

concentrated embarrassment which overcomes many people in
the presence of someone wearing a clerical collar. The man gave
Aisley a quick smile. The woman continued to stare. Aisley
smiled stiffly and nodded. The man would be about Alwyn's age,
he thought. Twenty, twenty-one. He had not kept in touch with
his brother and his family. From time to time, on impulse, there
had been letters, photos, greeting cards. After Katherine's death,
Aisley and Russell again remembered the existence of each other,
and in the way of families who possess this characteristic of
spasmodic communication, there had been a confused, pleasurable
exchange of letters, of invitations, none of which had been accepted. Eventually this flurry of memory would have collected
about itself and family affairs, have become a sturdy, weighty
whole, and would have sunk like a stone wrapped in snowflakes
into the usually undisturbed depths of family unconsciousness,
had it not been brought to the surface in the agitation following
the news of Aisley's illness and impending resignation from the
Church.

"You must come to stay," wrote Greta, whom he had seen
only once, the day of his wedding, ten years ago. He remembered Alwyn then as a beautiful child of ten, an extraordinarily
happy child, strong, clever, with an emerging arrogance which
was charming. Russell, more than ten years older than Aisley, had
remained aloof, as if sensing the danger to his separate existence
of sharing too closely the Maude characteristic of unfashionableness, the subversive denial of "the times."

Aisley thought, studying the woman passenger, Perhaps I
should liken her to Alwyn's friend, Jenny Sparling, who, it
seems, is staying at Clematis Cottage. Perhaps she and Alwyn are
engaged to be married. Aisley did not think, with the usual resentment, If so, no one has told me. He had no preference to
being told or not being told—another characteristic which had
not endeared him to the members of the Church, who had mis-
taken command of titbit knowledge for Christian awareness.

"This is Ipswich, isn't it?" the woman asked, appealing to
Aisley.

Out on the platform the woman and the man linked arms. Aisley saw that they were laughing. He did not hear their conversation.

"I wonder was he real?" the woman said.

"You mean the clergyman?"

"Yes, they're got up to look like clergymen these days, and no one suspects them."

"There could have been fifty thousand in his luggage."

"Clergymen. And cripples demanding to have their wheelchair put on the train. And old women hiding the loot in the folds of their clothes!"

"There could have been fifty thousand in his luggage!"

Greta was standing at the gate. She held a knotted stick in one hand. Aisley had the idea that before his arrival she had removed all the furniture from the cottage, set it on the spacious front lawn with the neat hem of wakening garden, and systematically, with her knotted stick, beaten the dust from it; dust, or some other substance which had accumulated since she began living in Little Burgelstatham. She looked tired. She looked burdened, like an old woman from Greek drama about to join the wailing chorus.

"Isn't it strange," she said, smiling formally and shaking Aisley's hand, correctly interpreting his glance at her, "how the after-effects of a dose of flu give rise to wild speculations of unaccountable tragedy? I'm so glad you've decided to come, Aisley, though you might have asked British Railways to organize the trains. You're Russell's brother," she continued, almost wonderingly.

(So it was still, Aisley thought, You're Russell's brother, you may *influence* him.)

"Jenny has picked lilac for your room."

"And Alwyn?"

Greta smiled, and said vaguely, "Oh, Alwyn."

"And Russell?"

"Pulling out teeth. Or filling them. Pounding away at his National Health mortar. Perhaps you'll like Little Burgelstatham, Aisley. Did you know that a *burgel* was originally the burial place of the heathen?"

I shall be praying, Aisley thought. Indeed I shall be praying. But I shall keep the movement of God to myself. I shall pray a kind of hammering, insistent prayer which wounds and indents metal but does not penetrate it. There's such a wide choice of instruments given to Man to make his rhythmical too ineffectual thrusts upon a cold, remote will. It is the striking power which matters; they say; men and nations do say: the striking force . . .

Upstairs in the small bedroom with the low black-beamed ceiling ("the spars of ancient pirate ships, Aisley," Greta had said); with the dormer windows opened to admit the scent of the lilac hedge in full bloom, and the cake-mixing cries of the pheasants; with the prayer-chair rescued from a demolished church placed in the corner opposite his bed (there was a red patch in the seat of the chair, like a kneeled-on rose or a bloodstain), Aisley submitted to the pressure of change, unaccustomed journeys, solicitude of relatives, the fresh country air, and went to bed early, enacting, with astonishment when he remembered it the next day, the behavior of fictional heroes who "sleep immediately their head touches the pillow." He slept deeply, and, like common fictional heroes who are blackmailed into dreaming plot-unravelings which the author has not the skill or inclination to describe elsewhere, in cold daylight waking, Aisley dreamed, but his dream was the kind that happens when the troubled mind wishes to repeat an outline of the facts. He dreamed that he was a clergyman, that he was a widower, that he had quiescent t.b., that God had moved; and at the end of the dream he saw a yellow field of mustard, and his nephew Alwyn standing in the middle of the field, turning and turning his huge, flat, crackling body and smiling with his crackling silver face.

5 Many of the villagers who went to the Baldrys' farm to share with Vic and Muriel the colored slides of their second honeymoon voyage round the world, and to listen to Vic's tirelessly enthusiastic descriptions of life in Australia, would have liked to refuse the monthly invitation, and had refused during the dark winter months when the weather provided excuses, but it was now May, officially summer, the evenings were growing longer and lighter, therefore most who were invited came, if not for the slides of Muriel and Vic sitting in tropical gardens, then for the refreshing drinks, the tasty sandwiches, and the chance to siphon with a gossip-sucking movement the latest news from the pooled events of Little Burgelstatham.

The Baldrys' social net was small and firm, cast discreetly; they did not indulge in "coarse" fishing. This particular evening they had (as it were) trawled Greta Maude, the dentist's wife; Alwyn Maude, the handsome young student son who (the gossip went) was writing a novel between helping to renovate the Unwins' old farm cottage; a stranger from a summer cottage near Withigford —a young American, Eustace Glee; Alwyn's girl-friend (some said fiancée), Jenny Sparling, a fellow student; and a clergyman, Russell Maude's brother, who looked ill. The Sapleys had not arrived; an Italian farm worker, expected at the White House Farm, had disappeared between the station and the farm.

"So I follow in the path of Orson Hyde, Heber Kimball, Joseph Field, Brigham Young, and William Pitt, who founded our Ipswich temple . . ."

"Brigham Young? But wasn't he? . . ."

He looks quite harmless, Muriel thought. Everyone seemed to be staring at him. He was young, with blond hair crew-cut, with a pale skin laid delicately over prominent bones. He wore sports clothes—gray pants and a tweed jacket wtih splits at the sides. Looking at him, Muriel pitied him. She knew the course of persecution Little Burgelstatham followed when a stranger came to live there.

"I know that we are persecuted by the enemy, but the fields are white for harvest . . ."

"I'd go back there any day, I'd sell up and return. I've never felt more at home. It's the place for me!"

Vic's voice was loud. Eustace Glee, the handsome young Mormon, retreated. Someone began to ask about immigration prospects Down Under.

Before this second marriage both Muriel and Vic Baldry had been widowed. There were no young children. Vic's married only son was farming in another county. Instead of taking over the usual stepchildren, Muriel had been confronted by the problem of trying to inhabit and control a strange house which seemed as difficult to possess as a new human relative, for it had also been the home of Vic's first wife, with the furniture and decorations chosen by her, while the garden had been Vic's and Joyce's shared offspring. Muriel found the house too big; she felt that she did not have enough spare personal fluidity to occupy all the rooms. She thought despairingly that Joyce must have been a limitless ocean compared to her own shallow drought-afflicted pool of influence. She seemed always to be discovering new rooms which did not belong to her and Vic. Even one of the traditionally most private yet neutral places, the bathroom, had the formidable aspect of a throne room with the w.c. raised on a kind of dais, and the bath deep and capturing, like a gleaming coffin. Muriel had set to work carefully to change the appearance of the house. There was one change she was working obstinately to bring about—the installation of a wonderful chandelier which had been left to her by an uncle whom she had never met.

"You'll sell it, of course," the executor had said. A Venini chandelier—fifteen thousand bulbs—you'll have to reinforce the ceiling of any house where you install it. You'll get a good price for it. Venini, you know."

Muriel had not known. She was not a connoisseur of glass, and she knew no one who was, yet she had become obsessed by the image of herself walking into the drawing room, switching on the chandelier, and sitting beneath thousands of tiny bulbs enclosing her and the room in soft prison-gray light.

She had little hope of realizing her dream. She had been surprised at Vic's meanness. After an extravagant world tour, whose
items were, however, carefully and economically planned, she
had come home to face everyday irritations in Vic's niggardly
use of electric power from their private generator. None of the
bulbs in the house were more than sixty watt, and even then
there seemed not to be enough light; in such vast rooms the night
was always more shadow than brightness; reading small print or
sewing was out of the question. When Muriel had driven into
Murston to buy more powerful light bulbs, she had been astonished by Vic's refusal to let her use them; they stayed unwrapped
on one of the shelves of the coat cupboard. Now, this evening,
when Muriel walked among her guests, she found herself apologizing for the dim light.

"It's our private generator. It doesn't always work too well."

She hoped the guests had not noticed the White House pigsties
with their welcoming café-style brilliance.

"It's the place for me, all right."

Muriel was startled to realize that Vic had adopted the appearance and manner of an Australian. He even spoke with the
twang. She knew that he had been impressed with the country,
that he had enjoyed himself (and her) with an abandonment he'd
not shown before or since his visit. She realized gloomily as she
watched him demonstrating the birth of a kangaroo (method
style) that their honeymoon had resulted in a new unofficial
marriage which would never be dissolved: Vic was living in a
state of geographical bigamy.

"Though I'm here on holiday it's natural for me to seek friends
and fellow travelers to eternity. Back in Salt Lake City . . ."

"These Americans," someone said softly, in the tone that only
Englishmen use when referring to Americans.

"Oh, no, we're not bigamists!"

Muriel hoped the Reverend Maude was not being offended or
disturbed by the young Mormon. She had read somewhere that
the English Church was worried by the growing popularity of
Mormonism.

"This farm, miles from anywhere. The wattle. Do you know
the *real* meaning of 'Waltzing Matilda'? You might be interested,

by the way, in the fact that not every Australian sings 'Waltzing Matilda' from dawn till dark."

"Well," Muriel said, since it was evident that Vic was not going to say it. "Well."

She wondered what Alwyn and Jenny were whispering about in the corner, what Greta Maude was thinking as she sat staring at the Reverend Maude, who stared back, without speaking. The room was hot. The curtains had been drawn to exclude the light. Muriel wished they had been able to look upon the garden, to admire the roses and the neat lawn.

"Well," she said again.

The guests looked at her, at her tall, well-built body with its large hands and feet; at her face with its stored quietness of expression. Her voice was slow and soft. Had it been a fraction slower, it might have given her the appearance of one who gropes inarticulately for thought; instead, her hesitation made her seem to weigh and measure her words, to determine their accuracy and full value.

There was a foreignness about her, a characteristic so easily and often perceived by the inhabitants of a small village. What was she doing, the guests might have wondered, married to this swashbuckling colonial? She came from another country. This was not her real home. Had she a past? Who were her people? What was her background?

"Well, everyone, here's the next stage of our journey—Calcutta. From there we went to Darwin, our first glimpse of Australia."

Among the guests there was the usual questioning murmur—people find it so hard to *believe* or absorb the simplest statement —as attention was focused again on the screen, and Vic, with a triumphant down-under stride (those cattle at the water hole had to be driven back to the station before nightfall) made ready the apparatus and switched off the light. In the dark, Muriel's face burned with her shame. It had been weeks since they began showing their slides of the tour, and here they were only at Calcutta. Vic had photographed everything possible; did ever a journey progress so slowly? How bored the guests must be!

Glancing about her, Muriel told herself, with surprise, that they were not bored, they were sitting passively ready to accept a further account of the voyage. She was glad, then, that in her determination to take part in the social life of the district, in spite of her shyness in giving direct invitations to teas or parties, she had arranged to show films of their tour. Vic can't wait till we get to Australia, she thought, listening to his monotonous description of Calcutta.

Yes, Muriel thought, moving unobtrusively from her seat to prepare supper, they *are* bored. It would surprise me if anyone is thinking of Calcutta. Jenny Sparling—she's thinking of young Alwyn, and no one knows what *he* is thinking. It's the first vacation in years, they tell me, that he's spent at home. They say he's helping to renovate the Unwins' cottage, getting paid for it, I suppose; but why does he stay the long, long summer vacation? And this Jenny: pale face, no make-up, long blond hair, duffle coat; I'm told bed follows naturally with that uniform; they'll be restricted, though, with a clergyman in the house. Clergyman, dentist. Why did Greta Maude marry a dentist? She spends most of her time in the garden, and he spends most of his time at Murston in or out of his surgery. I must sign up with a dentist. They say Russell Maude's work is mediocre, but I'd be pampering Vic's fantasies if I chose that young Australian who's just set up practice; they say he's brilliant; everyone's signing up with him. I shouldn't have thought Russell Maude would have a clergyman for a brother; the Reverend Aisley Maude looks ill and tired. Oh, that Eustace Glee—fly-by-night. Mormons are in the news . . .

"On this day, I remember, we set out from the hotel . . ."

Muriel clenched her large white fists and looked down, blushing. At least supper was prepared. The guests were bored, bored, bored, and enjoying their boredom.

"You didn't enjoy it, Aisley, I knew you wouldn't. We shan't persuade you to go again. One feels sorry, though, for Muriel Baldry. Oh, and fancy a Mormon in Little Burgelstatham! You didn't *mind* the Mormon, did you, Aisley?"

Greta looked curiously at her brother-in-law. She hadn't had a
clergyman before in the house; she hadn't been close to a
clergyman before. She'd had the idea that, studying him, she
would be able to discern the physical shape of his religion or the
wound from beneath which his reputedly lost faith had been
excised. Was it a limb, a dream, a memory, a habit (cloth and
custom)?

"Mormons are not monsters from the sea, you know," Aisley
said gently, with conscious self-righteousness. "Now, in Anglo-
Saxon times . . ."

There he is again, Greta thought. Anglo-Saxon times! I knew
he was old-fashioned, but not as archaic as that.

"Even further back in time the sea flowed over this land,
Greta. Little Burgelstatham has always been a drowned place, in
one way or another. Yet sometimes the tide goes out, we are left
high and dry, shriveling under the sun with no place to escape to
or be buried in, for the sand is burning too. You might almost
plead for the return of the tidal wave—after all—a boatload of
Mormons . . ."

"Jenny's beautiful, isn't she?" Greta said suddenly.

"Now, in Anglo-Saxon times," Aisley persisted, smoothing the
way to the past, almost as if he deliberately troweled the present
and recent centuries with layers of fast-congealing concrete—the
kind which sets the memory irretrievably into memorials.

"We're dead here," Greta said bitterly, feeling the time and
place hardening above her, enclosing her. "They say there's a
woman journalist in Withigford, writing letters from the countryside to one of the London newspapers. I've never seen her. I'm
curious about what she writes. Little Burgelstatham. The countryside in May. Influx of foreign labor. They're taking an Italian
worker at Sapley's . . ."

Sudden laughter from an upstairs room startled both Greta and
Aisley.

"Alwyn and Jenny," Greta said uneasily.

"Is Russell away somewhere for the evening?"

"There's a stamp auction at Tydd. Didn't I *tell* you? Didn't
you *know* that for years my only rival in matrimonial affairs has

been Penny Black and others of her kind displaying seductively their exclusive official marks and perforations?"

Aisley did not answer. He had guessed that Russell was not happy in the time described as "the modern age." He would have liked to comfort Greta at this moment, but he was feeling pleasantly soothed. He was remembering the flowers in the hotel gardens at Calcutta. He was daring to admit to himself that he had enjoyed the evening at the Baldrys'. Usually he had been too busy to go to social gatherings which were concerned with a second honeymoon instead of with affairs of the church. At the same time, he felt, now, obscurely worried by the fact that Russell had so openly proclaimed the unfashionable ways of the Maude family. Aisley hadn't yet seen Russell's surgery in Murston, but he had learned from Greta that the furniture was old, the equipment was out of date, that Russell's ideas of dentistry seemed to belong to another age, that he deliberately practiced in the country because he was convinced that the country was "behind" the city and must remain so. Even his speech was full of archaisms. Aisley had been astonished, during the first few days of his visit, to hear Russell muttering on some simple domestic occasion, "I durst not do it, I durst not."

The sight of the stamp collection had depressed Aisley. He could not help noticing how much time Russell spent cataloguing his stamps, speaking of countries by names which had long been changed and which few people now remembered. Aisley had felt responsible for this antiquarian trend. Had not Katherine so often urged him, too, to "live in the present," to inhabit a century where he had never felt at home—and why should he be at home? How could he surrender to this terrible pressure to "move with the times" when he (like Russell) seemed to be not equipped constitutionally for such a way of life? He was nothing more, he thought, than an ecclesiastical dinosaur. The solution had been put to him that he must adapt or be threatened with extinction. But was that the only solution? Somewhere in time and place there were fields where he could put his third eye to profitable use without submitting to its being blinded by an unwanted growth of temporal skin.

6 Each week there were two occasions when Bert Whattling, with special care, washed, shaved, put on his best shirt and suit, polished his black boots till they shone like blobs of country darkness. These were preparations for his Tuesday or Wednesday evening visit to the Unwins, and his Friday morning bus journey to the market in Tydd.

He was halfway to the Unwins' house now, riding past the Hall, the wood, the gamekeeper's cottage, the Bull, on to the London road where the traffic would frighten anyone, not least a pensioner of seventy-four who was short of breath, who had a stiffness in his knee that made his control of his bicycle erratic, whose eyesight played tricks, especially in this twilight when great alarming shadows that belonged to no substance but the phantom wind or scudding clouds suddenly rushed across the surface of the road, causing the handlebars to veer, for a moment out of control, and making Bert's heart stab out of its usual rhythm against his chest. On these warm summer evenings there was always the further menace of the tiny flies that swarmed into the cyclist's face, into his eyes, nose and mouth, slapping and stinging, putting him in danger of falling blindly into the roadway at the mercy of the broad pounding tarpaulin-covered lorries charging along the crown of the road.

It was no help for Bert, facing the hazards of fifty yards of A-class road, to remember that he'd once been a soldier, in the First World War. Danger seemed not as simple as it used to be.

He turned down the lane, under the oak trees, toward the Unwins'. He leaned his bike against the hedge, and as soon as he opened the gate, there was Mrs. Unwin at the window waving to him, and the white-aproned geese advancing around the corner of the house, warily, not yet sure whether Bert was friend or foe; then their noisy cries did not increase to their usual frenzy, but stopped, and one by one they lost interest, retreating, as if to say to one another, "Only Bert; not the baker, the butcher, the postman, the paraffin man—only Bert Whattling."

34

All the dogs and geese in Little Burgelstatham knew Bert. Everyone knew him—the older villagers because he had been born in the village, had gone to school there, had lived there all his life, except for the short period during the War; the newer inhabitants like the Sapleys, the Maudes, knew him because he was a pensioner who would garden for them at half-a-crown an hour, a careful conscientious worker who needed no supervision. Bert was proud of his round of "clients"—the Sapleys (hedges and lawns), the Baldrys (hedges and lawns), the woman journalist, Miss Unity Foreman (caretaking in a cottage that was almost always empty), the summer tenants of one or two cottages beyond the church (gardening, fetching eggs), the Unwins (wood-chopping, taking geese to market).

Mrs. Unwin, who was eighty-five, was wearing gum-boots and a shapeless old floral dress covered by an apron. She was waving the *Eastern Daily Press*.

"Bert," she said, "there's a chill in the air, and the fire's smoking again; there's a down-draft."

As Bert followed her into the kitchen, she brandished the newspapers at the smoke.

Lex, her son, who had not inherited the farm when old Mr. Unwin died and who was thus in a continual state of grievance at being forced to earn his living as a milk-roundsman, was sitting morosely in a chair by the door, with his shirt rolled up, while his wife Dot applied liniment to his back. Lex was forty-five. He was Ruby Unwin's only child, and as far as she was concerned, he remained her child: she had never recovered from the insult to her vanity made by his marriage to a woman who was a stranger to the district, who came from London one summer to help at the Sapleys' farm, who until then had never lived on a farm or been within cooee of one. It was just as well, Ruby often thought, that Bob hadn't willed the farm to Lex, for surely Dot Graves would never have been able to play the role of a farmer's wife. Even now, again and again, Dot had to be reminded (by Ruby) of Lex's delicate health.

"His back is bad again," Ruby Unwin explained to Bert, who nodded, sat down in the chair by the fire, and began to smoke his pipe.

"The smoke's clearing. The wind's dropped. Why don't you get a cowl for the chimney?" he asked. "It might help."

"A Colt cowl?"

"A Colt cowl."

"I'll mention it to Mr. Bedford," Mrs. Unwin said. It was Mr. Bedford who had taken over the farm when old Mr. Unwin died and who now managed it, though he allowed Mrs. Unwin to live in the old farmhouse, which was becoming more and more dilapidated. It was common knowledge that Mr. Bedford refused to have the farmhouse repaired, that he was waiting for both house and occupant to fall into their final decay.

"Yes, I'll mention it to Mr. Bedford," Mrs. Unwin repeated. She knew, with shame and resigned indignation, that she and the old house were partners in decay. She remembered other items she had "mentioned" to Mr. Bedford—the upstairs front window, the leaking roof at the back, the door that wouldn't budge once it was shut, the new washer for the tap that brought the water from the mains to a hole in the kitchen wall and then dribbled it in a never-ending stream across the cold stone floor.

Three years before his death Bob Unwin had taken the dog Gyp and gone to live in the farm cottage (which he left to his son and which was now being renovated) and had broken off communication with his wife, appearing only twice a day to receive the meals she cooked for him and brought to the door of the cottage. Then one day Gyp ran out into the lane in front of a car and was killed, and not long afterwards old Bob died, not knowing who he was or where or why, recognizing no one.

Now that Lex was helping to renovate the cottage, Mrs. Unwin didn't expect *him* to repair the farmhouse. It was Mr. Bedford's responsibility. Yet she had never been a helpless woman. During the war she had worked side by side with her husband, milking, harvesting the sugar beet, cooking meals for the billeted soldiers. Now it seemed as if she was unable to perform the simplest task. The sight of the farmhouse crumbling around her brought the fear that this loss of control over decay, this gradual, unchecked dissolution of her surroundings would soon make its way closer to her, would become a general anarchy invading her entire body; and then, she knew, death wouldn't be far away. The smoke running riot in the room, the water trickling over the kitchen floor—these represented a sinister abandonment of everything which held house, body, soul together.

When feelings of helplessness overcame Mrs. Unwin she found comfort in cherishing two fantasies—rather, she cherished one, endured the other. Dot, who was kind to her, came in the morning to light the fire and make breakfast. "Lex and I have talked it over," she would say. "We think you'd better come to stay with us. You're getting too old to be alone in the house at night. And you know how cold it is here in winter. In the semi-detached there's electricity and hot water."

Electricity and hot water! How strange, at the end of one's life, to be offered these as comforters! No one seemed to understand that Mrs. Unwin didn't want electricity, that the small oil stove where a kettle could be kept on the boil all day (and wasn't that "constant hot water"?) suited her just as well. Yet, from time to time, Mrs. Unwin would begin sentences with, "When I come to live wtih you and Lex," "When I'm living with you in the semi-detached . . ."

Her own dream, the more precious because she felt that it would never be realized, was to return to Stamford, where she had been born and spent the years before her marriage. During all her years at Little Burgelstatham she had been careful to tell everyone that she did not belong to Suffolk, that she did not even look upon it as her adopted county. In contrast, her daughter-in-law, coming from London, had easily and swiftly wrapped herself in a rural mantle. She is something of a yokel, Mrs. Unwin would think to herself, while I retain my delicacy.

She had resisted adopting the Suffolk ways and speech; her consonants were neat, her vowels quick and precise. She shuddered when her son and his wife spoke in their thick, porridgy dialect to which each speaker added a cloudy earthy mix and stir that bubbled with slow, rhythmical unintelligibility.

In her dream Mrs. Unwin saw herself, a young girl, arriving at Stamford by bus, at midnight. She was the only passenger for Stamford. The bus stopped. She got off and stood alone in the

market square in the sleeping town where the air was cold and
sharp, and the buildings, glistening with night, stood dark-gray
and worn smooth, like stone pillars, by centuries of leaning darkness and rain. Mrs. Unwin had not been born "a lady," but several times in her childhood she had seen the Duchess of Rutland,
and even now she would cut from the newspaper any reference
to the Duchess. In her simple dream it was the Duchess who came
to speak to her as she stood alone in the market square: such a
dream had more meaning in her life than hot water and electricity.

"Well, Bert, what's the news?"

The liniment had been put on Lex's back and Mrs. Unwin and
Lex were sitting near the fire while Dot made tea.

"I've been around a lot today," Bert said. "Along the road (he
pronounced it "rude") at the Sapleys'. They wanted their hedge
cut, the front hedge, cut like a bird, and I said I'm sorry I can't
cut it like a bird and anyway which bird, there's nothing but
wood pigeons everywhere. So I cut it the way I always cut the
hedges, and then I had to be getting after my dinner or my wife
would have sued for a *dee*-vorce. I went to that woman's place
—Miss Foreman, the journalist—to clear up. Then I went a quick
way to the Maudes'—they've a preacher come to stay, so I looked
lively. Then away past the cottage . . ."

"The American's?"

"They say he's got three wives."

"Then Mr. Baldry asked me about some wire netting from the
auction on Friday."

"There are two geese for you to take on Friday."

"I'll come early and kill them."

"The bus goes at ten o'clock now—did you know?"

Bert looked startled. But it's the eleven o'clock bus, the eleven
o'clock bus at the corner, from Little Burgelstatham to Tydd,
stopping at Murston."

"They've changed it. There's a notice in the paper."

Bert looked worried. The many changes at Little Burgelstatham
had not disturbed him; they had provided him with material for
conversation and complaint; he did not panic, as trees do not

panic when the seasons are born and die; he knew, like trees, the superiority, the inviolability of a being whose roots are too deep to be disturbed. Yet the change in the bus time-table made him uneasy, for his weekly visit to Tydd was a consolation, a pilgrimage, a dream which never varied.

"The bus has always left at eleven o'clock," he said obstinately, almost using the words as a spoken charm to try to frighten the Eastern Counties number to 132 to revert to its normal timetable.

There was silence. The little group sat staring into the fire, thinking about "them," the invaders from the city who rented country cottages which they did not live in; the Americans and other "foreigners" who didn't belong; the rich Sapleys who had everything their own way because his brother was a minister of something in Parliament (they had electricity, new lorries to transport their fruit, grants from the government, and now that the countryside was suffering an official drought, they had installed sprinklers and hoses in the black-currant fields and kept them switched on from morning till evening, day after day, while anyone else who dared to hose a garden with a trickle of water was swooped on by the Council and fined. And now there was talk of closing the little Burgelstatham station!

"They're closing the station," Lex said bitterly.

Dot handed round the tea and sat beside Lex. She was a buxom woman in her late thirties, with brown hair and brown eyes, and sad, feminine features contrasting with her masculine clothes— trousers, boots, wind-jacket—and her unusually large hands and feet. There was no suspicion of frailty in Dot. It was she who every morning, wet or fine, delivered the bottles of milk while Lex, who drove the van, stayed warm at the wheel. It was Dot who waded through the flooded ditches and snow and suffered the piercing blast of the East wind, who got up early to light the fire and warm their own house before she drove with Lex to Mrs. Unwin's where the milk-crates were waiting to be loaded. There she lit Mrs. Unwin's fire and cooked breakfast for the three. Apparent happiness in women like Dot is the subject of torturing curiosity to others who feel excluded by not being able to discover what such women "see" in a life of subjection and toil. "There must be something in it," they say, "or she would leave him."

Perhaps they reckon without the comfort of habit which is warmer, certainly safer, than love; and is not safety in fashion? As for love—was there ever such a state of mind or body? There's intolerable human need, the promise or threat of mortality. You thrust love on the scales, and snatch it off again before you can read its meaning—like the fruit-sellers in the market who tempt you with cherries and strawberries.

Dot's life was the subject of much gossip among the villagers because it was felt that sooner or later something would "happen." The villagers longed for something to happen. Their lives were centered in crises human and agricultural. They might hear talk of "foreigners," of bombs, of great military powers, but their real interest lay in their neighbors' life and land. Neighbors were strictly defined as those living in or around Little Burgelstatham, Tydd, Withigford, Murston. Love thy neighbor meant love the man who owns the next farm and is trying to grab more land by cutting the hedges and planting his crops to the edge of the road.

Dot smiled when she heard her husband say so bitterly, "They're closing the station at Little Burgelstatham." She could not recall a time when any of the Unwins had traveled from Little Burgelstatham in the train. *She* was the only one who had ever been as far as London, though that gave her little prestige, for no one cared about London or had any desire to go there. She had been surprised at this. Living in London, along with the rest of the swirling mass, she had the impression that anyone who lived beyond London was surging toward it in a great sweep of desire and longing; one could feel, in London, the pressure of the whole population of Britain wanting to visit, to stay, to get in at all costs; one had a feeling of privilege and importance. When Dot came to live in Little Burgelstatham she had therefore been surprised, and hurt, at people's indifference to London. They had never heard of Fulham, where she had been born and brought up. Moreover, they did not want to hear of Fulham. (London will never come of age as a city until it can acknowledge that the scramble to arrive at Paddington or Liverpool Street or King's Cross or Victoria is a self-created myth.)

For five minutes Bert and the Unwins talked indignantly about the bus time-table and the closing of the station. Usually at this time they played cards, but now, when they had exhausted their complaints about "them" and their autocratic ways, they began to feel themselves exhausted, and to remember that the next day would be long and tiring.

"Your back easier?" Mrs. Unwin asked, for her thoughts of the next day included her son, and the fact that a milk-roundsman could never lie in bed in the morning.

"He gets a sore back at this time every year, Dot. He was such a frail little boy. I always made him wear flannel next to his skin to soak up the perspiration and keep him from catching a chill. If only his father had left him the farm! Then he wouldn't need to go on these long journeys so early in the morning."

Lex listened without protest. Unlike some men who would have been embarrassed and angry, Lex felt comforted to hear his mother speak in this way. Sometimes he wished he had never married, for though Dot was well trained and a help with the milk-round, she couldn't massage his back as well as his mother could, and she wasn't as skilled at bandaging or putting embrocations on bruises; and sometimes her remedies were unfamiliar London remedies.

"I've had inquiries about the cottage, Lex. Every day a car passes, someone wants to know is the cottage for sale, and the price."

"I can't sell until it's painted. The new fireplace is in."

"I saw Alwyn Maude today. That girl was with him. They're both university people with a good education. You'd think he wouldn't care to turn his hand to carpentry, but he seems to enjoy himself. What a happy lad he is! Of course," Mrs. Unwin added carefully, glancing at her son's dark gloomy face, "he hasn't had your ill-health to put up with."

"Happy? He takes his time over the work!"

"But he's thorough, Lex. He's had a good education. They say

he's a novelist. Still," she added vaguely, these university students haven't got the feel of the country; half don't know wheat
from barley."

"Writing books?" Bert said. "I wouldn't know about that. I
was talking to Olly Drew and Olly says he knows how to mix
cement but he's got his own ideas where to put it."

"I took tea to Olly and Alwyn this morning," Mrs. Unwin
said. "I didn't know the young woman was there, but she said no
thank you when I offered her a cup. She's refined. She's had a
good education."

Dot changed the subject. "Did you know Milly was getting
married in two months?"

Milly was Dot's niece in London.

"Oh, yes."

No one seemed interested in Milly and her London marriage.

"She's invited me," Dot said.

Again no one was interested. All knew that Dot couldn't go to
London with the milk-round so busy. Lex would never be able to
manage it on his own.

"She's invited me," Dot repeated, suddenly breathless. "And
I've decided to go."

Lex flushed angrily. "You can't, Dot. You know you can't.
What about the milk-round?"

"You can work it on your own for a few days, surely!"

There was a hush of horror.

"Oh, Dot, you'd never dream of leaving Lex to work on his
own! What about his back? I told you it was worse at this time
of year."

Bert took no part in the discussion. He sat peacefully smoking
his pipe and thinking that soon he'd have to be going home or his
wife would be after a *dee*-vorce, and Bert didn't want a *dee*-
vorce, though it gave him much pleasure to refer often to it,
especially as a *dee*-vorce would be for Bert a major final disaster.
Though he had only once in his life traveled beyond East Suffolk
he knew, instinctively, that a man can be a daring explorer of
ideas and feelings as well as of distant new places; that thinking
can put anyone in as much peril as journeying on foot through
wild lonely places.

"What do you think, Bert? Should she go to London?"

"I don't know about that," Bert said mildly, unwilling to take part in the argument. "But I'd better be getting on my way."

"All right," Dot said. "But I thought I might be able to go. I'll have to get a new dress."

"You, a new dress!" Lex looked at his wife with amazement. "Why a new dress? What's wrong with your brown one? A new dress!"

"All right," Dot said. "I just thought I'd like to go. I'm fond of Milly. It'd be nice to go to her wedding. I'd see London again."

"London's a place that it's best to keep clear of," Bert said wisely. "Smoke, fog, thieves with guns and iron bars, traffic. Country people are best off."

"Oh, I know that," Dot said loyally. "It's nice in the country here."

She looked vaguely out of the window at the sealed complete country darkness. She bent over and smelled a branch of lilac that Mrs. Unwin had put in a vase on the window sill. Mrs. Unwin thought, watching her, She's a handsome woman, but she hasn't a lady's type of beauty. (Mrs. Unwin, small, delicate in appearance, had a "lady's" type of beauty.)

She wondered again why Lex and Dot had married. They seemed unsuited, like two people who had met in the street and had decided to walk the rest of the way together, though not really toward the same destination. Yet Dot had taken on country ways so completely. Hearing her speak, you would never dream she had been born in London.

"Couldn't Milly get married in Little Burgelstatham," Mrs. Unwin suggested. She was attracted by the idea of a wedding. Though she had unpleasant memories of the most recent one— Lex's—she thought perhaps Milly's would give her an opportunity to enjoy herself. She would stand the small rusty oven on top of the oil stove and bake a cake for the reception. And Dot ought once in a while to dress up and not always be in gum-boots and sou'wester. . . .

"But she doesn't belong here, she's a Londoner, why should she want to get married in Little Burgelstatham?"

"Let her stay in London, then," Lex said stiffly. "If she thinks

Little Burgelstatham's not good enough for her. It's time we were going home, Dot. There's a big day tomorrow, collecting the milk-money. You know it takes us all day to get through."

Lex, Dot, Bert went home. Mrs. Unwin bolted the door, put the chain in its groove, and went up to bed, and outside the moles, rats, bats, owls snuffed, nudged, swung and whisper-yodeled, and in all the fields of wheat, barley, sugar beet, maize, in the orchards and gardens, the scarecrows crackled in their sleep, leaning with the wind against the stone-solid impenetrable country darkness.

7 Country stuff, not too much sweetness, not too much tooth and claw; mix the dead toads discreetly with the crushed lilac; a single toil and trouble laced with blackberry and balm; don't forget the broiler houses (cross between mortuaries and school gymnasiums). But then you're writing it, get on with it.

Unity Foreman smiled, considering the editor's letter.

The Charming Village of Little Burgelstatham.
Letter from the Countryside.

Dear Reader.
The distant and near fields do look green
with wheat and summer perfection of trees, the peacetime
mapping
of cloud reveals no sinister shape, the wild creatures run
free,
the ditches and ponds are deep where swimming things
may swim—
surely nothing is drowned, face-downwards,
turning in violence from the Olde English dream?
Conservative ladies pursue their habits of roses,
honeysuckle,
blackberries, display wild sweet peas and pink may,
bridal nettle, muscle-bursting hogweed, Mr. Universe of
the hedges . . .
Is there place for the dying toad, like a lump of wound
lava? spurt of blood,
the adder, grinning rat, deadly nightshade?

"Oh," Unity said, kissing out with crosses what she had written, and beginning again.

In this peaceful rural Suffolk village where I've come to describe to readers the kind of life lived today in the countryside of England, the window of my thatched cottage looks out upon a ripening field of wheat, upon hedges of roses and honeysuckle, blackberries in blossom, tall grasses that glitter in the early-morning dew. But what of the people who still pursue this pleasantly rural way of life untouched by the turmoil of city pressures? Now, as I look from my window, I see—

a bus ticket coming over the wall. That's the third thrown over this past ten minutes. Why do I have to live in a flat so near a bus-stop?

A jet screamed overhead. The harsh June traffic, which, in winter fog and snow, had been reduced to a restrained felt-pedaled murmur, ran riot with noise under the high sky extravagant with summer light. Unity went to the window and shut it. The room was stuffy, full of carpet dust and invading soot. She reopened the window, in time to see another bus ticket drifting over the garden wall.

"Hell," she said. "Hell."

She returned to her typewriter.

Here, in the peaceful village of Little Burgelstatham, where I've rented this country cottage for the summer, life pursues its peaceful way. At the same time modern progress has made way for subtle changes not always appreciated or understood by the inhabitants. The poultry farms are an example. Only yesterday I was invited to inspect a broiler house. Not without some trepidation I entered and saw—

the Piccadilly crowds at rush-hour traveling up and down the escalators feasting their eyes on little X-tras and Living Bras.

God, what a life.

Unity realized suddenly that she was tired, and leaning on her typewriter, she dozed a few minutes. When she woke there were marks on her forehead, for she had removed the typewriter cover: bbbbb,,,787654££££; the £££££££ marks were prominent.

She quickly finished her "Letter from the Countryside," posted it to Cornstalk, and relaxed in a hot bath.

8 Greta was planting lettuces in the corner seed-bed at the back of the cottage where the main garden was laid out. She was expert at planting lettuce-seed, chiefly because her hands, like the remainder of her body, were small and firm and held the tiny seed fast, as if it were gold-dust, so that the trickling seed was controlled and she was not faced every two weeks with an uprush of lettuces so close together that they strangled one another before they could be thinned. It used to be Greta's admired childhood accomplishment that her hands were so small she could not separate her fingers to let in enough light to see, and therefore could never be accused of cheating when the game demanded hands over the face and no peeping. She remembered now, smiling at the memory, that in the short time she and Russell had spent together before their marriage they had tried to forget the war, to behave like lovers in an "ordinary age," and had returned again and again, as lovers do, to the confidences and comparisons of childhood. She remembered explaining about her hands, how they were so small. She remembered that Russell had answered as seriously and boastfully as any schoolboy that *his* hands were so large that he could stretch well over an octave on the family piano.

I never found out, Greta thought suddenly, who played the piano in the Maude household. Was it Aisley?

She finished planting the seed and began to label the rows, because she knew that no one would remember the seed was lettuce. It always happened that when seed disappeared into the earth it became dumb about its being and its future, and chose its own time to break into speech; one had to rely for identification upon the brilliant outsize dream portrayed on the empty packet. Therefore Greta pierced the packet with a stick which she thrust into the earth. It would be rained on, the colors would smudge, yet she would still be able to discover the truth from it and not be made to look foolish by trying to place two overconfident poses of tiny green leaf.

47

She rubbed her hands on her dress and was about to take her usual evening walk up and down the rows of beans, peas, Brussels sprouts, spinach; to consider their progress; to share the pleasure of their growth by attributing some of their such *lawful* intention, direction, tirelessly inbred family likeness, repetitive beauty and pattern, to the regularity with which she had brooded over them, hoeing, watering, dusting. Suddenly she heard laughter at the gate, and there were Alwyn and Jenny, arm in arm, heads close. Jenny climbed on the lowest bar of the gate, and Alwyn swung her to and fro, then lifted her to the ground, and hand in hand they walked up the path.

Greta stooped to stroke the broad bean-leaves. What stupid floppy summer hats the beans wore!

She listened to the laughter as Jenny and Alwyn went into the cottage. They had not seen her.

She remembered the dreadful seriousness with which she and Russell had approached their courtship and marriage, the intellectual books with the small print which they had read together, and the instructions they had tried to follow. Then she recalled, with surprise, that it had been she who had insisted on the books, the serious approach. It occurred to her suddenly that she had never really known what Russell thought of her fads and anxieties. For the first time, here, now, after putting a few trails of lettuce-seed to bed, she felt herself blushing with shame at the thought of the agonies of self-reproach she had suffered when she found she could not share the enthusiasm of the manual of instruction for lovemaking in the sunlight. Poor Russell had been embarrassingly sunburned! "Oh, God," Greta said, "I wish life were not merely a series of echoes! Why don't Jenny and Alwyn seem to *care?*"

How glossy the bean leaves were! And the runners, those tiny spurts of scarlet! And the riotous peas—a green frivolity that would soon need staking, training, shielding!

The garden was in shadow. Greta looked around her helplessly, with a feeling of having been abandoned.

"Tea, Greta. Like a cup?"

She went inside to share tea with Alwyn and Jenny, who

seemed so happily in step, who'd months ago put in take-over bids one for the other, and had no doubt paid colossal prices. But Alwyn was not yet twenty-one. What a happy child he had been! Greta remembered the anxiety she had felt over Alwyn's happy nature, for, according to her books, a child with a "griev-ance" was thought to be particularly intelligent, because he had evidently lost little time in learning to appreciate the ways of the wicked world, whereas a happy child, who stayed happy, was more likely to be a happy idiot.

"So much for modernizing," Alwyn said. "The old fireplace is out, the new fireplace is in, and the result would make you shud-der. Yet someone's going to pay over a thousand for that cot-tage."

"You'll be getting material for your novel," Greta said vaguely, out of touch, and of control at the bold direct way in which Alwyn spoke. He looked at her suddenly. She smiled at him, a small proud smile. She felt herself trembling.

"My novel? Maybe I do plan to write a novel."

"I don't think you *care* enough to write a novel."

"Care? What about?"

"You're too happy."

"Yes, yes," Jenny said. "He is, he is."

While Jenny and Greta spilled sentences beginning "He is," "He does," "He used to," "He thinks," Alwyn drank his tea in the silent amusement and slight annoyance of one who is sud-denly an item of property, a possession to be described, valued, bought, sold. The more Jenny and Greta talked, Alwyn noticed with satisfaction, the more the price went up. He gave a shout of laughter and stood, brushing his paint- and cement-spattered overalls.

"I wonder," his mother was saying, "what kind of life his happiness has equipped him for?"

Jenny looked dreamily at Alwyn. Oh, he was so clean; even with his paint-spattered overalls he was shining with cleanliness! She shivered, as if a dark, indelible, near-freezing liquid were being poured over her body.

"Good grief," Alwyn said. "I've a mother who equates gaiety

and laughter with happiness. I laugh because my face finds it convenient, my jaws feel comfortable that way, and I haven't yet got false teeth. Why shouldn't I laugh?"

"I've been telling Jenny," Greta said seriously, "that you always seemed such a happy child. Everyone remarked on it. I've never known you to cry."

She made the last remark as a statement, not with pride. She screwed up her face and seemed to peer at Alwyn's face as if to discover the hidden tears. Do we have a store of them, she wondered, to be offered at intervals as part of our unique gift? As a former nurse I should know: the supply of tears is unlimited and is used chiefly to wash grit, dust, and other foreign bodies from the human eye. It seems that Alwyn has never had to contend with foreign bodies . . .

"Oh, Mother, we've talked about this so much, you'll drive me crazy. I am born. I laugh instead of crying as soon as I 'smell the air.' I go to school. I enjoy myself. I haven't money worries. The personal allowance from Uncle Tom has been useful. I find Jenny, I enjoy myself, we enjoy ourselves. Why shouldn't I write my novel out of my enjoyment?"

"But all the great novelists," Greta said primly, aware that she was trembling with anger or love, "wrote from the point of view given them by suffering. You've never known want or death or suffering.

"Have you never seen anyone dead?" Jenny asked, wonderingly. "Has no one close to you ever died?"

They went to the sitting room. Aisley had returned from his walk through the field on the other side of the cottage. He was sitting in a chair by the fireplace; the fire was not lit. Greta, Alwyn, Jenny were immediately apologetic. They had had tea, they hadn't dreamed that Aisley was home, why hadn't he called to them? Greta wished she knew what to do with him. She had fallen into the first trap prepared by a hostess for herself—the belief that one must manipulate one's guests. There he was, sitting so quietly in the chair, and everything in the room was quiet, with a quietness that seemed like neglected silence rather than peace. Greta was suddenly conscious of the meaninglessness and deceit of the teatime conversation as opposed to the steady evenly distributed silence of the sitting room.

"Reading, Aisley?" she said falsely, determined to establish the scene as one of contentment.

Aisley turned the pages of his book and began to read aloud:

> " 'The ashes of the oak in the chimney are no epitaph of that oak to tell me how high or how large it was; it tells me not what flocks sheltered while it stood, nor what men it hurt when it fell. The dust of great persons' graves is speechless too, it says nothing; as soon as the dust of a wretch whom thou wouldst not, as of a prince whom thou couldst not loop upon, will trouble thine eyes, if the wind blow thither; and when a whirlwind hath blown the dust of the churchyard into the church, and the man sweeps out the dust of the church into the churchyard, who will undertake to sift those dusts again, to pronounce, This is the patrician, this is the noble flower . . .' "

He stopped reading and looked at Alwyn, who was listening attentively.

"Beautiful prose," Alwyn remarked. "But it shelters behind 'couldst,' 'wouldst,' 'hath.' It's easy these days, when you know the trick, to think a fancy trite thought and make it sound meaningful by adding a few 'wouldsts,' 'dosts,' 'haths,' 'thous,' and 'thees.' "

Aisley turned the pages again.

> " *'Maeg is bw me syklum sogied*
> *calde grfrungen*
> *waeron fet mine forste gebunden*
> *caldum climmum.*

> " 'Whither has gone the horse, whither has gone the man? Whither has gone the river of treasure? Whither has gone the place of feasting? How that time has passed away, has grown dark under the shadow of night as if it had never

been! Now in the place of the dead warrior stands a wall wondrous high covered with serpent shapes; the might of the ashwood spears has carried off the earls, the weapon greedy for slaughter—a glorious fate; and storms beat upon these rocky slopes; the falling storm binds the earth, the terror of winter. Then comes darkness, the night shadows cast a gloom, send from the earth fierce hails in storms . . .' "

Is Aisley getting better or worse? Greta wondered. I've no experience of how clergymen behave when they're convalescing. Even as little as I've had of brothers-in-law.

"Do you know," Alwyn said, looking serious, "I've a father a dentist, an uncle a clergyman; a father concerned with the extraordinary darknesses of the human mouth, with the power, should he wish it, to strike the world dumb; and an uncle concerned with the darknesses of the human spirit, in keeping with the times, of course. Isn't it the fashion in religion to move with the times?"

"It always has been," Aisley said slowly. Then he sighed. "It seems many weeks since I prepared a sermon."

Then he took out his handkerchief and began to cough into it, while Jenny, Alwyn, Greta looked at him and at one another with expressions of alarm which said, "It *is* quiescent, isn't it?"

"I'll get your biscuits and milk," Greta said.

"Thank you," Aisley murmured, aware that this was new. His biscuits and milk? Greta hadn't offered these before as a nightcap.

Greta left the room, Jenny and Alwyn went upstairs to Jenny's room to talk about and act their private lives, and twenty minutes later Aisley, eating biscuits and drinking milk, was sitting on the edge of his bed listening with that extra keenness of hearing given to a man who has lived a celibate life since his wife died, to the murmurs and movements of Jenny and Alwyn. What is Greta thinking of? he wondered. Where is Russell, to allow it? The girl is only a child and the boy is all that everyone thinks he is not. The only certain thing about him is that he's living in the twentieth century—that remote age.

9 Aisley's bedroom, which overlooked the promised fields where partridges and pheasant hens morning and evening escorted their chicks through the grass and baby rabbits bobbed and played chasing games, had been furnished and arranged for his spiritual and physical comfort, the latter with more discretion: the old-fashioned bed, Spartan in appearance, held a luxurious inner-spring mattress. On a small table by the bed, Greta had placed a copy of the Authorized version of the Bible side by side with the New English version; as if Aisley were indeed "passing the night" and Greta were a member of the Gideon Society and not his sister-in-law. Or had Russell supplied the Bibles? Or Alwyn? Jenny? The visits of Greta and Russell to the church in Murston seemed, to Aisley, to be social occasions rather than acts of worship. Russell returned from church in high spirits, like one who has wined and dined at a party. Not long ago, Aisley, examining this effect of church-going, would have pronounced it "a good thing," for was not faith a state of being in constant celebration? Yet now, he knew that Russell seemed happier because he had worked hard among teeth all week, among stamps almost every evening, and the visit to church gave him a breath of fresh air, and the self-confidence brought about by his noticing the approval of patients visiting the same church, rather than the approval of God. It was possible, Aisley thought, that the Maude family and the young Jenny lived in the place inhabited by most people—the cloud of general belief called Goodness, the outside of a prison, gazing cautiously through the bars at the chained "committed," not realizing that one wall of the prison was open to the sky.

Aisley considered the prayer-chair. He remembered that when Greta had said that it came from a demolished church she had used the word "demolished" with brisk familiarity, as evidently one must who is at home in an age of demolition, extermination, the wiping clean from the face of the earth of the smears of ill-arranged, unproductive, superfluous buildings and people. In spite of the mountains of refuse and litter, and the opinion of historians that the twentieth century will be remembered chiefly as an age of Clutter, I think, Aisley said to himself, that the age is one of Neatness, of clean polished surfaces reflecting the skimmed, carefully contained lives; an age which can be symbolized by an immense sewer where the dead are drained discreetly away, vanishing in turquoise transparent seas where the population is encouraged to bathe in cleanliness and safety. It is an age of Safety, but Safety from poorly perceived and falsely identified dangers.

The fact that a prayer-chair had been put in his room struck Aisley as another example of the approval of Neatness. A place for everything. It would be necessary for him to kneel on the bloodstained rose to get in touch with God.

It was early morning. He stood in his room, undecided about what to do. He could hear no sounds from the kitchen or the bathroom or the bedrooms, and he was as much a stranger in his brother's household as to feel diffident about publicly "stirring" when the others might be asleep. He listened to the early-morning noises—the pheasants, partridges, wood pigeons; a clatter of milk cans at the Unwins' farm; the distant sound of roosters crowing at the poultry farm at the end of the lane.

Aisley looked at his watch. It had stopped. He crossed to the table near the window and turned on the portable radio. A woman was singing:

> "*Morning has broken*
> *like the first morning.*
> *Blackbird has spoken*
> *like the first bird.*
> *Praise for the singing*
> *Praise for the morning . . .*"

A voice said, "So I thought to myself when I saw this youngster dressed in his strange, fashionable garb, God cares for you. God cares for us all—for the city businessmen, for the humble laborers on our farms, for the dukes and the members of our beloved Royal Family . . ."

"Oh God," Aisley groaned, swtiching off the radio. He thought of the early days of his preaching when his own sermons used to emerge as platitudinous homilies, often with no biblical text, or if there were a text, its truth suffered from his distortion, interpretation, fanciful spiritualizing. Though he was still eager to seize examples from daily life for use as text or pretext, he understood that too often his sermons and prayers had been sandwiched with a false filling of holy generalizations and en-treaties—"Oh Lord we pray Thee we beseech Thee, Jesus my sweet Lord." He was repelled now, having listened to the complacent clergyman beginning his program, "Be of Good Cheer," by the cozily patronizing atmosphere, as if religion were a not too strenuous daily arms-bend-upward-stretch-running-on-the-spot which would make the believer who practiced it handsome, rich, envied, nearer to Mr. Universe himself than to God, and able, one fine day, to balance a dumbbell on his shoulder in the belief that it was the world.

The idea, it seemed, was that God was a privileged secret which all could share. In Aisley's view, God (supposing He existed or had not moved, and Aisley was too tired and depressed to argue) was less a privileged secret which everyone clamored to share than a *dirty* secret (incongruous, in an age of Cleanliness) swarming with foul bacteria which could be used, nevertheless, cultivated, like a kind of penicillin, to wipe out plagues that had persisted for centuries too long in the human spirit.

Aisley's room was the only one on the top floor. He heard beneath the sound of Jenny and Alwyn, talking and laughing. Sometimes it seemed to Aisley listening to their enjoyment, that the time and place swarmed with youth entwining and copulating with the shameless abandon of troops who kill and die (embracing enemies and death) on a permanent battlefield, who possess all the force, the power to destroy, the sealed commands, the knowledge of the objective, of the target; who simply wipe the blood from their eyes and the semen from between their legs and get on with the war. Aisley wondered if, in the end, they would capture the City.

The City?

Allegorical musings, he said to himself.

Then a hollow query from his inside reminded him that it was time for breakfast; he was hungry. He listened. A tap had been turned on in the bathroom. Footsteps sounded down the stairs. A door opened. There was a smell, real or imagined, of bacon, something sizzling, toast burning.

Aisley began to gather his small civilized collection of toilet articles—towel, soap, toothpaste, razor, Old Spice shaving cream. He waited. Then, thrusting his toilet bag on the bed, he took the two Bibles and began to read from each version:

> When I was a child I spake as a child, I understood as a child, I thought as a child but when I became a man I put away childish things. For now we see through a glass darkly, but then face to face . . .

He turned the pages to:

> Beareth all things, believeth all things, hopeth all things, endureth all things. Charity never faileth; but where there be prophecies, they shall fail; whether there be tongues they shall cease; whether there be knowledge it shall vanish away. For we know in part, and we prophecy in part. But when that which is perfect is come, then that which is in part shall be done away . . .

Aisley could feel the peace and love steal over him as he read. Peace, love, and the stranger—the undesirable—the nostalgia for the vanished age. But why not? he told himself. Human beings will forever imagine there is but one entrance and exit, when the years are perforated with them—rat holes, escape holes, doors to wonderland.

He opened the New English Version and began to read:

> When I was a child, my speech, my outlook, and my thoughts were all childish. When I grew up I had finished

with childish things. Now we see only puzzling reflections
in a mirror, but then we shall see face to face . . .
There is nothing love cannot face; there is no limit to
its faith, its hope, and its endurance. Love will never come
to an end. Are there prophets? Their work will be over.
Are there tongues of ecstasy? They will cease. Is there
knowledge? It will vanish away; for our knowledge and
our prophecy alike are partial, and the partial vanishes
when the wholeness comes . . .

Though Aisley knew that he could not compare the two ver-
sions dispassionately, for the "glass darkly" had dissolved so long
ago in a shining sea that flowed close, omniscient as the blindfold
tunnels of his blood, yet, to him, the translation "puzzling reflections in a mirror" seemed nothing more than a linguistic fun-fair
or a disappointing glimpse of incorrectly applied religious
cosmetic. The group of scholars, Aisley thought, who sat at the
conference table to make this new translation had undertaken the
task of convicts breaking stones, monotonously striking day after
day until they destroyed a quarry of jewels which they still
imagined to be stones; and their imprisonment in their scholar-
ship had compelled them to work thoroughly, to obey the laws
of language, as if they were indeed men under sentence. What
had been their feelings when they shattered the "glass darkly"
into so many pieces that they could not restore it, could merely
hastily rescue a few fragments which gave, as some small comfort, a "puzzling reflection"?
The partial vanishes when the wholeness comes . . .
And that, Aisley thought wtih despair, would do very well as a
before-and-after advertisement of wholeness as a patent medicine.
We clergymen who criticize this new version of the Bible have
been labeled "out of touch" with the modern needs of the
church. We have been urged again and again to "move with the
times," to "adapt to present conditions." The scholars, in replying to our criticism of their translation, have said their work is
not meant to be a stream of dark mystery flowing close to the
blood, it is a form of modern highway, tar-sealed, hard-shoul-

dered, complete with lay-bys, which can transport the facts, history, purpose of Christianity swiftly to the ignorant ones in the outlying areas. It's a Utility Bible they say—a version for times of war. I'm old-fashioned enough to believe in undreamed-of paths and underground streams, to remember migrating clouds, seeds, swallows. But who is to decide whether we should live our Christian lives by punting on now detergent-soaked backwaters, or riding to a hundred-miles-an-hour head-on collision with our "puzzling reflection"?

Russell, the bacon-and-egg Englishman, was glancing quickly at the morning newspaper. Clematis Cottage was privileged to have it delivered so early.

"It seems . . ." Russell pronounced in his irritatingly archaic tone. (He was fifty-three; his hair was completely gray, his paunch showed under his shirt and beneath the top of his trousers. He didn't "look like" a dentist. His marriage to Greta had been peaceful and happy enough, if one remembers that after ten years it grew into a fossilized numbness which could have been described equally well as happiness or unhappiness. Greta's contribution to the marital "one flesh" had grown numb, to Russell, like an embarrassingly unabolishable dead limb; Greta herself was more conscious of movement, energy, throbbing of habit, pain, pleasure, in Russell's area of the after-marriage metamorphosis. It was more social pride and necessity which interpreted their embalmed state as happiness.)

"It seems," Russell said again, anxious for a spurt of family communication before he set out for his rooms, "that we have a death in Little Burgelstatham."

Listening to him, Greta felt anger. "It seems." Why was he always so many removes from the actual? There was no "seeming" about death when it happened: it *was*.

"It seems that an Italian farm worker, just arrived in Little Burgelstatham, has got himself drowned."

Polite "Oh's." Eyebrows raised. Jenny prodded her immodestly bleeding fried egg; it lay up to its neck in dark-red crepe bacon.

"Murder? Suicide?"

"Anyone 'helping the police with their inquiries'? Alwyn quoted playfully.

"It seems he had an English phrase book in his pocket, and a sheet of paper with English phrases written on it.

" 'The pen of my aunt?' "

Russell looked surprised. "Why, no," he said seriously. " 'My wounds are bleeding. My tailor is rich. These photographs are underexposed; please will you intensify them?' Also," Russell disclosed in a satisfied way, "two of his upper molars had gold fillings. Now, how could an Italian peasant afford that?"

Looking at him with her customary appraising breakfast glance, Greta felt envy for his specialized knowledge of the human mouth and its absurdly cumbersome and painful dental habits, and the blackmail put upon the whole body and soul by the finality of "second" teeth, and the ridicule, the loss of dignity brought about by the toothless mouth. If only Russell had gone on, she thought. If only he hadn't buried himself here in the country! He would have been at the top, the top! In London!

"No, he may have lost his way in the dark, and tripped."

Oh there's mold growing on him, green mold, Greta thought. If only he had gone on!

Greta had tried to understand the make-up of people who did not "go on" as a matter of course. She had never been able to fathom their motives. She looked impatiently at Aisley sitting there wrapped in his Anglo-Saxon wadding, safety-pinned by his God.

Aisley frowned, thinking of death, taking upon himself the clerical burden of it; were he at home now in his parish, he would be writing in his notebook, in black ink, as required. "To die," he said, "so far from one's own country!"

"One's own country?" Alwyn questioned. "You're behind the times, Uncle Aisley. The modern world is international. You don't just belong any more to a 'country.' Breakfast in Rome, etc, etc."

"All the same," Aisley replied, "one does need a country."

"If he hadn't the gold already in his teeth and hadn't just

arrived here, I'd say he's been preying upon the National Health."

"Why not?" Jenny asked. "Isn't the National Health there to be preyed on?"

"He would be a Roman Catholic, I suppose."

"Priests are so calm. They will see to him."

"There's the question of dealing with the teeth of our own people first."

"Our own people?"

"Do you remember, Mother?"

"Yes, Alwyn . . ."

"Years ago when I came home for the holidays I put up a tent in the garden, and I imagined it was waterproof, and so it was. It kept the rain out, that time it rained for days and nights. Then one day I touched the canvas, the spell was broken, the rain came in. By night, the tent was flooded."

Russell snorted. "Riddles again. Well, they used to tell me I was mad to take up dentistry. I hear you're going to write a novel. That sort of thing's fashionable now."

"Sometimes I wish," Alwyn said, "that no one had ever learned to touch the canvas. But you don't *learn* to touch it, it's an instinctive movement."

"Oh, Alwyn, not at breakfast!"

"I've an Approved School boy to fill," Russell said, thrusting the paper aside and getting up from the table.

"They always tell me," Greta said, "that the thing to do when they file past here on their Sunday walk is not to answer when they say hello, not to smile when they smile. Then they know you're someone to be reckoned with. Little Burgelstatham has such a precise book of rules! Watch the wall while the Approved School boys go by!"

"That clematis on your front wall is dead."

"No. Almost, not quite. I think I've saved it. Clematis needs such care."

"When they escape they're always guided by the light of the TV station. The police always know where to look for them."

"The new Magi."

"Yes," Aisley said, in reply to Greta's questioning glance, "no doubt I'll go walking today. The weather promises to be fine."

"Walking will do you good," everyone seemed to say at once, while Greta sighed to herself. Thank goodness Aisley was disposed of for the day.

What did one *do* in Little Burgelstatham with a sick clergyman?

10 Alwyn had taken the work of helping at the Unwins' cottage chiefly because he thought it might give him "experience" of the people of England who, according to tradition, had been "smiled at, passed, paid," but who had "not yet spoken." He had not kept secret his idea of writing a novel, and therefore had been overwhelmed with advice from his fellow students, his family, and anyone who was interested. Experience is what counts, they told him. Get experience.

But I have it already, he said to himself, fingering the fattening purse within his skull. Simply by belonging to the twentieth century I've been granted so much experience as a birthright. My father and Uncle Aisley poking around in yesterdays numbed by toothache or Godache are like infants in this modern age; their limbs and their minds are flabby, their brain won't support itself, they crawl, mumbling, through concentration camps and extermination posts, and have no knowledge or understanding of their surroundings. They think *The Voyage of the Lucky Dragon* is the latest Hollywood pirate film or an advertizing campaign to sell a new brand of cigarettes; the sun goes down on the summer sea, the sky is yellow, soft music plays, leisurely the members of the crew unflip their flip-top cigarette packs . . . life is good . . . teeth and God are profitable concerns.

Alwyn wondered: How does Aisley *stand* with God?

He was enjoying his task of partially demolishing the cottage. Destruction gave him special happiness. He had to keep reminding himself that he was going to write a novel, to write it, not to live it. If you lived experience you were too easily drowned in it. Writing about it, you could flail and splash your way to the shore, thrusting away those desperate fools who tried to cling to you for survival; you could then clamber out alone and sit, chilled, exhausted, but *alive*. What is more—you got such a *good view!*

There was Jenny. Something would have to be done about

Jenny. She was sympathetic, and so definite, geometrically definite, like a clear line drawn upon a blank page, with the same clear line for arms and legs and a circle for a head; children understood when they drew men and women as fleshless lines and circles with their feet wanting to walk in opposition to their bodies and their eyes, amazed, like suns that never set, and their hands like starfish poised to sting, and their mouths extravagantly ear to ear, greedy to swallow and vomit what they swallowed, and to kiss, deeply, like knife-blades. Scientists, Alwyn thought, were truthful in their masculine and feminine symbols—the circle, the arrow, the straight line.

He thought: Jenny compels me. She gives a precision to my life. An acrobat, I tread the high wire; an arrested drunk, I walk the white line. She confirms my cleaving power, like the sea arranging its waves and foam about the bows of a ship; she provides belief in my physical presence. As a ship, I'll travel on and on. She and I are not safe together. I agree with Aisley that it's a good thing to be safe, as long as we've worked out an *intelligent* scale of perils. Only someone living at the beginning of the world of civilization could say with truth and dignity, "I'm not safe, I'm in deadly danger."

"Why?"

"Because the sun disappears each night, and the world grows dark."

Alwyn discarded his thoughts for a moment to concentrate on fitting the hinges of the new wrought-iron gate. He began to sing. All right, so he was happy, and why not?

I'm extravagant enough to want to live, he thought. And to live beyond my spatial and temporal means and menaces. Thank—God?—for extravagance. Thank God for emergence from the mud, for loss of my third eye. I'm a happy man with a shirt, a bank account, a woman . . . In an age when it's so dark, with white darkness, we need those scratches of scientific or childish symbols to distinguish man from woman; even then, it is love among the skeletons with no time to construct the differences and luxuries of flesh, to soften the lips and withdraw the poisonous sting from the hands. How the bodies mutilate each other!

There should be time and light enough during the white winter darkness to build a softness of flesh:

> *With what shall I hone it, dear Henry, dear Henry,*
> *With what shall I hone it, dear Henry, with what?*
> *With water, dear Liza, dear Liza, dear Liza . . .*

"Enjoying yourself?"

Alwyn smiled at the woman who stopped her Vauxhall car in front of the cottage. She was Beatrice Sapley, the wife of the fruit farmer whose brother was a member of Parliament. Alwyn had been listening most of the morning to Olly Drew's complaints about their waste of water on their crops.

"I'm busy."

"We haven't seen you since you've been home." Beatrice pouted and made as if to search up and down the road. "It makes a change to have a university student around."

Beatrice Sapley, Alwyn noted, was dark and smoothly cellophaned in the usual affluent after-birth. She was safe enough. One could, of course, remove her transparent covering. He swung the gate to and fro.

"It's such a lovely day. You'll have heard about our Italian. I'm trying to dispose of him. I'm also thinking of buying this cottage. For the land."

"He was found in the ditch, the pond?"

"The pond. He hadn't any relatives in this country. The Consul is arranging everything. The whole thing is sordid and stupid; there may have been foul play. It makes one feel responsible without knowing what one's responsible for."

"Perhaps it would have been more convenient if he had died in what people would have called 'his own country.' Though I believe he didn't have a country? Dead exiles, expatriates, are always an embarrassment."

"Why are you wasting your time doing this kind of work? I know students like to get out and about during vacation, but to come to one's native village—and this!"

"I enjoy it."

"How can you? They say you're writing a novel."

"Everyone is. These days you have to start publishing early in the writing game. No one seems unduly shocked by teenage novelists; they're not regarded as depraved. It hasn't got to the stage where literary contraceptives are being issued."

"You're not a 'teenager' now, are you?"

"Twenty-one this vacation."

"I remember one late summer, you helped with our deep freeze."

"Oh?" Alwyn shrugged and began singing softly:

> " 'Well mend it, dear Henry, dear Henry, dear Henry,
> Well mend it, dear Henry . . .' "

He laughed suddenly.

> " 'Hang down your head, Tom Dooley,
> Hang down your head and cry,
> Hang down your head, Tom Dooley,
> For you are goin' to die.' "

"You're in touch with folk music," Beatrice said cynically. "Maybe you'll be a pop-singer instead of a novelist?" Then she said, smiling, retreating, and restarting the car, "I hope you and your fiancée will come to us one evening for drinks. About six. Any day." She waited for Alwyn to comment on her use of the word "fiancée," but he said nothing. She drove away, along the land.

> " 'Hang down your head, Tom Dooley,
> Hang down your head and cry,
> Hang down your head, Tom Dooley,
> For you are goin' to die . . .' "

Beatrice Sapley, Alwyn thought, was a fool, an animal without the animal discipline which defines and keeps to territorial rights. Her photo, they said, appeared every three weeks or so, hard and bright, in the glossy *East Anglian* magazine. Her two children, Abby and Judith, at boarding school during the term, were in France for the holidays. Evidently she had looked forward to the arrival of her Italian protégé; she was said to have arranged for his work while she and Bernard were in Andorra.

Every Sunday Beatrice Sapley rode, a head higher than the rest of Little Burgelstatham, higher than the hedge roses and the spray-withered blackberries, while the keen wind stung her cheeks, outlining the long scar curving toward her mouth.

Yes, Alwyn thought, when I was a small boy our eyes met over the deep freeze, above the strawberries and stringbeans . . . " 'Hang down your head, Tom Dooley . . .' " I'm almost twenty-one, in the prime of life . . . Eyes have to be plucked out before they meet, there must be "horrible steep" land, a cliff overlooking the sea; madness comes, not from the overwhelming complexities and possibilities of youth, but from the drying up of tributaries, the narrowing of the main stream to a single obsession of age. I'm almost twenty-one, there's no cliff in view, and the only people I know approaching senility are my Uncle Aisley cataloguing saints and my father cataloguing stamps—unused and used storks; pelicans; statesmen; islands; queens reigning and dead; causes; ideals; anniversaries . . . Here comes the dear old lady with the tea, and the ancient thermos flask with rust around the grooves of its throat.

" 'With an ax, dear Henry, dear Henry, dear Henry,
With an ax, dear Henry . . .' "

But Alwyn hadn't used an ax to kill the Italian. His hands had been strong enough. He had met El Botti near the Unwins' farm. They had walked together. Botti Julio had said "My tailor is rich. These photographs are underexposed; please will you intensify them?"

The scarecrows, like the secret, solely important remnants of mankind, crimson and faceless at last, had crackled like flame in the field. Then—the final blotting country darkness, reversing the writing of trees and quill-grasses, with the faintly gleaming surface of sky providing no mirrors, no means of interpretation.

Alwyn unscrewed the thermos and poured his cup of tea. He smiled at Mrs. Unwin. Her eyes were bright, intelligent. She had had a long life of adaptation to the age in which she lived, but he knew that now, when she looked out at the fields, at the relentlessly unjudging combine harvester that had no understanding of the subtle differences between corners, sun, shade, the golden center field thick and bright with light, she saw only the men with their scythes, herself there too, close to the field mice and poppies and the larks' nests; and abolishing a lifetime of tenacious clinging to the present, she set herself adrift with almost every word she spoke. In *my* time. In *my* day. It used to be.

Alwyn finished his tea. He smiled again at Mrs. Unwin. He knew they understood each other.

"Dear Henry, dear Liza," he said. "There's a hole in my bucket. Dear Henry, dear Liza."

PART TWO

Maplestone's chart

11 "We used to play a game," Jenny said. "You had three wishes. Most of us used to grant the first wish an everlasting power. What would you wish, Alwyn? Your first wish."

They were alone in the cottage. Russell and Greta were visiting the Baldrys for another installment of the Honeymoon Tour, and in spite of their promise not to include Aisley, they had invited him and he had accepted willingly. The evening was cold, edged with frost, and Jenny had heaped coal and wood on the fire. She poked a collapsing log; its almost hollow interior was honey-combed with soft gray ash and golden embers. She and Alwyn were sitting opposite each other; usually they sat side by side, as close as possible; and when they walked together they locked arms and hands, and at every seventh step Alwyn would turn to Jenny, grasp the blond hair twisted or falling free at the back of her neck, pull her head back until her body arched, turning toward him; then they would kiss, the movement of their tongues rising from deep within their bodies, their mouths a porch-place of sudden surprising but looked-for shelter, with light glowing from the inner room.

Tonight they made no attempt to touch. It could have happened that their being alone in the cottage, in charge, had caused them to project themselves so far into a fantasy of married domesticity that they became a Derby and a Joan sitting by their evening hearth, exchanging the time-polished signals that make speech unnecessary, even undesirable; or walled in irritating aloneness because the code has been forgotten, the signals have not been relearned, rehearsed, given new meaning.

Alwyn and Jenny had looked forward to being alone in the cottage.

"Some night," Alwyn had said, "when our clergyman, our dentist, our lady gardener have gone out and we have the place to ourselves . . ."

"I wish," Jenny had said, "that we could be together one eve-

71

ning, alone in the cottage. The inconvenient fact about people is that their minds and feelings have no boundaries. Skin's not a very efficient hedge. People *do invade*."

They sat now, moodily silent. Jenny had made coffee, and they had smoked a few cigarettes. The coffee was sour and the cigarettes tasted like straw.

"What would I wish?"

Alwyn was staring into the fire. He was distressingly handsome, Jenny thought, quite unlike his mother or his father or his uncle. Yet one of her delights during her stay at Clematis Cottage had been the scrutiny of the Maude faces, with Alwyn's as the center permanent reference that one labels *Important: Do Not Remove, Deface, or Otherwise Abuse*. She was comforted to see a faint family resemblance, for the uniqueness of Alwyn contained a sinister element which frightened her, with a fear that lay, like ice-cold steel rods, along her blood, close to her bones. Space-needles, she thought, would seem that way, lying close to the light. As soon as she was able to note a family likeness her fear would vanish, for whether a person's characteristics are sinister or endearing, the multiplication of them casts a spell of submission and acceptance; the warning signal is switched off, which flashes in the human mind at the appearance of anything or anyone strange or solitary. Jenny, whose parents were dead and who had no brothers or sisters, had thought this collecting of likenesses to be one of the reassuring advantages of family life. Often at Clematis Cottage (at times when she and Alwyn were together in bed) she had thought, His eyes are his uncle's, his voice is his mother's; and thinking this, she had been conscious of an immense feeling of relief, of a burden removed, as if the blame had at last been laid elsewhere.

She thought Alwyn's father was an old fuddy-duddy with his teeth-filling and stamp-collecting; and his mother was quite dotty about her runner beans and the red spiders on the shrubs; but Alwyn's occasional resemblance to his parents softened their eccentricities, made them endearing rather than irritating. Conversely, when Alwyn seemed to stray from his pattern as the Golden Knight of Happiness and Love, a swift reference to similar moods in his parents or his uncle would calm Jenny's apprehension. Indeed, during the first days of her holiday she had spent most of her time knitting the Maude household, twirling threads of Alwyn's mother and father and uncle on her needle or measuring-rod, to create a neat warm pattern that might keep out the cold for the rest of her life.

For she meant to marry Alwyn. She was not sure that his mother approved of such an early marriage for him, but Alwyn's mother—well!—out among the red spiders and the black fly!

"Yes, what would you wish?"

"While I think of it, I'd wish I didn't have this everlasting reputation for happiness. Happiness is laughter is a quirk of the jaw is lack of shame because you've got your own teeth!"

"But you *are* happy, Alwyn. You said so yourself, and I *know* you are."

"I sing, I smile, I make love, I love. I've catalogued worries like lack of money, education, prospects . . ."

Jenny burst into a giggle. "Alwyn, sitting there in the chair your uncle uses, you've taken on his persona. You're not really enjoying Little Burgelstatham, are you? The vegetation's so aloof, an affront to human dignity, all this defiant secrecy in fields and ponds—how did you manage when you were little, living here? Why not go away? You said Spain was a good country to write a novel in. Let's go to Spain."

"It seemed the place. A lot of the chaps go there."

"Oh!"

Jenny felt disappointed at Alwyn's sudden tone of ordinariness. She searched for a hint of excitement in his words "a lot of the chaps go there." The words had the effect of the leveling of a mountain; do I have to stare and stare at that plain all day, every day of my life? Once again Jenny found herself playing the game of references and resemblances. Though she was as much in love as to want Alwyn not to resemble "a lot of the chaps," it was really of no consequence if he did resemble them, for the reward of loving was enjoyment of a special view of the beloved, the view extending from intimate close-ups to privileged poses against a background of commonplace other people in a commonplace world.

"It would be nice in Spain," she said dreamily. "I could get a job teaching English."

"I could be a courier."

"A courier?"

"A lot of the chaps do that."

Jenny shrugged, to try to remove the vaguely irritating disappointment at the phrase again—"a lot of the chaps."

"It would be experience for my novel. Your teaching English would be experience."

"Oh," Jenny said lightly, "shall we exchange experience as the unenlightened exchange wage-packets? What shall I do with *your* experience?"

"Return it to me. I wish I had a motive."

"For what? Marriage or murder?"

"Both."

"Alwyn, I don't feel like being bright and—"

"Who's borrowed a persona now? My mother sits in that chair. She's apt to complain about not feeling 'bright,' as if human beings were meant to resemble copper kettles."

"It's not that, Alwyn. You seem to be so in step with the times. You don't seem to mind being surrounded by *time*, you're extravagant with it, you don't seize it, you let it be, almost as if it were no value to you; or as if it were a part of you; whereas I go stabbing desperately here and there at the stray moments. I'm like the old park-keeper picking up the leaves."

"You mean the hunchback in the park,
           the solitary mister,
           propped between trees and water . . ."

"Like the birds, he came early,
like the water, he sat down."

"Isn't that a perfect description of water?"

"You asked me what I did here at home, as a boy. I remember a few weeks of the long dark quiet winters here. My mother used to give me an old magazine and a pair of scissors to cut out pictures—I was very small; it was just before I went to school—

and I'd paste them in a scrapbook, and just when I'd begun past-
ing, my mother would come and she'd move the oil lamp from
one corner of the room to another, looking for something small
and unimportant—a dropped hair-clip or book-mark—and I'd get
so angry that my share of the light had been stolen; and then,
when I had the light again and I came to the last of the pictures
that it would make sense to use, I would be so angry, I wanted to
keep on cutting out pictures and pieces of words. Everything had
to be made into a picture; I'd feel scared if I couldn't make a
picture. They were mostly from old geographical magazines, and
once or twice a *Nursing Mirror* (Mother used to be a nurse),
where I would collect an attractive page of nasal tubes, seaside
homes for elderly gentlefolk, operating tables, enemas and vacan-
cies, and once, I remember, there was a little boy with a monstrous head and tiny wasted hands and feet; my mother snatched
the picture away from me.

"You know, it's strange how she's put up with living with my
father, when he's so much in the past. You ought to go to his
rooms to see his out-of-date equipment, his collapsed oxygen bag,
the frayed cord on the drill, the stained rinsing basin—it makes
me sick. I think it's a crime to desert the age you live in. It's like
phoning for the fire-brigade with a message that the house is on
fire when you don't know whether it is or not, and you don't
really care to investigate, you've seen only wisps of smoke, or
smelled something burning—it could have been dust, or people,
you don't know, but you make a run for it to the place where
they've never heard of fire, where they sit in caves, trying to rub
two sticks together to make a spark of warmth."

"I wouldn't say it's a crime. It's so hard to know. What if the
house *is* on fire—wouldn't it be best to get away?"

"I remember I cut out a blue sky, from the geographical. You
couldn't have known it was a sky, because it was all blue. I
showed it to my mother: she was very keen in 'interesting herself' in my progress. She didn't approve of the sky because she
didn't know how to name it, she couldn't identify it. 'Very nice,
very nice,' she said, but she looked afraid, with the same fear she's
had of the boy with the monstrous head and tiny wasted hands

and feet. She's been brave, you know, to move with the times when Dad's so far in the past."

"What did you do when you fell in love for the first time?"

"I searched the ground for clues, I tracked her in the sky, at night. But I haven't said my genuine first wish, have I?"

"Who cares about wishes! Marry me, and write your novel," Jenny said suddenly, gulping the words as if she were swallowing a medicine with acid base and a surface scattered with rose petals. The taste of the rose petals came last.

Alwyn did not say Yes, I'll marry you, or No, I won't marry you. He looked surprised, frowned, laughed.

They went up to bed together, and when Greta, Russell, and Aisley came home from their journey near the Tropic of Capricorn, Alwyn and Jenny were fast asleep, skin to skin.

Perhaps I ought to make a stand, to speak of it, Aisley thought, as, long past midnight, he heard Alwyn return to his room.

Russell, dreaming of the Cape of Good Hope, lay like a palm tree latticed with green light—bilious light, Greta thought, as she listened to the wind in the leaves. Groaning, Alwyn pressed his hands against his head. He piloted a space-craft. His dreams rose, drifting from his grasp, weightless. He fed himself with a tube. His monstrous head, aching, pivoted among the stars.

12 So refreshments are served. . . . If you look closely you will see that the marks on the edges of Russell's stamps are not perforations at all; they are Russell's teeth-marks. If you have enough imagination of the possibilities of human behavior you may also realize that the holes in the young cabbages are not made by garden pests named in the chart—Maplestone's Chart— but by Greta herself; that the scar on Alwyn's chest is not the result of an arrow shot in a childhood game in Sherwood Forest, but of a savage attack by Jenny. And Aisley's refreshment? It is invisible and ambitious. He does not attack leaves or stamps or people. Already during his stay at Little Burgelstatham he has provided himself with a satisfying banquet of the East Suffolk neighborhood. The country surrounding Little Burgelstatham is now scattered with small islands like bitten mouthfuls of earth. Aisley has swallowed a handful of centuries with more desperation than if he had been a starving man snatching bread-crumbs, not stopping to think whether he might be devouring pellets of poison. He has returned to the Anglo-Saxon world of East Anglia, of Northumbria. He has got rid of the troublesome terrifying years by the first means a human being ever uses to get rid of, and thus to more securely possess, what he hates and loves: he has devoured the intervening centuries. At times, now, when he looks from his window at the pleasantly rural scene he is not the Reverend Aisley Maude, he is St. Cuthbert himself, saying his prayers in the sea while his astonished fellow monks follow him, watching while the two seals come out of the deep water to warm him *"mid heora flyce."*

Yet at times you can see Aisley smiling to himself, mockingly. He knows the infectious nature of apparent simplicity. He smiles to think how he has adapted the quiet rural scene to his own true time and nature—is he not, then, the truly Adaptable Man?— how he has whittled away the world, the people, the land, the time, and because simplicity itself must have an end, he has ar-

77

rived at himself, close to the first fluid world, the sea; he is inhabitant of an island, gazing through the grille of loneliness at the few curious observers—the sea, the marsh birds, two seals; he re-enacts the life of St. Cuthbert. He wonders if, in this first simplicity, there is room for God to return to the picture.

The self remains: a complex doodle or pattern, like those menacing structures you see in the lonely places of East Anglia— the incongruous temples built upon prayers of destruction, where bombers fly in and lay their eggs in the concrete towers, and the bell tolls for all. When men are like flies to be exterminated, there is no refinement or distinction of "me" and "thee." It is "us," and "all." A yellow fire of light streaks down the sky, there is a taste of ashes in the mouth, the eyes expand, like frogs' about to commit a spring vision on the surface of a weed-infested pond. Me, thee, all, whilom, whilst, durst . . .

> Whither has gone the horse? Whither has gone the man? Whither has gone the place of feasting? How that time has passed away, has grown dark under the shadow of night as if it had never been!

> *Hwaer cwom mearg. Hwaer cwom mago? Hu seo þrag gewat genap u der nihthelm, swa heo no waere!*

13   Years ago, when Greta left her home in the Northeast to begin nursing in a London hospital, she had been full of excitement, longings, eagerness to extract as much life from the city as the city was prepared to give. In a characteristically direct way, she had decided upon nursing, because, as she thought, it would introduce her immediately to Life and Death attentively studied, provided for, administered to, in neat, clean surroundings. She had scorned the other girls from her home town who had gone to London without having made any plans for the full apprehension of its drama, who hoped to find the elements of Life and Death in untidy, uncontrolled places like streets, railway stations, lodging houses—without realizing that here there would be such confusion that Life would be indistinguishable from Death, and that both or either, without clinical restriction, would prey upon the observer.

On her days off, Greta used to practice elocution. She had been in London only a few months when she was able to speak without her northern accent. It was then she realized that she wanted more than the observation of "living," that perhaps her friends had been right when they chose the kind of "living" that has no obvious boundaries or controls, where one is sucked, helpless, into the terrible "swim."

The war came. Greta's new desires were fulfilled. The pace of life quickened. A skilled ward sister, her examinations passed with honors, she moved among the wounded and the dead, conscious of her part in the drama. She thought of Florence Nightingale, Nurse Cavell. She experienced, during the war, a sense of timelessness, or some alteration in the measurement of time. She noticed that her pulse-rate increased, as if her body were accommodating itself to a new element, as if she were an earth-creature who had entered the sea and immediately adapted to the conditions there, living and breathing in water, in "the swim" without any homesickness for earth. Yet in a way this process of change was as casual as if she had merely moved from one part of the country to another. It seemed that her childhood training in economy, in "making do," had decided that the first feelings of loneliness and fear that she experienced when she left home for the first time were enough to "last" through future changes in her life.

There had been no crisis for her when war came, when she witnessed so many deaths occurring with such violence that they seemed more a part of a festival, a celebration, an explosion of lives in a firework of blood and flesh. The dead were dead without the wholeness of hospital death. It seemed that the same urge for plunder which drove so many of the Londoners to seize what they could from the shops where articles were blown into the streets (she had seen, once, an East Ender, his face holy with triumph, carrying away a small bronze-legged coffee table as if it were an altar) also propelled an unknown force to seize human limbs, to carve and remove slices of bodies, to whirl away in the ransacking wind anonymous heads, like toffee apples that could be walked upon in the rubble, then discovered, without a feeling of horror, only with the accepted certainty that they belonged to the dead and had been used by the trampling panicking feet acting in the interests of the body's safety, as stepping-stones, as if they had been clean, bright, obliging as those ancient worn stones that were laid across water and are still used in time of flood and flight from danger, but are more often found now jutting parched, smooth and white from the beds of old streams where the water does not flow any more.

Greta fell in love. He was a doctor. They planned to marry when he returned on leave from the Middle East. He talked of setting up a practice in the city, for he did not care for the country. Greta saw herself as a doctor's wife in an orderly London house in a pleasant residential suburb where the power of the purse kept at bay such disquieting features as factories, dance-halls, mental homes. She saw their house as the kind referred to in advertisements as being "situated in best part of." "Best part of Bromley, Hampstead, Streatham." Later, when Christopher had tasted a little more success in his profession, they would live in one of the London districts described as "sought-after," where distinctions like "best part of" and "part growing more popular" cannot be made with dignity.

Christopher was posted missing, believed dead. When the authorities issued such messages, they assumed that their belief and the belief of the notified relatives would coincide. Greta had seen so many of her friends, grief-stricken, refusing to believe, that when she heard the news about Christopher she accepted at once the fact of his death. The surprising smugness of her feelings revealed to her that she and Christopher had been bound by a relationship that was not "love." She had been planning to marry a fashionable suburb!

She grew thin. When she brushed her dark hair she drew it closer to her head, pressing it, pinning it neatly, as if to meet an answering pressure from within. Her bones found at last their exactly desired covering from her flesh and skin. She became almost beautiful. She looked beautiful, pensive, self-contained when the dentist on leave met her at a friend's house, fell in love with her, and proposed within a fortnight. She smiled her "quiet" smile, accepted the proposal, and within another month she and Russell were married, and within three months Russell was again with Dental Corps while Greta had returned to the Northeast to await the birth of a child. During her melancholy stay in the country, among people with different accents, with aging parents who did not understand, she comforted herself with dreams of the future, conveniently switching possessions and suburbs. Beneath the constant disguise of his army uniform, which had seemed to cling to him even in nakedness, Russell gave the impression of a young man (thirty-four) with ability, with a stray self-sown ambition that would have to be cared for if it were to grow and blossom. Greta found his passion for dentistry both alarming and gratifying; here his ambition could be trained, she thought. The suburbs loomed pleasantly once more. Wife of the fashionable dentist, Russell Maude. Reception at the Royal College of Surgeons. Mingling with those at the Private View, I met . . . Russell Maude and his wife Greta.

She knew these were hollow charms and dreams, yet they echoed in her brain during the months of waiting for Alwyn to be born. The Northeast was a land of marsh and ice. There all sign posts had been removed from the villages and towns. Day after day, night after night, the bombers flew overhead, and the local inhabitants were cut off from the rest of the country, entrusted with terrible secrets which they could tell to no one in the South or the West. There was talk of invasion. The pewits flew crying over the fields where the grass had been flattened and thinned by the trampling soldiers. The country blackout was more terrifying than that of the city.

Neither Greta nor Russell had wanted a child so soon, yet when its birth was certain, each was careful to avoid giving "responsibility" to the other. Russell's letters, hampered by censorship, were filled with nationally harmless domestic longings and comments that made Greta think, with fleeting horror, What has the war done to him? He has let himself "go." When, after Alwyn's birth, Russell came home on leave, Greta knew that the war had made him into an old man. His body and mind seemed to have sagged, like an exhausted double bed. It seemed to promise the end of her life when, with the war over, Russell came home, bought a practice in Murston, a cottage in Little Burgelstatham, and began to bury her, himself and Alwyn in the depths of East Suffolk. At first Greta tried to think of him as a pioneer who would bring modern dental treatment to the backward natives of Little Burgelstatham. She had never forgotten her first visit to his "modern" surgery. The equipment might have come out of the ark; the place needed painting, renovating; the rubbed worn linoleum might have been chewed by rats. Greta had thought, Of course he'll change this, everything will be neat and clean, so clean and white and shining. With my nursing training I could help as a receptionist. There'll be a sitting room with a bright fire burning on cold days and the windows open in the summer, with the lace curtains blown gently by the lilac-scented breeze: the countryside has compensations.

Greta sought in marriage the orderly controlled encounters with life and death that she had experienced in the hospital. She was pleased, happy, but intuitively incredulous when Russell said, seeing her disappointment at the state of surgery, "I'll keep up with the modern trends, of course. Though," he added, his archaism finally making its runaway unashamed victory, "I don't agree with the modern world. I've had this modern age. Otherwise I'd have found a smart practice in London."

Greta flared. "But you don't have to *agree* with the age in which you live. It's not there to *argue* with you. Neither you nor it will win an argument. It's there to be adapted to—isn't it? You've got to *adapt.*"

"Basically," Russell said, almost as if he had not noticed her outburst, "I'm content to let things stay as they are. Basically."

Greta had noticed that the word "basically" was becoming a habit with Russell. (Or had it always been? In wartime one does not spend moments studying the merits of a lover's vocabulary.) "Basically" seemed to be his favorite word now. It was beginning to irritate her.

"Basically, I think," he would say, "Basically, you know . . ."

Also, there was his increasing absorption in his stamp collection. Teeth were bad enough—but stamps! What had come over him? He would place the album, the new stamps, the hinges, the tweezers, all the paraphernalia upon the dining-room table immediately after dinner, as if to say, "Well, we've had a token meal. Now this is my true nourishment."

It might have been more interesting, Greta thought, if he were involved in that part of philately which entailed wild dashes to London to bid for some rare stamp that he'd set his heart on and was prepared to pay the highest price for. But he's not enough money anyway, she reflected sadly. She could not remember any talk of stamps during their courtship and the early days of their marriage. Perhaps if their life were lived now at the same pace as in wartime there would be no irritating concerns and hobbies that leaked, like rising damp, through formerly weatherproof foundations of love, and that stained, with a stain that could not be removed.

Only fools blame the war, Greta thought, for such changes in a man's life and habits. I do not even know if they *are* changes.

It was true, however, that the war acted as a catalyst, changing predisposition to disposition, having the effect of a cloud-burst that either uprooted characteristics and swept them out of sight, replacing them with stray diseased branches borne with the storm from the mountains, or provided more fertile soil for the growth of a new personality. If Russell's way of life were to be at all related to the effects of war, one might say that war had acted upon him like a drought, draining and parching. He had withered. Anticipation and satisfaction of pleasure, a spendthrift salt seminal energy, tears and tastes of pain, had been sucked up by fire-bombs burning like the sun. And now, twenty years later, when Russell was fifty-three, he was an old man with the kind of old age which stops midway in life and spends the remainder of the years not in change or gradual dignified or undignified descent to the grave but in a continual level unchanging plain of proclamation that it has already reached the limits of life. Though Russell was "old" at fifty-three, he would never grow older. He was trapped, like a pitiful English counterpart of the "bold lover" on the Grecian urn.

"Bold lover never never canst thou kiss, nor she be fair. Nor she be fair"—Greta preferred to ignore this part of the poem.

Russell's condition could now be summed up in his fondness for the word "basically." His life was now (or *seemed*) simple and level. Perhaps it was an affirmation of the individuality that afflicts more than blesses human beings that when all the tides had gone out, Russell was found clinging, not to the basic wreckage of sex (which men of his age seize as a new pirate's treasure), but to inadequate uncomfortable promontories of Postage Stamps and Teeth. And he did not even plead for rescue!

Greta had learned, too, that when Russell said, "I'll leave things as they are," he was making an understatement. His real interest lay in things as they *were;* he yearned for the past.

Though as a young wife Greta would have liked a new home, when she, Russell and the baby Alwyn moved to Clematis Cottage she was prepared to accept it as "period with exposed oak beams" and to furnish it accordingly. Her neatness of mind found satisfying expression in the way she bought everything "to match"—the way she hung the brass warming-pans over the inglenook, placed the unused but polished copper kettle on the hob, filled the log box with huge logs saved from a poplar that had been felled but that in all the years the Maudes lived in Clematis Cottage had refused to die, and each June put forth from its withered stump soft fronds of light-green leaves, so that by August of each year the stump was a mass of tiny branches. Greta never stopped marveling at the persistence of the felled poplar.

Her concession to Russell's archaic pursuits and sympathies ended with the furnishing and care of the house. To every other pastime or duty she applied her determinedly "modern" outlook.

Though at first she resented the garden (for she was not interested in it, nor was she built as a Juno who would tramp about in heavy boots with a spade flung over her shoulder), she had learned to find an almost contemptuous pleasure in gardening. She had long given up interest in the flowers; their Olde English associations made her shudder. Clematis Cottage! One could enjoy the fragrance without making it an excuse for nostalgia. To the cultivation of vegetables and fruit she brought as much modern knowledge and scientific technique as she could acquire. Her garden became her compensation for not being able to "modernize" Russell and his attitude toward his profession.

Alwyn grew up, as modern a son as any woman would wish for, yet it seemed to Greta that no sooner had she realized the fact of his growing (in the brief time he spent away from boarding school), and become conscious of new pride in him, than he had removed himself from her to be the companion and lover of Jenny Sparling. When Greta thought of Alwyn she was conscious of having missed a treasured share of time, as if the monotony of her years at Little Burgelstatham had been accepted too readily as a time of patient waiting, like a child haunting a solemn birthday party, until the cake is cut; Greta's eyes had grown amazed, hurt, angry, when she observed that the knife had been thrust deep, the slice had been taken out of her reach; it had

never been meant for her to share. She was surprised to discover
that in her secret dreams the treasure and reward of a son had
belonged entirely to her.

Alwyn had been a strangely happy boy. Sometimes Greta
knew that her heart was beating very fast, her body was trembling, when she listened to him discussing his plans for the "future." He was so ready to accept the responsibility of the twentieth century! He seemed to her to be all Russell had never been,
yet no one had persuaded him that way, he had grown effort-
lessly into the space-age air, up through the everlasting pressures
of history and habit, like a blade of grass innocently thrusting its
way through concrete; dark, crumbling fragments surrounded
him, debris of the barriers of human habit that are broken twice
only—when the heat of the inner sun is so intense that the solid
covering melts, flows, bubbles, glues the feet and burns black
holes in the hands; and again when the inner surge of growth is so
powerful that no pressure or prison can outlaw it from its free
thrusting toward the sun.

If there were a war, Greta wondered, would the effect upon
Alwyn be as cataclysmic as upon Russell? Would the apparently
inherited archaic tendencies of the Maude family ever reveal
themselves in Alwyn? Or was this determined acceptance of the
age in which he lived merely another facet of antiquarianism?
Was time, perhaps, so disorganized (or man so disorganized) that
the farther one traveled into the future, the nearer one came to
the past? Would it be Alwyn, after all, who was first into the
Anglo-Saxon dream? Would it be he and not Aisley who retired
to the lonely island among the sea birds and the seals, or who
heard in every Suffolk lane the swish swish of the reeds, the
splash of the craft as the Northmen made their invasion?

Would Alwyn at fifty be a withered old man like his father,
satisfied in his final "basic" marooning with the equivalent of
stamps and teeth? Alwyn had said he was writing a novel. Most
students had such ambitions. Had Aisley? Greta did not think so.
Aisley's life seemed to her as much a pretense and evasion as
Russell's. When she had invited him to Clematis Cottage after his
illness she had hoped that he would not accept, that he would

reply with a combination of derision and fortitude that he could not leave his parish, that Katherine's death and now his illness had made him determined to "carry on." Greta had been disappointed in his swift acceptance of her invitation. She had a respect, strengthened during the war years, for people who "carried on" with their work in spite of illness and bereavement. She did not care to realize the truth—that such behavior is a myth, that nobody ever "carries on in spite of all." Yet Aisley *had* seized her invitation too readily, or had been seized by it, like a man who, circumspectly pacing the floor of truth, treads suddenly upon a loose board that gives way, plunging him into the dark joyful secrecy of falsehood.

Greta was not always practical; there were times when she knew surges of romantic feeling, when the rainbow bubbles floated in her mind to hide the clear vision of fact. Pretty bubbles to look at, they always burst; she did not weep for them. Often she still longed for the sense of power that she and Russell might have known had he brought "modern dentistry" to Little Burgelstatham; yet here he was, surrounded by storks, elder statesmen, bright-red empires, pounding away at his tiny National Health mortar, trying to persuade the farm manager's children not to eat iced lollies—even, once, when the vet was on holiday and the locum ill, taking out a cow's tooth! Impatient with Russell's futile preoccupation with teeth, Greta used to lose her temper and complain ("nag" would have been the objective description), "Teeth! I understand your reasons for being a dentist . . ." (Here the thought of Christopher rose like a released pain from her memory and lay close to her heart.) "But what are you doing to keep up with the times? Where are all the conferences, the modern techniques? I'm always reading about doctors and dentists who fly abroad for conferences."

Flying abroad! Oh! Russell Maude and his wife Greta on the jet for San Francisco!

Russell had answered in his slow way (he was like a toy man whose mechanism had run down, whose key had been lost; yet once he had had bright whirring sharp edges, capable of wounding), I don't have to hold conversations with the present or with posterity. I leave it to the teeth. They talk well enough, even without tongues or throat or face or flesh. Teeth from a million years past are still talking—and telling. I don't care for the present time, though I do often think, Greta, of the scene a million years hence when teeth that I have cared for are dug from the ice or the desert and begin to talk . . ."

"Hence!"

"What's wrong with 'hence?' I'll say 'from now' if you wish, Greta." He had then looked at her with that elderly helpless gaze that summoned her protective feelings.

"But why?" she said, "with your interest in teeth . . . as such . . . why don't you keep up with the times in your profession? You could have been . . . you could have been . . . and look at Alwyn . . ."

"Well?"

"I'm sorry. I'm behaving like a hospital matron. I'm nagging."

He hurt her by not protesting. He said smoothly, "At your age, you know . . ."

"Oh!" she said furiously. "*My age, my time* of life!"

"It's hard for a woman. So many changes . . ."

"Oh!" she said again, defeated. She looked at him suddenly hopefully, but it was no use; there were licked stamps—wild animals, generals, buildings, heroes, commemorations—adhering to his body. *Post Early*, the caption said. *Beware of Forest Fires!*

Hoe in hand, she was loosening the soil around the rows of leeks. The plants were tough and strong, their layers interwoven like green and cream plaited flax. She was thinking of Alwyn, of his absurd trust in his future.

Aisley was coming down the path. She had time to snatch one or two thoughts. I'm forty-seven. It's not unknown for a woman of my age. He is not human.

Aisley loomed. She tried to forget about Alwyn.

"Do you know," Aisley said, "I didn't know you were a gardening woman, fond of country life."

How tactless he was, in that blind way that is at times characteristic of people who are ordinarily so perceptive! "I love the country, Aisley," she said obstinately.

"Have you seen Alwyn?"

A wood pigeon flapped its gray and white wing in the mass of leaves in the tree above the pond; it was a sharp, swatting, destructive movement.

"Alwyn?"

They went inside.

I can't face it, Greta thought. It is *not unknown.* The double negative gave her a feeling of security, as if the fact itself could thus be canceled.

14   When Aisley was near, the Maudes did not care to mention God, partly because God was an embarrassment to them (like a senile parent who kept making outrageous remarks, performing wanton illogical acts; who, in spite of the fact that the ill-will toward him outweighed the attempts to keep him alive, simply refused to die) and partly because, not being sure of Aisley's "view" of God, they felt he had the first say in any discussion, that he knew more about God than they, that his knowledge might be combined with criticism of them and their way of living. Aisley was used to this attitude among many people, strangers and relatives. It depressed him. In his present state of lapsed faith it was no help for him to be living with a family greedy for punishment. The Maude family needed God, there was no doubt of that, but only for punishment: they had the expectancy of fear, not of love. Every time they look at me, Aisley thought, there's guilt in their eyes. This simple narrow white band worn with a difference around my throat has the effect of a whip: people cower; they suddenly turn upon themselves in panic, beating down all apparent or hidden swarms of evil; they put on a timid yet self-satisfied smile that pleads for the suspension of judgment; or they mock, how they mock, thinking, He regards himself as perfection; he is prolific as a fly in his breeding of self-righteous homilies; he buzzes forth to settle on our moral decay—and why not? He sucks his livelihood from it.

There were others, Aisley noticed, who, recognizing his clerical collar, relaxed, spread their minds in an easy chair because fires were lit suddenly, the maid-of-all-work had arrived, consolation, deliverance were near, sleep would come soon. And these few, lulled by their religion and its human symbol, at last opened their mouths and snored, and it was as difficult to wake them or to stop their snoring as it is to deal with someone prone in a feather bed, his face toward the ceiling and the sky, his heart beating rhythmically, free from the difficult personal pressures and jealousies of left-side, right-side. Such an attitude of complete submission is like that of a woman waiting for her lover to make his delayed contraceptive arrangements, or of old people, their head thrust back, the film spreading slowly, like weed on a stagnant summer pond, over their eyes, face to face with death.

With Aisley in the house, Greta realized she had never known such a scene of comings and goings: Aisley out walking, returning, out walking, making vague gentle remarks about "seeing how the morning is going," "observing the heat of noon," "enjoying the evening before it becomes night." He must have walked miles, Greta thought, since he came to Clematis Cottage.

(Aisley was so thin; his feet moved like planks or flat paddles along the summer-dusty lanes. The dust rose in a thin cloud about him; he looked like a portrait of an aloof creature, new to earth, skimming along the lately abandoned surface of hell.)

Aisley seldom talked of the people he met in his wanderings. He sometimes mentioned, vaguely, the result of his observation of the morning, noon or evening. He did not rhapsodize about nature, as so many do, using the natural scene as a keyhole to peep at God, returning with the shining triumphant expression of a voyeur who has seen all and wants only to retire to his solitude where he may relive the experience with himself as the chief actor.

Aisley was matter-of-fact in his talk of hedgerows, ditches, drought. He was interested enough to ask the name of plants picked from the hedgerow, but not interested enough to remember the names. When again and again he brought the same leaf or flower to Greta, she perceived with a sympathy that she did not often feel the fury and determination of the human memory to have its own way, to bring back the named again and again for renaming, the dead for reslaying. Why, Greta wondered, did Aisley never remember that hogweed is hogweed, balm is balm, that the words "hare" and "dawn" have the same etymology; with his knowledge of language he ought to have known and

remembered this. Greta herself had lived for so many years with
vegetation as her nearest neighbor that she gossiped daily among
it, using names and nicknames, respecting the endless vanity,
deceit, innocence of so many plants. It had not been easy for her
to live her social life among vegetables and hedgerows when she
might have been enjoying the prestige and satisfaction of being
wife to a professional man, if not in London, then in Little
Burgelstatham; but Russell's metamorphosis had been so complete (he had not even emerged, as some insects do, with the dry
husk of his former life lying near him as a kind of trophy), his
refusal to "move with the times" and live in the present had been
so determined that Greta found, like Lady Macbeth, but with less
dramatic potentiality, the need to "catch the nearest way." Had
she been a milder, more patient woman, had she been able to find
for Russell an extra supply of the love that some women do
provide at such times, she might have been content to wait beside
him in his archaic world for the change that would never happen;
but she had not the care and hope for him as the Princess had for
the Frog Prince when she brought him to eat and sleep with her
in the belief that he was other than he seemed and that one day
he would bring the fulfillment of all her desires; such hope was
only for the *young* who were *princesses* who had servants to
attend to the embarrassing needs of the Frog Prince while he
remained a frog.

Sometimes, sitting in the garden or the garden summerhouse
where she rested in the afternoons, she deplored and was afraid of
her sense of "empire" as she thought of the seeds, the seed-beds,
the plants, the pesticides, and realized that no plant had ever
spoken to her, that she was not the imaginative kind of person to
whom plants revealed their "secrets." They obeyed her, they
worked hard at their growing, but she knew no *encounters* with
them. She longed to be in situations where she might once more
use the dead (if she could not use the living) as stepping-stones
over streams of blood to a new land.

"It is ladywhite, Aisley," she said.

"Thank you," he replied humbly. "I'm a city man, there's no
doubt of that. My sermons are not in stones and trees."

It angered her to think that he, too, now believed her to be "involved" in the countryside.

She was concerned with infinitesimal things. She had not dreamed what had happened to her. Since Alwyn had been home she had observed him more closely than she had ever dared. He and Jenny were in love? She wondered why she had not objected to their sleeping with each other, for she cared for conventional behavior, believing it to be favorably economical in its dealings with one's temper and time as well as with one's future. It was strange, too, that Russell had not mentioned it; nor Aisley— surely he had a right to comment? This supposedly modern way of living had invaded a stronghold of archaism and was safe there, almost like a thief who, to avoid capture, conceals himself in the very house that he has burgled.

Greta envied Jenny. She wanted sometimes to strike her. There had been the evening when Greta, deciding to have a bath and seeing that the others were absorbed—in stamps or in each other—had crept upstairs and had begun undressing, when Jenny, not knowing she was in the bathroom, came in and saw her. She saw her touching the folds of her skin and thinking (for surely her thoughts were visible?), I'm like this. I never noticed it happening. I used to see it on old women when I was young. They shrink, the area of skin no longer fits edge to edge and bone to bone, it wrinkles like sand in a desert. And look down here, between my legs, hair has no color now, it's not even gray, it looks like ashes when the fire is out and there's no one in the room.

Greta knew that Jenny had seen her thoughts. Her face burned with shame, but she was grateful that Jenny had not seen too deeply, not as far as her knowledge of Alwyn and the fact that his love-affair was not really with Jenny or with any one person. He was a man who from birth had been provided with a huge set banquet of people. It had taken some years for his appetite to grow. He was satisfying it now. He would go on and on to the Last Supper that would mean as much to him as another Last Supper had meant to Aisley.

It is not unknown, Greta thought again.

Russell was asleep beside her. She wished some light would

show in the dark beyond the window. The bats were winging, dipping; they thudded against the window. A star showed in the sky; a planet; she had never been able to translate the pattern of the stellar system from paper to sky; there was a hemisphere unaccounted for that one could not leave on paper while one gave the Bear, the Hunter pride of place in the sky. The heavens whirled, but the Southern Cross did not show.

It is not unknown, she said to herself again. I can't think that I've sinned. It will be long and difficult. I may die. The news will spread. He will be a little prince with wrinkled skin.

15 Aisley was beginning to feel free. When he thought now of Katherine and their life together there was little depth in his images; it was a shallow, gentle process of thinking, a lazy punting through the past, stopping under the willows for picnics. As a clergyman who had practiced for fifteen years, he had grown used to the routine associated with dying. Katherine's death had almost become one death among many. When someone died in his parish he would go home, retreat to his study, find his bottle of black ink, uncork it, take his pen and his parish notebook and record the death. This routine never varied. Clearly in his mind he could see that part of the textbook from which he had learned his parish administration. The chapter had been headed "The Memory Tickler," and the instructions read:

> Memory ticklers must be consulted in a parish where there is such a large turnover of births, marriages, deaths. A good way is to make three hundred and sixty-six pages in a book with a plain date at the head of each page; enter the event as it happens on the appropriate date with a note of the year; red ink can be used for marriages, black ink for deaths and funerals.

How neatly and precisely, Aisley remembered, a year and its human events had thus been dismissed! At first he and his fellow ordinands had deplored the prosaic way in which this black-ink–red-ink routine seemed to rob their year's work of its endeavor, its difficulties, even its glory, by reducing it to a few strokes of red and black. There had been so many ordinands who had not been able to bear the strain put upon their ideals by the overloading and burial of them by such details as Commonplace Books, Parson's Freehold, Benefice Property, and all the administrative and theological material used to tailor the ordinand's belief in Christianity and in his vocation into a shape that would fit most readily without wear or tear or attack by moth or rust (the

95

traditional aggressors, the more familiar and invisible remaining
unnamed) upon the souls of the parish suffering from religious
nudity or wearing some outlandish unacceptable spiritual dress,
or uneasily chafing within a misfit means of salvational warmth,
or exposed in lonely places to undreamed-of winter privation—
"cracking winds, howling storms." Yet it seemed, more often,
that the shape of Christianity which was to enclose the congregation with love had adopted the texture and menace of those
plastic bags fashionably used by intending suicides as a means of
suffocation.

Aisley, as a born antiquarian, had found the disillusionment
easier to accept than had his fellow ordinands. They needed the
strength and the faith of the true pilgrim to sit in the G.O.E. class
(Aisley had no formal degree) while a lecturer spoke movingly
of the simplicity of Christianity and at the same time tried to
persuade them to face the duties, traditions, disciplines of trying
to perform a "cure of souls." Some of the students found it hard
to juggle God in one hand, Man in the other, and not lose their
sense of humility or their capacity to relate each hand to one
body. There was a tendency to grasp in a miserly way at the
gathered souls (to count them like coins before one slept) and to
feel in control of the seemingly imprisoned God. And then, in
the early days of training with an overworked harassed encumbent, some found themselves cursing instead of blessing,
moving irritably to free themselves from the tightening bonds
which left as many wounds in the hopes of the young clergymen
as the flesh wounds suffered by the ancient persecuted holy men.
There was little comfort in trying to decide which brought more
glory to the sufferer—the gashed faith at the sight of the elderly
encumbent counting the church collection and muttering, "Pray
there is enough to restore the South Window, to install heating,"
and the seemingly more distinguished ravages resulting through
the contemplation of the saints wandering alone in the wilderness,
tortured and put to death by mass fear and hate. It was easy to
forget the struggling encumbent by thinking elevating thoughts
about holy men of the past who had at least been canonized for

their pains and who were not close enough for their irritating personal characteristics to be observed.

During his first years of training and after his ordination, Aisley, like his fellow clergymen, "came down to earth"; but Aisley went further, he went *to* earth, like a fox; he burrowed into the past. Some might have said it was an act of cowardice, others that it proved his unsuitability for his calling. It was really a form of compromise. Some abandoned the church to take up medicine or teaching or farming or manufacturing; others made their compromise. By the time the young clergymen were ordained and had received a call to their first parish, each had decided his course of action. A compromise, by its nature, excludes conscience. Here it was a kind of flight square granted to those whose simple valuable beliefs were placed in danger by the stalking surrounding pieces of traditions, disciplines, official duties.

Aisley found that it was no longer possible for him to say "Let us pray," and then to pray. His mind was too full of church concerns: missions, pastoral letters, visiting lists, jumble sales (which he attended, peering at and prodding tangled heaps of pajama tops, skirts, old overcoats, while his face tried to keep an expression of spiritual ardor). He was not one who would make his personal compromise by rationalizing the need for these distractions, by asserting that his prayer would gain in dignity and power if it made its preliminary journey through a landscape of pajama tops, dilapidated pews, the storms of bridge-night jealousies; that this touch of simple sleeping, loving, quarreling, and mean humanity would make more "appeal" to God (as if God were involved in box-office ratings or a popularity poll) than a prayer which drove immediately, cleanly, capable of wounding, like a sword, or like that less obsolete, more pertinent weapon (of attack or defense)—the homely spike that records payments made or received, a year's or a life's profit and loss.

So many of Aisley's fellow clergymen thrust their prayers through moth-eaten overcoats or through rotting church beams, along paths to God pioneered by woodworm. They became successful vicars, loved by their congregation, approved of by the

Diocesan committees. Others took refuge in their ability to preach and conduct public worship. Others turned to the more subtle eloquence of church decoration and ritual, or made a success of misssions and of personal contact. In the banqueting halls along the ecclesiastical highway, as one by one Aisley's contemporaries were ordained, individual lights were being lit under the "meal-tubs."

Aisley, who would have been content with nothing less than a "candle under a bushel," took refuge with St. Cuthbert, the power behind the gray stone corner church in the East End of London. He was not without vanity. When he met Katherine and she agreed to marry him, he was for a time put off his course by her wonderful enthusiasm for his work. As Greta had tried to rescue Russell, so Katherine tried to reclaim Aisley from his drab parsonic Anglo-Saxon dream. Unlike Greta, Katherine had more chance of success, as she had been used to manipulating people rather than vegetation.

It was Aisley's vanity, not his faith, that grew during the years of his marriage to Katherine; she possessed a scattering brilliance as if, when she walked, she shed polish about her; whereas so many who must distribute the jewels clustered in their decorative personality are inclined to cast away only drab uncut opaque stones that must be pored over, cut, polished, before their true worth is realized. Katherine endeared herself to the parishioners. She had a quality of immediacy that Aisley had not met before. He thought sometimes, uneasily, that she seemed like a short-cut being; there were no leisurely ways in her. She was like a bird whose wings are so much a part of its body that it forgets them, and falls like a stone out of the sky; the wind cannot blow it or help it here or there, it cannot change its course or rest on a gentle current; yet, unlike a stone, it falls softly; the few blades of grass crushed beneath it spring to life again when it flies away; falling on water, it makes no dent in the waves; it harms nothing, yet its directness of aim is like that of an eagle swooping upon its prey, to bury its beak in nothing.

Or Katherine was like a whirlwind—no, a hurricane, those that are given Christian names, women's names, that rage across seas to doomed prepared cities, and then lie down, quiet as drowsy kittens, to sleep outside the walls.

It was this short-cut power that made Aisley feel his marriage to be a thing of wonder rather than a reality, and that helped him to accept his widowhood as a natural state. During Katherine's lifetime his reputation had begun to grow; his congregation increased. Recognition was sweet, but in the end it stank; Aisley had the image of God holding His nose and looking the other way. Though Katherine had never persuaded him to adopt the "modern approach," people came with an air of anticipation to hear his sermons. Taking up his newspaper, he read once, drawing his breath in horror:

> In town today is the Reverend Aisley Maude, that up-to-date clergyman who with his model-type wife are doing so much to transform the church from a medieval white elephant to a bang-on space-age tiger . . . with prey between its jaws . . .

Oh, God, Aisley thought.

The complementary quality of their marriage had been its ruin. Two pieces of human jigsaw, evidently fitting so neatly, are disarranged by a leverage of ideas, and the resulting gap made between them becomes a ravine; the pieces are violently scattered. Who will now carry the tree to its root, the hand to its arm, the jigsaw green or blue to merge with the appropriate piece of sky? If an attempt is made to reconstruct the picture, it is likely that the hand finds itself clutching roots, the sky in the west looks out from a woman's eye, the door becomes the lid of a safe, coffin or treasure chest; the roofless house stands forever open to the storm, its furniture covered with snow in winter, warped by sun in summer.

Katherine had tried to take over the running of St. Cuthbert's. There were certain changes that he had not been able to avoid; people approved; they looked upon the husband-and-wife team as an asset to the parish. It might have remained so, had not Aisley obstinately torn apart the whole idea by his devotion to more rare (not necessarily more worthy) visions than those of space-age unity. Aisley resisted the pressure to unite, "unite at all costs." Is it not the stray threads, he thought, the untidy sucker-roots that weave and flourish in new places—not new in the illusory sense that "tomorrow" is new, but very often with the kind of newness that draws its food from the past, reaching down through outcrops, volcanic folds of rock and soil to a former age?

To put the thing crudely, and Aisley did this almost as soon as Katherine died, her death, for him, was a piece of good luck. The physical act of loving had seemed glaringly like shopping in a supermarket, and, as in a supermarket, everything was ready, arranged, displayed, even priced; one had only to enter the door marked *In*, take up the two-toned basket, and, to soft background music, dazzled, proceed.

Aisley anticipated more from marriage than public acknowl-edgment of "suitability." Should he have asked for more? He thought so. The complement of the bee and the honeysuckle makes a pleasant picture to those who observe them, but bees and honeysuckle are far from resembling people who, when they draw close to each other, suffer that terrible deformity of eyes in the back of the head, so that the nearer they draw to each other, the farther their visions range until, often, united in their appar-ently self-contained complementary world, they perceive a tiny speck at the most distant outer edge of their vision. Often they quarrel over the nature of the speck; some say it is a spark, a drop of poison, a stain, others that it is a tiny shadow whose substance must remain forever invisible to man, that although it may seem small viewed from the world, the magnitude of its reality fills that other world beyond the range of human vision, where the light stays at perpetual noon. Spark, poison, stain; and some said God. Aisley had said God. The human eye is not consistent. Aisley began to say, not indelible God, but indelible stain. Then, at this stage of his faith, unlike many of his fellow clergymen, he did not put a telescope to his eye or in any other way enlist the help of science to discern the nature of the nature of the stain or to refute the fact that it *was* a stain. He did not say, "Agreed, it

seems to be a stain, but does not the biologist sprinkle his watch-
glass with XXY XX and do not these, to the uninitiated, have the
appearance of a stain?"

Just as it was Aisley's preoccupation with the speck in the
distance that caused him to study for the ministry, so it was his
preoccupation with the nature of the speck-become-stain that
absorbed him since his wife's death, his illness, and the morning
when God unexpectedly moved. Since that morning Aisley had
experienced all the sensations of grief. He recognized the state:

> After great pain a formal feeling comes,
> the nerves sit ceremonious like tombs,
> the stiff heart questions . . .

He knew that during this period of "formal feeling" it is easier
to make dialectical progress toward God, who, though He may
have moved or disappeared from the picture, is at this stage believed calmly, inevitably, to exist. A man believes He exists, as a
perfect sentence believes in its right to punctuation—whether
inwardly with no visible marks or outwardly—all the riotous
speeches, conclusions, pauses, exclamations, question marks, those
hundreds and thousands that illuminate meaning, all the glittering
seed put out for the starving flocks of continuity pecking desperately at the snow-covered pages . . .

Aisley wore his grief like mourning wear. He let it be known
that he still mourned for Katherine. And so he may have
mourned. But it was God who occupied his thoughts. Just as
Greta preferred to "catch the nearest way" in dealing with her
problems, so Aisley sought "the highest way," with, perhaps, a
naïveté unusual for him who takes it for granted that air and
feeling are more pure at the heights, that climbing is superior to
descending.

How he dreamed of Northumbria, the home of St. Cuthbert!
He thought he should be there rather than in East Suffolk, yet
with geographical economy he "made do" with the East Suffolk
countryside to conjure dreams of his saint. Day after day he
walked and walked. He did not really care if hogweed was hogweed or balm was balm or if the hare and the dawn had the same

origin; yet he drew his breath in suspense at the idea that hares do not need eyes in the back of their head for their sight to encompass wheat sky briar toad man gun road pigeon clod home blood God in one swift glance.

"Happy the hare at morning who cannot read the hunter's waking thought," Aisley quoted to himself. It is comforting to know that men are not hares; but men, also, cannot read the hunter's waking thought. And why suppose, as the poet does with the hare, that not being able to read it may bring happiness? Why not the torturing curiosity to *know* the hunter's waking thought? And remembering another poet who writes of hares, I'd ask why, merely because the poet belongs to the countryside, must he assume that hares "run races in their mirth"?

> *All things that love the sun are out of doors;*
> *The sky rejoices in the morning's birth;*
> *The grass is bright with rain-drops;—on the moors*
> *The hare is running races in her mirth;*
> *And with her feet she from the plashy earth*
> *Raises a mist, that, glittering in the sun,*
> *Runs with her all the way, wherever she doth run.*
> *I was a Traveller then upon the moor;*
> *I saw the hare that raced about with joy; . . .*

Aisley was fond of Wordsworth's poetry—another aspect of his make-up which made him seem so sadly old-fashioned! Who but the scholars reads Wordsworth now? he wondered. He had sympathy, too, for the poet's descents into banality:

> *At length, himself unsettling, he took the pond*
> *Stirred with his staff, and fixedly did look*
> *Upon the muddy water, which he conned,*
> *As if he had been reading in a book:*
> *And now a stranger's privilege I took:*
> *And, drawing to his side, to him did say,*
> *"This morning gives us promise of a glorious day."*

Aisley had suffered similar compulsory descents in his vocation. What would Jenny and Alwyn think, he wondered, if they knew I read Wordsworth? I, who have lived in the city, walking beside houses, parked cars, railway lines, bridges, factories, and not once thinking, when a car passed, driven erratically, "Ah, the Ford is happy, full of delight." Nor have I looked upon the television aerials and mused: "How calm they stand; they do not know the future." Surely it is curious, Aisley thought, to argue that hares, roses, trees are alive while cars, factories, television aerials are not? Does man kill *everything* he touches?

No one knew, not yet, he thought, when not-life became life, or if there was any not-life; there were restless movements of patterns even within the speck stain drop of poison. Aisley wished he could sleep again in peace and call the speck God.

16 There was still no sign of rain. The farm workers—stout women in summer dresses, gum-boots, head scarves; men in hayseed suits, all with rustic sunburned appearance that one associates, had one the experience and knowledge, with crumpled, dream-ridden mental patients—cycled on their way to work in the Sapleys' black-currant fields, through rainbow mists formed by the streaming fountains of hose-pipes and sprinklers. This extravagance appalled the farm workers. Little Burgelstatham was divided in a feud of water. In the small household gardens the leaves of the vegetables drooped, turned yellow; white butterflies crowded like summer snowflakes; the heavily flapping wood pigeons held meetings and orgies that no wielded truncheon of wind could disperse; when the shots rang from the carbide bird-scarers the pigeons rose, beating their wings in the air, then descended, spreading softly like tents or gray and white skirts, as if the sudden disturbances had been part of their ballet arranged with carbide and scarecrow accompaniment. In the midst of the drought, day after day, the Sapleys' farm was obscured by a water-mist of rainbows. People complained, grew angry, "His brother is in Parliament. Electricity came to *their* end of the lane, and stopped there; what about us? They bring in foreign workers, taking away our jobs . . ."

Day and night the wind moved in perpetual restlessness. It was the East wind; it had never been known to blow for so long in spring and summer; it was by tradition the autumn and winter wind, bringing frost and bitter cold; it had not yet its wintry chill, yet strangely, while the drought persisted, the wind was still cold enough for summer to be spoken of as a season almost past. People's eyes, gloomy and autumnal, said, "There's been no summer this year. Spring was late; there was no spring, and now there's been no summer." There had been no hordes of people from the cities, setting up their picnics in the first green lane they drove near, erecting their splint-legged formica tables, tubular chairs that converted quickly from dining to lounging position; drowsing in the midst of the pleasant murmurings and rustlings of June; thinking, lazily convalescent after city afflictions, *This is the countryside, our countryside. Who said our land was not green and pleasant, that it has been spoiled by overspill, ribbon development?*; looking curiously at the dogged rustics tramping by with their farm implements, their fox-tanned faces, their secret mole-thoughts contoured beneath their dry skulls; or rushing to buy derelict country cottages whose thatch crumbled like mold in their hands; or packing the stout tourist buses that struggled to pass through the country lanes while the passengers inside glowed like Christmas presents within the sealed golden wrapping of the modern windows described in the brochures as *Panoramic*, extending over the roof where the gray-white light, turned yellow, shone on the straw-hatted elderly women, the white-haired close-shaven skulls of the Americans, with a strange yellow-rippled glare, like that inside a furnace.

Few tourists came. The lanes were quiet. The trees were not even yet fully leaved, the hedgerows had not blossomed completely, the tissue-buds of the blackberry flower had not opened, the holly berries were few, their dark-red skin blotched with yellow, presaging, some said, a bitter winter. Yet the honeysuckle thrived, the grass sprang tall, necklaced with morning dew; in the early morning the fields were lakes of mist; always, walking in the lanes, one walked toward water, sky-shadows, mirrors.

People said, "Do you remember the cowslips this year?" The stalks of the cowslips were now withered, but it was said there had never been so many before in spring, nor so many daffodils. But why didn't the sun shine? Why didn't the rain rain? The wheat was on the ear—men and women talked of it in the buses and in the train to Tydd. "The wheat is on the ear," they said, and strangers traveling through rural Suffolk, thinking Ye Olde English Countryside, shivered at the significance and mystery of the phrase, and returning home to the city, they found occasion to murmur it, as if the phrase, the experience and knowledge of it were theirs *by right*. Englishmen believe in their inborn *right* to the countryside; that is why they scatter about it the share of

their country selves, their love-gifts, their evidence—the empty
packets and bottles, the fat-stained blue and yellow striped crisp-
containers, the salted-peanut packets that they've needed fingernails like swords to open.

"The wheat is on the ear." But how could it ripen?

Only the true natives of Little Burgelstatham knew how to
discuss the ripening of their crops. The Maudes could not properly be described as natives, for though they had lived many
years in the district, they were from "outside," they spoke with a
different accent, they had visited London, they received letters
from London or from places abroad—airmail letters. The Sapleys, the Baldrys, the woman journalist, on the rare occasions
when she came to stay in her cottage—all received mail with
foreign postmarks. Airmail letters caused excitement in the
Murston Post Office. If the postman had decided not to deliver an
afternoon mail, to wait until the following morning, he swiftly
changed his mind at the sight of an airmail letter, for he too was a
native of Little Burgelstatham, and he believed, like the other
villagers, that no one wrote airmail letters, just as no one sent
telegrams, unless the matter was one of life and death. His heart
raced with excitement when an airmail envelope flashed before
him its familiar blue and red emblems of speed and urgency.

Perhaps Bert Whattling was the one true native of Little
Burgelstatham. When Mrs. Unwin recalled life "as it used to be,"
she returned in her mind to Stamford and dreams of the Duchess
of Rutland. When Bert thought of the past he had no places to
think of except Little Burgelstatham and the First World War
battlefields. On his visits to the cottages in Murston Lane, the
Sapleys' farm, the Baldrys' farm, he experienced a sense of
power, and he knew that he received glances of respect when he
remarked, with shrewd old-identity perception of the old-identity role, "I knew this land when there were no big farms, no
roads, only cottages. I helped to make the roads."

Creation brings the prerogative of destruction. Bert's voice ex-
pressed a devilish enjoyment of power when he compared the
land as it was now and as it had been.

"Where the Sapleys' farm is *now* (he pronounced it in the

Suffolk way—"*nu*"), and the Baldrys' farm, the Maudes' garden, all these cottages, there were flowers growing as far as the eye could see; a market garden; roses, daffodils, snapdragons (these were Bert's favorites), carnations, chrysanthemums. No city people with cars and picnic baskets, living in the cottages in summer and leaving them empty in winter for the rats to run in and out."

From the way Bert talked, one would think he'd been born on the spot, in the midst of the market gardens, watching over it and its ghosts all his life; when he walked about in his heavy wellingtons it often seemed a wonder that he was able to lift his feet from the earth without pulling up his own roots. When he talked about the local way of life "within living memory," he gave the impression that everything since the time of the flowers was superfluous, temporary, and could be removed, and would be, in time, leaving no trace; then the flowers would grow once more, and all would be as it used to be. One might suppose, then, that Bert was an antiquarian like Russell and Aisley, but that was not so; his life was lived strictly within his own time, which, since he was now an elderly pensioner, had the privilege of being referred to in the superior phrase "within living memory." Though he had had little formal education (he was making and mending roads for the Council when he was fourteen), he had heard of the time when the North Sea flowed around Tydd and Murston and Withigford, and the land was marshland full of nesting and sheltering sea-birds, and the Northmen came on their raids up the reed-enclosed waters. He thought of this time with a vague dreamy disbelief; it had been "within the living memory" of people who were dead, whom he had never known; who, after all, cared about them now? They had had their say and had slipped neatly (like people getting into bed, between the sheets) into the pages of history books. You couldn't sit in the Withigford Bull on a Sunday morning and talk about the Danish raids and the number of Saxon dead, but you could enjoy reminiscences of the time when lightning struck the Hall and the two cottages in its grounds and the flash could be seen for miles around.

No, Bert was not concerned to dive off into possibility and fantasy and the dark waves of other people's memories; his own memory was a long enough and firm enough plank to parade up and down on without his ever needing to take the plunge into the past.

Or, like a tree that records and expresses only its own span of time, that cannot or does not think, When I was a shadow in the ice, when I shall be ashes in a coal fire, Bert's contemplation was bounded by his birth (hearsay inevitably creeps over the border) and by his "going" or his "passing," when he would be, as he described it, "laid to rest" in the cemetery on the outskirts of Murston, next door, alas, to the new broiler factory. Bert joked about this. "Say how will I feel," he said, "when I'm lying there with the hens next door squawking in one end and coming out plucked and ready the other end; say how will I feel if those that own the factory get ideas to build on an' they take over me last resting-place an' the tombstones are stacked up close the way you see them doing in Tydd, getting ready for the overspill, trying to make more room.

"Who's going to buy the cottage?" Alwyn said.

Mrs. Unwin, who always stayed now when she brought the morning tea, to have a cup herself and to talk to Alwyn, whom she admired, said she didn't know who would buy it.

"There's been a lot of work put into it," she said, in a tone that was meant to sound businesslike. "We have to ask a good price for it."

(A tiptoe greed, not often seen in her, looked out from her eyes.)

"They want everything these days. There's no electricity, and they all ask for it. They want a bathroom, too. We're putting in running water, we're bringing it to the sink. They'll want a new kind of lavatory, too."

Alwyn sympathized with her. "They may not like the thatch," he said. "The fire risk."

"Oh, there's some that like the thatch. The Americans like the thatch. There's an American Air Force base not far away. But I'd like a nice educated gentleman from London to buy the cottage. They're very rich in London. I had someone call the other day, someone from television. The agent told me, after he'd gone."

"He wanted electricity?"

"Oh, no. He said he wanted to live like us. He liked the outside lavatory too, but I'm sorry we couldn't show him the roses in bloom on the roof."

Alwyn took Mrs. Unwin's cup and filled it with the remaining half-cup from the thermos. "I might be sorry to leave here," he said. "I'm enjoying my holiday, and this work."

"Oh, you needn't leave, you could get a job on one of the farms. But," Mrs. Unwin added respectfully, "you're educated. You're going to be a teacher or a doctor. (My doctor in Murston went to Cambridge; we often talk over old times.)"

She did not explain the nature of the "old times" or how her doctor's going to Cambridge necessarily involved her in them, but she flushed proudly when she spoke of her doctor.

"Or perhaps you'll be a nuclear scientist? They're very important these days. I've heard you're going to write a book. I used to like reading but I didn't take to book-learning. When I was in Stamford . . ."

They finished their tea. Olly Drew was away, sick, and in the meantime Alwyn was working alone at the cottage.

"See you, Mrs. Unwin," he said, smiling.

She returned his smile. He had no airs at all, Alwyn Maude, he was a gentleman. He was doing a good job at the cottage, too. There was talk that his morals weren't very clean, but anyone could see they were, from his happy boyish face. Lex should be paying him more for the cottage work—no, no, of course not, for he wasn't trained, and Lex found it hard enough to make ends meet, though he would not have done had he inherited his father's farm. I must remember, Mrs. Unwin thought, as, prodding with her stick, she walked out the gate and glanced a moment at the spot in the road where her husband's dog, Gyp, had been killed—I must remember to put some flowers on Gyp's grave.

Gyp was buried under the mimosa tree near the front window of the farmhouse. Mrs. Unwin had hated Gyp, but no one but herself knew of this. "Now, you ought to have seen Gyp," she would say, when people admired the farm mongrel—a doe-eyed, deformed, potbellied bitch called Nelly. "Oh, you ought to have seen Gyp! We were all very fond of Gyp. No dog could match up to Gyp. He's buried in the front garden, just there," she would say ostentatiously like a courier defining and describing the spot, "under the mimosa tree," implying that anyone who buried a dog under a mimosa tree must surely have been fond of him.

Mrs. Unwin did not really care at all for dogs or cats or other domestic animals. She liked the geese with their white aprons and yellow beaks, and she liked the birds flying around as small graceful objects in the air, and she liked "nature," or claimed to like it, but she cared most for, and spent her time enjoying and collecting news of, the stately mansions and their inhabitants.

She opened the farmhouse gate. Nelly came waddling toward her, sniffing, tail-wagging, shameless, as only dogs can be.

"Out of the way, Nelly," Mrs. Unwin said sharply, brandishing her stick. She frowned. "Get inside!"

And opening the front door, she called to Lex, forgetting that he had been away on the milk-round since early morning. "Lex, Nelly's that way again. You know what happened last time."

No one answered her. Nelly climbed into the chair by the fire and curled, head between her paws, watching, waiting, in a manner that sickened Mrs. Unwin, for an excuse to show pleasure and affection.

Mrs. Unwin sat in the chair opposite Nelly and closed her eyes. She was tired. Her sight was getting worse. The preparations for the cottage worried her; no one knew what type of person would be coming to live there, and even though the cottage was being sold, she knew that she would still think of it as belonging to the farm. It was a secret still, but Lex had had an offer—the television producer from London who had stood at the point of the boundary between the farmhouse and the cottage, where there had never been a fence and where a track had been worn with the comings and goings to and from the cottage.

"Where's the boundary?" he had said sharply.

"Oh, we've never bothered," Mrs. Unwin had replied.

"That wouldn't do me," he said. "You understand that, of course. My wife and I would have a fence built. My son will be coming here to stay in the holidays. He's at Oxford."

"Oh? At Oxford? My doctor went to Cambridge," Mrs. Unwin told him. "That's Dr. Finch. I've never had any other."

The television producer then explained that he wanted to get away from the noise and bustle of London, that he and his wife had often dreamed of a little country cottage like this, with no modern conveniences to spoil the simple way of life.

"All the same," he said, "we'd have running water, that's one thing we need. Running water, a bathroom, electric light, an inside lavatory. One has to make concessions," he said.

Mrs. Unwin had been unwilling to have the Dutch oven removed, but she had agreed with Lex that anyone who bought the cottage would certainly—if not at once, then later—ask for modern conveniences. She knew that people might *say* they wanted to live in the old way, with candles, oil lamps, Dutch ovens, coal fires, no bath, no water; but after they had moved in they would discover they wanted everything, and they would keep making excuses to themselves and others for wanting everything, as if it were a crime. Mrs. Unwin also knew that by the time winter came, if all modern conveniences had not been installed, those who had rented or bought the cottage would leave, they would not even stay to watch the packets and packets of seed (Cottage Garden Variety) they had planted in the spring appear and blossom. People had no sense of responsibility to the landscape.

Most of the wall between the kitchen and the sitting room was being removed, the oven with it. Alwyn's clothes were layered with brick-dust and plaster; he pulled and probed at the last few bricks, which were so old they almost crumbled. He had dropped the pick and thrust with his hands to dislodge the last section of the wall, heaving it away in another cloud of dust and a shower of broken bricks, and now the wall was ready to be cleaned, restored with new brick, the back of the chimney made safe. He noticed a yellowing sheet of paper upon the wall; it was a poster, over a hundred years old. He gently eased it away, shook the dust from it, spread it on the floor, smoothed the crumpled surface, and studied the printing and the picture that were disclosed. He saw a Negro woman advertised for sale. *Slave Sale.* He read the information given in smaller print: "For Sale at Tydd Market, Friday. Sarah, fifty-five, a hard-working servant. Cleans, cooks, gardens. Price five pounds. No bargaining."

Alwyn folded the poster and put it in his pocket. "What happened, Sarah?" he asked. "Who bought you? Who sold you? Did they, in the end, bargain for you? Perhaps Aisley is right in removing himself so far in history that he can avoid the embarrassment of too recent events. He's happy enough with his Anglo-Saxons. I can almost see him getting about the marshes in a coracle. There's a saint on his mind. I'd rather have Sarah, the slave, on *my* mind. I imagine that while Aisley has a saint on his mind he's finding it hard to concentrate on other things: it's a matter of filling the gap; Cadbury's snack would do just as well; God is convenient enough to be pumped into the human mind till it swells and floats with its own importance; but there's no doubt that the human mind has got moving somewhere under the inflationary power of the gods; also it has been given a good view from the heights. Aisley's religion, I'm afraid, in spite of dreams of floating and flying, is old steam travel, the puffing billy way to glory."

(What television tycoon is going to live in this cottage, and sit reading the Letters in the *Radio Times* or the *Kama Sutra* in that lady's bonnet of a lavatory? Who's going to sleep in this old iron bed?)

It's the space age; they keep telling us so often that it makes me suspicious. It's the time when you wink a golden eye at the world, shout through wind-tunnels of distortion, "A wonderful view, a wonderful view," and then return from your glory to have psychiatrists and physicians prodding at you, entreating you to count backwards in sevens, to supply the missing word—*cat, kitten, dog,* blank.

All things Bright and Beautiful. Oh love that will not let me go, so hangs my helpless soul of thee, I give thee back the life I owe

. . . and so on. Peace perfect peace . . . we are but little children weak . . . *cat, kitten, dog,* blank.

Alwyn had expected the face, and was prepared for it. It was not frightening, because it had appeared so often in fact and fiction. He glanced at it casually. "Botti Julio," he said calmly. I'm no Raskolnikov, he thought.

There were no Raskolnikovs now, not in the space-age. If one wanted to live in the twentieth century (though "living in" an age was rather like making a succession of dives at revolving doors and spending the time breathless with relief that one had found a small three-cornered compartment in which to travel to the next room), one didn't want to make heavy weather of an occasional murder. There was no question of the sweat of guilt, no "frightful fiend" treading the Little Burgelstatham lanes in the evenings; there just wasn't time to sink a shaft of guilt into one's mind and bring up on misery-creaking chains the dregs of conscience, using them to try to flood the so pretty landscape of Now.

The face receded. Its dark eyes were shining like tenpin bowls. It opened its mouth to speak. My tailor is not rich, it said. A brace of partridges and two rabbits. The boxers are skipping in the gymnasium to strengthen their legs. These photographs are underexposed; please will you intensify them?

Jenny came to walk home with Alwyn. He thought that she looked assured and trim, like the Mrs. Nineteen Eighty-Four of the advertisements who is pictured having a love-affair with a washing machine. He did not mind, he was not jealous. He put his arm around her waist. He thought, I'm fond of you because you have so many *plans*, they even come out of your ears, like those multicolored streamers used by conjurors; and there are plans in your eyes, like millions of those lively not immediately identifiable creatures that spawn in dark ponds in springtime.

They passed the farmhouse. Mrs. Unwin was standing belligerently, stick in hand, while the heifers were being driven through the gate from the field at the back of the house. She smiled proudly at Jenny and Alwyn. Her smile said, I'm over eighty but I'm still useful on the farm, even if it doesn't belong to me any more. Both Jenny and Alwyn knew the meaning of her smile, because she had told them so often.

"I'm over eighty, yet I still help bringing in the calves, feeding them, driving them into the field. Each one knows me. I don't know what Mr. Bedford would do without me."

She waved her stick at Alwyn and Jenny, who waved back.

"Will she ever go to live with Lex and Dot?" Jenny asked.

"She won't leave here. I don't think she could bear it."

They walked on, holding and swinging hands, "the picture of innocence," past the wheat and barley fields, while Mrs. Unwin, watching them, remarked to Mr. Bedford as he shut the gate behind the last heifer, "They're so happy together. He's a real gentleman."

Mr. Bedford grunted.

Mrs. Unwin sighed. She *knew* about Alwyn.

One of the little Friesians thrust its head over the gate; she went over to it and patted it on the head. "It knows me," she said. "They all know me." She spoke gratefully, as if being known by anything or anyone were an everlasting miracle, as mysterious as the sentences "And he knew her," "And she knew him," in the Bible.

She said good evening to Mr. Bedford and went indoors. It wasn't the right time to tell him about the leaking tap, she thought. Or to show him the upstairs room where the damp strikes. I'll tell him about it soon, though, I can't go on living here with the kitchen floor always a pool of water; I can't live here another winter. Why, when we lived at Stamford. . . .

17 Muriel Baldry was driving home from her weekly visit to the bank in Withigford (bank in Withigford, go to church in Murston, shop in Tydd) when she saw Greta standing forlornly on the side of the road, with her arms full of wild flowers that she seemed about to throw away. Muriel stopped the station wagon.

"Oh, don't throw them away, Mrs. Maude. I'll take them home. I haven't yet got as far as walking in the lane to gather flowers."

Though the two women were about the same age, Muriel had addressed Greta as if she were older; the note of respect was for Greta's length of residence in Little Burgelstatham. Muriel wondered what Greta "saw" in Little Burgelstatham, to have stayed so long.

"Do you really want them? They're all insect-bitten, or they've been affected by spray. Some of my ways are still city ways. I can't resist a flower blossoming in a country hedgerow." She passed the bunch of foxgloves, ladywhites, and evil-smelling daisies, with centers bright as cake-mix or custard, through the window to Muriel, who exclaimed, taken aback, "Oh!"

She had thought they were *real* flowers, not a child's wayward assortment of limp rejects. She thrust them in the chromium vase by the front seat, taking out the pink plastic roses. Her movement was leisurely, for a woman who was claiming to have little leisure. Her body, too, in rest or motion, had a leisurely aspect; the large bones were smoothed over with enough pale flesh to make them seem like a luxurious possession, like furniture covered with velvet. Her appearance contrasted vividly with the slight, tense Greta, who seemed in her movements to be meeting or escaping from a secret challenge. Greta's body had an aura of dissatisfaction that came partly from her belief that if a woman is pleasantly plump during adolescence, she returns to a similar shape at middle age. It had not been so with Greta; somewhere, at some time, her body had deceived her or had been deceived, and now there was another deception that could not remain hidden for long.

From a neighboring field a sound like gunshot made the two women start; oh, it was a scarecrow crackling in the wind.

"Are the birds really afraid of red?" Muriel asked. "Last year, they tell me, blue was the rage in scarecrows; another year it was white. Bert Whattling tells me that torn newspaper scares them. I use newspapers on the beans—or rather Vic does—but nothing seems to be effective."

There was a pause. Then both Muriel and Greta spoke at once, but it was Muriel's slow, assured voice that won. "Would you like to come back to the White House for a sherry or something?"

"Why not? Thank you."

Greta got in the car. The smell of the dog-daisies was unpleasant, but Muriel seemed not to notice it, or perhaps she was being tactful, Greta thought, as she suffered the stink. How many roads, Greta thought, are made impassable between person and person by these avalanches of tact! Then Muriel, as if reading her thoughts, gave a prolonged sniff.

"These daisies!"

"I don't know what came over me, picking them," Greta began, and instantly felt ashamed—there was no need to explain, as if she had been shoplifting. She wished she had Muriel's slow assurance. Her own appeared to be deserting her. She would have liked Muriel Baldry to know that she, also, did not really have leisure to wander in the lanes of Little Burgelstatham, like Proserpine gathering flowers.

Muriel poured two glasses of sherry. They sat in the big light dining room of the White House Farm, where the furniture had been some past cabinet-maker's dream. It had not the pallid goose-fleshed appearance of wood that had been snatched from the cradle, as it were, ravished too early, given a guise of maturity or even of old age. The grains of growth in the farm furniture showed uniquely, personal as fingerprints; one was invited to bask in the warm glowing color of the wood. A different invitation was given by one wall that had been almost covered, like a bulletin board, with magazine pictures of Australia. There was one of a sheep station, wtih a flock of deep-eyed pudgy sheep, their wool like white chrysanthemums, standing staring with a properly tourist gaze at the Australian sun going down beyond rolling brown hills.

"We stayed there," Muriel said, noting Greta's glance at it. "Right at the back of beyond, as Vic would say." Then with a self-conscious air she stood up, tugged her skirt down over her knees, and bracing her shoulders slightly, she crossed to the wall and in a dogged manner began pointing to and identifying some of the Australian scenes, speaking at times in the Australian vernacular, adding, "As Vic would say . . ."

Watching her, feeling pity for her (and for herself as she remembered Russell's stamps, which—thank God—were not pasted on the wall!), Greta said boldly almost as a way of acknowledging that though she and Muriel were the same age, hers was the superiority of having lived longer in Little Burgelstatham and having known Vic Baldry's first wife, "They're your husband's pin-ups, aren't they?"

"Yes," Muriel admitted, surprised. She was not the type of woman, she thought, to begin confidences. Her doorways didn't open immediately onto the road, thank you, there was a long stately driveway, with formal borders . . . yet . . .

"Yes," she said again. "He talks of emigrating to Australia. Buying a farm there."

"Would you like that?" Greta's tone was shrewd. Again, her manner was now that of an older woman whose husband had presented a similar problem.

Muriel was unwilling to commit herself. "I don't know," she said. "I think I'm truly English. I get on very well in this country with the light, the mist, the cloud effects, the absence of brilliant color." She smiled bleakly. "I think some personalities are not suited to sun, to brilliant striped reptiles, and birds beating crimson wings in the air."

Greta felt like saying, "I'm English too, but I would never

describe myself thus, in a roundabout way, as a kind of female leech-gatherer sitting in state with the climate." She supposed that Muriel was less phlegmatic than she was willing to admit, that vivid colors and birds flashing their crimson and turquoise wings were not unknown in her dreams—she "supposed" this, with that imaginative possession of another's mind that is more often self-reflection than intuition.

Vic Baldry, waking and sleeping, had certainly been over-powered by his trip Down Under. One evening, Greta thought, as she recalled the "slides" and films shown at the White House, we shall reach the climax of the tour, we'll set foot on Australian shores.

She smiled to herself. In public presentation the honeymooners had still not sailed from Calcutta.

Greta put down her glass. She declined another sherry. Mention of one subject slightly distressing to Muriel had given her leave to mention one distressing to herself, for one must keep continuity of permissions—and who was there to tell? Who, if the need arose and persisted? Not Russell. Not Jenny, or Aisley —certainly not Alwyn. There was no one. All her years spent in a cottage garden instead of among friends in London and the north were of little help now: one did not confide in Brassicas.

Muriel refilled her own glass. "Has the affair of the Italian been dealt with?" she asked.

"Botti Julio? Yes."

Muriel shuddered. "The Sapleys were so keen to get foreign workers. I believe others were supposed to arrive, but it's all been canceled. Vic was rather keen to have some here. The Italians do marvelous farm work in Australia."

"He won't be buried here," Greta said. "I used to nurse—did I tell you?"

"I nursed too, for a time. I married early."

They were rivals.

"I married early too. I suppose the Consul sees to everything. Was he married, with a family?"

"I don't know. A postcard came for him the other day. I don't know why it came here. I felt so guilty about having it, and of course he's dead. I put it in *Pears' Cyclopedia*, in 'Household Pets,' the white mice and cats page . . . Silly, isn't it . . . It was in Spanish."

"Alwyn knows a little Spanish," Greta said, simply and boldly, as if she had been reading large, clear print upon an outsize page: The dog is on the mat. The cat is on the mat. The white mouse is on the mat. The cat, the dog, and the white mouse are on the mat. The house is tall. John sees that the house is tall. Run John run. Run Jenny run.

Greta remembered suddenly that most elusive experience of learning to read: the John and Jenny books they had used as primers; how as the grade of the books increased, the print became smaller and more secret until it adopted the full deceit and disguise of "grownup" print. It was the first book that Greta remembered at this moment so vividly: the words so tall, tall as a house; the pink wooden-seeming drawings of John and Jenny; their names; the capital letters unadorned, entwined with none of those plants that fill the story (and the capital letters) of the Sleeping Beauty: bindweed (was it bindweed?) clematis, nasturtium; the words so tall, the letters so unconcealing. No matter how fast or how far John and Jenny were running, they could find no place to hide—not in the first books. Ah, the adult print was different; there, a forest of hiding-places!

"I hear Alwyn's going to write a book. Is he writing one now?" Without waiting for an answer, Muriel began to tell how, last summer, a poet had been staying in the cottage at the corner of the lane, and one afternoon he had asked her to drink wine with him on the lawn. The wine had been rich and red—the kind, the poet told her, that Keats used to drink. "I've never met a poet before," Muriel said, still amazed and pleased at the interlude. "It was just when we'd come back."

"Oh, yes. I never met him. He stayed only six weeks, didn't he? Isn't there an American there now, a Mormon?"

"Eustace Glee? Oh, no, he went after staying only a few days. He came here one night—remember—the night you brought the Reverend Maude. I didn't know he was a Mormon then. He was

very handsome, wasn't he? Crew-cut, smart suit, but there was
no chance of drinking wine on the lawn with *him*. Did you
notice he even refused *tea?* He talked of sealed boxes, secret
plates being carried up to heaven . . . and someone, Moroni. And
in Little Burgelstatham! He was pretty soon edged out of Little
Burgelstatham! Anonymous letters, threats, gossip. They're so
handsome!" She laughed.

Greta's answering laugh was hard. "A useful scapegoat. They
spring up everywhere—so naturally and opportunely, it makes
one wonder why a goat was ever used in the first place."

"And *is* Alwyn writing a book? We shall have to be careful, or
he'll be putting us all into it!" Muriel spoke with pleased anticipation.

Greta moved toward the door. "I don't know," she said. "They
never confide in you," she parroted.

"Look," Muriel said, immediately on Mothers' Union terms
(Oh hell, Greta thought), "why don't you come to W.I.? I
didn't think I would like it, but I've enjoyed myself there." She
had enough egotism to make an unconscious switch of pronouns,
to present a picture of Greta enjoying *herself*. "Last week there
was a talk on rug-making. There's to be one this week on artificial flowers. An expert is coming. Haven't you ever thought of
going along?"

Greta was beginning to realize that Muriel's rather slow, gentle
manner was no mask; there was a simplicity, a folk quality in her
make-up. "Expert," she had said, in that dreamy, revering tone
that was not really in keeping with her self-awareness. Expert.
Specialist.

In her domestic life, Muriel would show at times the nature of
a witch, Greta thought. Had she lived in former times she might
have lived as a witch. Greta supposed that Muriel was the kind of
housewife who kept recipes allegedly "handed down" over hundreds of years; who would perceive an element of magic in
"Household Hints" (hadn't she put the stray postcard from
Canada between "Household Pets," White Mice, and Cats? It
was likely that she saved pages from magazines—*How to Remove Stains from Carpets, Old Country Recipes for Nettle Beer,
Slow Wine, Rose-Petal Champagne.*

"Yes, I found it interesting. I hadn't expected to. And there was a quiz. You know. I won it." Muriel sounded almost shy.

Greta was surprised to find herself speaking gently instead of with the impatience she felt. "It's not my idea of a social evening. No. Thank you for asking, but it doesn't appeal to me."

"No, of course not," Muriel said quickly, wondering: What does Greta Maude *do* with her time, other than garden, garden? She waited. Perhaps Greta might explain. But Greta made no excuses.

As she was about to leave, Muriel said suddenly, "You knew Anna, didn't you?"

"Yes, slightly."

It was a question and answer on the edge of a precipice; there was nothing to be done with question and answer but drop them over the cliff. And now Greta and Muriel were smiling and saying good-by and Muriel was saying, "Do come again, not only to these *evenings* of ours—Vic's so determined to reveal the glory of Australia. Also, I must show you (she was going to say "someone") the new decorations, and there's this remarkable Venini chandelier."

Her voice became dreamy. "Isn't it strange? A relative of mine was a dealer in glass. In glass. He left me this magnificent chandelier. I have to reinforce the ceiling to put it in—there's that big long room overlooking the garden—but we've no electricity to light it."

"I hear Eastern Electricity's coming this way quite soon, now the Sapleys have got it."

"Yes. Vic isn't all that keen. But we do expect it soon. I'll have to throw a combined party to celebrate the coming of electricity and the installing of my chandelier!"

When Greta had gone, Muriel returned to the dining room to look at the Australiana upon the wall. Gum trees, kookaburras, kangaroos. Good God. When she had stood with Vic that day in the desert when they had been trying to trace the path of starvation followed by Burke and Wills, she had been terrified, the sweat had come out like dew on her forehead, her face, hands, between her breasts, and Vic had said, embracing her in the exuberant manner he had adopted since his visit to Australia (almost as if he were trying to prove to the Australians that he too was an Australian), "It's the heat. Imagine how Burke and Wills felt!"

She had been too exhausted for anger. A honeymoon with a husband who spent his time being concerned about two stupid dead explorers! It wasn't the heat that exhausted her, it was fear.

She studied the picture that Vic had brought home—Burke and Wills struggling through the desert, their knife-edged ribs carving at the heavy blocks of sun, their skin yellow as sand. They were naked. A dark-blue stain the color of ink on an old stamp-pad (years of days impressed upon it) blotted and dried by the sun showed between their legs. In spite of their lack of flesh, their bodies, so taut in their yellow skin (more like sand-grained airmail paper than the traditional "parchment"), their elongated hands and feet (like rafts made of bones with blood instead of sea glimpsed between the cracks), seemed to surge with growth. Flowers blossoming in the desert? No, only the buoyancy, directness, almost military confidence shown by men who had clearly concluded and signed their treaty with death.

This ironic victory of the two explorers was vividly portrayed in their feet, which had so little flesh they could no longer be thought of as "Burke's feet," "Wills' feet." They seemed like the feet of kangaroos, hares, apes; they had even abandoned their right to be recognized as human; after many more years, lying undiscovered in the sand, they would secede finally to the empire of the inanimate, that is, inanimate to human eyes, yet perhaps somewhere still conforming to the compulsive pattern and route of growth that would lead them again within the boundary of the living human state.

Staring at the picture, Muriel was not concerned to read deeply an articulate portrayal of the men's desperation. She saw only starving explorers. Even as skeletons they looked to her like Victorian gentlemen set neatly side by side under a tropical sky. Muriel feared incongruity. She feared going to Australia to live under such a sky, by such reputedly shark-infested seas, near so much terrifying desert where Englishmen had perished. Yet it was these features of Australia, and the new cities, and the burning sun that, she knew, had captured Vic's imagination. Life had been rather too swift for Muriel. It had been a strange honeymoon. She and Vic had agreed that a voyage almost round the world was an ideal way to spend their honeymoon, that having both been married before, and not being so young, they would not have cared to rent a crofter's cottage in the wilds of Scotland, or booked a suite at the Metropole. A voyage seemed to be the perfect answer. The voyage itself would be the "third party," the discreet distraction that would give their honeymoon the quality of a honeymoon more suited to middle age and second marriage, that would prevent it from being a blasé repetition of the obsessively narrow self-destroying self-resurrecting activities of a first honeymoon, where the ambitions of union are pitched too high, and the world and the future are lost if one partner lives while the other dies, where the anxieties of the new officially blessed state reduce the eye of the needle to such a narrow gateway that no two people, no camels, nor any thread, even a spiderweb, nor even rich men (like Vic Baldry) on their way to heaven, could ever hope to pass through it together.

At first, then, until Vic and Muriel reached Sydney, their voyage had been all they had wished for. The idea of a "round trip" had been prompted by Vic's middle age, where the aim in life is often not so much a laudable desire to "see how the other half lives" before it is too late, as a need (pathetic when one considers the thimble-sized human container) to replenish the store that is slowly draining away; if one has lived in valleys, one dreams of some new prize, some compensation, not in mountains, for the mountain people experience the same yearning, but in a leveling of heights and depths, a presentation of a comprehensive view. At this age one looks not up, not down, but along, around. For men and women who belong originally to the mountains, middle age can be a disaster: the former "peak in Darien" from where they gazed beyond the edge of the world is flattened to a meat-pie eminence. A delicate adjustment in the art of looking is imperative, but such adjustment may be so violent that a mental squint

results or (here the prognosis is more favorable) one is granted
double vision. This is to be envied, for here both substance and
shadow are visible, not the shadow only; perhaps it is worth
waiting half a lifetime for this experience?

For practical purposes Vic chose Australia because a shipping
company offered "round-trip" voyages there. Also, a chap in the
bank in Murston had a cousin who had gone to Australia, and a
chap in Tydd had married an Australian girl. There had been a
TV series—*The New Continent*.

So the obscure desires and needs of a middle-aged honeymoon-
ing couple were arranged for. They paid their passage and set sail
and all had been blissful, with the voyage as the discreetly invisible third person intervening to subdue any memories or thoughts
Muriel might have of her first husband and any comparisons that
might cause Vic to think too often of Anna. Vic's pride in the
obvious success of their venture made him a gay companion.
Muriel had not seen him so happy before. It promised well for
their future together and it flushed Muriel's usually pale cheeks
with a new surge of life and warmth. Her small permanent store
of romanticism increased, and instead of cherishing it, brooding
over it occasionally in solitude, she indulged in a calculated
squander of it. She dreamed. She dreamed of Vic and of her new
home. (She was not ashamed to note that husband and home
appeared of equal importance in her dreams.) Their happiness
together grew. Their lovemaking was intense, with a kind of
comfortable intensity that Muriel had not known before. She
would sleep immediately, more deeply, and not feel the occasional resentment of being awake while a satisfied animal snored
beside her. Sleep, too, seemed to extend its boundaries to include
part of waking life. Had Muriel considered this to be a natural
accompaniment of growing old, she might have felt more fearful
than blissful, but using the new defenses that replace the lowered
or removed defenses of youth, she looked on the gently invading
sleep with a feeling of gratitude.

Vic became the life of the games and gambles on board. Someone remarked that he didn't seem like an Englishman, he was
more like an Australian sheep farmer than an English farmer,

frustrated monarch of three or four fields and a ditch, rented by Grace of the Lord of the Manor.

Muriel did not know what to blame—the voyage, herself, life on board ship, her first husband, Vic's first wife, those returning Australians with whom Vic surrounded himself, laughing, joking, drinking with them. She was disconcerted to notice that many of the Australians on board were quiet men not given to "shouting," drinks, and back-slapping; they might have been Englishmen! This discovery was irritating: exceptions are such a violent threat to the peace and ease of generalizations. Muriel put out of her mind what she had seen when she wrote to Meda, her sister-in-law by her first marriage, who lived on a remote farm in the north of Scotland; to Meda she described "all these back-slapping, joking, beer-drinking Australians," but she could find nothing and no one to blame when the ship sailed into Sydney harbor and Vic, seizing from the unobtrusive third party, the reliable "companion-help" round tour, the seductive, stimulating, youthful *Australia*, decided once and for all who would be the real partner of his honeymoon and future life.

Muriel took up the empty sherry glasses. She looked again at the Australian pictures and, briefly, at Burke and Wills collapsed under their burning southern sky. She moved toward them. An observer might have thought she was about to offer them, cruelly, the empty glasses. Then she turned and went out of the room.

I'll ask Greta Maude to come over one other day, she thought. I must show her the chandelier. Vic's keen on it too. If I can get him to be enthusiastic about electricity (there's nothing to lose; generators are out of date and too cumbersome) and we get the chandelier installed, I think . . . I don't know why . . . I'm sure everything will change, things will be different, happier.

18 A garden shed was a conventional place for it to happen. Yet it was not the shed featured in so many stories—the door half on its hinges swinging to and fro, the broken windowpane pasted over the newspaper, the camp bed in the corner, or the pile of old spiderwebbed sacks; and the weather—rain, storm, vivid flashes of lightning that struck through the window, back and forth like the swinging lantern of the Searchers combing the night for the lost, tired, hungry travelers. It was not a shed where the very discomfort evoked visions of eventual warmth and peace when the lights of the Searchers at last picked out the huddled, forlorn figures of the travelers, who were then taken to the Great House for feasting and fires. For thousands of years these same Searchers have been moving in and out of fables, myths, histories, stories. When Adam and Eve found each other in the Garden, the Searcher was there, waiting to help, for there has always been the desperate need of man and woman to be *found*, for a light to shine out of the darkness, kind words to be spoken, the Searchers to lean down to soothe, reassure those who have been kept alive by their hope, or to cover with blankets or layers of forest leaves those who have died before rescue came.

Don't you remember? Haven't you yourself experienced these things? Forests, lanterns, dwellings on the edge of the wood where only a witch might live and where those who have lost their way in the forest may seek shelter; the lights and sudden cries; bowls of steaming soup; charms; mirrors that will show the future and the correct path to take to reach it; beasts that speak; branches that are loud with messages.

Then, at last, sleep, with the storm already asleep whimpering its dreams in the leaves (autumn leaves; it is forever autumn, or winter; snow is falling); the little shed is warm, a bright fire is burning, a great black kettle suspended from the ceiling swings gently when the breeze blows beneath the floor of the forest room.

126

It happened here. Oh, the circumstances were different. Were they like those of myths and fables, there might have been some understanding: charms, mirrors, rescues, youngest daughters, only sons, withered crones—the formal ruinous patterns of the everlasting mythical family—the youngest son who sets out on a journey, crossing the bridge over the forest stream; the daughter who defies her mother and is changed to a wayside flower; the eldest son who becomes a hare; all the pains and penalties of misbehavior, greed, refusal, denial, love, hate; the fixed (three-year, seven-year) period of punishment, of lonely wandering, before the flower resumes its human shape, the hare becomes once again the eldest son; the conspiracies—foxes and sons against fathers, creatures from the pond who entice daughters from their faithful or faithless lovers; a mother's temptations, mysterious, menacing—If the bough breaks three times between midnight and dawn, then—the penalties are always clear.

It did not happen that way; it was not that way at all.

When Greta had given up trying to persuade Russell to "modernize" the cottage, she had transferred her efforts to live in "contemporary" surroundings to the layout and management of the vegetable garden and the small cedarwood summerhouse. After Alwyn had been sent to school and she had accepted the fact that she would not be having another child, she began to spend most of her time in the garden. She found the cedar summerhouse illustrated in a garden catalogue.

"A cedar shed is best," Russell told her. Though she did not know how he had come to get knowledge of garden sheds (between teeth and stamps) she had felt grateful for his advice; then she rebelled. How was it, she wondered, that men could go through life without ever, so to speak, "crossing the path" of cedar sheds, yet knowing so much about them, so much that when they spoke you would have thought garden sheds had been their life-long involvement. It was very mysterious. Whereas a woman, to know anything of the subject, had to send for a garden catalogue, and when the catalogue came, to let eveyone see it, to be given more advice. Almost as soon as she had withdrawn the catalogue from the envelope, Russell had taken it and, without using the index, had turned quickly to the correct page.

Again, that was very mysterious. It almost seemed to Greta that their long-lost pattern of sharing had been rediscovered. She had thought, impulsively, I'll give up the garden, we'll forget about the catalogue: *Couple United by Garden Shed. Garden Catalogue Works Miracles.*

She wondered how, in the days before mass distribution of newspapers, people coped with this need to simplify and proclaim the substance of their personal crises. Surely they had lost themselves in the confused complications of detail with no experience for seizing isolated facts. *Cedar-Shed Woman. Teeth-Stamp Husband. Reunion.*

"This is the one," Russell said definitely, with his superior intuitive knowledge.

"Yes, yes," Greta said eagerly, "that one."

Solemnly Russell returned the catalogue. She wondered about the possible news items in Russell's mind. *Valuable Work Interrupted to Choose Garden Shed. Teeth Second Place, Complains Dentist. Cedar-Shed Wife . . .*

Oh, but she was not being fair to him. She moved toward him. She was not surprised when he came to her room late that night (they had slept apart for many years) muttering that he had lost something, some article of clothing, some valuable stamp; she couldn't now remember what it had been, but he had asked did she know where it might be found? It was an excuse, of course. She had hated him for needing an excuse.

"Sorry," Russell said.

Why apologize, she thought. But she said, "Never mind, I understand."

Quelled, Russell retreated toward the door.

"It was some stamp, rice fields, a commemoration," he muttered as he left the room.

The shed—more a garden room, a summerhouse—was put at the bottom of the garden. Greta furnished it carefully. She had bought new gardening tools, fertilizers, pesticides, and arranged them on the shelves along one wall where above them she pinned the chart distributed by the chemical company—*Maplestone's Pest and Disease Chart*—with its printed injunction: *Hang this chart in your garden shed.* It was bright, lucid, with columns for identification, location, and treatment of pests and diseases. In the center, in very br ght color, some of the more notorious pests and diseases were illustrated: a mass of green shaped like an elf-cap—green fly; a rose stained with rust-colored blood—black-spot; a tiny black-faced creature emerging from a frothy yolk of yellow—codling moth. Apple scab, white fly, leaf miner; fruit-tree buds afflicted by green tip, petal fall, fruitlet; millipedes, moss, peach-leaf curl, botrytis, gall mite, mealy bug, thrips, wasps, cutworm, carrot fly, leaf hoppers, clubroot; rats, mice and voles . . .

It was comforting to return to a chartered world where the enemies could be located, stalked, and destroyed—some in what the chart described as "The Dwelling-House"; others "Under Glass"; or "in fruit trees in early summer." Greta was proud of the Maplestone Chart. She believed it almost rivaled any classical or modern painting that she might have chosen for her garden room. She was equally proud of the collection (in "puffer"-packs, bottles, bags) of lethal smokes, dusts, powders, selective weed killers, chrysanthemum mildew specific . . . and the ferti-lizers—Foliar Feed, Soil Sterilizer, Winter Wash, Hormone Rooting Powder . . .

Had it been ten years later, she might have thought, seeing herself in these surroundings, Who is the witch? I or Muriel Baldry? Recipes for calve's-foot jelly and sloe wine are nothing compared with this lethal array!

Now, after some years, the garden tools had lost their shine. Some had gathered rust; they had been supplemented by the domestic casualties of twenty years of housekeeping—broken kitchen knives, old spoons, gadget toys, a miniature gardening set—legacy from some uninspired Christmas shopping; oil lamps, bicycle lamps, a rusty scooter; wellingtons, sou'westers; Russell's old raincoat. Many of the insecticides and weed killers were out of date now and had been replaced by new, handsome packs, like containers for cosmetics. Along one wall where the camp bed had been there was now a comfortable divan and bedroom furniture, separated from the rest of the summerhouse by a curtain; one walked through the garden section into a small guest room, with all conveniences.

It had been early afternoon, after lunch. Aisley had set out to walk the two miles to the Little Burgelstatham station and from there to catch the train to Tydd. Jenny had gone alone to shop in Ipswich. Russell, Greta supposed, was at the surgery or finishing his lunch at the White Horse, where he often dined late with the bank manager, the postmaster, or the solicitors from Silk and Silk.

Alwyn, in a quieter mood than usual, having the afternoon free from the Unwins, had gone walking by himself. As Greta watched him go, dragging his footsteps, she thought, remembrance mingling with tenderness, that if he were a young boy now, with that look on his face and that hesitation in his step, he would go out into the lanes and walk, hitting idly with a stick at whatever took his fancy; or he would stop at the pond (the same pond where Botti Julio had been found dead) and throw stones into it; and he would stay in that mood until by chance a friend, one of the village boys, came on the scene; then together, enlivened, they would perform acts of mischief—poaching, robbing orchards; the hitting of sticks would have an aim; the stones would be thrown with calculation and skill at a definite target. If Alwyn had met no other boys in his wanderings he would keep walking, perhaps until twilight or night, and then come home, going first to the garden room to see if his mother was there, and if she was, he would stand by the door, saying nothing, only staring at her. Then suddenly with a whoop he would race from the garden into the house, emerging a few minutes later with his fist and mouth full of bread.

Greta wondered, as she watched him going down the lane, what had taken the place of sticks and stones, gangs, solitude, bread. She was depressed to realize that she did not know. Merely to say, quickly, *Jenny*, was too simple a way of answering. Perhaps Jenny represented the fist and mouth full of bread? Or she might not feature in the mood at all.

Feeling suddenly depressed, aimless, as if an unidentifiable new burden had been placed on her, Greta lay on the bed in the garden room, arranged the pillow for comfort, drew the green rug over her, and closed her eyes.

Half an hour later, returning from his walk earlier than he had expected, and, with a dreamlike urge, re-enacting his boyish ritual, Alwyn came to the garden room. He opened the door, and saw his mother lying with the green rug over her, her face pale, her eyes closed, dead.

19 He stared at her. He made a sound like a small scream, and rushed forward. He seemed to lose all control of his limbs. They seemed to operate beyond his body, like those great mechanical shovels and jointed steel arms that lean and turn and grasp far in the sky, far from the center; you gaze up at them in wonder; they glint in the sun, dazzling your eyes, then heave slowly toward the earth.

"Greta!"

She opened her eyes, looked at him in a puzzled way, and yawned. Then she sat up suddenly.

"What? Were you speaking to me? You called my name?"

She saw that he was trembling and flushed. She noticed he had a stick in his hand. So he *had* been a boy again, and walked by the hedgerows aimlessly hitting at shrubs and clumps of grass; and he had gone to the pond and thrown stones, those pieces of flint with blue and yellow embedded in them, sharp flints the color of midnight, mottled with silver; and he had met no friends on the way, but had come home, to the garden room, to find her; and now he would run up to the cottage for a fist and mouth full of bread . . . how strange . . . had he called her name?

"Alwyn dear."

Alwyn had regained control. He no longer trembled. He stood tall, hard, compact. There was an opaque quality about his body. Usually when Greta looked at him she would think, placing him like a transparent ornament, There is Alwyn. She could see through and beyond him; she could see the current of happiness passing through him, like a golden vein. Yet at this moment she could see nothing beyond him. He had set himself immovably in the door of somewhere—where?—and was blocking the light and the view—which view?

"I'm your mother, Alwyn," she said, in a trance, adding in a Run-John-Run, Run-Jenny-Run manner, "And your father is a dentist. And your uncle is a clergyman. And there's Jenny, and there's the village, and your university career . . ."

132

She did not try to stop him. She wished she had a view from somewhere. Why wasn't she standing on a hilltop, why wasn't the sunlight in the background?

"I'm your mother, Alwyn. Your father is a dentist. Your Uncle Aisley . . ."

She sobbed.

It seemed very dark though it was early afternoon. The East wind was at the door, swinging it, rattling the too-early fallen leaves like dry bones. On the days when the wind was quiet everyone listened for it, waiting. The air seemed empty, without destination.

She gasped for breath and sobbed again, embracing Alwyn.

"I thought you were dead," he said.

They did not speak any more for a long while. At last they were calm together and slept. Waking, finding him gone, she was still too deeply tired to accept the distasteful truth—that what he had done had been an impulsive desperate attempt to preserve his own life, rather than restore, rekindle hers.

20

They told me you had been to her.

If I or she should chance to be
involved in this affair,
He trusts to you to set him free
exactly as we were.

This must ever be
a secret kept from all the rest
between yourself and me.

He sent them word I had not gone
(we know it to be true)
If she should push the matter on,
What would become of you?

They told me you had been to her . . .

PART THREE

Red ink, black ink

21 Greta was amazed that no one guessed; that Alwyn, except for the midnight stain spreading in his eyes when he looked at her, betrayed nothing. He and Jenny flirted together as usual. Aisley sat poring over the *Church Times*, and when he glanced up to speak to her, he did not say suddenly, "Ha, I know it. Your secret is out!"

What he did say was, "Listen to this. 'Fund-raising. Let us help you with your appeals; collecting boxes in wood, collapsible collecting boxes, miles of pennies, perfume cards; jig-stamps for Building and Organ Funds; Book of Bricks, Book of Tiles; Death-Watch Beetle Book . . .' "

He sighed. " 'Death-Watch Beetle Book!' What has my church come to?"

He returned to his reading.

Then, when the house was quiet, and everyone seemed to be asleep in bed, Russell did not tiptoe to her room, and instead of inquiring about stamps—anniversaries, rice fields, red-footed storks—he did not say, "Ha, I've guessed it, Greta. I know. Nevertheless"—pressing his foot subtly on that old-fashioned mechanism that operated the dangling-armed drill that bore into her brain—"I forgive you, my dear."

"The blackberries don't seem to be growing as usual," Russell remarked, between the Cape of Good Hope and the Chinese Republic. "They're small and hard and green."

What is he doing? Greta thought irritably, jealously noticing the blackberries? He never gives them a thought until they appear topped with cream on the table before him.

"Stop it, Alwyn. Philidor's defense. Keep the precious language for your novel. No one will read it."

"*En passant*. I always feel that a pawn *en passant* is making a move against its own nature. I can't think whether bestowing this right has proved a curse or a blessing to the pawn."

"Will your book be about us, Alwyn? You know, two students, two young people trying to 'fit in' with the world, and all
that corn; rebelling, arguing; every second word or phrase italicized; your mother uttering sentences like: *'Don't* put your
books there, Alwyn. I've *told* you. No one in this house *knows*
anything. Can't you do *something* about Jenny? How can I keep
any kind of *order*? I can't think why I didn't give birth to a
normal son?' Is it that kind of novel, Alwyn? Or is it: 'Looking at
her with infinite tenderness, he sank on his knees before her and,
in response to her unspoken appeal, whispered, I can't manage. I
thought I might be able to, but I can't . . . Later he looked at her
and murmured, a tremor in his voice, as he drew her toward the
bed: It's going to be all right, I know it's going to be all right
now.' Will it be that kind of novel, Alwyn?"

"I still think the pawn has no right to take *en passant*. It should
press forward with all single-mindedness."

"Single-minded? I think narrow-minded. Discovered check. Or
shall it be: 'The bacon and egg is before him . . . his hungry eyes
. . . he will break it, plunge his fork in it, the punctured sun, the
earth reeling . . . noon . . . he is trying to escape the smear . . .
afraid of too much daylight . . . now the dark-red bacon . . .
sandpaper surface . . . salt-filled newborn skin . . . a moment ago
. . . a moment ahead . . . he knows the significance of *breakfast* . . .'"

Jenny began to giggle. She could not keep her happiness hidden, and she was annoyed that it should show itself in
such a schoolgirlish way. To have a long-standing desire fulfilled
and to show her pleasure in it, after all her adult experiences, as if
it were a fourth-form joke! One's personality was not fair. She
was sophisticated, grown up, she should let a small, serious light
of happiness play around her mouth and in her eyes, to let Alwyn
know her complete joy in the arrangements they had made that
afternoon—marriage, a journey to Spain to live . . .

"Or shall it be after the contemporary style, Alwyn? 'Eccen-
tric jackal, he he palinode raw, human—once, once he was reso-
lute lava.' Or shall it be a verse or two, just another playful verse
with sinister implications?

'*They told me you had been to her*
and mentioned me to him;
She gave me a good character,
but said I could not swim.

He sent them word I had not gone
(We know it to be true.)
If she should push the matter on,
What would become of you?

I gave her one, they gave him two,
You gave us three or more;
They all returned from him to you,
Though they were mine before.

If I or she should chance to be
involved in this affair,
He trusts to you to set them free,
Exactly as we were.

My notion was that you had been
(before she had this fit)
An obstacle that came between
Him, and ourselves, and it.

Don't let them know she liked them best,
for this must ever be
a secret, kept from all the rest,
between yourself and me.' "

"We learned that poem at school. It frightens me. It is full of
mysteriously anonymous entreaties, a terrible fluidity of pronouns—'me,' 'she,' 'him,' 'you,' 'we' . . .''

Jenny began again to giggle. "Or shall it be, Alwyn, as a novel
to end all novels, one of the old style: 'On July twenty-ninth,
nineteen hundred and sixty-three, a young man with fair hair,
blue eyes, humorously creased face' (isn't that how they describe
it?) 'stood waiting at a number fifteen bus stop to catch the two

nought five bus to Port Strange to visit his recently widowed aunt at number nine Chaucer Street . . .' All the best novels begin with such a plunge into numbers . . ."

"Perhaps you should write this novel yourself, Jenny?"

Jenny looked in pretended dismay at Russell's sudden attention. She felt pleased, she wanted everyone to be looking at her, to know that at last, beneath all sophistication, education, incorrigibility, italicized parodies and postures, she had *got her man*.

Greta appeared in the doorway with tea, sandwiches, and cakes. She looked tired. The edges of her nostrils were a pinched white, and there were sooty shadows under her eyes for conventional or unconventional reasons. How kind, how conservative the body was in its expression of mental and physical states! It gave nothing away, if it could help it. In spite of all anxieties and fears of being "discovered," the body was still the best-kept secret; and in spite of its slow evolutionary advances (a cast-off appendix here, a shriveled gland there, a forever-sealed third eye, skin-enclosed flightless wing), it was still a piece of machinery in the habitual groove, putting forth the daily unsurprising sweat, smile, frown, tremor; the cause of tears was still a guess between peeled onions and death.

"Oh," Jenny said. "You look so tired. If I'd known you were getting supper . . ."

Warm, glowing, bathed in her nineteen years as with a luxurious brand of soap that, used at forty-seven, had worn flat and sharp as a stone, is split, gives no lather, must be stored in an old bathroom jar or "boiled up" before it is of any use again.

"No, no," Greta said vaguely. How radiant Jenny looked!

"Did I hear something about a number fifteen bus stop?"

Jenny began quoting her parody. "On July the nineteenth, nineteen hundred and sixty-three . . ."

Greta gave a cry that sounded like a stifled scream.

"Your birthday, Alwyn, your twenty-first birthday. Next week."

The urgency in her voice made all turn to stare at her. Jenny smiled at her, a smile of sympathy, of dutiful love, sharing with her the knowledge that Greta and she had been shipwrecked together, floundering in the dark ocean, and now rescue had come, and there was room only for Jenny to be rescued, and here she was, being helped out of the water, being wrapped in warm blankets, with a piping-hot drink thrust to her lips; and now the rescue craft was moving swiftly away, out of Greta's sight, and Jenny, appreciating her good fortune, and feeling natural sympathy for the lonely figure struggling in the water, and unable to throw her a lifeline, and unwilling to abandon her own place of safety and warmth, was therefore smiling, smiling, casting out little hooks of love that did not reach, however, as far as the drowning Greta.

Greta's cry had been for survival.

"I mean," she said, "you'll be twenty-one."

Alwyn flushed.

"Promotion," he said, moving his pawn to the final square. "Another choice thrust upon him now. He spends his life in restricted movement as a pawn, until victory comes, and he must choose what he will be. It's damned unfair!"

"It's only a game, Alwyn," Jenny said, with the futile tenderness of a mother who tells her child, "It's only a dream, there are no bogies in the wall."

"Coming of age," Aisley said, with a shy pleasure which made Jenny, looking at him, at his pallor, his big brown eyes, think, I hope he's not *that* sort of clergyman after all. Poor Uncle Aisley.

"Well."

Russell smiled, guiding his craft carefully around the Cape of Good Hope. He looked at Alwyn and felt envy and pity. He felt an exhilaration and clarity of purpose unusual for him. He felt that he had failed as a father, a husband, and as a man who could communicate his feelings to his family. There seemed to be no hinge by which he could be attached to them, or they to him; there was no appropriate page to put them or him; he could find no definite value. The horror of his failure came home to him when he realized that he thought of his problem in a metaphor of philatelic jargon—"new," "used," "mint," "first-day cover" . . .

Soon Alwyn would be twenty-one. Russell took grateful hold of the catalogue of age. His family and his life within it became clear: fifty, forty-seven, twenty-one. It would have been comforting to have had a daughter; he had an idea that his marriage might have been a success had there been a daughter. He liked to balance people—mother, son, father, daughter. She would have understood him, asked his advice. She would have been interested in his profession, not dismissing it with a contemptuous "Teeth, what can you see in teeth?"—the idiotic remark made by strangers, friends, relatives alike. Was there something so unusual about teeth that forced people to mock in that embarrassed way? Or was it fear—the dentist as villain, the childhood tortures, cloves, cocaine? So few people seemed to understand; perhaps it was only members of the profession who understood. Those in allied professions—medicine, psychiatry—adopted an equally embarrassed tone; dentistry was something vaguely indecent, unworthy, undramatic; centuries of pain, fear, the horrifying inevitability and finality of teeth had caused man to look upon his dentist as material for comedy; perhaps, in a way, that was the highest tribute that could be paid? One laughed, seeing a film of a man having teeth pulled out; did one roar with laughter at the sight, say, of an operation for appendicitis or stomach ulcer?

Russell had chosen his profession because he was passionately interested in dentistry. Had it not been for the war—which war? oh, that confusion: the limbless man, his shot limbs lying tucked beside him like a child's toys; yet with all the blood and ripped flesh, so many of the screams were caused by toothache; and here comes the dentist with a pair of forceps, a tiny silver hook to go gardening with, neatly, precisely, in the mouth of a man whose legs are tucked uselessly beside him, so that there's nothing but a twitch of phantom legacy, a memory of standing, walking, running; the legs tucked up in shawls of blood; this dentist walking so surely, neatly; it was or was not the war—had it not been for the war, there would never have been so many blows struck to Russell's pride, ambition, desire.

He wondered if Greta would understand and not put renewed pressures upon him to "keep up with the times" when he told her

that during his coming fortnight's leave he was planning to spend
a week in London, to "call" at the Royal College of Surgeons and
Dentists, not as a member—oh, no, he had no urge to "keep up"
with his fellows—but as a visitor who would walk in, walk out,
recognized by no one. Would Greta understand? A daughter
would have understood. She would have traveled with him to
London for the day, two days; he did not think now that he
could endure a week there. The visit to the College would be a
time of triumph: "Oh, of course I remember you. That paper of
yours in the *Dental Journal* had us all (not literally! ha ha) at
each other's throats for weeks. I've often wanted to meet you.
Why are you buried in a place like Murston, a man of your
brilliance? Have you ever thought of trying—"

"By the way, this is my daughter—Carla, Sarah, Catherine . . ."

You fool, he whispered to himself, returning to the Gold
Coast, not even aware of having forgotten that there was now no
such region on the earth.

So my nephew will be twenty-one, Aisley thought. It's a pity
Katherine and I had no son. He might have entered the Ministry.
He might have made more of a success at it than I. His success
would have atoned for my failure to keep God in the picture.
When I was Alwyn's age I thought sometimes of being a poet. . . .

Unlike Russell, who was not used to public pronouncements of
his thoughts, Aisley looked swiftly around the room, ready to
seize the opportunity to speak. Though at the moment there
was no actual conversation in progress, and all were apparently
busy eating supper, there seemed to be such a burden of words
and thoughts in the air that speech would have been unwise until
the unspoken sediment had distributed itself and settled below
the level of consciousness. Aisley was longing to talk, not of
Alwyn, but of himself when he was Alwyn's age. Alwyn would
be interested to know of that early ambition to be a poet. He
would be surprised to learn that Uncle Aisley was not such a
dead creature as he may have appeared, not entirely a moping,
coughing widower, turned to the past, looking at God through a
telescope directed backward in time.

"When I was twenty-one," Aisley began, and stopped, think-ing, No one's listening.

"Have a cress sandwich, Aisley. Cress is a most comforting plant to grow."

"Indeed?"

"Mother . . ."

"Most students call their parents by their Christian names these days."

"Do they, Jenny?"

If only I hadn't become so determined, Aisley thought. Every-body listen, listen to me, I'm not going to preach a sermon, I've lost the urge to preach, I want you to know, here, now, that when I was twenty-one I thought I'd be a poet. *I* have been twenty-one in my life as well as you, Alwyn. *I* was a young man. *I. I.* Life was not much fun, but who wanted fun? I, I, I. Jenny is radiant this evening.

"So, Alwyn, you will be twenty-one?"

"Free, sane, able to vote, sign, die, the disposition of my body and soul to be arranged according to my will."

"Oh?"

I'm not entirely a middle-aged fuddy-duddy church mouse, Aisley thought. I appreciate the need for heroes, for young gods to live and move in the twentieth century. Ah!

"I recall," he said slowly, "that my favorite poet used to be Stephen Spender, when I was your age."

Greta sighed. Christopher's favorite poet!

Everyone looked respectful, interested, as Aisley murmured (he felt that he had not lost the power to command an audi-ence):

> *"I think continually of those who were truly great, . . .*
> *The names of those who in their lives fought for life,*
> *Who wore at their hearts the fire's centre.*
> *Born of the sun they travelled a short while towards the*
> *sun*
> *And left the vivid air signed with their honour."*

Greta's face was rapt.

"Don't you remember, Russell? When you and Christopher . . . before I knew you . . . when I knew Christopher . . ."

"Of course," Russell said calmly, quoting:

> "Far off, like the rumour of some other war,
> what are we doing here?
> The poignant misery of dawn begins to grow . . .
> We only know war lasts, rain soaks . . ."

Greta frowned. "Aisley," she said, "do you know there used to be a portrait of Stephen Spender—very young, ethereal, handsome?

Jenny spoke crisply. "Stephen Spender. Oh, yes, we've studied his poems, among others. It's strange that you mention him now, for there's a photo of him in that Sunday paper—isn't there, Alwyn?" she said cozily.

She lifted the magazines and *Nursing Mirrors* on the table near the window, found the newspaper, and spread the page on the table for all to see. She sounded triumphant. "There!"

They looked on the photo of a middle-aged man, going bald, jowls about his cheeks, his face clouded more from general vagueness than from being radio-photographed. He was boarding a plane; he carried a small, square, black case, like a lunchbox in which workmen carry sandwiches.

"There!" Jenny repeated. "So much for the landscape near an aerodrome, 'more beautiful and soft than any moth.'" She spoke sharply, as if her words were a bitter attack upon something that she could not or dare not name.

Alwyn, her immediate ally against all that was old, tired, vague, memorially rosy, said, "So this is the beautiful young poet who 'thinks continually of those who were truly great'? You've been tricked, of course; but don't worry, we'll be tricked too when our time comes." He began to quote softly:

> "One by one they appear in
> the darkness; a few friends, and
> a few with historical

names. How late they start to shine!
but before they fade they stand
perfectly embodied, all

the past. . . .

"There is today's 'beautiful poet,' still pursuing the heroes. When's it going to stop? Is it ever going to stop? In thirty years we'll see his blurred telstar-photographed face as close to the stars as his own heroes who

turn with disinterested
hard energy, like the stars.

"No doubt he, too, will be carrying his little black box of salt beef sandwiches or spy equipment or after-shave lotion to make him smell sweeter when he comes back to earth. It's tough work, you know, to try to smell sweet on this earth—not only sweet, you've got to exude the right kind of sweetness, blue for a boy, pink for a girl. If you're a man, you must go about smelling of newly washed decks, the moon in the rigging . . . and now having said that, I have the penalty of looking on a company which is puzzled, curious, and 'doesn't understand'?"

Greta smiled. Her voice trembled. "All the heroes," she said. "All the heroes."

"They needn't stop," Aisley said. "Just because the poet grows old and takes to salt beef sandwiches instead of ambrosia, and cares to smell sweeter when he descends from the stars."

"You're safe in saying that, Uncle Aisley, because your particular hero, St. Cuthbert, lived so long ago that even if we were endowed with extra-perceptive senses we'd never dream of sniffing the pong of his stuffy little Farne Island cell with all the bird-dirt and seal-droppings in and out of it."

"Alwyn, don't. Let's talk of . . ."

"Of what, Jenny?"

"I don't know. It frightens me when people climb outside all generations, even their own, and look upon— I don't know, it's dangerous. A cosmonaut must stay inside his space craft and dutifully press the buttons, turn the levers, do what is required of him."

"Has it occurred to you," asked Russell, who had taken the photo of the poet and was studying it, "that the little black box might contain books of poetry or writing materials?"

"It contains," Aisley said pompously, "what you wish it to contain. You lament the death of heroes because you have no wish or use for them, you have killed them."

"I, a murderer?" Alwyn looked surprised. "But did I not say that heroes go on and on, that these poets spring up, their heroes with them, like nettles in the lanes of Little Burgelstatham?"

"Your mother's tired, Alwyn."

"Oh, no," Greta denied. "At least if I am, my tiredness is not caused by heroes."

"Naturally St. Cuthbert had no flush lavatory in his cell, nor did he have television . . ."

Alwyn pounced. "Ah, another sheriff who wants to shoot the badman television!"

"I heard in Murston today that electricity is coming here in six weeks. That's definite, I believe. So in six weeks' time you'll be able to switch things on, Alwyn."

"If we're still here. Jenny and I are getting married. We're thinking of going to Spain."

Silence.

Who will perform the ceremony? Aisley wondered. An occasion for writing in red ink!

"Why Spain?" Russell wanted to know. "I don't know about their way of life, but their stamps are all El Caudillo, El Caudillo."

Greta looked at Jenny's fair freckled face and thought, The sun in Spain is strong. They say that freckles are a form of skin cancer which the sun aggravates. It will be autumn in a few weeks. I shall have to get in a store of winter wash. Perhaps I shall be desperate, having learned the truth.

"We're having a registrar wedding. At Murston. It will stop the local gossip, anyway."

"And you've no parents, no relatives, no one at all?" Greta said, wondering, Who is she? She tried to trace identity in

Jenny's face. What is her secret that she's able to pull my son up by the roots as if his life were a simple clump of field poppies?

"I haven't a brother to be best man," Alwyn said.

"It's unlike you to be concerned with convention. No, you haven't a brother."

Russell looked vaguely at Greta as if to say: Has he a brother anywhere? He hasn't a brother, by chance, has he? Then he smiled, feeling heroic. "Well, we'll see what we can do," he joked. "Won't we, Greta?"

Aisley cleared his throat. "Good night, all," he said, and, glancing at Jenny and Alwyn, "Any advice you need . . . upon the holy estate . . . from a clergyman who's old-fashioned enough to believe that marriages are made by One Higher . . . or I used to think . . ."

So both Russell and Aisley have delivered their reprimand, Greta thought. As Alwyn's mother I should have something to say, or something to think.

She was silent.

Russell put away his stamps. Jenny and Alwyn abandoned their game of chess; Alwyn's pawn, after all, had had no opportunity to practice its new life of individuality. All knew that they'd been waiting for Jenny and Alwyn to announce their news. Everyone seemed at once jovial and cautious. They called cheerful good nights as they went upstairs.

"Decisions should be made, things should happen more often," Russell said.

"You've worried over them, haven't you?"

"Yes, Greta. But marriage, like death, is no solution."

He came to her room and stayed the night, the first time in many years, and Greta was appalled at both her and his self-deceit, at the virtuoso tunings of sex that could make it sound so many themes which were not strictly the exclusive "love" she had once dreamed of, but were instead variations of mutual pity, comfort, weariness, a sense of the passing of time and the approach of age and death, even an apology of one partner to the other for what both had made of their lives.

22

The most appalling piece of reasoning that man has ever concluded, against all evidence, is that death is a prime, convenient, perfect solver of problems. If ever there was a need for the human race to be proved insane, this piece of reasoning would provide all proof. Death solves nothing. An exterminated race is not a vanished race; an assassinated ruler does not cease to exercise power. These are commonplaces, yet men everywhere continue to equate killing with getting rid of. It works with flies, vermin, weeds; how inconvenient that people who swarm, breed, suck, prey on others, strangle their blossoming neighbors, are yet not flies, vermin, and weeds, but remain people! People persist!

Botti Julio persists. A happy Italian-born citizen of Andorra who has pleaded for the underexposed photographs to be intensified, who has spent weeks and months trying to learn English, is not going to be silenced by death. He will speak. He may not speak in English after all. He may not say My tailor is rich, my tailor is not rich. The boxers are skipping in the gymnasium to strengthen their legs. I am wounded, see my wounds are bleeding. A brace of partridges and two pheasants. Do I need to report to the police? These photographs are underexposed; please will you intensify them? He will not be silenced by a young university student who, believing himself to be a product of the twentieth century, and wishing to identify himself more fully with an age in which genocide is the basis of survival, and wishing not to be known as one who retreated, like his uncle the Reverend Aisley Maude, into the mists of an Anglo-Saxon era, or like his father, who had built a picket fence of teeth about him, and paved his life with colonies, commemorations, celebrations, nations, has taken the first step toward being the truly Adaptable Man, a Child of His Time, by murdering someone whom he did not know, whom he had never seen in his life before, whom he neither loved nor hated, a man whose only qualification for being murdered was that he belonged to the human race.

Alwyn is proud that he killed successfully. When he has learned in Little Burgelstatham the few facts that are known of Botti Julio's life, he has not let himself become emotional over the matter. Botti has appeared to him once or twice in his day or night dreams, but that was to be expected: the magnitude of murder is not to be believed until the act is accomplished. As a twentieth-century man, Alwyn does not feel guilty because he has killed. If Raskolnikov had lived now, Alwyn thinks, two pages rather than a novel would have been needed to describe his feelings after killing.

Alwyn supposed that his own murder of Botti Julio had been such a normal twentieth-century act of a normal twentieth-century man that no suspicion had been attached to him. The coroner's verdict at Botti Julio's inquest had been "accidental death," with a rider addressed to the County Council expressing concern at the treacherous ponds in the district and the need for adequate lighting in the lanes. The County Council replied that with the coming of electricity to Murston Lane the problem would be solved. After the inquest the headlines in the local paper referred, not to the death of an unknown Italian worker, but to the fact that within two months or before, Murston Lane would have electricity: thus even the newspapers were striving to belong to the age in which they were printed, by setting up a new system of priorities. One had to remember that man was of first and last importance, his place made according to his nearness, power, and wealth. An Italian whom no one knew was of as little importance as the sixty-five passengers in the foreign plane lost over the Andes, or the inhabitants of the village buried by earthquake or avalanche.

No one knew. No one suspected. The affair was finished. It had to be finished. People living in the modern world have to know where they are; they can't be haunted by the dead, chiefly because if the dead did decide to haunt, their mass pressure would bring madness.

Alwyn had successfully learned the furious adaptation of his age; no stick insect could have managed better, dry, hard, and gnarled on the dry, hard, gnarled ranch in the sunlight; giraffes weaving through patterns of forest leaves were never as clever as man weaving through his light and dark patterns of ideologies, safely concealing his nature from the enemy and, incidentally, from his brothers and himself.

After murder, the seducing of his mother had come easily. He felt as if he were now responsible for building a new world. He looked inward to his personality, admiring it. His adaptability in an age where uncles and fathers fled to the past, where almost no one stayed his temporal ground, positively rippled with power, like displayed muscles that could be trained to perform further feats. His fondness for Jenny, his plans to marry her, to go with her to Spain, where he would write his novel, caused him some disquiet; his chief concern was not his fondness or his plan to marry but that fact that in being so adaptable he had deceived himself into letting others deceive him into thinking that like most young men he would write and publish a novel—one only, of course—that would be declared brilliant and promising and allow him to set further novel-writing aside forever. He had no inclination to write more than one book. He liked to read, to think, to consider the world, the times, and his place in them; he had been trained to appreciate literature, yet he had no desire to create shapes with words, paint, stone, sound. His aim was to be at peace with his time. He was tired of watching his fellow men run forward, backward, out, in, refuse to stay in the here and now. His aim of adaptability had become so intense that he now confused it with taking orders from fashion. Fashion decreed violence, circuitous sex . . . Sometimes when Alwyn thought of Aisley's way of solving the problem, he despaired (fleetingly) to realize that time was deeply grained, that perhaps the most precious dregs were stored in the dark cracks between forgotten years, where Aisley and Russell were so happy to lurk their beetling lives. What was there for anyone who stayed exposed to the four and more winds blowing from so many directions, to the terrible hurricanes of moment after moment, but a slow, resistive hardening of the skin over the body and the mind, a growth of new armor: the so-old, so-new plan for survival? Down there in the darkness Aisley could get in touch with God, for it was known that gods emerged in the dark, confined places like blood-sucking insects from the night walls; to have a God set like a leech upon one's life was a painful but relieving state; one fed the despairs of man through the pipe-mandible-line to a God whose appetite and being were built to meet the strain of overfeeding.

And then Russell, setting up camp in the human mouth . . . Both Aisley and Russell were Adaptable Men—adapting only to themselves and their needs. What of the World?

For Alwyn, at twenty, the World still held itself together by capital letters. He was riding on the globe, he was standing astride it. When Jenny was married and domesticated, he would get her to scrub with a scrubbing brush all the cowards and concealed gods from between the cracks; the only difficulty was that seeds (of man, beast, and flower) were more fertile when planted there in the dark, between the cliffs.

And his mother was still not dead. She had been attended most of her life by Maplestone's Chart, botrytis, leaf miner, peach-leaf curl, thrip, thunder fly . . . the fairy courtiers as real as Moth, Cobweb, Mustardseed surrounding the fairy queen, Titania.

Exposed and alone against the buffetings of time, Alwyn yet had his dreams, reflections, memories. He knew that the incident with his mother had been less a "contemporary" act than a prompting urgency drawn from his childhood when closed eyes and sleep meant death, when absence was removal and burial in a dark, suffocating hole in the earth, when limited experience had not yet been able to provide the material to build barriers between thinking and doing, so that one walked alone, seeing clearly and responsible for the massacre of those hated or merely disliked, one's head and heart full of the results of brandishing so many weapons of love and hate, with no one to explain the phantom nature of thinking and dreaming, to distinguish between the shadow and the substance, or to point the existence of shadow, how one may walk through it, tread upon it, strike it, without harming oneself or the shadow. One learned, furtively; one learned from the sun that one did not stand perpetually in the noon-deed of existence exposed to the precipitate dreams flying as deeds out of one's heart.

Where were the clear divisions of time if the present could thus reach out of the past, like the hand "clothed in white samite, mystic, wonderful" emerging from the lake, to draw one's life, like the sword Excalibur, out of sight into the deep obscure past? Perhaps Aisley with his gods of yesterday, his Anglo-Saxon wandering in their coracles through the marshes of Little Burgelstatham, were at the same time living a life more "contemporary" than anyone else knew or dreamed of? Perhaps Russell walking alone around the last durable monuments of extinct mammoths was more concerned with the present and the future than he supposed, was rehearsing the time when the hero emerges, not as poet, philosopher, statesman, but as *dentist* with the task of identifying, classifying, the sand- and ash-buried teeth, the tiny white pyramids erected as almost the last tomb enclosing the human race? In that future time the "traveller from an antique land" who brought news of how "two vast and trunkless legs of stone/Stand in the desert." Who talked of nothing remaining, of how "Round that decay/Of that colossal wreck, boundless and bare/The lone and level sands stretch far away" would be referring, not to the tomb of "Ozymandias, King of Kings," but to the dental relics of the human race!

Well, there had been News. In Little Burgelstatham. Not news of tombs, deserts, destruction. It was not brought by a "traveller from an antique land," but by the officer of the Eastern Electricity Board. They were to begin work to supply Little Burgelstatham with electricity!

23 Alwyn, his mind concerned with murder, seduction, teeth, God, time, was helping Olly Drew to install power points in each of the rooms of the cottage.

"No matter what they say," Mrs. Unwin had told him, "they'll want electricity. I've seen it happen before. They come to the country, wanting to live a primitive life, and the first thing they try to do is switch on the electric lights and turn on hot-water taps. As for digging a hole to empty the lavatory tin! Mind you, this television man and his wife insist that they want everything, as they say, 'in keeping.' That means they want the timber to show, the paint scraped off the beams, and so on, and the lilac hedge to grow and grow to the sky. I'm very fond of lilac myself."

Olly fitted the dark-brown fuse cap over the wires.

"Putting on the cap," Alwyn laughed. "Like a judge pronouncing sentence!" The he began to sing in one of his bursts of gaiety:

> *"Duncan Gray came here to woo,*
> *Ha Ha the wooin' o't,*
> *Duncan Gray came here to woo,*
> *Ha Ha the wooin' o't . . .*
> *la la la la*
> *For a haughty tizzy die . . .*
> *You may go to France for me,*
> *Ha Ha the wooin' o't."*

"Not France, Spain," he corrected.

He and Jenny would marry, go to Spain, enjoy themselves. He would forget this now frightening preoccupation with Time. It was almost as if he had sold his soul to Time instead of to the devil so he could act the Complete Contemporary Adaptable Man. And what would be the reward or penalty? Would Time, like the devil, haunt him to claim repayment?

> *"You may go to France for me,*
> *Ha Ha the wooin' o't."*

He could not believe that the payment would involve death. Why, already the result of one of his so-called destructive acts was beginning to make itself known—a slight disturbance, he knew, of suspicions and hopes in the mind of his mother. She was thinking that perhaps she would have a child. Was birth such an evil result? If only acts had not such deep shafts, such capacity for wounding or scarring all who foolishly leaned too close to acknowledge, identify, claim, or disclaim them! Pelicans jabbing at their own breasts were not as self-destructive as human beings in their investigation of consequences, effects.

"That's a Scottish song," Olly said approvingly. " 'Duncan Gray.' Ever been to Scotland?" He spoke as if Scotland were a foreign land.

"Yes, I've been there."

"You students get around. I've never been out of the district," Olly said proudly. "I was born and brought up here; I went to school here; I was in the same class as Bert. Bert Whattling. He was a little devil. He stuck a pen nib through my hand. See the scar? There to this day. The teacher said, 'Bert Whattling come out here!' "

"*Ha Ha the wooin' o't. You may go to Spain for me.*"

"Now Spain. The chemist in Murston has been to Spain. Fancy sticking a pen nib through my hand!"

> *"Hang down your head Tom Dooley*
> *Hang down your head an' cry,*
> *Hang down your head Tom Dooley,*
> *For you are goin' to die.*
> *Hang down your head, Tom Dooley,*
> *Hang down your head an' cry . . ."*

"Now, that's somewhere I wouldn't want to go. Not to America."

"Why not?"

"I'd rather stay here."

A tree might make the same reply, Alwyn thought, if it were asked to transplant itself, roots, branches, leaves, birds in branches, bats, nests, squirrels, insects, even the pattern of sunlight in the leaves. Oh the swelling pressure of a being standing tall againt the battering assault of space! Oh the tension between living things and space, the hostility of space against a being, man or tree, that it cannot break or flatten or dislodge!

"You must be very proud," Alwyn said, "to be winning the war—at least to be holding your own."

Olly frowned. "I am indeed. We don't fight now, though. But he must have been a fierce little devil to take to me with a pen."

He smiled. "It was all over a girl, of course. The girl sitting by the window. But it's a long time ago now," Olly said, extricating himself from the slowly encircling tentacles of memory. "Yes, it's a long time ago now."

Olly returned to the Present. His memory, revolting against his determined escape (after all, old men should be captured and held prisoner), emitted a dark, poisonous, painful cloud of realization that life was not much fun, had never been much fun.

But who ever wanted fun?

I, Olly Drew, pensioner, round, fat, pink-cheeked, white-haired, scarred with a pen made for hitting and jabbing, not for writing.

"One thing's certain, then," Alwyn said. "The pen that Bert used to stab with couldn't have been used again to write with."

"Oh, no. The nib was broken in me hand. It could've turned poison. The pen broke too. All over a girl." Olly smiled an old man's wicked smile that is wicked only in the dreams of the old man who smiles it.

Alwyn, glancing at him, thought! He looks like a baby smiling with an attack of wind. A baby. My mother, he said to himself, has begun calmly, deliberately to prepare the nest, lining it, making it warm with all those odds and ends of material that only women know about who can even think the thorns from the stalk of a rose-bush so that it may be used to shape the bed of their maternal dream.

24 Can't you see him? He came to the beginning of this century, dragging his dreams with him, deadweight, like an animal that had been stalked and killed, bled, the superfluous unappetizing portions discarded. He wanted only to fulfill his promise to himself, to haul his dreams to some quiet lair within sight of the stars, to feed upon his prey, in privacy, no judgment put upon him for his way of taking his food, for his posture, his use of knife or claw, for his going mad with the madness of having arrived at last in the haven to attend his dreams with the grace of a ritual accorded to his living brothers. Or whether, hoarding the decayed bodies of his dreams around him, he merely dreamed his fulfillment.

All the deceived pilgrims!

So the door of the century shut fast. It was dark inside. He might have been lured into the deepest and darkest cave. Where were the stars, the sky? He panicked. He turned to escape but it was too late; he was man; man is no traveling salesman to go thrusting his foot in the doors of time; man has many tricks, but not this trick.

One thing that prevented his deadweight dreams from being recognized as flesh-and-blood victims was the neat way they had been packaged; the label said *Untouched by Human Hand*. The outer covering sparkled in the pretense that the package had been Someone's Gift; the curiously festive air contrasted with the secret knowledge of the blood-soaked inner wrappings.

There was dancing at the entrance to the new century. Celebration. A pitiful hope among those who study the everlasting outstanding success of morning, that the new world was near, that this time was the new time, that man could at last, feeding upon his burden of dreams, *become* his dreams, prove the truth of "we are such stuff as dreams are made on"; dreams would blossom from dreams. Man would at last be free of time, his journey would take a new course in which he did not close his

157

eyes and turn away from any part of his history, whether through fear, shame, horror, incredulity, vanity, hate, or love; beyond the imprisonment of time man would learn to stare at himself, at the truth of the strange history of his life upon the earth.

Stare, stare. If he does not learn to stare soon, he will be destroyed forever. Do you remember the childhood rhyme, chanted in derision and annoyance?

> *Stare stare like a bear*
> *sitting on a monkey's chair*
> *when the chair begins to crack,*
> *all the fleas run down your back . . .*

The human race is peculiarly sensitive to the effects of staring and being stared at; staring is a conscious destruction of the thing or person stared at. When you stare at another being, destroying it slowly piece by piece, your own world falls apart, the blood- and soul-sucking insects are let loose in revenge upon your own body.

No wonder man has never learned to stare.

He came to the beginning of this century, dragging his dreams with him, but he's found no place to feed upon them. The Great Escape is on. There are more ways out than through the doors of time. Is there any one human being who has stayed, who has truly stayed, not merely made an eloquent pronouncement that he would like to stay, that he feels he ought to stay, that he would stay . . . if . . . and if . . . and if . . . or shouted the colossal lie from his caves and coracles that he *has* stayed to be a child of his time?

Alwyn is learning to stare. The convenience of rhyme will have it "like a bear"; but it is more accurately described as "like a god."

He had never meant it to be this way. He thought he must be going mad. He was enclosed, sewn up in the present time, as a body is sewn at sea in a canvas shroud, before burial.

25 If Muriel had not spent one afternoon of her life drinking wine with a poet, she might never have known or realized the need of her gentle, commonplace, domesticated existence to be illuminated and made more vivid from time to time by the romantic glow provided by some other person's habits of behavior, speech, thought. She was not, like Greta, chiefly a self-contained being, though she managed as well as Greta by allying herself with inanimate objects—household furniture, rooms, decorations—rather than with people, in the same way that Greta led most of her social life among the beans and cabbages with Maplestone's Chart serving as an interesting variation of Who's Who in Little Burgelstatham. There was a quixotic element in Muriel's nature which demanded, at intervals, a Sancho Panza to complete the short-lived rare visions of the exciting mystery and menace of being alive. The appearance of the poet had been a stroke of good fortune. His invitation to her to sit with him on the lawn to drink Keats' favorite wine had seemed like a miracle; Muriel could say to herself with certainty that never again would she sit on the lawn of a country cottage drinking wine with a poet. She hadn't known his name, or read any of his poems, though she *had* read a newspaper article about a poet who had taken a cottage for the summer, but there had been no photo of him and no mention of the village or county. She was surprised that when she told Vic about it he had said he didn't even know the cottage was let.

"A poet," he said. "Drinking wine on the lawn with you!"

His manner of saying it was not insulting; the "you" was spoken softly and possessively; but it acknowledged, though the incident had happened long before Muriel spoke of it, a need in her that he could not always fulfill.

He's going through the bush-ranger phase now, Muriel thought. He can't live for much longer in the English landscape, with or without the occasional rivalry of poets.

So the affair of the poet became a memory to be supplanted or
at least overlaid by other rural excitements—the last Women's
Institute meeting when she won the prize in the quiz competition. The haphazard, undirected romanticism of her nature was
made evident by the fact that poets, when they were available
were fine, but a quiz competition at the Women's Institute could
satisfy just as well. She was not a sly romantic who fires arrows in
chosen places with skill and precision; she was honestly unable to
handle the weapons that her rarely felt needs put before her from
time to time with the command "Take aim!" Arrows, bullets,
blades flew in all directions; it was no surprise that a poet and a
toy stuffed dog, first prize, lay side by side with equal honor.

Muriel's latest interest was the coming of electricity and the
installing of the Venini chandelier. Art as art had little appeal for
her; she cared most for things of beauty if they could be used and
enjoyed, if they could affect people not by rousing obscure emotions of pleasure and wonder but by directly and visibly changing the shape of the environment and a person's attitude toward
it; for instance, she would appreciate the beauty of a wine glass
that comfortably, glowingly held wine that would be drunk and
enjoyed; someone would touch the glass, twirl it, move it up and
down, sniff the wine; for a time flesh and glass would be close as
lovers; then, the slow retreat, the final rejection; the glass had
been *used*, had adapted itself or had been adapted to fit a special
moment, but the fact that it had been put down empty and was
no longer needed did not detract from its beauty or value. Wine
glasses, chairs—Muriel appreciated these; pictures also, if she
could identify the thing painted, for, like many people, she had to
know what the picture was meant to *be*, which way was right
side up and which was upside down; those startling belches of
shapes and color put forth by some painters with contemporary
indigestion and technical constipation left her puzzled and angry;
there had been an exhibition at the institute by some fellow from
London who wore a black velvet band around his throat.

"Whatever for, I say, whatever for?" the women said to one
another when he had gone.

Though Muriel was not especially interested in art, she tried her best to look fairly at the painting; she felt, ever since her meeting with the poet, that she had a responsibility toward artists; but this feeling lasted only during an exhibition when she walked from painting to painting, murmuring, "I see, I see, how clever, he really is clever."

The cleverness struck her with gloom; it depressed the other women too.

"We'll be blown up in the end, they're so clever," someone said.

Did the painter who had spent weeks in London planning his exhibition to bring Art to the Villages, did he know that after his paintings had been removed from the walls and he had folded the used sheets in his room at the White Horse, and cleared his few clothes (and a supply of hotel coat hangers) from the wardrobe, that only two memories of him stayed in the minds of the women of Little Burgelstatham?—the black velvet band around his throat and the disasters he might bring about by his cleverness.

The chandelier had arrived in a huge padded crate pasted with notices: *Fragile, Caution, This Way Up*. Feeling the excitement of having at last received the dead uncle's legacy so long after he had died, Muriel followed the workmen to the storeroom, watched them set down the crate, and when they had gone, she stayed dreaming over it. What a serene world! she thought. When people had remarked enviously, "You're getting a Venini chandelier?" Muriel had not known what to reply; she had looked for "Venini" in a twentieth-century encyclopedia; it should have been near "Venice" ("Once did she hold the gorgeous east in fee"), "Venizelos," but she could not find it there; nor was there any space for it between "Velvet" and "Ventilation" in the General Information of *Pears' Cyclopedia*.

She had been disappointed in the chandelier itself, in spite of her anticipation and excitement at the thought of layers of tissue paper casing the separate bulbs, as if they were rare tulips being cosseted for market. She could not quite capture in her mind the vision of the chandelier when it would be hung and every bulb lit, the delicately poised sparkling glass fingers knuckled with light; the magnificent way it would control the shadows in the long drawing room. She had rubbed the dusty gray bulbs, and exclaimed with disappointment, "Gray light. I thought it might be gold. Or silver. But gray, like wasted snow!"

Vic was enthusiastic. "How much do you think you could get for it? Who is this Venini?"

She could not tell him whether Venini was a place or a person alive or dead. "I should say it's the name of the manufacturer," she said. "A Venini chandelier. Or a place. Sheffield knives. Nottingham bicycles."

"We'll get it priced," Vic said. "Out of the question to hang it anywhere."

"Oh, no, there's the long drawing room!"

"Where's the power coming from? You'll need enough power for a whole house to supply the chandelier alone. Our generator has barely enough for the cowsheds, the pigsties, and the battery units. But wait till we get down under. There we'll have enough electricity from all those rivers. Remember the rivers, Mu, the day we . . ." And so on.

How theatrical he is, she thought. Australia is part of the world now; we, the arrogant English, have *accepted* it; nobody talks of "down under" these days except with a trace of self-consciousness. Also, Australians are no longer (if they ever were) swashbuckling, uncouth; they don't spend their lives panning for gold or sitting under gum trees. (She thought with panic, If only I were not forced to change my view of them. Why can't we go on believing that they're vulgar, uncouth? Just when everything about everyone is settled, we have to disarrange everything, to begin again and again.)

"But electricity is coming to Little Burgelstatham. There's definite news of it." (Oh, to get rid of the fifteen- and forty-watt bulbs, to break forth into a blaze of light where a thousand needles can be threaded, words from a book or newspaper planted in my eyesight as clear, firm, and sparkling as fence posts in the great Outback. *Outback. Outback. Down Under. Pommie. Swagger.* He has me using these terms now—part of the mingle of marriage.)

"The chandelier's certainly worth a lot," Vic said. "But what use will it be to us?"

"It will look fine in the drawing room. I'm having the ceiling reinforced to bear the weight. We'll have a party to celebrate our Venini chandelier."

"It's all right with me," Vic said.

He liked parties. He liked a sober beginning, a drunk ending, with plenty of gaiety between.

That's Australian, she thought, labeling him. All Australians are like that. Downright. What is downright? It means you land from the moon with a thud. You open doors without knocking.

She smiled to herself. It means he grabs my breasts at night like those little boys we saw, who run after a lorry because it's moving and because they want it, and they dart out their hands and grab whatever part of it they can find to hold on to, and then they haul themselves up, climbing, climbing, always moving, until at last they are safe, going the whole journey, rocked to sleep in the dust and the sun. And that's lovemaking with Vic Baldry. If I knew how Australians made love, as distinct from human beings and Englishmen, I would say he did it the Australian way, with its own kind of violence, risk, and outback glory.

"No one in the neighborhood has seen the chandelier yet," she said.

"Need they? Before it's hung?"

He could never understand why women had to go through such a ritual before they took any form of action; it was a special characteristic of women; it puzzled him, enticed him, almost roused the slight uneasiness of envy. Women could make so much of everything; they could enlarge, elaborate, decorate until the thing itself was almost forgotten; the wonder was that all this elaboration, decoration only served to make the thing decorated more mysterious and exciting. Women were wraithlike.

A more accurate description of lovemaking, from Vic's point of view, was that of a desperate male who grabbed at the mists of a wraithlike female in order to make reassuring substance of shadow.

On a more commonplace and less personal level the ways of
women amused Vic. Every week when he drove to Murston to
the bank and the broiler factory he used to laugh aloud at what
he called the "antics" of the Women's Conservative Association
in their selling of cakes, hot scones, sausage rolls, and other home
produce to the public. It seemed to him to be a kind of prostitu-
tion. There was the long trestle table set up outside the bank,
the group of chattering women lined up behind it, the goods
neatly displayed on the table, the notice in outsize letters: *Nothing sold before eleven a.m.* People (mostly other women) walked
by, peering, almost prodding and touching; gazing, gazing, building an image of the cakes and rolls in *their* possession, on *their*
table . . . It was all part of the mysterious feminine need to
display before offering or bargaining; to display, arouse, entice.

Vic supposed that this need lay behind Muriel's words: "No
one in the neighborhood has seen the chandelier."

It would have to be shown, it seemed, before it was hung in its
full glory.

"I thought of showing it to Greta Maude. They've been a
long while in the neighborhood, haven't they?"

"Yes. Anna knew Greta, only slightly. The husband's a bore.
He's a good dentist, knows what he's doing, more so than some of
the younger chaps, but he's twenty years behind the times. They
say his drill makes a noise like a road drill. That sort of thing.
Hasn't caught up with the refinements of the modern age. In
fact, he seems to have stopped somewhere back along the line. My
God, it's dangerous to stop. If I'd stopped when Anna died,
where would I be now?"

Muriel took his arm. How massive he is, she thought.

"Did you really drink wine with that poet on the cottage
lawn?"

"Yes. Keats' favorite wine. I've got a supply in the house
now."

"It's good?"

"Yes."

"Let's have some."

"Now?"

"Yes."

"But not now—why . . ."

"Yes."

They drank a glass of Keats' favorite wine.

Vic was disappointed that Muriel hadn't argued with him about the wine; he was feeling in the mood for an argument. He looked out of the window at the formal rose-beds. English landscape depressed him more and more; there was nothing to struggle against, there were no real mountains, no desert where a man could die of thirst and never be found; there was no room in England for a man to experience all the emotions that were part of his nature. Oh, the Englishman (Vic no longer thought of himself as an Englishman) managed well enough by constructing a series of boundaries, deserts, mountains, in his head, by confining his destructive movements to a jab with a rolled umbrella or some other more personal weapon; but some men needed to flow over into their surroundings, to attack mountains and deserts, to seek revenge against rivers and bush. Since his visit to Australia, Vic had been overwhelmed at the thought of what he had missed: a mountain like a punch-bag in his backyard! God!

Muriel was beside him, slow, strong, peaceful, more landscape, he felt, than woman. He explored, searched her, staked his claim, and each time he trembled with pleasure and gratitude at the little sparkling store of gold he brought back with him, to cherish in secret.

"Greta's coming this afternoon to see the chandelier," Muriel said. "The roses are especially beautiful this year."

Vic frowned. "There's fowl pest at the Sapleys'. God for Australia!" He turned to go, but he caught sight of part of the Australian landscape out of the corner of his eye. It was Muriel. He kissed her. "I'm sure she'll like the chandelier," he said soothingly, his heart beating rather faster at the thought of the rituals of women.

"Well, it's a fine day," Muriel said.

Vic strode, in the approved Australian way, to the door.

Women were exciting but senseless, he thought. A fine day for a chandelier! Of all the . . .

> *"And he sang as he watched and waited till his billy boiled,*
> *You'll never catch me alive said he . . .*
> *Once a jolly swagman camped by a billabong . . ."*

If Burke and Wills could go, he could. He and Muriel. She might protest about it, she *would* protest, but she'd go with him. How else could he get his regular and necessary supplies of gold?

26 When Greta first learned of her pregnancy she had a wild notion that perhaps she would disappear. So many people seemed to make successful disappearances; twice in two days before the eight o'clock news the announcer put out an S.O.S. for a woman who had disappeared, leaving no trace; this caused Greta to think that perhaps this news was an omen, a secret instruction to her to plan her own disappearance. Russell would come down to breakfast one morning and find a note pinned to the tablecloth near her plate: *Please Don't Try to Find Me*. Did such things happen? Greta wondered, as she sought over and over in her mind to think of a way of breaking the news to Russell. She knew without answering her question that such things did happen, but not to a person of her nature. She was the kind of person who stayed and stayed, like a pyramid or Egyptian god, even while the flood waters were rising about her.

It had been nearly six weeks since the episode with Alwyn—no, two months; and not much later since Russell came to her room without searching for stamps to commemorate lost empires. A woman of forty-seven, particularly one whose bed relations with her husband have lapsed or are episodic, hasn't the calendar complex of the young wife. Any attention that Greta paid to the effects of her impulsive surrenders was not based on anxiety about her "condition" but upon a small joyful hope that took her so much by surprise that she thrust it out of sight, refusing to acknowledge it. It was hope, not anxiety, that took her to Dr. Finch's surgery in Murston. Dr. Finch used the words she herself had used in her thoughts: " 'It's not unknown for a woman of forty-seven.' There may be complications, but these are not as frequent or usual as people sometimes believe. Extra care, of course. We'll soon be able to put your mind at rest." Dr. Finch fat with medical clichés.

"I see young Alwyn's home for the holidays. Which university is he at?"

"Manchester."

Dr. Finch, looking unimpressed, nodded politely. Greta recalled that he had gone to Cambridge, that he and Mrs. Unwin
(according to Mrs. Unwin) often talked together of the "old
days" in Cambridge. She wished she had signed up with a
younger doctor; if she was going to have a baby, it might be
wiser to have a younger doctor. He would be more likely to have
kept up with the times. The hospital, she reflected suddenly, was
next door to the cemetery, and that was next door to the broiler
factory: ingenious juxtapositions.

At the end of her examination Dr. Finch said, now irritatingly
pompous, "I think we can fairly say . . ."

It was only then that she began to tremble and tears ran down
her cheeks. "What's fair about it?" she cried. "What's fair about
it?"

"I'm sure everything will be all right, Mrs. Maude," Dr. Finch
said calmly. "Shall I phone your husband?"

Greta smiled. She was once again small, compact, cool. "Oh,
no, I'm having lunch with him at the White Horse."

"A celebration lunch?"

"Yes. Yes, it may be that."

Dr. Finch called the nurse to make arrangements for future
appointments and the application for a hospital bed.

It's ridiculous, Greta thought, as she went out into the lane off
the market square. The light was yellow; the town was preparing
itself for a noonday sleep. Veterinary surgeon. Fish monger.
Lawyer. Chemist. Ironmonger. News agent. Estate agent. Mu-
nicipal offices. The Town Hall, with the public conveniences
roped off because they were being repaired. The library. Greta
felt a longing to be in touch with a world apart from plants and
insecticides. She was not a regular church-goer. She had never
been to the Women's Institute. She had joined the library, but it
was open only once a week, and the opening was such a physical
complication that one tired of waiting for it; the books were
arranged in the Town Hall, in rows of shuttered cases which had
to be unlocked, the shutters removed, before the books could be
seen. If one arrived too early, there was always the feeling that
one ought to help "open" the library; then one spent ten minutes

carrying heavy shutters about the room. After this struggle to get at the books, Greta found their range disappointing—fiction, domestic affairs, a row of books on water-skiing, coins, old china. She had lunch with a blood-spattered Russell. (Blood had dropped on his sleeve, unnoticed.) They had salad, ice cream, and coffee; in public, each noted secretly, with pleasure, that they made a "good couple." They joked, laughed. They knew that the other diners, looking at them, thought, with smug possession: The dentist and his wife. There's the dentist and his wife.

Greta caught the bus back to Little Burgelstatham without having told Russell her news.

Place Used Tickets in the Receptacle Provided. She did so with the customary correct obedience of a true inhabitant of the "modern world" used to being helped in the difficult journey by gnomic injunctions, no longer on the boughs of trees, *Shake Me,* the lips of golden horns, *Blow Me,* the bottles of magic, *Drink Me,* but chiefly on tins and cartons in pantry and bathroom: *Place Thumb Firmly on Perforation before Tearing Back Top; Twist Lid to Right; Pierce with Pin, then Lever Off; Snip with Scissors before Using* . . .

As the used ticket crumpled in her hand she remembered her promised visit to Muriel, to inspect the famous chandelier. She had been weeping, she was tired, she wanted time alone to think about her news. There was no one to tell. Broad beans and Brassicas had not yet evolved ears.

Aisley was sitting, cozily convalescent, in a sheltered place by the south wall. He was passing what he liked to call a "quiet afternoon." He was reading. She saw with irritation the title *Anglo-Saxon Riddles,* and knew that Aisley was more qualified than she would ever be, in the mysteries of bringing and breaking news. He could ask the help of sun, storm, horn, shield, night, book, bow and plow; speak in softening circumlocution as these or as bird—nightingale or jay—"I announce to men many welcome things with my voice."

Then, seeing him there so quietly and unobtrusively passing the time, she forgot momentarily her worry about herself, Alwyn, Russell, and felt the pangs of conscience too often suffered by a conventional hostess, reminding her that she had done little to "prepare" or organize Aisley's holiday; she had left him alone; in his tourist time-table she had marked every day: *Morning Free, Afternoon Free, Evening Rest.* He had wandered everywhere on his own, in apparent enjoyment.

"I'm going this afternoon to look at a remarkable chandelier at the White House Farm. Would you like to come, Aisley? You may be interested."

"You look tired, Greta. Is something wrong?"

"Oh, no. I had to go to Murston to see about gardening things. You know what the ironmongers are like; unless you're on the spot, they don't seem to understand what you want: I like to get in supplies a season ahead." She moved her hands as if she were indeed "getting in" supplies "in" to herself, not merely gathering them around her. "I had lunch with Russell. We don't often have lunch together. There was blood on his sleeve." She laughed nervously. "The chandelier's an obsession with Muriel. I haven't much knowledge of works of art in glass."

Aisley shut his book.

"The chandelier sounds interesting," he said, implying with the habitual clerical undertones of a man in consultation with God, Though what God thinks of it we shall never know.

Certainly if God had thoughts, there was no compulsion to tell. The exchange of thoughts between God and man was chiefly a one-way process unless man learned the language of God, by constant analysis, repetition, practice, and finally by creation, where the words and phrases of the language—but they were not these, there was no name for the components of God's language —struggled and fought like fish on hooks to get free; more often they escaped, there was a stain of blood in the water, cold blood, it may be remembered, that keeps fish alive; then the nameless agents of creation were lost, until man tried again.

Yet when he did succeed in capturing part of the language of God, his treatment and use of it were not always worthy. The fact that he had captured it gave him, he thought, permission to mouth it, and swallow it as accompaniment to an agreeable orgy.

27 Muriel Baldry showed Greta and Aisley to her sitting room, mellow now in the afternoon sunlight. (The Australian wheat marched golden along the wall, disturbed by an invisible wind; the sheep grazed or stared, eyes narrowed, their wool creamy-white, tangled with sun; the flanks of the farm horses shone dark and warm as plum pudding.)

Aisley sensed that he was not welcome; the inspection of the chandelier was to be shared by women only; Muriel had frowned when she saw him, but had immediately replaced her frown with a "hostess" smile. She was obviously dressed for the occasion; she wore a soft green velvet dress becoming to her pale skin and making of her large, awkwardly shaped, but distinctly feminine body (the pear shape, often seen in women, where the hidden pelvis becomes a mountainous dream of bone and flesh, where the head is poised clean and firm as a bud on a stalk, and the bosom is a slight curve above the swelling base) a graceful mountain covered with—sward.

The word "sward" came naturally to Aisley's mind. It pleased him. "Sweard," the Old English "skin"—*sward, turf*. Muriel Baldry's appearance was happily at home with the ancient and the modern. He realized again that in some way his arrival had quelled her excitement. She looked self-consciously at her dress.

"One would think I was going to a party," she said, apologizing.

Greta came swiftly, sharply to her support, with the habit of people who, being part of a group of three, have for the moment anyway identified the intruder. (One has to be swift in such moments, for in the exciting fluctuations of a human group the identity of the intruder changes, enemies become friends, friends become enemies; it is likely that when the group separates, the hated and resented may have become the most needed and loved, and the most welcome may then be the most alone and rejected.)

"Of course not. It's an occasion anyway, isn't it, from what

you've told us of the chandelier. I should have thought it might
be an occasion for wine."

"Wine." Muriel smiled and murmured:

> *"O for a beaker full of the warm South,*
> *Full of the true, the blushful Hippocrene,*
> *With beaded bubbles winking at the brim,*
> *And purple-stainèd mouth."*

She had never forgotten the words quoted to her by the poet on
the lawn. She remembered them because she liked to remember
the time with the poet, not because she liked the words quoted;
they did not appeal to her; she thought them extravagant; a
purple-stained mouth implied an impending heart attack rather
than the pleasures of wine. All the same . . .

She sighed. "We'll keep the celebration for when the chandelier is hung, and there's electricity at last. I'm having a party then.
The place will be extravagantly lit."

She looked doubtfully at Aisley. Perhaps as a clergyman he
would not approve of extravagance, if only with light, though
God Himself had shown little economy in bestowing it. She
thought Aisley seemed a quiet, shy, kindly person. It must be a
handicap when others knew your vocation. If you were a clergyman, they always put you in the position of judge and wise man;
clergymen in company, like doctors and lawyers, were beings of
convenience and inconvenience. "Use is everything." Why,
Charles Dickens said that, she thought, pleased. Use did apply to
people as well as to objects; the chief fascination of people was
their natural skill in using and being used by others.

"I would never regard light as an extravagance," Aisley said,
again with maddening parsonic undertones. "Let there be light.
The light of the world. A man does not light his candle under a
bushel." Good God, he thought, why do I say what is expected
of me?

"It's really nothing to see," Muriel said, suddenly bashful. "The
chandelier, I mean. Oh, yes it is. It may be one of the few Venini
chandeliers in the country."

"Venini?"

Muriel was glad she had driven in that morning to Murston to the library. She had seen Greta coming from Dr. Finch's surgery. Was Greta ill? she wondered. Troubles of middle age, perhaps?

"Paul Venini, the Venetian glass designer. He's very famous. He's made some beautiful modern glass objects."

The encyclopedia had given no further information. There had been such a large space devoted to Vegetarianism, Veins, Venereal disease, and two pages to Venice. Encyclopedias were always unsatisfactory. Going to them for information was like going to a lover wanting him to say "I love you"—a simple, well-known declaration—and receiving nothing but "I like you, it's nice to be with you, I'd hate to be alone again after this" . . . and so on.

"I'm longing to see it now," Greta said.

Aisley gave a murmur of interest.

"Well, I'll show it to you," Muriel said, trying suddenly to look around for obstacles that were not there, that would prevent her from showing the beloved chandelier. After all, it was not in its full glory, it was unlit, it was lying unpacked in that great box in the storeroom. The occasion seemed to be getting beyond her. She had merely wanted Greta to take a peep at the chandelier, as friends will take a peep at a sleeping child without disturbing it. And why had Greta brought the clergyman relative? Here they were both hunter and huntress, almost after her blood, *demanding* to see her precious chandelier! She resented them. She forgot that she had gone as far as dressing for the event.

"It may be difficult to get into the storeroom," she said warningly, leading them from the dining room through the dark passage to the small room at the end, opening off the long drawing room where the chandelier would be hung.

Muriel flung open the door of the drawing room.

"See, it's big enough to take such a magnificent chandelier. But you haven't seen it yet, to judge."

She turned toward the storeroom.

"It's so cluttered with things. While the decorators have been here I've had to pile everything in, higgeldy-piggeldy. It's always like that, changing over a household."

She smiled shyly, pointing to the huge box near the door.

"Well, there it is. I'll show you."

She lifted the lid, withdrew a handful of straw and corrugated paper, clearing a small space for them to look in. Aisley leaned over, peered in, and saw two bright small eyes peering back at him; there was a scurry, a scuffle, and a large black rat with tapering triangular jaws laced with sharp teeth sprang from the box and ran across the floor and out of the room. Greta gave a small shriek. Muriel exclaimed, "Oh, oh"; then calmly she withdrew a handful of straw, revealing the opaque gray bulbs of the massive chandelier.

"Do you have anything for them?" Greta asked. "I've rather a good supply of pesticides. There's one that attracts them. They run to it straightaway, swallow it greedily with apparent enjoyment, then lose consciousness, passing simply and painlessly from sleep to death. Or so Malpestone's Chart describes it. I don't know from first-hand experience, as we've never been troubled with rats in the house."

Greta's voice had adopted the slightly triumphant tone that women use in their comparison and challenge of households.

Muriel frowned. "It's the first I've seen indoors. Imagine. Asleep in the chandelier. The chandelier!"

"There may be a nest," Aisley warned, moving toward the door. "It may be wise to leave it until it can be dealt with."

"Yes. Vic will have the right poison," Muriel said calmly, aware that Aisley, who had shown no revulsion at Greta's quotation from Maplestone's Chart, had given a pained shudder at the outright reference to "poison."

"I'm afraid, he said, "that modern preparations for dealing with pests have got beyond my comprehension; their measure of sophistication is alarming." A pleasant poison, he mused—administered, no doubt, like a shampoo or perfume, in one of those so-called puffer-packs.

Aisley had the common maddening habit of referring to things new or strange as "so-called," implying that those who secretly darted forward to add a new component to the conveyor belt of language (often being burned in the act) had shown more courage than judgment and accuracy, whereas if *he* had been entrusted with the job . . .

"Why, yes," Greta said. " A blue puffer-pack with pink sprays of blossoms round the base . . . I know my Maplestone's Chart."

"At least you can see some of this magnificent glass," Muriel said, bending over the small exposed view of the chandelier. Reluctantly Greta and Aisley came toward the box.

"The decorators probably brought the rats in," Muriel said comfortingly, at the same time finding a solution and creating a myth, for is it not strangers to a household, "foreigners," who "bring in" these unaccustomed pests and diseases to the formerly pure, whole inhabitants? "Yes," she repeated, satisfied. "The decorators. We never had rats before. Not in *my* time."

Vic's first wife, of course, may have been responsible for so much that was irregular; there was that hole in the corner of the bathroom. Vic had sworn he had never seen it before; and she, certainly, had not been responsible for it. She had accepted it as part of the show of intractability put on by a new house threatened with invasion.

"We'll leave it, then," she said, "and you can all see it when electricity's here and I give my party." But she thought: I dressed up for a black rat. Oh, rats are such nasty creatures. Harbingers of plague. And then there are those soft-bodied toads, all dead in the mornings in the lanes . . .

"If there's a nest, I don't think we ought to disturb it. Vic will see to it. There's nothing really to stop us from unpacking the chandelier. All the same . . ."

They agreed. All the same . . .

Muriel closed the door softly, aware that some of the derelict furniture had the appearance of leaning forward, trying to get out. She turned the key in the lock.

"But if that was the mother rat, how will it get back into the room?" Greta asked.

What stupidity, Muriel thought. Now that she had definite evidence of rats in her house she had almost accepted them; even without realizing it, her mind was busy putting them in their place, allotting them their share of the "blame," fitting them into the mythology of a well-run household. "I've heard," she said, as she poured wine for them—they had agreed that a glass would help to soothe their disappointment—"I've heard that this was Keats' favorite wine."

Aisley felt annoyed with himself for replying with such certainty, as if the others had not known the fact, "John Keats."

"The poet," Greta said stupidly, superfluously.

They looked at one another in the glow of recognition and personal accomplishment so often lit by shared irrelevant knowledge.

"I had someone quoting Keats to me last summer, just before our tour," Muriel said. "I'm not up on poetry at all. It amazes me that poets still write."

"I've known it only through other people," Greta said. "I've not cared greatly for it, except in association with people I've known." She looked horrified. "I mean, I don't *read* it for its own sake. Do you?"

"Oh, no!"

"Aisley does," Greta said, as if Aisley were not there. "Alwyn too. And Jenny. But it's not the poetry I'm used to, not the war poets, or even your John Keats."

Muriel smiled, shy and pleased at her momentary ownership. Then, freeing herself from her dream of nightingales and blushful Hippocrene, she said, letting the sharp disappointment sound in her voice, "Vic will be able to get poison for them. They must be got rid of. Meanwhile . . ."

"Yes," Aisley said, taking the hint and putting down his empty glass, "I must be going."

"And you're enjoying your stay at Little Burgelstatham, Reverend Maude?"

"Indeed, indeed."

What a stupid word, Greta thought. Indeed. In deed. In *deed*. "Alwyn's birthday is quite soon. His twenty-first. We're having a small family party."

"I'm not a party-goer or giver, not really," Muriel said. "But the night the chandelier is installed I want my friends to come to celebrate. Even old Mrs. Unwin. She can bring her stick and her Friesian calves, if she cares to."

"You show them the chandelier," Vic said curiously, returning from the desert interior and speaking in the sparing way of a man deprived for too long of food and drink. He exploded with laughter when Muriel told him about the rat. He went to the storeroom to investigate, and Muriel forgot about the matter until they sat down for their dinner.

"What did you find?" she said.

"You were right. A nest."

"You got rid of them?"

"Too right. We don't want rats in the house."

Muriel smiled warmly at him, thinking, Now, if he were any other husband he would surely begin the next sentence with, "When Anna was alive . . . In Anna's time . . ."

We have the time to ourselves, she thought happily, trying not to see out of the corner of her eye the ghost towns, the shanty towns white with dust, blue with the brittle leaves of gum trees.

28 All would have been well, Mrs. Unwin thought, if she had not noticed the rust on the oven. It had been there for years, but now the fact of it haunted her; and the thought that it was so many years ago since she had baked bread there. In the smart brick semi-detached on the way to Little Burgelstatham station, opposite the coal merchant's, where Dot and Lex lived, there was a new oven white as a mountain, with a surface smooth as the best royal icing; but nobody baked bread in it. Dot was too busy with the milk-round to bother about such things. Nobody baked bread now—nobody.

Mrs. Unwin, standing alone in the big smoke-blackened kitchen, rubbed her finger along the coarse rust of the oil oven. She felt like weeping; at the same time she felt too tired to weep. She crossed to the window and looked at the polythene-covered stack of hay that had grown during the past week; at the stubble fields, naked again, plucked golden birds shivering with the first cold touch of autumn; then a green flock, now a gold flock. Now everything was revealed: abandoned nests, partridge and pheasant plumes, stones colored blue, pink, gray; and the flints with their black night hearts.

"And the television people'll not bake bread either," Mrs. Unwin said, arranging the red plastic flowers in their plastic vase on the windowsill. Her niece had brought the flowers on a visit from the city. She had brought meat pies too, one veal-and-ham each, and one pork each, and Mrs. Unwin had said afterwards to Dot and Lex, who shared them, "What a pleasant surprise that was! Weren't they delicious?"

Yet when the meal was over she had felt troubled, not knowing what to do with the small aluminum-foil containers that seemed so perfect, so useful, for she could not quite determine their use. She had felt ashamed to be asking, "Are the pies always made in these little dishes?"

"Oh, yes," Dot had said, helping her to clear the table, and crumpling one of the dishes in her hand and throwing it in the fire while Mrs. Unwin thought angrily, watching the little silver dish blacken and lose all shape, Londoners don't know how to save, I'm sure I could have used that, somewhere.

Returning from the window, Mrs. Unwin looked up at the wall, at the remnants of her husband's service in India—a rifle, a sword, Indian Army colors. I don't want to leave here, she thought. What does it matter if the roof leaks, if I find it a struggle to get up and down stairs to bed, if I get more and more muddled when the telephone rings and I must answer it (my voice gets so breathless with excitement). But the Colt cowl hasn't stopped the chimney from smoking; there's still a down-draft.

And the oven is rusted. *Out of all recognition.*

Things seemed to come to an end, to have no remedy or point of return, when not in exaggeration but in fair description one used the phrase *out of all recognition.* The shape of things fell away, like the useless silver dish twisted in the fire.

Mrs. Unwin had been proud to say, "I'm over eighty. The calves know me. The geese come when I call them. I can remember the days when I worked in the fields alongside the menfolk, during the war. I can recite, word-perfect, the recipe for sloe wine. I'm over eighty, still living at the farm."

She had been so proud. Now she was afraid. And one night when Dot and Lex called in for supper and asked her once again if she would come to live with them in the semi-detached, telling her that she worried them, alone in the farmhouse at night, even with the telephone, and there was the Approved School not far away, and one never knew, therefore to set their minds at rest would she . . . ?

"Yes," she said, she supposed she had better leave the farm. Only that day one side of the oven, thick with rust, had come to pieces, had crumbled like a stale burned biscuit in her hand.

She worried over what to wear; she apologized for her clothes. I used to have a neat figure. And it's still neat, she thought, looking down at herself, but again the phrase *out of all recogni-*

tion came to her. Her hair had once been dark and thick and soft, the color of melting chocolate; now it was like ashes. They say, she thought, that old people express the desire to die in peace, in their own home—but do they ever have their wish? They say that people die almost as soon as they retire or move house; but I don't think so many do. You only hear of them over the wireless or read of them in the paper, while the others who have retired or moved house go on living and trying to get used to new places. I know, I can tell what Dot and Lex think . . . and the boy Alwyn—he and I are good friends, I think, but only friends by privilege—he knows and I know that I'm too old to bother about it, to question him and find the answer: what was he doing that night? Now, if it had been an Approved School boy . . . But they don't escape this way any more, they make toward the television mast and the main road. Yes, I can tell that even Bert and Olly . . . all the people in the village think that as soon as I move from the farmhouse I'll follow the example of those whose sad stories are printed in the papers: *Retired. Collapses. Moves house after forty years. Dies.*

So Mrs. Unwin prepared to leave the farmhouse. People said admiringly, "You've adjusted yourself to the times, Mrs. Unwin," yet beneath their congratulations ran a vein of warning: "You know what to expect when you move house at your age."

During the weekend the farm manager drove up in his new Volkswagen, stopped it outside the house, and for the first time since he had bought the farm he looked carefully at the old farmhouse, noting alterations and repairs to be made.

"Things are moving at last," he said to himself, and without getting out of the car, he drove to his home a mile beyond Tydd, went immediately to his office, and began to make Plans.

29 There seemed to be a wild howling of wolves, and Mrs. Unwin found it a long journey struggling through the snow by herself, up and down stairs in the snow with her thin cotton apron wrapped around her thin body, and only her slippers on, no stockings, and her ankles jutting and bony, the way old people's ankles grow, like pegs with nothing much left to hang on them.

She woke suddenly, shivering. The howling had not ceased. Not wolves. A dog. Outside the kitchen door. She wiped from her eyes the sealing ooze that again in old people is set flowing as soon as they sleep, in preparation for the final sealing of death, and she reached out, fumbling for the matches, and lit the oil lamp by her bed. A yellow rod-shaped shadow stood tall against the wall opposite the window—the television mast. She could not understand its mysteries, why it was lit, why it was so tall, whether or not it held a supply of television pictures to be "beamed"—that was the word, "beamed." Well, she wanted no beaming in her farmhouse, but she would have to put up with it when she went to live with Lex. She preferred to think of herself "going to live with Lex" rather than "going to live with Lex and Dot." She would have to take orders from Dot about where to hang the saucepans, the tea towels; which drawer to put the cutlery in; and Dot would say, "This is the place, Mother, this cupboard here, this shelf, at the back, at the front, at the midde; lay them side by side, crosswise, apart: I make a habit of it; it's best for you to fit in at the start with my ways." At least, Mrs. Unwin thought with relief, they won't keep wanting me to have a bath. I haven't had a bath since I went to consult Dr. Finch, and yet I'm as clean as a newborn babe. I'm glad that Lex and Dot haven't these modern ideas about bathing; evidently they don't bathe in London, either, or we'd have heard about it from Dot.

The lamp was lit. She was fully awake now, as far as one can be fully awake at night when the area of waking is ringed by a darkness and drowsiness that must be kept in its place, otherwise it moves ceaselessly in and forward, encroaching like a tide. Downstairs the dog began howling again, and was answered by a whimpering and scratching from within the kitchen. Nelly.

"Nelly, Nelly!" Mrs. Unwin called. "Do you want to go outside, Nelly?"

Downstairs, Mrs. Unwin put the lamp beside the telephone as she looked for the card with the Baldrys' phone number on it.

"It's the Baldrys' black dog again," she muttered. "I'll have to get them out of bed to come and fetch it. I told them about Nelly, and to tie their dog up. It happens like this every time. We're besieged in the house. I can't put Nelly out to do her business."

A pile of newspapers on the chair where the telephone was kept slipped to the floor. Mrs. Unwin was fast returning to the doddering state of sleep. She found the Baldrys' phone number, picked up the telephone instruction card, and began laboriously to follow the directions. No matter how many times she used the phone she always needed the instruction card. *Lift Receiver and Wait for Dialing Tone.*

She did so. There was a scratching noise in her ear, then a tingling. She supposed it must be the dialing tone. Carefully she dialed the number, repeating it aloud. There were two pink spots spreading in her upper cheeks as the excitement of the task took control of her. Ah! The answer noise! She swallowed, getting ready to speak, waiting.

"White House Farm."

"Mr. Baldry?"

Her voice was breathless.

"Oh, is that you, Mr. Baldry, it's your black dog again, it's loose, I can't move out of the house, it's at the back door, after Nelly, it's late to ask you to come and get it but remember the last time Nelly was that way, and your black dog stayed and stayed."

"I'll be right around, Mrs. Unwin. It's only just after twelve."

"Oh? Oh? Is it? It seemed later. Do come. I'm alone in the house. I can't open the back door."

"Don't worry, Mrs. Unwin. We had it tied on the lawn this afternoon and it broke the chain. It's a cunning devil."

"Thank you, Mr. Baldry. I can't do a thing with Nelly while he's here. I'll expect you, then."

She hung up. Her heart was thudding against her ribs; she breathed quickly two or three times, then sat in a chair to recover. She always had to recover in this way after using the telephone. She thought, Perhaps I'd better see to Nelly, spread some newspaper on the floor in case she wants to do her business.

Sitting there with the still darkness outside and the persistent howling and shuffling of the Baldrys' black dog in her ears, she let her feeling of loathing for Nelly surge inside her. If it hadn't been for that clause in her husband's will she would never have kept the bitch: a bow-legged flea-bitten mongrel more often in heat than out of it. It was getting to be too much of a task to spend one's old age trying to keep the neighborhood dogs (especially the Baldrys' black dog) at bay in order to prevent the worse nuisance of having a bitch in whelp. Of course there were preparations you could buy—tablets, and stuff you squeezed in a cloud all over the dog's private parts to remove that so secret yet so public smell; there were all kinds of disinfectants to use, also; Dot knew about them, but again she hadn't time, with the milk-round, to look after Nelly, and you had to keep on using the puffer-packs and tablets, for once the slightest scent escaped, it was the end, all the dogs in the neighborhood *knew*, there was no peace.

A car drew up outside in the lane. It would be Vic Baldry. Mrs. Unwin pulled aside the curtain in the dining room and looked out. The howling had stopped. Nelly fawned and slobbered at her feet.

"Get away, you bitch," she said sharply. For a moment she fancied that her husband was standing in the room watching her, saying, "I knew you never liked either of the dogs, that's why I put a clause in my will, for you to look after Nelly."

"Get away, you bitch."

Snow, stoves, people, my son's wife, bread-baking, my son, and that smell of dogs escaping and going round the world, full of power.

"I said, get away!"

"She was sitting upright," Vic said afterwards. "Smiling. Most likely had been talking to Nelly, for company. It was lucky she sent for me when she did, but it was too late—to help her, I mean. The dog will be lost without her, she seemed fond of it, it followed her everywhere. What a name—Nelly!"

The farm manager looked guiltily at his plans, as if death had surprised him.

"It's no fault of mine," he said.

Aisley wrote in his diary, in black ink: *Mrs. Ruby Unwin, aged eighty-five, born Stamford.*

The black dog sat on the hearth between Vic and Muriel. Muriel patted its head.

"That night," she said, "when he escaped from you he came running back home trailing his chain. I'm not given to fancies, but he seemed like one of those legendary black dogs of the night."

She laughed self-consciously as Vic raised his eyebrows. She changed the subject.

"What do you think of it?" she asked. "You'd never go back to the old ways, would you?"

They were sitting full in the glow of the one-hundred-watt bulb lit with the beautiful electric light.

The black dog blinked, moaned, leaned on his paws and slept.

30 "It's something we have to talk about, Lex," Dot said. "You know that before your mother died I had made up my mind to go up to London, to Milly's wedding. In my new dress." Since Mrs. Unwin's death, Dot, extricating herself from family relationship, had preferred to talk to Lex of "your mother," rather than accept the shared burden of "Mother." She had been fond of Mrs. Unwin. She had not realized before how much she had looked forward to the morning visit to the farmhouse—lighting the fire, sweeping the kitchen floor. There had been more satisfaction in sweeping the farmhouse kitchen than in sweeping the cramped linoleum-covered room in her own home; the dust had parted so willingly from the mellowed stone, and the light from the fire had leapt and flickered, and the scrubbed wooden kitchen table had glowed with cleanliness, with the breakfast dishes and Mrs. Unwin's tray for her cup of tea placed ready; while outside, Lex would be stacking the milk-crates (delivered before six by the Stowmarket Co-operative Society Dairy) onto the back of the van, and inside, all would be homely and shining and warm. Even old Nelly (occasionally sprinkled with flea powder that Dot bought chiefly to rid herself and Lex of the fleas they picked up from Nelly), curled in the worn chair by the fire, had the faithful look of a true farm dog, a thoroughbred! Thoroughbreds were so acceptable. They moved admirably, powerfully; one respected them. Their bodies had been planned to perfection by those who knew how to breed animals in order to please the human eye. There had been talk that long-haired poodles were going blind, that dachshunds suffered from their deformed legs, that bulldogs had difficulty in breathing because of their curiously shaped chests; even so, one did not turn from them in disgust as one turned from *mongrels* which had escaped such meticulous planning and care. Poor Nelly. Dot thought she had never seen an animal so repulsive to look at, so without pride or shame, yet so alive; how could that be? Once or

twice Dot had given Nelly a bath, more to restore her own self-respect than to give the dog an appearance of being clean.

Now that Mrs. Unwin was dead, Dot longed once again for the special peace of those early mornings. They had had to arrange a new place where the lorry could deliver the milk-crates. It meant getting up earlier, having breakfast at home, making a longer journey, finishing the milk-round late in the evening. Though the fire burning brightly, the kettle boiling, the table laid with the breakfast dishes had helped to give the feeling of peace, it had been the *convenience* of everything which, Lex and Dot discovered, had mattered most; convenience can never be overestimated in plans for a peaceful life.

"We must talk about it, Lex," Dot said again. "And about the clause in your mother's will, the burial in Stamford."

"I've said we can't afford it," Lex replied. "What's wrong with burial in Murston? It costs a lot these days to transport bodies. You know how much the undertakers have robbed us already. And we can't keep Mother in cold storage forever."

"It's only three days since she died!"

"It seems like years—all this arranging about the milk-round."

"Your mother was fond of Stamford, Lex. She often used to talk of it—*you* know that. I don't think she ever really settled in Little Burgelstatham. She was always taking out the photographs of Stamford to show me. And those cuttings she saved, about the Duchess of Rutland! If I died today I don't think I'd want to be taken to London to be buried; but it's different with an old woman. And then there's Nelly. She was so fond of Nelly."

"I didn't notice it," Lex said.

"A woman notices these things. Now, this letter from the undertakers—they want instructions."

"There are winter repairs to be fixed up. New tires for the van . . ."

"But now that the cottage is sold to those television people—There are firms, by the way, that would charge less than the undertakers."

"The broiler lorry goes twice a week to the north of England."

"Lex!"

"Well, it does. And the crates from the White Horse come here twice a week. And there's any number of removal men who'd be glad of a chance to take a full load . . ."

"Lex!"

"I'm only saying it, Dot. There's a difference when you're only saying it. I don't know why the farm wasn't left to me. I could have had the farmhouse repaired. You and I wouldn't be working from morn till night delivering milk if I'd been left the farm. Mother should have come to stay with us long ago. She was the only one who ever understood about my back. And as soon as she's dead you're off to London to a wedding."

"You know Milly asked me weeks ago. And your mother wanted me to go. She said to me, 'Dot, get out of those heavy gum-boots and that shapeless dress and go and enjoy yourself at the wedding.' "

"I can't meet the expense, Dot. Burial in Stamford, a wedding in London . . ."

Dot spoke with her rich country voice. (A native of Fulham, how had she managed so easily to speak with a Norfolk accent?) "I've a surprise, Lex. You remember I asked about a dress for the wedding?"

"It's not that I object to a little enjoyment; it's that you can't be spared from the milk-round."

"I've a surprise, Lex."

"If you're going to tell me that Milly sent you the money for your fare, then I know already."

"You've seen the letter?"

"I saw it."

Dot did not protest. She accepted the fact that Lex read her letters as she accepted working with him on the milk-round, getting out of the van into the cold and rain and wind to deliver the milk-bottles; then, when they got home at night, preparing a hot nourishing dinner for him and herself; warming his slippers; rubbing the liniment into his back.

"Yes, the fare," Dot said eagerly. "And not only the fare. If you read more of the letter you'd know that she sent me the money for a dress also. There!"

In all Dot's married life her strongest gesture of defiance which she found satisfying and effective, if she used it sparingly, was a vehement "*There*," spoken now so forcibly that she blushed and her big brown eyes grew moist. "*There!*"

Lex was cool. "What of it?"

"But I'm going to do as you said, Lex, I'm wearing my old dress, my brown; it can be touched up. I'm going to the wedding, as your mother said I ought."

"What about the milk-round?"

She tossed her head. "It can do without me for a couple of days. Why not take on Alwyn Maude? He's hanging around, he's finished at the cottage."

"Him! He doesn't know a thing about delivering milk. If I went with him he'd expect me to be running back and forth in the rain and cold while he stayed safe and snug in the van."

"Oh? But it's still summer weather; there's no rain and cold yet."

"Call this summer!"

Playing the role of the legitimately annoyed housewife, Dot said sharply, "Let me tell you it's all the summer we're going to get, so we'd better make the most of it."

"It's funny not being able to go to the farmhouse any more. She had to die sometime. Perhaps it was better than coming to live here."

"I think she'd have liked it here. There's the television."

"She wasn't interested in television."

"Oh, they all say that, but once they start watching they enjoy it well enough. Which reminds me . . ."

Their dinner was over. It was late; the clock on the tiled mantelpiece said half-past nine. Lex crossed to the corner of the room and switched on the sound of the television. The picture had been showing ever since they came home; while they had been eating their roast beef and vegetables and apple pie, statesmen in raincoats, chorus girls, swooping jets, trick cyclists, lions and their cubs; detergents, laxatives, and jeans had been quietly crossing the screen.

"The weather report," Lex said.

"What I was going to tell you," Dot said, anxious to tell her news before she and Lex were submerged in the compulsory silence of watching television, "was that I'm giving the dress money for your mother to be buried in Stamford."

"No, Dot, we don't want to do things that way. I'll put up the money myself."

"But you haven't got it, you said you hadn't."

"I haven't. But we're not poor as church mice. It's just that I can't understand why she need be buried in Stamford when there's all of Suffolk to be buried in. We can get a nice plot in the Murston cemetery."

"People are beginning to talk. They're saying, 'When's the funeral?' They look at me as if she might be . . . might be . . .' "

"They keep them in deep freeze nowadays," Lex said practically. "It's so funny. Vic Baldry said she was probably having a conversation with Nelly just before she died. I'll bet she was calling Nelly a dirty bitch."

"Lex! Your mother never said an unkind word to Nelly. The animal was company for her. They were never apart."

"You didn't know my mother," Lex said, while the isotherms and isobars whirled unheeded on the television screen and the announcer with the ashamed face prodded hopefully with a long stick.

"It was she who drove my father out of the house to live in the cottage. He couldn't stand her. He knew that as soon as he died she'd get rid of the dog too, so he put that clause in his will about our keeping Nelly no matter how old or ill she became. The dog's old, she's going blind, it's time she was destroyed, but now *we* have to keep her until she dies a 'natural death.' What's a 'natural death'?"

Dot sighed. "Oh, Lex, don't be against your mother. I know with my woman's intuition that nothing happened as you've described it. Your mother was the kindest woman. We'll get in touch with the undertakers at once, shall we, to arrange the Stamford burial. Your aunt in Stamford is waiting to hear from us; we're to ring her neighbors any time; after six it's half rates.

The announcer, in final despair, rubbed the isotherms and

isobars from the television screen, then vanished, and a tiny imp, popping out of a beer bottle, said, "Why don't you drink away your summer thirst?"

Dot and Lex went upstairs to bed. Dutifully Dot rubbed the liniment into Lex's back. They were both feeling tired and married, that is, so close that there was no need to separate before they came together. Their grief drowsed to a vague sadness and regret, and Dot was surprised by an unexpected feeling of calm rejoicing, as if she had finally got rid of an obstacle that she never dreamed had existed. A moment before she fell asleep she thought, with a stab of wakefulness, that she was giving her dress money toward the burial in Stamford, not entirely because she felt obliged to respect the clause in the will, but because with Mrs. Unwin at a greater distance, and with her son and daughter-in-law having had the final say by taking command of the distance, Dot felt safer, more truly herself. She found herself in that embalmed bland state so often enjoyed by politicians: she was "looking forward to the future with confidence."

She dreamed of Fulham. World's End. Lot's Road—all the pavements and roads there to be walked on and walked on; everything "for use," as the landladies say. The country was a lonely place compared to Fulham. Dot hacked away in her dreams at new roads and paths and her feet were sore with walking on and on to Stamford. A lorry passed—the broiler lorry going north—with the cramped hens cackling and fluttering, and just inside the back of the lorry, Mrs. Unwin's coffin, traveling cheap, midweek but not return; while Lex, driving the lorry, never stopped or leaned down to help, and the wind and the rain ripped at the clouds and the trees, and Dot walked on and on. So high and dry Lex seemed with his chattering and silent cargo that Dot, in despair, was about to beg mercy from him when she remembered she was not going to Stamford to a funeral, she was going to Fulham, to a wedding. World's End. Lot's Road. Lot's Road.

She laughed as Lex looked back, dark and biblical, and he, not she, changed to a pillar of salt.

31

On August 17 Aisley made another entry in his diary, in black ink:

Funeral: Mrs. Ruby Unwin, farmer's widow, buried at Stamford.

Then, from information received (for country hedges, even when they are barely a foot high, have a habit of communicating the important events of country life), Aisley wrote in red ink in the future spaces that were yet smooth and blank:

Marriage: at Fulham, London, Milly Street, niece of Dot Unwin, to Harry Collins.

Birthday: Alwyn Maude, aged twenty-one; celebration to be at Clematis Cottage, Little Burgelstatham.

Halfway through the birthday entry Aisley's pen refused to write; he blew on it, licked it, shook it, waved it vigorously in the air, but it was no use; his supply of red ink had run out. He finished the entry in black ink, adding the comment: *A very pleasant evening for one on the threshold of manhood.*

When he had finished, he held his pen poised in the air, uncertain whether any more entries would be needed; if they were, they would have to be written in black ink. Births? Marriages? Deaths? He could think of none. The marriage of Jenny and Alwyn seemed too far ahead to justify an entry, and he was unwilling to forecast death, or birth, except the birth of the seasons; but these arrived almost unnoticed. The hay had been gathered and stacked in the great red-brick barns; the crops had ripened and were harvested; it was time for the glory of the grasses, deep in morning dew, and the bare fields lying in lakes of mist, and blue smoke drifting against the horizon. The sun, rising farther south, had a streak of blood in it, at least for those, like Aisley, who were old-fashioned enough to cling to animism and poetic fallacies; others spoke of chemicals and fall-out; yet all agreed that summer, which, the more one thinks of it, the more one realizes had never been, had vanished, playing a trick of existence that is tolerated only when it is performed by seasons, aided and abetted by man who remembers chiefly the cold, the wind, the rain, and the long, lonely night.

Aisley realized, with a characteristic autumnal dismay, that his convalescence was over. His sickness had vanished as surely as the late blackberry flowers in the stunted hedgerows. The completeness of the vanishing alarmed him, prompting him to the more sinister elegaic reference that seemed to imply the departure of his whole being to inaccessible worlds—"The bloom is gone and with the bloom go I."

32 The "small family affair" planned as a twenty-first birthday for Alwyn developed in a way unusual for such affairs; it became smaller and smaller. Alwyn was scornful of the celebration of being twenty-one; it was primitive, out of date, he said, adding boyishly that he didn't like cake with icing. Jenny was happy to follow Alwyn's view, but she confessed that the presentation of the traditional key had appealed to her. Greta had her own worries; she had not yet told Russell about the child. How incredulous would he be? It was doubtful if he even remembered his impulsive night with her. He was the only one who seemed to look forward to the birthday tea—it had dwindled from "party" to "tea"—with a firm in Murston baking a three-tiered decorated cake. Russell had ordered champagne—from London. Why from London? Greta asked herself as, preparing one of his suits, she found the memorandum on the notepaper Russell used, with two big red words—*Don't Forget*—printed at the head of each page. *Champagne (Fortnum and Mason's). Needles, porcelain, dental supplies. Royal College of Surgeons. Hell let loose.*

What on earth did he mean ?

She found out three days before Alwyn's birthday when Russell, impressively dealing with perforations literal and metaphorical, said, "I'm going up to London tomorrow for a couple of days.

He had not been to London for years; Greta couldn't remember the last time he had visited there. She was at the same time depressed and relieved that he had not suggested their going together. Her first thought about her pregnancy had been—London; the traditional refuge, the city which, one assumed, was capable of absorbing and dealing with distress from whatever source—love, ambition, politics, pride, poverty; the city whose deep-rooted myth of generosity is strengthened year by year by young travelers from the provinces and near and far countries, who, giving their heart to the city, believe, with that character-

193

istically human need to try to abolish the effect of action that
involves the doer with the pain of both willing and doing by
switching the suffered verb to the suffering, that it is the city
which offers its heart to them. I am loved, not I love. I am taken,
not I take. The very buildings are of stone porous enough to
receive all—time, weather, and the cast-off human burden.

Run away to London! Greta could scarcely believe, now, that
the idea had risen so spontaneously in her mind, almost as if it
were a communal idea stored, like an iron ration (in sand, beneath ice) for use in emergency. It was, she realized, the emergency of youth risking the dangers of desert and mountain; it had
no relation to her own middle age, her married respectability.
Her years for running away to London to hide and lean her heart
against the generous eternal pillows of stone had gone. She had
known that when she made her appointment in Murston with Dr.
Finch. It was a relief, in a way, to be beyond the reach of the
exhausting sweep of dramatic action that plays like a searchlight
upon one's earlier years; she had made no desperate visit to London to consult a specialist. Yet when one was close to youth and
moved impulsively, as she had done, in and out of the range of
restless light, one discovered that the body had too few layers of
skin; there was deep, first-degree burning, as in time of war.

Greta remembered the war when Russell talked of London. It
seemed that he was going for two days to a place of fire and
darkness. She wished now that he had asked her to go with him.
Russell. Christopher. She was mad ever to have come to live in
Little Burgelstatham, to have stayed year after year plotting her
life according to Maplestone's Chart, "measuring out her life" in
puffer-packs, in slugs and snails, in all-purpose Winter Wash.

That night she and Russell stayed up long after the others had
gone to bed. Journeys for herself and for Russell were so rare
that though she accepted with outward calm the fact of his visit
to London, she was surprised to feel a mounting excitement that
she knew was shared by Russell. It was past one o'clock in the
morning. Aisley had gone to bed earlier than the others, making
of the occasion an invalid's custom that seemed out of place
lately, as he had so much recovered his health. (In company, for
his own protection, he still kept his life to the pace of a theatrical

limp, when no doubt he was capable of greater physical and mental mileage.)

The fire was lit against the first autumn frosts. She and Russell sat opposite each other, close to the fire. Greta remembered the evening before Alwyn had gone away to school for the first time; she thought of the night she had learned of Christopher's death, of night vigils in the hospital when she blinked tired eyes beneath her green-shaded ward lamp and listened to the snuffles and snores of the patients; she was reminded, too, of Christmas, of the religious hush, depressing in its fulsomeness and falsity, of the endless waiting for something to happen, the bells tolling suddenly with the news that nothing had happened, yet one pretended it had; there were congratulations, goodwill; kisses, a birth.

She clasped her hands. "I'm having a baby, Russell," she said, hating herself for the glow sounding in her voice.

"My dear!"

My dear, my dear—he sounded like a Prince Consort!

"My dear. That night?"

She was surprised and touched that he remembered. "Yes," she said, with a feeling as if golden syrup were trickling down between her breasts.

Puppet-like, he moved to her and kissed her. He seemed to have grown shorter. She looked with quick dismay to make certain whether he had acquired a club foot.

"An accomplishment," he said, "on our son's twenty-first birthday!"

Greta felt herself blushing. Tears ran down her cheeks. She sobbed. "I'm so tired, I'm so tired, as if I've been—fire-watching."

Russell looked thoughtfully at her. "How are your teeth?" he said.

Her tears vanished. "My teeth?"

"Yes, it's important, you know."

"Oh, of course."

When I tell Aisley, she thought, he will ask after my soul, and perhaps Jenny will ask after my diet. And Alwyn? It's a game I shall play to determine who shall ask after my heart.

33 Fiction has so clouded with romanticism and drama the actions of a husband from the country who spends a day and night in London that if a writer were to set down the story of a "real" person such as Russell Maude, and try to describe his time in London, the result would fall far short of the reader's expectations. Russell, respectable dentist of Murston, kept no mistress in a West End mansion flat, frequented no weird parties in Notting Hill Gate, was not even interested in strip clubs or casinos or other more sophisticated entertainment provided by the use of tape recorders, cameras, one-way mirrors. He had not been fretting all his years in Murston for the opportunity to buy, in person, the plainly wrapped merchandise of Fulham Road or Strand Alleyways. Russell was one of the lucky men of this world—self-sufficient in vice—whose common humanity explores the less popularly condemned but no less vicious avenues of possession, power, deceit, selfishness. Among these men are those of such innocence that their exploration takes place in dreams only; waking, they commit the prime sin—the denial of responsibility.

No one is saying that Russell Maude was a "bad" man. No one is saying, He doesn't go to London to have a good time with women, but ah! if you only knew what goes on in the depths of his mind! Russell was just an "ordinary" respectable dentist, not as skilled as he might have been, since for so long he had lagged behind in his profession, not keeping in touch with modern developments, yet conscientious in his daily fillings and extractions, and quite a clever sculptor in the task that now took most of his time—the fashioning of National Health false teeth. His reputation as a maker of teeth had extended as far as Tydd; one or two patients came to him from Norwich. It was said that in making teeth he showed an astute knowledge of facial expression. He did not say, "Smile, smile, we'll see if your teeth suit you, they must match your smile!" In this Russell was as up to date as anyone;

the time was gone when one paid extravagant homage to smiling. Today, people weep and moan when their true photographs are taken.

"Relax, close your eyes, snore as if you're asleep, then I'll know if your teeth suit you," Russell would say.

In this also, how modern he was! He had abolished waking; the age was an age of dream, the only shape in which many were able to accept it. Yet for all these special skills Russell as a dentist, husband, father, belonged to the numerous Great Incompetent, and like his companions there in the vast limbo of moments, speeches, thoughts, actions, machines, lives which through some trick of faulty engineering just failed to work, he suffered abuse from the Competent. Competence is one of the chief gods in the history of Adaptable Man.

So, Russell went up to London by train to visit the Dental Supplies Company in Fulham, and the Royal College of Surgeons in Lincoln's Inn Fields. He planned to stay the night in a hotel in Russell Square and return to Little Burgelstatham the following morning for Alwyn's birthday tea in the evening. He would also bring the champagne, he said, from Fortnum and Mason's. He did not explain why he had suddenly decided to visit London after all his years in Murston. No one was anxious to demand a clear reason from him. The two important events of the moment— Alwyn's approaching twenty-first birthday, and the news that Greta was expecting a baby—seemed, as such events do, to supply with unique generosity peripheral more ordinary occasions with a reflected glow of reason and rightness—as, in the presence of miracles, ordinary unexplained happenings are seen in the light of the miraculous.

Even Greta was too absorbed to question Russell's journey; "absorbed" is the precise word to describe her state, for while her body was preparing the usual nest-lining for the crude red-as-plastic creature whom Russell and she or Alwyn and she had begun, her mind seemed to be lining itself with a similar kind of protective material—warm, absorbent—to accommodate the thrust and struggle of many new no less crudely colored thoughts and feelings.

The sun shone. Russell remembered London in rain, mist, fog. He left his bag in the hotel and set out at once for the Dental Supplies Company. He smiled to himself as he thought of his apparently commonplace mission. For some time he had not been satisfied with the delivered orders, nor with the attitude of the representative, who, when Russell, paying the high cost of carriage, had sent the dilapidated dental chair to be mended, had without warning forwarded a brand-new chair, cash on delivery, with the advice that the old was so out of date that nothing could be done with it, and that the firm was sure that when Russell saw the new chair (a very popular brand with other customers) he would not hesitate to accept it. Russell had been horrified and angry—horrified at the design of the modern chair with its push-button controls; angry that after all his years of dealing with the firm and their assurance of "personal service" its representatives had so little understanding of his needs and wishes.

He had arrived at eleven o'clock at Liverpool Street. It was now past midday; the pavements were soft with heat-bubbled asphalt; men had taken off their coats; women wore sleeveless dresses. As the Fulham bus passed through the city, skirting the parks, Russell, noting the summery people sprawled in deck-chairs or on the grass, the bright umbrellas and little painted tables and chairs set on the pavements outside the cafés, felt as though he were visiting a foreign land. The street was full of foreigners —women in saris, Africans in magnificent gold and brown robes, people crying out in French, Spanish; the slow down-under drawl of: "Can you let me know when we get to Westminster Abbey? Oh, am I on the wrong bus?", the American: "Say, can you tell me where's the Old Bailey?" All seemed bright, gay, without cohesion—a pebbly kind of life, too close to the other pebbles.

A man and a small boy got on the bus. "Is this for London Airport?" the man asked.

"Hammersmith only. You'll get the bus for the airport at Hammersmith."

"Daddy, how many planes do you think we'll see?"

"Scores. Perhaps hundreds."

"Viscounts?"

"Viscounts."

"Caravelles?"

"Caravelles."

The child climbed on his father's knee and pointed excitedly to the people, the shops, the traffic. The woman sitting behind Russell began to talk to her companion of her last plane flight. Russell could hear other passengers talking of flying. A strange feeling came over him, as if, while he had been all those years in Murston, his countrymen had been transformed into a nation of birds. He knew that many more people made journeys by plane, for even in East Suffolk the sky was noisy with jets putting their mercerized white writing from cloud to cloud; yet Russell had not been aware of the vast migration to the air. The three stages of development, he thought. Sea, land, air. Where next?

As an unadaptable man (the race is so easily recognized) he spoke in disparaging terms of all new movements and discoveries. At the White Horse in Murston where he so often had lunch he knew moments of real happiness or some feeling which he thought he identified as "real" happiness when he and others of like mind murmured to each other, between mouthfuls, that television was "bad," computers were "bad," all so-called progress was "bad." When Lawrence Silk, his solicitor friend, used to ask Russell why with all his education and intellect he could so far descend to the bottomless habits of thought of the "rabble" quaking in their time-life swamps of emotion surface-weeded with fear and love, Russell would try to explain that he had deliberately chosen the past and must remain loyal to it on all counts (though occasional disloyalties slipped by even without his noticing them), that any word spoken in praise of the present or the future was sabotage of the precious past and should be avoided by those few who cared for the past. A man was as free, Russell said, to choose his time as to choose his wife, whereupon Lawrence made a cynical remark about *that* kind of freedom:

"What if you marry the wrong time as you may marry the wrong wife, and can't escape from it? What if the time *chooses you?*"

"It's the choice that is important," Russell said. "So few people know how to choose their time or their wife."

You haven't been so successful with one yourself, Lawrence thought, but did not say so.

"You've got to choose with your whole being—your body, your mind, your fingernails, your teeth."

Ah, teeth.

"How is it you're so keen on teeth, yet—you know this and won't mind my saying it—you subscribe to no modern dental journals, your equipment is out of date, you do a good job with the stuff you've got—better than most—but you're not carrying out your responsibility to the profession—are you?"

"Here it is again," Russell had said in a tired voice. "The profession. I believe in ripples, the wider the better. It means a big stone has been thrown in, and *that* means the sediment of what you call 'bottomless thought' has been disturbed. I'm crazy over teeth. Do you want to know why? They endure. The past endures."

"You're a fool, Russell," Lawrence had said. "And like most fools, you're happy. Ever flown in a jet?"

Russell was remembering Lawrence's words now as he sat in the bus. It turned to Fulham Road, his stop.

"Hammersmith only," the conductor called, barring the path of the extra passengers trying to crowd on. "No standing. Hammersmith only."

Russell stayed on the bus as far as Hammersmith, where he got off, crossed to a waiting ninety-one B, and boarded it. Sitting behind the man and the child still engrossed in their conversation about aircraft, he traveled through Chiswick, Hounslow, to London Airport, where he followed the man and the boy to the observation platform (paying his half-crown at the turnstile) and sat staring down at the runway.

"Fulham Dental Supplies, Royal College of Surgeons, Lincoln's Inn Fields; champagne from Fortnum and Mason's," he repeated to himself in a cynical tone. "Ha!"

The reader (once courted in novels by the attribute "dear")

may think that Russell's sudden abandoning of his visit to the
Dental Supplies store and the Royal College represents another of
the countless commonplace examples of people (called in the
context "worms") who turn. Russell's journey to the airport was
caused by the curiosity of the persistent earth-dweller to study
closely the machines that fly and the people who fly in them. His
archaic way of life was further emphasized by his reference to
"machines that fly" instead of to "planes." Once, he ventured
"aeroplane," and the holiday schoolboy leaning over the railing
beside him gave a short glance of scorn, as if to remind Russell
that if he wanted to stay alive, as a man of his time, he would
need to take care of his language, to make it swift, brief, highly
powered as the jets in the sky; stumbling over an unnecessary
syllable in the race for speech might be a matter of life and death.
Weighing both life and death and finding them equally balanced,
Russell felt old, calm, tired; he was aware for the first time in
years of the self that had once been Russell, standing beside him.
He stared disapprovingly at it. He scarcely recognized the young
man in army uniform, ready to fight and fill teeth for freedom;
he remembered his vigor, enthusiasm, the plans he had made for
his future practice, urged by the charming small dark woman
whom he'd met and married while on leave. He remembered, too,
with bitterness, for his sense of humor had never been robust or
liberal, the mockery that pursued him everywhere because he had
chosen dentistry. He realized that people's attitude toward dentistry was as complicated, deep-seated, irrational as their numerous
racial and religious hatreds.

At the front, among the wounded during the war, he had
been baffled and angry by the ridicule directed at him. Had he
been a more forceful personality, he might have overcome this
obstacle as surely as members of some races and religions survive
the campaigns against them to rise to fame; yet here the past that
Russell had chosen was against him. Who had ever known a
famous dentist? The most famous dentists were the most notorious with emphasis laid on their brutality. He had heard once of a
novelist who contemplated writing a novel with a dentist as hero,
but who gave up halfway because even he could not take seri-

ously the unheroic history of dentists. How could a man suffer, think, feel, fall in love, live an interesting or tragic life when most of the hours of most of his days were spent not climbing mountains, exploring caves, tracing or creating the right word; not flying, fighting, pioneering, deciding the future of nations and worlds; but in pursuing the career of exploring the tiny mouth-cave of vulnerable man suffering an undignified personal pain that began and ended in ridcule? "Why did so few people understand that the wearing of false teeth could dominate, subtly change a man's habits of eating, speaking, laughing, weeping, sleeping—even of dying? To Russell, dentistry had once seemed to contain material for heroics; but the weight and prejudice of history had subdued him. He who might have been a hero had become a potterer; on the other hand, he had surrendered a prospect of tortured heroics for a calm, cozy wrapping of yesterday —not *his* yesterday, a vague "other" time, woven with words and habits as frayed as the cord on his old-fashioned dental drill.

As he watched the planes landing and taking off he had the feeling, in a kind of self-defense, that his feet were being more firmly rooted in the earth, or rather in the wooden floor of the observation platform, which, though there were so few people there, was already littered with the leavings of plane-spotters sharing the need of humanity for drinks on sticks, in cartons, sweets in wrappers . . . Directly before him, on the runway, space was prepared for a Viscount to land, and beside it another Viscount stood ready to load and take off. Small airport station wagons darted and whizzed around each plane like clerks before the manager; yet far from resembling a manager, the Viscount seemed to Russell to be like an old tired woman submitting without interest while the life-giving, flame-giving, possibly death-giving fuel was pumped into her belly. She was not even dressed for the occasion; her red and black coloring was crude, tatty; her wings drooped; beside the sophisticated streamlined Comets and Caravelles she looked like an old whore who doesn't know when to retire.

The refueling finished, the stores taken on board, the airport bus appeared with a further last offering, of people, so insignificant beside the huge plane, which now seemed less a weary whore than a weary but still powerful dragon who suddenly swallowed with indecent greed and swiftness seventy bodies, minds, stamped carrier bags; two air hostesses, pilots; then withdrew the gangway, with a flick as of a serpent's tongue, into her belly, snapped securely imprisoned the assorted meal, guidance, satisfaction, then began to scream like an old hag who can scarcely wait to get her revenge upon all who have wronged or abused her. Looking down upon the retreating mechanics, the already swirling propellers, hearing the vengeful screaming, Russell was not alone in thinking the usual thoughts of spectators at an airfield when a dowager-drooping plane is about to take off: It will crash. Over Bombay or Bangkok or somewhere remote enough for the crash to be of little news value—unless the passengers are British, when, naturally, their age, appearance, profession, marital status and number of children will be announced. The Viscount will crash, its tail will drop off in mid-ocean, fuel will have to be jettisoned, flames will be seen, the plane will explode; the wreckage will be found floating in the Indian Ocean or the China Sea.

A fearful hopeful fantasy common among those who give vent to their secret urges of violence by watching planes.

Russell turned to look at the schoolboy beside him. They exchanged the understanding glances of people who *know* why observation platforms at airports attract old and young, mad and reasonable, rich and poor, equal and unequal—or any other convenient divisions of humanity. Russell was surprised to realize that the boy *knew*. Would Alwyn have known? He had never taken Alwyn to an airport; no doubt his school had gone there for an excursion; "these days" visits to places of public interest and excitement were included in a boy's education. Russell wondered how many other visits Alwyn had made and to where, and what he had learned, and how much he had told Greta and himself when he came home for the holidays; perhaps he had talked only to Greta; the time of Alwyn's education had been the time of Russell's decision to continue to live with Greta, though sleeping apart from her. There had been no quarrel, nor any of the tremendously dramatic moments that wrap important decisions in mothballs of memorabilia. Neither Greta nor Russell had a "sign post" temperament; in this they had missed much of the suffering and happiness experienced by those who apply lavish gold and black luminous paint to the events of their lives (one must note that luminous paint, while it gives a more distinct view of the dark past, may in time induce cancer of the memory). The decision made by Russell and Greta had not been remarked upon by either of them. Russell had "happened" to let it be known that he preferred his bed made up in the study-bedroom; Greta had "happened" to be tired, to want to sleep alone; one night spent in this way led to many nights; many nights led to every night, though the pattern had been broken at times in the interesting way of human patterns, when Russell impulsively wandered into Greta's room in search of his "commemorative" stamps.

Stamps. He thought of them now as he watched the Viscount taxi-ing out of sight in preparation for take-off. Stamps had given so much meaning to his life; it had been a vague longing for foreign lands, the spell of a miniature magic carpet that might transport him from the concerns of everyday existence, that had prompted his first interest in stamps. Had he not made his decision? He was now on the side of the Great Dull (though not by choice was he included so often in the Great Incompetent). There are those whose hobbies are fascinating, unusual, interesting: ships in bottles, tight-rope walking, skulls, bird-watching, and so on; others merely "have a hobby," pursue it, and, in talking about it, bore those who listen. Russell was not only on the side of the Great Dull; he was one of them. In the same tone that people used to ask, "Whatever made you take up dentistry?" they exclaimed, "What do you *see* in stamp-collecting. Why stamps? Messing about with perforations, First Day covers, Commemorative issues . . . it's all a racket these days anyway."

Then, their eyes lighting with understanding and pity as they gazed at the stay-at-home dentist, they would cry, "Oh, you're interested in foreign parts? Stamp-collecting is like traveling, isn't it? Of course, living as you do here in Little Burgelstatham . . ."

People need a million eyes or perhaps none at all; perhaps it is blindness they need to "see" more clearly what others "see." How desperately they need to see it, too—more desperately when the object of the seeing is a human being particularly one who is loved. Hate is so often taken for granted; people seldom remark, "I can't see why you should hate her or him," yet always there is someone, somewhere, exclaiming with indignation, envy, intense curiosity, "What does he *see* in her, what does she *see* in him." How jealous we are of another's private view, even when it is the view of common objects like postage stamps. It is the privacy we are jealous of, the joy in the personal vision, and because love and loving are important for all time, the "seeing" of the lover is constantly in danger of being ransacked as if it were treasure; often murder is committed to get possession of it.

Love? Murder? Passion? No one would be spending sleepless nights coveting Russell's private view of philately or dentistry; few people covet the vision of a bore. It is more useful to imagine a human race composed wholly of interesting people than to acknowledge the overwhelming population of bores—more useful, because more expedient in the struggle for survival. Bores are easier to hate, to kill, to imprison, to experiment on in camps, to refuse the privilege of owning a soul; they even contribute by their own actions to the denial of their soul. Should they be seized with poverty, hunger, sickness, they will find they are given less pity than the interesting poor, the interesting sick. They are not even made familiar to themselves and others by being described, analyzed, explained by novelists; their world is largely unknown. Novelists who write of them cheat by implying, This man is a bore, but *I* shall write about him in such an interesting way that you will not realize he is a bore, one of the Great Dull. Novelists are on the side of life; they understand the need to assume that all people are interesting; otherwise they agree to the death-sentence of the individual; part of their vast hostel of memory is filled with their private furniture and tenants; most of it is let to the history of life—beast, bird, man; they know but do not tell us of the many rooms let to those whose lives contained so little of interest to others that their death passed unnoticed, brought no protest or mourning.

Russell saw someone waving at the window of the Viscount as it moved heavily into the air. The plane might crash, he thought. And who cares? He had been alarmed at the way the passengers were hurried aboard. Now he felt equally concerned as he watched another Viscount landing directly beneath his observation post. He noted the usual formal ashamed procedure of hurrying the passengers from the plane to the waiting bus, as to a prison van. He saw a confusion of bodies, hats, umbrellas, overcoats, cameras, small bags, occasionally a pale, tired traveler's face seeming to float without attachment to body or brain, between the emergency gangway and the snaking bus. As soon as the passengers had been disposed of, the official nurses attending the Viscount adopted a more leisurely, tender pace. The flight-weary matron with the dented body was touched, probed, opened, smoothed, emptied, fed, consulted over by the airport gods—the fuel dispensers wearing clinical white coats. The plane, not the passengers, had become the reason, the being; somewhere, out of some incomprehensible urgency, the human race had been sidetracked, grounded, the main runway taken over by the machine. Aisley should see this, Russell thought. He'd compose a sermon.

Though Aisley was his brother, Russell had the same ignorance of his calling as most people have of the working of a clergyman's mind. It is usually supposed that a clergyman goes through life pouncing upon everything he receives through his senses as a topic for a sermon. In his early years, certainly, Aisley had made this the basis of his preaching and was still trying to rid himself of the homilitic tendency. It took years to learn that the only satisfactory basis for a Christian sermon is not something felt or observed in streets, stations, runways, but the recorded word of God, which practicing clergymen are trained to set, like jewels, inside their mind; it is the light of these jewels glittering upon streets, stations, runways that inspires and gives reason for the sermon. Russell seldom gave much thought to Aisley and his affairs. The ten years' difference in their ages, which in boyhood almost made them members of a separate generation, should have been diminished by time; but as they grew older their marriages, their separate ways of life, their habits had set them further apart. They had not even their appearance in common; Russell had grown stouter, more stolid; he had a "planted" look; the circle of his concerns had been set around him as immovably as Stonehenge; a personal solstice enveloped him; only the fact that he was human and not stone had enabled him to make this unexpected uncharacteristic visit to the airport. When people are Stonehenge they also have the privilege, sometimes the despair, of the longest day and night.

Their parentage, their devotion to the past were the only factors shared by Russell and Aisley; both with the inclination to stop had stopped and stayed, temporal fixtures, while the rest of the world went on and on, progressing, adapting, adapting.

More than generations separated Russell from Alwyn, though when he came to look for details of separation, for points of departure, he could note only seemingly trivial items like hairstyle, shoe-pattern, clothes, books read, choice of topics for conversation, choice of friends—the changeling Jenny. Like many people whose parentage and past are so solidly established that they can escape from neither, Russell had occasional fantasies of meeting and knowing changelings who glided, wraiths without origin or responsibility, through arches, in and out of doorways; who even entered, as Jenny had done, his own home and claimed his only son, shedding upon him part of the glow of her unworldly brightness . . . so Russell dreamed, with incredible inaccuracy. Tiny objects such as teeth and stamps, needing mirrors, magnifying glasses, tweezers to be observed, had for so long claimed his attention that when he turned to contemplate people he was impressed by their apparent enormity; he was inclined to deal with them in fragments—like a roving close-up camera that must present separately the blemishes of the skin on one side of a face, one fingernail, one eye, as if each were, for the time being, an entire human being. Jenny's youthfulness dazzled him. The time she spent in Alwyn's room disturbed him, more with envy than anxiety. He was happy enough to dismiss such a close family concern, perhaps problem, as a "sign of the times," the scapegoat owned by most people but seldom used by him. Why, was he not so far in yesterday that he needed artificial aids—telescopes, microscopes—in order to observe the present moment?

He swung the small telescope from its stand, gazing through it at the newly arrived Viscount being prepared for yet another flight. He was irritated suddenly by the noise of the jets, by the enthusiastic schoolboys surrounding him with their notebooks and pencils and their excited exchange of technical knowledge.

"It's absurd, he thought, to go on making ceremonies of twenty-first birthdays. There's no meaning in it. I haven't the complex My Son, My Son, which, if truth were known, is perhaps the reason behind Aisley's pursuit of religion. I care only for monuments—teeth as tombstone, as sculpture—I see a vast deserted world of burnt earth, with these tombstones rising from it to speak. My obsession with teeth may have begun when I was a child at the rectory (how like our father Aisley has grown!) and looked out at the churchyard upon the leaning tombstones that disturbed my symmetrical eye. In my mind I admonished the untidy dead. I'm a precise man still; I'm exact; I anesthetize, I operate. I've grown old—a self-pitying admission.

A surge of schoolboys crowded him from the railing. He left the observation platform, boarded the bus back to London. The driver, too early, filled in time by dawdling at the bus-stop near Lot's Road Bridge. At a church near by, there had just been a wedding. The bride and groom were standing on the steps, arm close in pledging possessive arm, being photographed; the bride frowned as a sudden belch of power-station soot clouded her flowing white dress. She brushed it quickly, leaving a dark smudge, while the bridegroom smiled, Never mind. Pigeons, clouds, gray light; World's End; the pavements on both sides of the street cluttered with second-hand furniture, old paintings, tapestries, statues bought cheaply at the Crystal Palace sale: naked weathered cherubs, dragons, men, women, gods; in the window two doors from the church a pink window pyramid displayed sensitized Durex; paper, packets, litter mingled now with confetti, blew along the street in that gusty breeze, seeming neither from north or south, east or west, which prevails forever over London.

Russell saw a familiar figure standing with the group on the steps of the church: a woman dressed in a brown costume with a brown hat tipped at the side with a small bunch of flowers. Dot

Unwin, the milkman's wife? The Little Burgelstatham milkman's wife here in Fulham? I'm dreaming, he thought, trying to reconcile the sprucely dressed figure with the raincoated, sou'westered, gum-booted person who every morning summer and winter, rain, sunshine and snow, delivered the milk to the doorstep of every home in the village. I *am* dreaming, he thought, as he saw the woman looking very handsome, laughing in a friendly way with the equally handsome man who stood near her, holding her arm. That's not Lex Unwin, Russell thought, with a stupid feeling, as if he'd been asked to work a sum in the new matrimonial arithmetic and didn't know how to arrive at the answer. As the driver and conductor, consulting their cards and watches, agreed that they had "made up" their time, and the bus began to move, Russell gave a last puzzled glance at the World's End wedding, with an uneasy feeling that things and people which ought to be in their correct places had shifted without his knowing; he felt some of the extravagant sense of promise and alarm, of commitment, of one who without preparation is baptized in anarchy, then thrust back into the kingdom.

"I saw Mr. Maude, the dentist, at the wedding. I mean he was passing in the bus at Fulham. He looked out of the window at me," Dot said later to Lex. "There was a woman sitting beside him. They looked very friendly. What was he doing in Fulham, I thought. I thought it was him, and then I looked again and thought it couldn't have been, but I couldn't make up my mind. They put Milly on half a page of the *West London News*. Remember when we were in the *East Anglian Times*, at the head of the list?"

Lex said that he remembered. He added that while Dot had been away the milk-round had taken all day and most of the evening; and she knew, without his reminding her, that the trip to London had cost more than he or she could afford.

"There's the money from the sale," Dot said softly but firmly.

"You're right," Lex said, looking less worried.

The sale of the cottage had pleased him. The television people had paid the price he asked; he regretted not having asked for more. He wondered at their eagerness to "get away" from London to a little place in the country. London was all right, he supposed, if you were something to do with television.

"And now everything's settled," Lex said, including vaguely in the "everything" Dot's visit to London, her return unharmed (with pork pies and wedding cake); the day-by-day routine of the milk-round set in motion again with less discomfort to himself; the check from the cottage put in the bank, the owners settled in; and, as a large significant part of "everything," his mother dead and buried. He did not grieve consciously for her, but he gasped with a sense of icy shock when he had seen Dot carrying a pile of her clothes from the kitchen to the bedroom; they were untidily limp, submissive; if his mother had been in them she would have been kicking and screaming at being carried off in that fashion. She had owned and mastered her clothes, wielded them as she wielded the walking-stick when she drove the Little Friesians in and out of the barn; and as her only son, Lex knew that his mother had belonged to him. When one possesses more than one loves, death is looked on as a thief more than a rival. Lex felt that his mother's death had been a kind of burglary that need not have been committed had the right precautions been taken, had all the doors and windows been locked and bolted.

But had not his mother's age advertised itself, like money or jewels left in full view while the tenants of the house are away?

"Well, the weather's good," Lex said. "The weather's good."

So much depended on the weather.

Russell returned home, without the champagne, for the twenty-first birthday party. There was a telegram from Alwyn and Jenny, from Durham: MARRIED. CELEBRATE WEDDING INSTEAD OF BIRTHDAY.

34 Upstairs in his room, where he spent more time now that his health had improved and he did not know how to break the news of its improvement without releasing himself once more to be the prey of the responsibilities of parish and God, Aisley, learning of the wedding, opened his record book, took his pen, and looked for the red ink. He could not find it.

"Perhaps I've used it," he said to himself. "After all, the color is not important," he told himself, "it's only a cunning shifting of the bonus of festivity from oneself to the color of the ink used. Some find celebrating a task as hard as mourning."

Therefore he entered neatly, in black ink, at the head of a clean page:

Marriage. Jenny Sparling, aged twenty, to Alwyn Maude, aged twenty-one. At Durham.

Why had they married at Durham? Perhaps it was a fashionable place to marry?

Memories of Durham returned to Aisley. He thought of his early and life-long obsession with St. Cuthbert, of the youthful way in which he as a student had imagined that simplicity in living meant always shutting the material shop and staring silently through the display window at the world. Such simplicity could mask, behind the glass of separation, an undreamed-of world of complexity; it had suited St. Cuthbert; it had helped to make him a saint; he had been the actor performing against the dark, bare backcloth; the light of attention and devotion had shone upon him.

Aisley remembered that he himself had wanted to lead a life similar to St. Cuthbert's. He had reckoned without the twentieth century. A man who shut himself on a lonely island, who talked to the birds and the fish, who in the early morning went walking up to his neck in the North Sea waves, might hit the newspaper headlines, appear in television interviews—but not as a saint. St. Cuthbert had led a life as simple as dewfall, when dewfall had

truly been simple and not an occasion for reckoning radioactiv-
ity. How would St. Cuthbert have lived, Aisley thought, if he
had been convalescing in Little Burgelstatham in the Maude
household, enduring the cliché situation of old and new generations, old and new beliefs, customs—even old and new Bibles?

Yet surely in St. Cuthbert's age there had been men like himself who chose to abandon their time, who disapproved of
adaptability as a necessary virtue of the human race, who believed in a certain control of human progress—forcing the trees
to grow tall to accommodate themselves to the tall people who
walked among them, forcing the air to produce a buoyant substance that could carry man simply because he desired so much to
fly—not leaving him condemned to life on earth because he did
not possess wings; a control by which man could achieve wings
first, then command the heavens "Fly me!" and the heavens dare
not refuse. Man had learned to build houses, to say to them
"Contain me!" and they did so; one day he would extend his
control to space and time and to the history which they enclosed.
Events happened; it was considered such a virtue to "adapt" to
them, to "accept" them, merely because they in their turn had
exhibited the admired virtue of happening, of taking an ordered
place in time. Someone has to begin, Aisley thought, to take
action against the tyranny of time.

But what of God? He's no longer in my picture as a benevolent elder watching over His children; there's no need for Him to
be made acceptable by dressing Him in pleasing comforting
imagery; the photo is as vivid, more truthful, perhaps, without
technicolor, without the "Smile, please" persuasions of the pho-
tographer. When I woke that morning and found that God had
disappeared, I assumed He had gone from the picture, I tried in
panic to identify the specks and blots near each corner as God. It
has only now occurred to me that after all my years of preaching on the kind-old-man theme, on the white beard, the blue
loving eyes, the peaceful countenance of God; or in other moods
of His righteous anger, His furious revenge upon wrong-doers,
His sword uplifted to strike, I have lost sight of Him, not because
my vision is obsolete, but because I see Him in His true form: the

adult image of a powerful invisibility, the final Power and Pressure—less a superhuman creature than a marvel of engineering
precision which, ultimately, will provide us with the power to
develop wings though the heavens cry "Fall powerless on rock
and stone"; to walk safe, alive, in the sea, though the waves cry
"Drown"; to choose and master the Time which cries "Submit to
my magical happenings, destroy because I have provided means
of destruction, cower because I train the weapon of progress on
you; you dare not now decide your own fate."

St. Cuthbert had the faith to walk in the waves; he saw God; I
would follow St. Cuthbert. Can it be that, returning to the Anglo-
Saxon age, I am yet walking more surely into the twentieth century? The last shall be first? Where are Greta, Alwyn, Jenny,
Russell—in a way, and for the time being, my parishioners—and
the other inhabitants of Little Burgelstatham, the burial place of
the heathen: the Baldrys, the Unwins, the Sapleys, the old gardener, the builder, even the Italian farm worker who dared to
enter this tiny world? How I have nursed myself to myself, as if
I were my own illness! What of my "cure of souls"?

Aisley, in a mood of rhetorical questioning—so much less demanding of precise thought than ordinary questions—read once
more the entry in black ink. He signed it, shut the book, and put
it back in his desk.

How kind of Greta to have provided me with this desk, he
thought. And with the prayer-chair, and the two Bibles by which
I may shuttle back and forth from Beauty to Abomination.
Greta's child will be born next spring. Sometimes a child born to
a woman of Greta's age is deformed or mongoloid; the fruit of
middle age—wizened almost as soon as it drops. Or is the idea a
myth in the mind of those who must explain and expiate the
magic and guilt of the unexpected, the incongruous, the miraculous? The dry seemingly dead tree bears fruit; it will be poisoned
fruit, they say, with envy and fear; and with Greta so it may be.
I wonder if some time between now and the birth of Greta's
child, Alwyn will confess to having murdered Botti Julio the
Italian . . . but why should he? I too can play the generalizing
facile game of Aren't We All Murderers, bestowing the magical

excuses on the majority, we're all in together this fine or foul
weather, the possession and legacy of the guilt is diminished because it is shared; there but for God's grace I hang, because I
killed. The worship of the big fat people-packed opinion and
behavior means that somewhere democracy has sprung a leak; or
its protection and roof have been sealed to exclude God, the
dividing Power which may still consider human beings one by
one, examining a man apart from his family, his neighbor, his
country, or wherever else a man clings safe as a member of the
ordered compulsive colony.

It's no use my dismissing Alwyn by claiming that he is not
"real," that what he has done is not "in keeping" with his nature,
his usual behavior; nor even placing the responsibility for his act
upon his being truly a "child of his time." Who knows? He may
even be the father of Greta's child. A spring child, to be born
before the snowdrops. I'll be gone from Little Burgelstatham
then. My latest X-ray at the Murston Cottage Hospital has been
read by those who are suitably literate in the language of the
body (as I once thought myself to be in the language of the
soul); the shadow has gone from my left lung. When I asked
why it had gone, I was told—the sun, the country life, quietness,
fresh air, rest. My feeling of helplessness increased—so man is still
at the mercy of the sun and wind, which like two thieves, can
steal in and take away the shadow from his left lung; or the fog,
frost, and rain that put the shadow there in the first place. Were I
as I had been in my earliest days at St. Cuthbert's, I would be
sitting down to write a sermon about the cruel shadows that
obscure the souls of men; how the literate clergy, with the help
of the wisdom of God, must read, interpret, banish the shadows;
I would be saying that the health of a man's soul is at the mercy
of God, the persistent spiritual weather.

I'll no longer deliver such facile sermons in a kind of pop-
preaching which, as pop-art tries to include all subjects by insisting that everything is significant, has claims to beauty, in its turn
fancies that the God-touch, like the Midas-touch, turns everything everywhere to a golden message of salvation or damnation.
The sad fact is that not everything has significance; the desperate

rage to make it so is only another habit of the Adaptable Man who has lost the center of meaning. I cannot smooth away an easy resemblance between shadows on lungs and shadows on souls by troweling with a God-cement . . .

My summer has been uneventful. My nephew has murdered the stranger who dared to try to enter the closed community, to speak its language. My sister-in-law is expecting a child after many many years. Old Mrs. Unwin has died. My nephew has turned twenty-one, has married. My record book, brought with me in a surge of clerical nostalgia, carries the usual entries in red and black ink. My brother continues to fill and pull out teeth, to collect and catalogue stamps. It used to amaze and shame me that two brothers could be so far apart; now it depresses me that we so closely resemble each other, though he reveals more of the secret —when he opens his mouth, the archaisms fly out like shot directed against the present age. His life, like a pair of forceps, takes teeth in its grip as a means of salvation, just as certainly as I've taken God, whole or decayed, diagnosing, trying to cure. That's an admirable skill Russell has—the fashioning of new false teeth that seem real. I've heard, though, that people with false teeth have a dread of bursting into hearty laughter—some are even afraid of smiling—though somewhere I've seen an advertisement for what is called a "fixative" . . . a Fixative . . . How shall I spend my life when I leave Little Burgelstatham? Who wants Christ as a fixative? It may be that at this moment some of my more up-to-date brother clergy are conducting shamelessly, enthusiastically, an opinion poll into such consumer needs of the soul. . . .

35   Dear Reader.
        Summer has "given way" to autumn,
        with so much grace and lament. The
stubble fields are deep in mud-filled pools; the swifts
plunge and rise in the air—as a city dweller I'd say they
are dancing, but having lived all summer in this dear
little thatched cottage, so kindly rented for me by this
newspaper, I know now that swifts are not lightly dancing in air, they are flying to seize and eat insects.

During the summer the peaceful village of Little
Burgelstatham has not been troubled by tourists; the only
strangers have been visitors at the dentist's house, and a
foreign worker who fell and was drowned in the pool
in the lane.

The hedges are cut, the wind from the North Sea
sweeps with more chill across the bare fields; morning
and evening are blue with mist.

"Good God," Unity Foreman said, pin-scooping the ink-filled
e, a, o, and *c.* "The setup gets worse and worse. Someone will find
out I've never been near the countryside, that I've never put foot
inside a dear little thatched cottage. I've the smell of the one and
only Elsan of my life still in my nightmares, that dark, suffocating liquid with its guaranteed 'film' over all offensive matter: the
rising damp, the gas-hissing lamp light (though I've heard that
Little Burgelstatham now has electricity), the spiders on the
beautiful beamed ceiling—spiders as big, hairy, long-legged as
those trick spiders for sale in the joke shop in Tottenham Court
Road."

Unity Foreman sighed, sniffed the autumn smog stealing
through the chained window, opened its permitted few inches at
the top. She crossed the room, shut the window, noted the backyard drains already blocked with brown leaves. (There had been
no interval when leaves were golden in the trees; the leaves had
caught on to the general trend of economy; green to dirty-brown

was the rule of the season; intermediate coloring was a futile waste when seasons, like railways, had to pay, pay, pay.)

How clean the *e*'s and *o*'s and *c*'s were now! They were such tiresome letters, too greedy for their share of ink from the typing ribbon.

> A hush steals over the East Suffolk countryside. The migrating birds for which this county is famous have gone, the marsh orchids have withered, now the empty remote sky is set like a shifting mirror above the bare, flat fields. Up north the summer bodies have been recovered from the Broads, delivered with the appropriate ceremony to their city homes; the white sails have folded neatly as butterfly wings; the level of the dark reed-bordered water rises; the remaining marsh birds splash and swim in the true loneliness and peace of their sanctuary . . .

Unity smiled. Well, a bit of fine writing a day keeps the . . .

She put the cover on her typewriter. Her hands were branded with *o, e, c, a*. She went to the bathroom to wash them, remembered that she wanted a bath because she was going to the theater that night, switched on the hot water, flopped in a chair with a copy of *Vogue*, Talking Points from the London Collections.

That evening on her way to the theater she posted her "Letter from the Countryside," after having hurriedly finished it, keeping closely to the editor's prescription: two-thirds flora and fauna; one-third people; one-sixth old customs; one-sixth progress.

PART FOUR

The chandelier

36 Progress. Recovery from illness; growth of plants and human bodies; new means of satisfying the old needs to move from place to place, to see in the dark, to swim, to fly, to explore, to understand; to subtract, divide, add, multiply; the need to speak, to be silent, to remember, to prophesy.

Only the young have hope of staying in the game. The old, under the autumn trees, play knucklebones or sleep with their mouths wide open, their stale breath drifting along the moss-grown track of their tongue.

Progress: allocation one-sixth.

Animals, including human beings; birds, vegetation, one-quarter.

When Mrs. Unwin died, Bert Whattling found the enforced change in his weekly routine more disturbing than the actual death. He missed the evenings spent at the farmhouse—helping with the blocked chimney, drinking the smoke-filled tea, making slow, wise remarks about marriage and "*dee*-vorce," gossiping about friends and strangers in Little Burgelstatham and beyond in his dream-world of Tydd; drawing from his pocket, in the hope of giving everyone a pleasant surprise, the titbits cut from the *East Anglian Times*—the story of the elephant that walked into the sea at Clacton, the write-up of the British Legion Mystery Tour that in spite of the intended mystery made Clacton its destination almost every year. "I were there that day," Bert would say impressively. Above all, he missed sharing his plans for the day in Tydd, helping Mrs. Unwin to round up the geese to be sold, acting as messenger between the old identities at Little Burgelstatham and Murston and those at Tydd.

Since Mrs. Unwin's death Bert seemed to walk more slowly, to lose his balance more often when he rode his bicycle; he preferred now to wheel it along the narrow grass verge of the A140 rather than to ride it near the charging Snowcem and milk-lorries

and the fast cars whose drivers seemed not to care about the
faltering rosy-cheeked old man, but would look briefly askance at
him, thinking perhaps, Old codger shouldn't be in charge of a
bike at his age! Few things make for as much enmity between
generations, sexes, professions, trades, as a long, straight stretch
of the Queen's Highway that by law may be used by all.

Bert missed, too, the evenings following his visit to Tydd when
he told his day's adventures to an audience (Mrs. Unwin, Olly
Drew, Lex, Dot) who seemed so enthralled by his account that
he might have been describing a visit to Damascus, to Egypt,
Japan; a few minutes spent in the ironmongers', a word-by-word
report of what he said, what Bert said, what he said, what Bert
said, could be made by Bert to sound as enthralling and mysterious as the conversation between man and prophet.

There was no one now for him to tell. He had never talked
much to his wife about the day in Tydd except to note whether
rabbits and other merchandise had "gone up" or "gone down."
He did not think it strange that he should choose the evenings
away from home to confide the exciting details of his pilgrimage.
Home was home—food, bed, things to be mended or painted or
planted or planned. Bert's wife had never visited the Unwins'; to
those who lived in Murston Lane she seemed to be more a dream
than a reality; no one ever saw her near the Sapleys', the Maudes',
the Baldrys'; she lived her social life "over the way, t'other side
of the Bull," as Bert described it, whereas he had made Little
Burgelstatham, two miles from his home, the center of his social
life, because so much of his work lay in the district, and the
Unwins had always been there to be visited between morning and
afternoon jobs, and Mrs. Unwin had always been grateful for
hedge-cutting, wood-chopping, weeding of the nettles, or for
someone to look after her bonfire to see that if the wind changed
a dangerous spark did not blow toward the newly thatched roof
of the cottage.

Nor had Bert anywhere now to stop at midday to eat his
sandwiches and drink his thermos tea. He could not go to the
empty grounds of the Unwins' cottage, for they were no longer
empty, and a wire fence had been built around them, blocking

the short-cut path to Mrs. Unwin's former home. Once, before the farm manager brought his repair team to the farmhouse, Bert had mistakenly gone to the back garden to "see how things were," and the new owner of the cottage, the television man from London, had called sharply over the fence, "Whattling, here a minute!" No one in Little Burgelstatham called Bert anything but Bert. *Whattling!* Bert's face had flushed a dark red. The television man had wanted help to shift some firewood from the front garden to the shed that was already stocked with firewood, and knowing that Bert was a useful, willing handyman, he had committed the double crime of imagining that he already belonged to the village, and that he could speak to Bert as a master might speak to his slave. "Whattling, here a minute!" As Bert said afterwards to himself—who was there now to say it to?—"For all his Oxford accent the man was ignorant. I nearly died laughing at the sight of so much wood."

Were they coming to live in the cottage for the winter? Bert had asked.

"Oh, no," the television man had said, confirming Bert's opinion that townees were barmy. "Just weekends in summer, but we like to have everything in stock."

That seemed fair. Bert might have been more sympathetic had he himself been the kind of person who was a strong believer in providing far into the future: he was inclined to be a reckless old man, he liked to take chances, he cherished the spirit of adventure; he knew how to have his pleasure without worrying too much whether his shed was full of wood for winter fires. It *was* full, of course it was full, but the wood hadn't been carried there to the tune of "Whattling, here a minute" played by an upstart television producer from London who deserved, if anyone did, the name of "foreigner." He was in television—and wasn't it television that was emptying the pubs, making people so sour that you couldn't speak to them in their own homes of an evening without being told *Sh, sh, sh,* setting a bad example with its violence? Also, this television producer was from London, and what good had ever come from London? Not only was it a wild city full of bank robbers, murderers, models, dukes, tourists, but

—so Bert had learned from the *East Anglian Times*—it had been given permission by Parliament to send thousands of its people to live and work in East Anglia. The process had been described in the newspaper as an "overspill." "One of the new words," Bert had said to himself. He had cut the article from the paper, but there had been no one to show it to since Mrs. Unwin had died, and though he'd heard people in the street and the Bull talking about the "overspill," he missed the wise remarks from Mrs. Unwin.

"I see there's overspill coming to Tydd," Bert would have said, taking the newspaper cutting from his pocket to support his outrageous statement. "See, it says here, there's overspill coming to Tydd and the neighborhood, thousands of acres of semi-detached . . ."

An exciting, controversial talking-point, but not nearly so enjoyable now that the idea was becoming a frightful reality. Sometimes now as Bert was clipping a hedge or mowing a lawn he would repeat the word to himself: "Overspill. Overspill."

Such a strange word to choose. Didn't something that spilled, spill over also? Or were they using "overspill" to try to explain that once the people of London began coming to East Anglia nothing could stop them, there'd never be an end of their spilling, as there'd never be an end of people from London. The television man and his family and others who had bought the empty cottages were only a beginning. And then the foreign workers, the truly foreign ones from abroad . . . When the Common Market came, there'd never be an end of them also, speaking in many languages, shouting in the lanes; but there'd be no lanes, there'd be motorways like the M1, and all the new words that motorways brought with them—"bypass," "flyover," "flyunder." . . .

Bert was familiar with all the fears and the arguments—well, not quite all: Mrs. Unwin, having come from Stamford, with a clearer view of the approaching disaster, would have supplied suggestions and solutions not thought of by others. She had said that the Stamford buildings were gray at night when the frost and the dew were shining on them, that it was a medieval town (when she pronounced it *medevil* no one had contradicted her), and in some unexplained way the image she gave of the tall gray stone buildings had seemed to support, to invite respect for any "foreign" opinions she might have. She had been a privileged inhabitant of Little Burgelstatham. Bert knew of no other foreigner who had brought with him so completely the influence of his native county. In contrast, it was amusing to see the pompous Londoners trying to get accepted into the village, talking in loud voices in the post office about how they liked the simple country ways, how they hated the city and its noise, declaring that Little Burgelstatham was the place where they felt most at home; then undoing all their good work by complaining that letters were delivered twice a day only, that it took up to six weeks or more for a book ordered at the local library to be found, and another six weeks for it to arrive, that the shops in Murston, or even in Tydd, which at least had a Woolworth's, did not cater to their sophisticated needs. The people of Little Burgelstatham resented this complaining from city dwellers who yet wanted so much to belong to the country that they would pretend to be able to distinguish wheat from barley!

As for the darkness that was so often part of their complaints, what did they think night was but darkness? They moaned about not being able to see in the lanes or even to find their way outside their own back door; they talked of nightfall as if it were a conspiracy against them. And hadn't there been a death lately, perhaps a murder, because a stranger had been unable to find his way along the lane?

In the days following Mrs. Unwin's death Bert spent his time alternately grieving for Mrs. Unwin and hating all foreigners; his resentment was directed in particular against the television producer. *Whattling, here a minute!*

There had been a place against the cottage wall, facing the lilac hedge, clear of the cold wind, where Bert used to sit for a rest after lunch. No buying or selling of the cottage could make it belong to anyone but him. He could think of it now only as a right that had been stolen from him by a television producer from London who had emphasized the impertinence of his theft by putting up a wire fence where a fence had never been. How often Bert had sat there, sometimes alone, sometimes with Mrs. Unwin or Olly Drew, looking beyond the lilac hedge to the empty field at the rabbits and pheasants and partridges and wood pigeons (curse them!); and he'd see the sky, no higher or lower than it used to be when he was a boy and the surrounding fields were full of flowers. Sometimes jets from the air bases would spread a scream over the whole sky, then disappear, leaving a thin white trail.

"Them jets," Bert would mutter.

Olly would nod his disapproval, then crack some joke. "How about going up in one?"

Olly, like Bert, knew how to meet change with one of its strongest challenges—a sense of humor. They'd agree then that neither of them would ever have a chance of going up in a jet; implying that were they to live longer—say, one hundred and sixty years—who could tell what they might do, where they might go. The adventurous no-time lured their fancies to extravagance while their few remaining years told them they were temporal paupers, and no invention had yet promised them such a their spending was limited only by their own imagining; of this, their share was small; they did not often indulge in fantasies of the fearful tomorrow; their talk was more of hedges, gardens, the Tydd auction, friends, relations, rumors. The overspill was the new topic. Mrs. Unwin had died, had deserted, had been buried in Stamford; any wisdom on the subject of overspill had been lost. During her lifetime Mrs. Unwin had shown herself to be confused, obstinate; the inconsistent legacies of death as opposed to the personal material legacies of the dying gave her memory gentleness and wisdom; and as few oppose the will of death, so there were few who did not accept, gratefully, the memory given to them.

Talk of electricity was replaced by talk of the overspill. The authorities in London had said the matter was urgent. The metropolis, they said, would choke unless the overspill did what its name required of it and spilled the population into the almost deserted places of East Anglia. Already Tydd had been named as the center of the overspill plan.

An Italian farm worker had come to get a job in the district, had lost his way in the dark, and had been drowned; there had been gossip, sympathy mixed with a sense of triumph that one intrusive foreign worker speaking a strange language, even a strange English language (I am wounded, see my wounds are bleeding. My tailor is rich. These photographs are underexposed, please will you intensify them?) had been dealt with, got rid of. It would be more difficult to get rid of these overflowing Londoners. What if the whole world, from the "teeming" Asians (the Asians were often described in terms of a menacing movement, while other populations were statically and calmly "densely settled") to the Russians, the Danes, the Spaniards, the Italians—the whole of the continent of Europe—were to try to swarm into Little Burgelstatham, Tydd, Murston, and the surrounding countryside? What would become of the farms, the fields, the cottages—and the villagers? Thought of invasion is a dreadful thought—the people of East Anglia had known it vividly during the world war—and though invasion may be by means of germs, bombs, ideas, new laws, it is the invading people themselves who are most feared, whether it is one person, invading, taking over another, or thousands directed by the government to carry out a menacing plan of overspill.

Overspill, take-over, possession, invasion—the meaning was plain: there would be no help from the government now, as there had been during the war, when the local maps were hidden, the sign posts and street names removed. Nor would there be any of the slick, urgent wartime advice—*Is Your Journey Really Necessary? Before You Travel Consult Your Conscience.* These Londoners had already spilled over into several parts of the country; it seemed to be their right and privilege to spill over. No amount of persuasion could convince the people of Little Burgelstatham that the government was not inviting, deliberately, bank robbers, confidence men, dissolute models, playboy dukes, pimps, touts, sly foreigners, to build multiple-story mansion flats and housing estates on the vast, flat, quiet fields of which the rightful tenants, depending on the age the villagers chose to live in, were birds, reeds, water; or crops—barley, sugar beet, wheat; or homely farm workers wearing their disheveled clothes in the way pecu- liar to two types of people—themselves, and the mental patients whom they most nearly resemble—those whose dissatisfaction with the vision of reality provided by an age of commerce and industry leads them to a dream where they are once again close to the earth and sky, while the folds of their clothes are caked with dung, animal or human, and their speech, if they speak at all, is set to the pace of trees growing and of the seasons that breed, nurse, destroy, and resurrect them.

Well, Mrs. Unwin was safely out of the world, Bert thought, with some bitterness, for he'd have to stay, to endure the over- spill. He'd no other cherished county to escape to. They were saying in the village (he thought with exuberant glee) that it was just as well Mrs. Unwin had been dead on her return to Stam- ford; she'd never have been able to face the traffic, the new buildings. She had never known (or if she had, she had kept quiet about it) that only she talked any more of a "beautiful Stam- ford," that to the newspapers and town-planning officials (the chief influences in the country), Stamford was a "bottleneck," a "deplorable bottleneck," and was given the attention in Parlia- ment which bottlenecks demand as their right, but which gray stone buildings glistening at night in the frost and the dew have to fight for, with petitions, thousands of signatures . . .

Bert was not such a gloomy man that his every visit to Tydd was colored by thought of the future changes. He was too busy for sentimental dreams. Yet from time to time as he walked by familiar landmarks—the statue in the market place, the river, the steep, narrow streets, even the poultry farm next to the station, displaying the yellow sign so well known throughout East Anglia: *Fowl Pest, Keep Out*—he would feel, as if it flowed inside him along his blood, a surge of helplessness that was yet not derived entirely from thinking about the overspill. It was brewed, also, from the season—now winter—from his age, his rheumatism, and from a distillation of his dearest most persistent memory of the countryside of Little Burgelstatham (who else but a native has the discrimination to choose the time that he may mix with his sentimental dreams?): his boyhood when the fields were market gardens full of flowers. It may have been this memory that led him, when he became a pensioner, to pass his time and earn his extra money in gardening, that drew from him the enthusiasm that so charmed people—both the villagers and the new arrivals in the village who saw in him their fiction-built image of a taciturn rustic "close to the soil"—that there was always too much rather than too little work for him, and only his age made him refuse the more arduous jobs; even in the season when his rheumatism or bronchitis was bad he still responded to people's requests to "look at the garden." He had talked so often to everyone of the "fields full of flowers"; it was little wonder that everyone claimed a share of his memory of the flowers, and found the task more difficult of facing the prospect of a "field full of folk."

The talk of the "fields full of flowers" appealed specially to the summer strangers of Little Burgelstatham, yet their own walking among these flowers was done in Oxford Street, in the Strand, in Kensington High Street, in the London parks; for the city is the place to dream intensely and fully of the country, of the cottage garden, even of the familiar dreams of Old Caspar on a summer evening. And if the "foreigners" had any fields of flowers in their head, at any one time, that time was now, winter, when the country cottages were shut up, and the summer tenants and the fly-by-winter owners answering the call of electricity, central heating, hot water, pavements, regular buses, had returned to the city. Home to London. (In Wales the deserted cottages spoke, "Gone home to Birmingham"; in the Lake District—"Gone home to Manchester"; in Cornwall, Devon, as in East Anglia—"Gone home to London." Yet in East Anglia, especially in Suffolk, one might think the notice "Gone home to London" betrayed the visitor's disappointment. Summer lakes, fells, broads, downs, weald, wild coasts had been the lure of other counties; Suffolk, obstinately, had promised almost nothing, not even the common fortune of the age, a view: only rustics, history, and sky; birds, and water arranged in the wrong places.

People and buildings help to make a city warm in winter. In Little Burgelstatham the bitter easterly winds, more numerous than the villagers, were enough to surround and isolate each person who dared to walk out of doors. It is true that more sophisticated and abstract winds completing the isolation of city dwellers are not less keenly felt and known, but the winds from the North Sea were concerned with bodies, with frost that turned plants white or black, with rain that filled the ditches and lay in deep pools on the roads, with blizzards that covered the visible world with snowflakes. The most efficient weapon against these winds, in an age of thermo-nuclear rockets and bombs, was a supply of warm clothing, and a waterproof hat, coat, and boots like those worn by the sailor in advertisements for the Lifeboat Emergency Fund.

Bert was wearing such clothes the Friday in late January when he set out for his visit to Tydd. If the newspapers had not been concentrating on letters and articles about the overspill, he and the villagers might have forgotten it all, dismissing it with the thought that who, in their senses, would want to live in the countryside in winter; who but those who were privileged to be country folk, used to the dark, the isolation, the silence?

37 Little Burgelstatham had been closed at the end of the year, and the station buildings had been renovated and newly painted, and two old railway coaches hung with bright curtains had been shunted to the siding beside the buildings, and all had been offered for sale or rent and described in the summer advertisements which each year began to appear in the newspapers and magazines as shameless bait for the green and yellow dreams dreamed in a gray world of winter, as "Ideal holiday homes, away from it all in rural Suffolk." In spite of the protests made against the closing of the station, few people had used it; it had been inconvenient to travel by train to Tydd, as Tydd Station was two miles from the market square, whereas the bus, though taking the roundabout route from Little Burgelstatham through Murston and Lakenthorpe, stopped in the heart of Tydd, in the street beyond the market square. Shoppers had always found it more convenient to take the bus. Bert, with his assorted load of geese, rabbits, and his returning booty of anything from ironmongery to furniture and drapes from demolished cottages and churches, looked on the bus with an abiding loyalty which had been hurt but not lessened by the summer change in the Friday time-table. He could have accepted the change more readily had it been made at the end of summer or the end of winter, for all bus time-tables were changed then, to deal with the fall or rise in the local population and the difference between summer and winter times; but to have changed it, without notice, halfway through summer!

Though Friday was Market Day, there was little buying or selling this day. The best place to be was the pub, with a glass of hot rum. The town was brooding and dark; country lanes were not so romantic when the storms came, making streams and lakes. Bert was used to the wet and the cold and the time of winter, from January to late March, when there would be talk among the old men of who had survived, who would survive, with the mood

of the talk now gloomy, now envious. Today, Bert noticed, there
was no talk of old age and survival and death; the topic was
"them"—anyone who was not a native of Little Burgelstatham,
Murston, Tydd, Lakenthorpe, Withigford—and of the overspill
that would come ("they" had announced) in the spring. Already
the architects and town planners were in Tydd; some might even
be in this very room of the pub, Bert thought, sitting here drinking rum in front of the fire.

He looked cautiously about him. He could always tell who
were the strangers. He was not inclined to begin laughing about
his wife, how she would "sue for a *dee*-vorce" because he was in
Tydd in the pub drinking rum. There seemed to be little to talk
about that was not either "Unwin conversation" (not spoken
now) or the overspill. Rumors became the tall stories of the hour.
"They" were going to pull down all the farm workers' cottages.
"They" would build Council flats in the barley fields, offices with
luxury penthouses (for directors) in the sugar-beet fields. If your
cottage was not pulled down, then it would be taken under the
Compulsory Purchase Order to make room for a motorway.
Noise, smoke, smell, crime, no jobs, and a race of strangers who
laughed at your dialect and your customs and your clothes and
your ignorance of the great world; a nasty television breed.

It's a puzzle, Bert thought, as the familiar condemnation of
television came to his mind and he looked around at his sympa-
thizing fellow villagers, most of whom owned television sets! It
was too late; the enemy had invaded years ago, and the outcry
against it was a ritual that served the purpose of most rituals by
bringing comfort when its original meaning had been lost.

"A television breed!" Bert said aloud.

The others agreed with him. Yet what could they do? Once
London had made up its mind about overspill, that was the end;
any protests made were token protests, ineffectual and a waste of
time.

So the villagers sat and talked and drank and smoked, and after
a while they became tired of the hopelessness of overspill, and
turned to the familiar hopelessness of the weather, and then to
gossip—about domestic affairs, prices, people. The Sapleys would

escape the overspill, they said, because his brother was an M.P. The dentist's wife was having a baby—at *her* age. Their son and his wife were away in Spain. Spain? Why in Spain? He was an artist, or a writer, an intelligent young man, one of those intellectuals, not the kind who wore waistcoats and leather patches on their elbows, the other kind. Yes, his wife Jenny Sparling came from the North. And that clergyman, the Reverend Maude, was he still staying at Clematis Cottage? He'd be there until the summer? To christen the baby? He'd been ill again; he was dying; the district nurse called regularly. The dentist's wife? No, she was strong, she'd always been strong, gardening in all weathers; but at *her* age . . . and Lex Unwin, the milkman, had said . . .

Thus the women gossiped while the men drank, smoked, half-listened.

Had said, had said, had said . . .

The Baldrys were leaving for Australia. Were they? Emigrating. They hadn't got their electricity yet—after all that talk and waiting. What had happened to the Electricity Board? Their house had been wired for it, they were getting ready to install that great chandelier, the roof was being strengthened. All that waiting. The farm manager (did you see how he renovated the Unwin farmhouse?) and the television producer from London, who had influence, had spoken for electricity, in a way that the Board couldn't ignore; it was coming in spring—with the overspill!

Here the men took over the gossip from the few women who had sustained it while the men (husbands, strangers) drank their rum.

"Overspill in spring, in March. Electricity and overspill. Floods and the flu."

"And other things," someone said wisely, that no one knew of, but none of this would be in spring, for spring wasn't in March; what fool had said that spring came in March? They knew March vividly: snowstorms, frosts, the first snowdrop. Death; people died in March just when they believed they had survived the winter. Would you call that springtime?

Some would, some wouldn't. They drank more rum. They

shivered. Their minds turned stiffly in the cold, like frost-hardened sods at the first plowing. The few women hurried away to get their shopping done. The men, more leisurely, enjoying a last-minute involvement with talk of prices, harvest, acreage, went one by one or in groups to complete their business of the day. Soon the pub was almost empty.

The town planner, in the deep chair by the fire, put down his glass and turned to his companion, a London architect.

"See what we'll have to meet?" he said. "They're a different race. Talk about New Town loneliness! That reminds me—there's that competition to name the new town. The psychologists say it should be held locally—you know, let the natives feel they have a share in the project. It pays dividends, overcomes hostility."

"Wouldn't you be hostile?"

"I'd shoot the invaders as if they were so many wood pigeons. So be careful. We're in a foreign land here."

"Should we try to fraternize?"

"Hell no, not more than usual. Just don't make the mistake of pointing out a wheat field and exclaiming in your educated accent, 'What magnificent barley!'"

There was one fortnight in March
when Dr. Finch attended three patients
at Clematis Cottage: Greta, Russell,
Aisley. After the long hibernation of the winter months each
of the Maude family, at the prospect of attaining the light
and warmth that all had dreamed of and longed for, surrendered
to panic in the predictable human way, and became ill, or, if
one may be more accurate, retired to bed to think. In spite of the
rumors otherwise, Aisley had recovered from his tuberculosis,
but his mind and body emerged with such clarity, excitement,
from the cool storage of winter that he went to bed for a fortnight, nursing, as an excuse, a gentle cough but moving his bed
near the window, where he could look down on the wet frost- and
wind-beaten grass, the bare trees, the deep, full ditches, and the
still muffled figures of the local tradesmen—butcher, baker, paraffin man, postman—and the villagers—Bert Whattling, Olly Drew,
Lex and Dot Unwin—passing by in the lane. Aisley had told himself that when the green and white mist of leaves and blossom had
gone from the fields and lanes of Little Burgelstatham and the
merciless winter came to take away all pretense of decorative
beauty and glory from the earth, then he would look out with a
camera eye onto the essence of God. He realized, however, as
soon as the time came, and he looked down on the bare fields,
that he had been deceived again by the old fallacy that meaning
lies more in the framework than in the cluttered picture, more in
the symbol than in the complexity it stands for; he knew that his
dream had been only another example of the human cunning that
tries to bring God or not-God within its own limits.

During autumn and winter Aisley had gone to churches of all
denominations and descriptions—buildings of thatch, flint, mellowed stone; Roman Catholic, Anglican; Methodist chapels of the
late nineteenth century. Only once did he attend a sermon—
Harvest Festival in the sixteenth-century church at the end of
Murston Lane which was opened once a year after a party of

235

boys from the Approved School had cut the nettles, tidied the grounds, cleaned the tombstones, piecing together their broken remnants of stone to complete the stained ciphers of name, age, place, and valediction. A carpenter had been employed to repair the broken seats inside the church, while women from the parish had volunteered to clean the woodwork and the windows and the stone floor. The notice of Harvest Festival had been pasted on a telegraph pole outside the Sapleys' fruit farm.

Aisley had gone to the evening service, with something of the hope that had once been a belief that a church by its concentration of faith may trap the spirit of God—as radar traps the wandering stranger, not distinguishing between friend or foe, supplying the shadow only; or as a flower with special luminosity may trap a night-flying insect; or even as an angler fish may use part of its body as bait to lure its own kind to its death.

During his fortnight in bed Aisley often remembered his visit to the Harvest Festival. Again and again he walked along the lane to the church. He sat in the porch on the moss-grown stone seat. He picked up the weather-stained parish magazine printed specially for the occasion, turned the few pages, put the magazine down where the persistent water drops from the leak in the roof would not stain it further, and waited for the congregation to appear. He was on time, surely; he had even hurried, thinking he might be late. Drip-drop, drip-drop. The light autumn rain fell more heavily; the water from the roof splashed on the stone, formed a pool in the shallow dent of stone that must have been a sitting-place over hundreds of years. Aisley looked out into the churchyard at the neatly cropped grass and the withered stalks of nettle and blackberry, burned by the weed killer, and he knew that he preferred the year-round wilderness of weeds and moss to this one-weekend blackmail or bribery of a supposed God.

He went to the door of the church, pushed it open, looked in, and was surprised to see the white-haired seventy-eight-year-old Reverend Timothy Pillow, minister of three local parishes, standing before a congregation of two women and a dog. The Reverend Pillow, announcing the hymn and seeing Aisley at the door, called with embarrassed heartiness, "Come and join us in our festival service!"

Aisley went in, returned the welcoming smiles of the two women, nodding to the Reverend Pillow's introduction, "This is my wife; she plays the organ. This is my wife's sister, on holiday from London. And the dog."

Then, returning to the formality of the service, the Reverend Pillow once again announced the hymn, while Aisley, taking his hymn book and mouthing the words, pretended to join the frail chorus:

> *Come Ye Faithful people, come,*
> *Sing the Song of Harvest Home.*

The church was cold and damp. The dreariness and loneliness of a year's desertion clung to it; one might have imagined that the pews were not empty but filled with tall stalks of white blossoming nettles; as it was, the true congregation was contained in the huge turnips, cabbages, carrots, leeks, the baskets of apples and other fruit that the attentive loyal parishioners had brought as their offering; but why had the parishioners not stayed?

The hymn ended. With a mixture of pride and shame the Reverend Pillow spoke his excuse and explanation, directing his words at Aisley, the stranger, himself a man of God who would understand the difficulties of a poor old country parson.

There had been a large attendance at the morning service, the Reverend Pillow was saying. There had been crowds, people standing; every year it was the same.

He then explained that he would not preach a sermon, that instead he would ask those present to pray for and give their thoughts to absent members of the congregation who had found so many family duties that evening that they could not attend the service—and was not Christ a family man? But what a hearty attendance there had been in the morning! As he repeated this assurance the Reverend Pillow looked round the church at the fat marrows, cabbages, the fleshy leeks, the tightly buttoned Brussels sprouts, the full-blown roses, crimson and cream, as if to them only he was admitting the truth: they were indeed the true and *only* congregation. Nobody cared about Harvest Festival while *Emergency Doctor* and *Stage Coach* and *Private Eye Cluney* were showing on television.

The door banged in a sudden gust of wind. The Reverend
Pillow shivered and began to cough. Then, presumptuously, with
a shocking display of theological bad manners that caused Aisley
to despair of all country clergymen, he said he knew "God would
understand" if they ended the service and went home early. He
said a short prayer and blessing while his wife played concluding
chords on the organ. The Harvest Festival was over.

"My wife, my sister-in-law from London."

"From Kensington, London."

"You live in the vicarage, in Lakenthorpe?"

The old man seemed pathetically frail. His wife, apparently
much younger, was tall with graying hair and a plum-colored
complexion of which the bloom, not as fresh and soft as plum-
dust, had been coarsened by years of close powdering; her face
seemed to have long ago accepted a new cosmetic skin for which
the powder-puff and cake make-up and not the body and not its
food were responsible for maintenance and renewal. (Aisley's old-
fashioned outlook still made him shudder at the thought of lip-
stick and powder on a woman.)

Mrs. Pillow answered Aisley's question. "Yes, we live in the
vicarage, Lakenthorpe. The Murston vicar has a smart new place.
I've never known such an undesirable place to live as our vicarage
—twenty-three rooms, and no servants, no heating, no hot water.
It's impossible. My sister from London is frankly amazed at our
endurance. And my husband" (she glanced toward the Reverend
Pillow as he gathered the hymn books and removed the *Reserved
for Warden* notices from the vacant pews) "is, as you see, an
elderly man. He travels to and fro—by bus!—from three parishes. And you know what a clergyman's salary is like."

Aisley, anxious to return to Clematis Cottage, had stopped
merely out of politeness to exchange greetings with the Reverend
Pillow and perhaps to make a sympathetic tactful remark about
the poor attendance. Once again he was dismayed by the un-
theological approach and excuse as the Reverend Pillow prepared
to lock the church, ushering Aisley, Mrs. Pillow, her sister, and
the dog (which she had kept on her lap during the service) into
the cold porch. Though it was barely autumn, the stone seats

were sweating with dew and the little pile of parish magazines
already had stiffened and set, frost-bound.

"I feel," the Reverend Pillow was saying, "that it's often a
good thing, indeed a blessing, to hold a service for such a small
congregation. I feel it is good for the Church."

He added, with another daringly impolite presumption about
the habits and opinions of his God, "At such times there's very
often more room for the presence of God. It may be—indeed it
may—that a full congregation actually frightens Him away! God
does not like publicity; He is no pop-singer seeking adulation."

Aisley thought, He's indulging in this theological twisting of
God's arm in order to force His approval. Has his religion
always been as easy, compromising, childlike? Has he always
looked on God as a kind of automatic pilot, to take over when
the human faith is too frail to steer around and near the dangers
of life, death and worship? The preaching of his religion, I think,
is used chiefly for his own comfort and appeasement. Most of the
twenty-three rooms of his vicarage are empty, yet day by day
they gather dust and there's no servant to clean them. That's
his wife's problem. He uses God in much the same way as his
wife would use her servant, except that he's in a better position:
God is permanently employable; the rooms are kept clean for
guests who never arrive. I suppose that in the early days of his
preaching the Reverend Pillow, at some time, maybe once only,
paid his God a wage that he could never afford; it left him in this
state of congregational poverty among plenty. How will he deal
with the overspill, all these parishioners wanting guitar-playing,
jazz sessions, insisting on reading out of the new New Testa-
ment? Surely they will mock at the vicar and his twenty-three
rooms, will petition for the vicarage to be used as a hostel. Poor
old man; senility may save him, if God does not. But what do I
care? This white-haired old man, his wife, his sister-in-law, the
dog, are like characters in a legend, and the assurance he tries to
give himself and us may be the truth; a congregation of four—
three human beings and a dog—may be seen to represent the
whole parish, county, world, to swell to fill the belly of the
Church like those foods containing cellulose that give a feeling of

repletion when only a small portion is swallowed, that, at the
same time, have little nourishing value.

Aisley accepted the hilly gray-green marrow they offered him,
said good night and good-by, and walked down the path through
the churchyard to Murston Lane. In a fortnight to three weeks
that path would be covered once more with nettles; vandals
would have unpieced and scattered the broken tombstones that
would already be growing their green concealing slime;
spiders would weave their webs in the porch; the stained-glass
window— the Feeding of the Five Thousand—would be obscured
by dust and streaks of rain.

Almost out of earshot Aisley heard Mrs. Pillow raising her
voice in complaint: "Twenty-three rooms, no servants." He
could imagine the old minister smiling gently—an image that
roused his anger: he had learned long ago that gentle smiles were
vanity only, not blessings or forgiveness or any traditional
prerogative of the clergy; the person best suited to smile a gentle
smile was a madman.

Aisley heard the dog barking. He turned to see it being set
down to lift its leg among the tombstones.

It was an interesting memory. When Aisley had returned to
Clematis Cottage he had looked up the Reverend Timothy Pillow
in *Crockford*'s: a Cambridge man; arts degree; theological prizes;
essays on doctrine. In spite of his gifts there had been no prize of
Bishop or Archbishop in store for him; he was a frail old man
with a quavering voice and a view narrowed by age and compromise, and he was spending the last days of his life going by
County bus (those low-slung sagging seats and windows that
would not open) to Lakenthorpe, Withigford, Oak churches, not
more nor less usefully employed than the straight line which
completes the triangle; though from time to time, Aisley supposed, parishioners would even now use the Reverend Pillow to
calculate (though ignorant of sin-cos-tan) their personal short
cut to God.

During his fortnight in bed Aisley drew up final plans for his
own future. He had made his decision. He was preparing to live

as St. Cuthbert had lived—not on Farne Island or on any other island in the North Sea or the Channel, but on the Northeast Coast, perhaps at or near Berwick—a recluse in a small cottage by the sea, his wall lined with books on religion and poetry. He would not describe triangles and circles for the rest of his life; he would look for God in one place and another time; the money from Katherine's parents, untouched in his bank, would keep him if he lived in the simplest most frugal manner. The vision pleased him. He would leave Little Burgelstatham in a month or six weeks and not communicate again with Russell or Greta or anyone else he had known. He would enter no monastery save the monastery of solitude. He would set himself in a lonely place as bait to attract the meaning of meaning; he would say, in the jargon of his young London parishioners playing Martians, "Take me to your leader!" He was aware that his plans, at present mixed with a kind of poetic nostalgia which he deplored, would emerge soon unsupported by the romantic dreaming that, inevitably, would separate itself, sink deep in his mind, and be forgotten.

With his usual imagined dignity of thinking, he could not bear to look on his life as a recluse in common terms like "opting out of the rat-race," "getting away from it all." He thought of his future life as the result of a long-considered choice that could not be summed up in vogue phrases, though he appreciated the irony of using words that were tied and trailed like kites out of, it seemed, the mouth of the modern world to describe the most old-fashioned huddle a human being could get into, apart from embryo posture: life in a one-room cottage; books; birds; the sea. He knew that in choosing to live in this way he was enacting a belief in the fallacy that sight and insight are more clear in the winter world; that touching the hard black boughs after the pampering richness of summer had gone would bring realization that the boughs only were the final clear fact and truth. Aisley knew that he might just as well go to Piccadilly, have the vision presented in an image just as truthful, on a neon dish; or, staying at Little Burgelstatham, getting more involved in the life at Clematis Cottage, free-floating spiritually like weed or a tiny fish in a pond, cling suddenly with a flick of half-developed faith to the developing influence of a human attachment—perhaps to Greta's expected son or daughter.

(Though Aisley had so often taken out his notebook to record a birth, and though in his East London parish he had been into homes where babies were being expected, born, slapped, fed, kissed, buried, he had never before spent a silent snow-bound winter in the depths of the country waiting in an atmosphere of reticence, anxiety, pride, shame, love, for a birth whose imminence had been communicated so thoroughly to him that already his notebook, pen, and bottle of red ink were waiting on his desk.)

As soon as the fact of Greta's child had been made known in Clematis Cottage, it had occupied every corner, taking up more room than anyone had dreamed of, or could spare. Russell, Greta, Aisley brooded over it as over an expected guest (welcome or not welcome as the mood struck them) whose presence had already arrived, invisibly, and who at the moment of its appearance as a human being could be possessed (what rivalry for possession!), influenced, the whole world poured into it from the moment of its first breath without its having the power to protest. Greta, Russell, Aisley, all had their dreams of what the child would be and do; they seldom shared these dreams with one another, but each could tell when the other was surprised in his secret thoughts of command over a future human empire, by the historically familiar empire-building light in the other's eyes. It is not often that one is given the prospect of owning something or somebody so brand-new. There was no doubt, though, that among the three yearning tycoons contesting future rights and ownership, Greta would control all shares. A son, a daughter, Russell thought, absent-mindedly eating for two and growing fat. A virgin mind, Aisley thought, with chaste consideration. He would need to watch long and secretly for the first signs of God-disturbance, and his task would be made harder by the fact that in spite of his years of study and personal seeking-finding-losing-seeking of God—or not-God—he still did not know what to look for, and was being tricked again and again, now by the cluttered scene, now by the stark frost-bound essence, into making his own irrelevant images. Nor did he know from what direction the child's consciousness of God would come; or if, like a plant, its roots already lay deep and warm in the unborn spirit. The problem was interesting and absorbing; but when Aisley, as he sometimes did, forgot its secrecy and saw Greta looking at him as though she divined his thoughts, he gave up hope even of temporary ownership and field study of another human being and returned to his plans for living the life of a hermit. St. Cuthbert, Wordsworth's Solitary—the Saint and the Poet—would be his companions in the wilderness. Perhaps in the peace that he must find when he had abandoned the twentieth century and the future and had settled in his own carefully chosen time and place, his own existence would be possession enough, and the opportunity it would give him to stare, stare, stare at the meaning of being:

> As a huge stone is sometimes seen to lie
> Couched on the bald top of an eminence;
> Wonder to all who do the same espy,
> By what means it could thither come, and whence;
> So that it seems a thing imbued with sense:
> Like a sea-beast crawled forth, that on a shelf
> Of rock or sand reposeth, there to sun itself; . . .

He would be Man returned to stone, to communion with stone and sea and the first forms of life. In such dreaming, the physical facts of existence did not intrude, though Aisley remembered vividly, in the numerous commonplace moments of his thinking, the vision he had known as a student of St. Cuthbert—too mercifully distant, surrounded by his own dung, the smell of which could not penetrate to the senses, conditioned by personal and public hygiene, of those who lived in an age that was versatilely thermo-nuclear, prewrapped, untouched by human hand.

So the winter cured Aisley not only of his last symptoms of t.b. but of the hope, born of his natural laziness, of getting, free, a human being who would provide him with the lens he needed to stare through to identify the speck or stain that he'd pledged his life to study and understand . . . while the Reverend Timothy

Pillow walked among the dust-covered twenty-three rooms of the rectory, his wife moaned about the lack of servants, their dog lifted its leg to bleach the moss on the broken tombstones of Henrietta Carveley, Josiah Prince, William Storey, whom no one remembered any more and whom only the Approved School boys came close to now, as once a year they painstakingly brought the little village church out of its weedy ruin to wear a neater dress, and the pomp and pride of plants that grow and are harvested, but not any more of people.

39 In Greta's view in her moments of depression, the child was an addition to the deadly poetic names on Maplestone's Chart: a puffer-pack of human skin that would spray the kind of life which might wither the tall blossoming inhabitants of the human garden. The association with Maplestone's Chart was as natural as the association in her mind with almost forgotten fairytales—the cottage in the wood, the lovers (brother and sister, mother and son) asleep under the leaves; people as plants growing thorns or blossoms or both.

In happier moments Greta thought of her baby as a new son or daughter, of its nearness to her, of the undisputed fact that it was she who sheltered and owned it. She felt close as a spider to its web, with at one time herself as the spider walking delicately along the strung dew-laden sparkling possibilities of the future she (and Alwyn) had woven; or she thought of the child as the spider, light-footed yet disturbing her strained nerves, so that her whole body quivered, staring with its unborn bulging eyes and jaws from its hide-out at the attentively buzzing neighbors, future victims, that were its father, uncle—and its mother, one moment the complex sheltering web, the next the fussy, doomed, inquisitive fly.

During Greta's pregnancy she kept her compact shape and was the envy of the women of the village, who noted with surprise that it was indeed Russell who had put on weight. There was none of the usual bulging blowsiness in Greta; if she experienced physical discomfort (which she did), she confided the details to Dr. Finch only; and in the last months, instead of blundering along with a backward sway, like a retired general with all before him, she kept her normal light gait; her basin shape, though visible, stayed small, as if she were in complete control of it. As a trained nurse she was impatient and scornful at the rumors which the women of the village could not resist, the usual rumors tinged with superstition, featuring hares' paws, dawn, frost, snow, herbs, the berries of the holly, the first snowdrops growing in rings, chance clouds in the sky, shriveled nuts, the harvest of last year— all the old links between nature and man and woman, with the new superstitions added: burned withered weeds where no spray had been; strangers in the village; swine fever; fowl pest (the beautiful buff Orpingtons rust golden in their funeral pyre); toads, dead in the road; the new harvest machines; television (the light from the screen, its effect on the pregnant women who watched it); all the multiplications of folklore in the fertile con- templative minds of the people of Little Burgelstatham. Even the overspill was drawn into the circle of superstition, and with the overspill the circle was complete; what use was it for anyone to be born into the time of the killing of the village and of the land for miles around? Into a time of invasion?

None followed the gloomy prophecy to its conclusion that the coming child was itself an invasion that would be made more surely and subtly than that attempted by the clumsy Italian farm worker Botti Julio. A being who had never heard a word spoken in any language could win where a man who could pronounce in a foreign country the universally perplexing and meaningful phrases I am wounded, See my wounds are bleeding, These pho- tographs are underexposed; please will you intensify them? had so failed in direction, purpose, communication that he had met his death, had perhaps been murdered by a hostile villager whose act had not even the excuse of being founded on knowledge of Botti Julio. It had been a neutrally bred hostility, the response of a self-contained machine to attempts at further programming.

Or it had been an anxiety about love—about the way love leaks, then floods, into a human being, his house, his country, his world—a desire to escape the confusion, to maintain separateness, to preserve an age when one adapted entirely or refused to adapt at all. Botti Julio's death had been the act of a twentieth-century man who would fight and kill to stay in his time. Alwyn.

So when the new member of the Maude family made its special invasion, there would be no public outcry as that against the overspill from London. Perhaps being born was the best way to enter a foreign land, although, even then, one's passport and other credentials were scrutinized.

A month before the baby was born, Russell went to bed with the flu, his first attack in many years. It was during this fortnight that Dr. Finch, attending Greta, who was not confined to bed, found three patients at Clematis Cottage, accepted them as part of his routine (Mrs. Unwin would have said his "Cambridge training" helped), and went from room to room listening, looking, taking pulses, writing prescriptions, in the detached resigned manner of a doctor who tries by treating the body to cure the ills of the heart.

And when Alwyn, who had traveled alone from Spain for two days and nights arrived that evening and walked in, he felt that the general confusion, the attitudes of self-defense adopted by his mother, his father, his uncle at his unexpected homecoming were reinforced with special power and meaning by the little arsenal of pills and capsules all had arrayed, as prepared weapons, on their dressing-table. Only his mother had not time to seek their help.

"Alwyn!" she said slowly, then burst into tears.

40 They sat around the fire. It was snowing outside, a March snowfall that even inside by the fire they could taste with every breath, knowing that its taste was different from that of the January and February snow that had been routine winter. March and April snow, coming when the snowdrops and crocuses had disturbed the hard cells of earth (each clod blobbed with white like a winter mucous, a remnant spat from the sky by winter), seemed to be more like a sky-blossom, with a smell of newness, of first green tips of grass so frail that they were struck and crippled again and again by even the softest waking spring winds; it was because of this promise of blossom that March and April snow was treacherous in its deception. It had been snowing all day, lightly but persistently. The familiar drifts were piled against the hedges and trees, and the few figures and vehicles passing along the lane became fewer until there was no one in sight. Night came, with silence and isolation. Dr. Finch had called at noon. By the time Alwyn arrived, the features that made Little Burgelstatham a particular place in a particular time had been almost obliterated. He became the traditional only (youngest, eldest) son returning from the wars in a far country.

This view of him was seen only by Aisley, who was forever willing to make the season and its weather his ally in the extermination of the present time, and whose preoccupation with the mysteries of beginning, being, seeing, led him to throw clouds (or silk handkerchiefs?) of apparent meaning, of abstractions, over any event that could give him the excuse or stimulus. The very attitude of seeing that he had learned as a clergyman to condemn had become a habit when he tried to look at his immediate surroundings. Having no need now, as a layman, to seek the prophecy behind the moment, he had learned to include it, without identifying and criticizing it: a kind of spiritual free-breathing that absorbed without detailed study what it had formerly

248

rejected. (One might say this was no mood of thought in which to begin life as a Solitary in a world of seductive woods, birds, rivers, and seas—the traditional lure of myth and legend.)

Because Russell's concentration in life was upon one item of the human body, his view, though the same in kind and need as Aisley's, was more limited, or of narrower range. He looked for details. His son, recently married and gone to live in Spain, had come home unexpectedly, alone. He wore a duffle coat, winter boots. His clothes were covered with snow. He was not the "happy" Alwyn of a year ago, but who would be, Russell thought, descending to the easy comedy of platitudes:

> *Once I was a bachelor free,*
> *Look what marriage has done to me.*
> *Fol-de-rol, fol-de-rol . . .*

Alwyn had grown older. We all grow older. The affirmation and its comfortable inclusion of all beings came easily to Russell, as a habit, a ritual where now, looking at Alwyn, he had at last exhausted the responses, he could find nothing more to repeat from his personal religious service of change.

He looks unhappy, Russell thought, searching desperately for dark comfort.

But not that kind of unhappiness.

Then Russell coughed (ah, escape). Aisley coughed. Then, allowing Greta the only legitimate physical attention, they looked at her, waiting for her to speak. (They had heard her cry at the door but had not seen her tears.)

"The baby's due, Alwyn. Soon. Isn't Jenny with you?"

With a feeling of self-satisfaction she had prepared Alwyn's reply: We've separated. She's gone back to the North. I've been alone in Spain for months now. Working. Writing. I thought of home, Little Burgelstatham—God!

Greta was smiling to herself, waiting for Alwyn to explain. "Isn't Jenny with you?"

"Jenny! You knew, didn't you mother—Greta—that after the day I found you dead and tried to revive you—"

"Me! You tried to revive yourself! It was your own life you cared about."

"But you did know, Greta, that Jenny and I would stay together, perhaps a few months, then separate. A fairytale son, bearing the legend of an age of dis-ease—botrytis, peach-leaf curl, black fly, big bud. Big bud.

"Hell no. She's too busy. We're getting ready for a baby. We've a house (not a white villa) in Lerida."

"A family? And your novel?"

"Off. Was never on. I've a job with an American magazine writing, letters from . . . you know . . . 'Letter from Spain,' 'Letter from Lerida.' The public wants—needs—letters from faraway places. Wasn't there a woman journalist supposed to be living around here writing 'Letter from Little Burgelstatham'? A Unity Foreman?"

"She never lived in the Cottage, as far as I know."

"Naturally. It's old-fashioned to *live* in the place you write from. I'm doing a 'Letter from Ohio,' 'Letter from London,' besides my 'Letter from Spain.' Did you know these 'letters' are the new tranquilizing drug?"

If you're enjoying it, Alwyn, why do you speak so bitterly? Greta thought. Yet it's not the bitterness of disillusion.

Aisley, noticing Alwyn's tone, was thinking, It's the fruit that gets you into the age, the *Eat Me* which, when obeyed, is the passport to the century.

"A baby brother or sister for Alwyn," Alywn said, laughing. "Eh, Greta?

> '*Brothers and sisters have I none,*
> *but that man's father is my father's son.*'

"Or perhaps we could compose a more up-to-date version such as:

> '*Brothers and sisters have I none,*
> *but my son's father is the father of your son'?*"

With the deference that had become a habit during Greta's pregnancy, Aisley and Russell had been looking at her in both a husbandly and a paternal way, and now, half-listening to Alwyn's babble and banter but recognizing in it (as habitual husband and father) an irrelevant—or too relevant!—discordant note, a hint of a voice raised relentlessly against the sacred tradition of *family*, both turned with startled exclamations to face Alwyn.

"Whatever your riddles mean, I don't think they're funny," Russell said sharply. Then he blew his nose and coughed, as if reminding everyone that, having got up from his sickbed, he might be in a position of weakness but he'd fortifications enough to withstand attack. Russell's feeling of weakness was increased (though none knew it) by the fact that he had never been able to agree with the accepted solution of the problem *Brothers and sisters have I none* . . .

"Just what I say," Alwyn said coolly. "My son's father is the father of your son. You are all saved from embarrassment by the last line of the problem. I must ask, '*Who am I? Who am I?*'"

"I think," Aisley said gently, "that it's not the time for riddles. It's been snowing all day."

"And we didn't expect you, Alwyn," Greta said. Her face was very pale. She leaned back in her chair and shut her eyes and looked at the inward rose-and-gold land, horizon and sea; the flicker of her lashes let in yellow beams that changed to rainbows.

"You've upset your mother, Alwyn. She's crying."

"I'm not crying."

"I'm sorry, Greta. I thought . . ."

"I know when I'm crying and when I'm not crying. I never cry."

"Some people never do," Aisley put in foolishly. "They hold it back. It's not good to hold tears back."

"Oh!" Greta said angrily. Then she smiled. "It's snowing, it's been snowing all day. And we didn't expect you, Alwyn. And we didn't expect you to talk in riddles, confusing us. Do you remember when you were a little boy and it snowed?"

Alwyn frowned. "I'm sorry. It seems that no one is wanting explanations. How will you feel, Dad, when you're a father and a grandfather almost within the same month?"

"I'd feel someone's been indiscreet, and as I'm past the age of indiscretion . . ."

"Oh?"

"Is Jenny well?" Greta asked quickly.

"She's fine. I'm flying back in a couple of days."

"Flying?"

"Flying?"

Alwyn looked indignant. "Stone Age commentary, as usual. You always get it in Little Burgelstatham. Why shouldn't I fly?"

"I nearly flew," Russell began, then stopped. "When I was in London . . ."

He stopped again. What was the use? Who cared what he had done when he was in London? It was what he had done in Little Burgelstatham that was of family consequence. He'd had enough of the sly jokes at the White Horse. Used to being ridiculed as a dentist, he had now to bear the ridicule of having fathered an unexpected son—or daughter. He looked quickly over at Greta almost as if he could surprise in her face the knowledge of the sex of their child. He knew that a daughter would change his way of life. He remembered that when she would be of an age to influence, notice, and respect the change, he would be an old man, a retired dentist who prattled about other people's teeth when his own were gone. His sense of humor, which was slight and seldom, came to his rescue and surprised him in this self-pitying reflection by reminding him that he was no King Lear, that there'd be no dramatic disposal of his kingdom unless it was the kingdom contained in his stamp collection, that the question *"How much do you love me?"* put to his son or his daughter would produce no interesting hyperbole. The truth would be terse and unpleasant, as it often is, unless the miracle happened and his daughter, with the intuition that had been obscured in her mother by a literal vegetable curtain, understood the secret intensities of his life, that he had not spent years in useless mixing, filling, extracting, but had been concerned always with the first and last evidence of man's life on earth; in his own way he had been as single-minded as his brother Aisley in pursuit of his more respectable verities.

Russell knew that it was a bleak, selfish hope—to give an unborn daughter the responsibility of vindicating her father's life, of explaining him to those who had never understood. Russell despised his hopes more because he was not usually one who felt the need to explain; he preferred silence to excuses. But a man who takes up a profession that is jeered at can never really get used to the ignorance of those who jeer; his explanation, though it may come only at the end of his life, is perhaps a means of education rather than an excuse; and as such the anticipation of it can be given an urgency that fills waking and sleeping life. My daughter will know, she will understand, she will explain. But what was that, why were Greta and Alwyn whispering together now? Drying his mother's tears (she *had* been crying), opening his mouth to speak more riddles (that man's father, this man's son); it was no use simplifying, putting convenient gaps between the generations . . .

> *Sisters and daughters have I none,*
> *but I am the father of my son's son.*
> *Who am I?*

"So you've had the flu, Dad?"

"I have it still," Russell said touchily.

"And Aisley?"

Aisley smiled with the satisfaction that he did not feel. "Quite, quite recovered."

(Like the blow of an ax cutting him clean from the nourishing roots of sickness. He lay helpless. The source was gone. He would never blossom again.)

"I'm saying good-by in a few weeks' time."

"Going back to London?"

"No. Besides, what is the need? London is coming here."

"The overspill?"

"Please don't talk about it," Greta begged. "It sounds foolish of me, but our milkman—you know, Lex Unwin—and his wife—that woman who wears brown, Dot Unwin—every morning they've something to say about the overspill and what it will mean. I know that giving a particular kind of plan or behavior a definite name is often a way of giving it automatic approval. They say that overspill is Progress. I cheer Progress."

"The lemmings, too, like to move forward," Aisley said.

Greta flushed. "As usual, you're trying to argue by comparisons. Why can't we ever learn, before we think, to empty our mind *completely* before we begin? Progress is a *good thing*," she added, contradictorily.

Russell saw that Greta's fist was clenched. She was really excited about this overspill business. Suddenly all the struggle of the past, of their married life, came to him, like the heart-burn taste of an old meal which, though it had changed in form and meaning, still haunted and sustained body and soul.

Russell thought, She believes she is talking about the new housing of a London population. Instead, she's describing and judging my life, and this, in me, is not an egotistic perception, it is an acknowledgment that now, if at any time in her life, when she is carrying the child I gave her, she has the right to criticize me, it's her means of self-preservation. What defense does a woman have when her body is so invaded and taken over by the seed of a man she hates who isn't even her neighbor in time, who lives in another century? Oh, I should have stayed in my commemorative world!

Alwyn, seeing Greta's clenched fist and hearing her passionate assertion "Progress is a good thing," said to himself, She has solved her moral problem in the emotional way women have. She's made a statement of it, a rationalization. She knows that her reasoning won't provide for her behavior (I've no need to provide for mine!) but she's taking it in—to the porch of her being, as it were—to shelter it until the storm is over. She's afraid, not of having committed incest—she can accept that with the fairy-tale part of her nature, the part she gives to the earth and its plants—but she's afraid of her age, of the process of birth that may demand more than her store of energy, of the fact that her child may be deformed or strange, a change-of-life Mongol.

Aisley had little response to the mention of progress. He had heard it all before, so often, round and round the merry-go-round—Katherine, the Church, the congregation, his fellow clergymen had set the gaudily painted urgencies going. Aisley had no fee to pay for progress.

Therefore, observing the curious unspoken passion of Alwyn, Greta, Russell, and wishing not to ally himself with it, he turned, as it was proper for him to do (especially as he has been compared in his separation from his illness to a felled tree), to the contemplation of nature, of the weather. It was still snowing. The mystery of unspoken communication both inside and outside the cottage wearied Aisley.

"Soon," he said almost cheerfully, surrendering to the delights of the senses (remembering that blue was his favorite color), "the snow will be gone, and the woods will be full of bluebells."

He had forgotten there were no woods in Little Burgelstatham, at least none for all to walk in. When spring came, the villagers, if they cared to, and if the gamekeeper of the Hall and the estate were willing, could walk a little way through the front gate to see the bluebells; or they could peer through the fence at them. It seemed to Aisley, thinking of them now, that he was surrendering to all the deceptions of thinking that he had so deplored during his training and practice as a clergyman. God is obviously not, therefore I surround myself with a comforting vision of God, as false as the popular dream "April in September." Handfuls of satisfaction and ease when I struggle on with niggardly *handouts*. Now, the ultimate vulgarity, bringing more than poets to bathos—bluebells in the snow!

"It's still snowing," Aisley said, repeating, "Soon the snow will be gone and the woods will be full of bluebells."

No one answered him. He saw that Russell, Greta, Alwyn were now whispering urgently together. Had the baby decided to be born now?

Aisley learned, three minutes later, that the whispered conference had been held to decide who should go to the kitchen to make tea.

41   "It would help," Lex said, "if the dog were run over."
     "But you can't get rid of it like that!"
"Or shot. Mother never liked it."
"Your mother was more fond of it than you know."
"I knew my mother. She hated the bitch."
"It will die soon anyway. It's so old. I'll dust it with flea-powder, now, before supper, and run it along the road to let the dead fleas drop off."

The dog ran dragging at the lead while Dot followed, walking. It was late, getting dark; the violet light in the sky was once again the soft light of a new spring; all the snow had gone except the hoof-shaped hollows ridged along the edge of the road, the frozen traces of winter that might have led a stranger, seeing them, to imagine that winter in East Anglia was a procession of snow-white cattle moving continually along the lanes and roads, leaving, when they had vanished to where snow cattle go in late spring, their trail of hoof-marks as the last visible scars of the season.

Dot avoided walking on the frozen mounds of earth. She had no thoughts for snow cattle. I don't want to twist my foot, was her wary explanation. It's easy to do, in these hollows. I'm stouter than I was, and one false step . . .

Nelly stopped running, slackened the lead, and turned toward Dot, sniffing her and ogling with that moist brown sickening look of gratitude which dogs used to control, shame, or repel human beings. (Aisley might enjoy the thought that when human beings, attached to a lead long enough to give the illusion of freedom, turn in a similar way to ogle their God, they get little response, they realize they've made a miscalculation somewhere in their working out of the slave-master relationship.)

Dot responded to Nelly's fawning. She bent and stroked her in an impulse of gratitude roused perhaps by the soft violet light hovering over the fields. In six weeks the cloudy haze would be

256

green, the leaves a loosely knitted shawl draped over the hedgerows and fields. Dot felt happy. She did not interpret or identify
her happiness, nor did she begin dreaming about leaves, sky, soft
green shawls; but she *did* exclaim with delight when she saw a
snowdrop whose tiny white green-fringed bell had burst from its
bud. She picked it.

"All your fleas have dropped off," she said to Nelly, and tug-
ging at the lead, she turned back to the semi-detached, walking
quickly while Nelly, wheezing and out of breath, waddled after
her. Dot tugged suddenly, violently, at the lead. What a burden
the dog was! Old, rheumatic, bandy-legged. And poor Mrs.
Unwin, so far away in Stamford! No one had appreciated an
early-morning fire and cup of tea as she had done. And poor me,
Dot thought, with a snowdrop stuck in my brown costume.
When the overspill comes, there'll be no snowdrops.

The semi-detached was one of a group of six on a corner at the
junction of two long straight roads, one leading to the old Little
Burgelstatham railway station, the other to Withigford Hall. As
Dot turned to shut the gate she saw a row of street lights shining
on the road to the station and the Hall. She could see, in the
distance, along Murston Lane, the lights of the Bull, of houses.
She'd forgotten. Electricity had come at last to Little Burgelstatham. The lights had been ready but so long unused that their
switching on came as a surprise, and in the moment of surprise,
Dot took over (as a wife may) the character of her husband,
anticipating his response in a way that confirms the cleaving of
two people to form one flesh, that may question the power of
individual judgment of those who live alone, that also may, in the
end, make one marriage partner superfluous.

"You'd have thought," Dot said aloud in Lex's complaining
tone, "that they'd have brought electricity along the roads for
the winter months. They might even have had it last summer, for
when that Italian farm worker lost his way in the dark and was
drowned."

Then, opening the back door and continuing in Lex's manner,
adopting the aggressive expression where his eyes (and now hers)
flashed with anger: "It's the overspill that has made them hurry."

"The what?"

"The overspill."

Then, resuming her own personality, if she could now be described as having a personality of her own, Dot unfastened
Nelly's lead, took off her own coat, wound an apron around her
waist, brushed aside the golden-brown streak of hair that fell
over her forehead and had brought indoors with it some of the
soft glow of the evening light.

"Telly on?"

"Get away." Lex was talking to the dog, who would never
learn not to greet people and expect greetings from them.

"All her fleas will have dropped off. Murston Lane's got lights
too. After all this time."

"After all this time."

It was strange, Lex thought, that if electricity had come to
Murston Lane while his mother had been alive, the thought of
having it would have killed her. Why could she not have seen
that it was such a blessing?

"Poor Mum."

"I know. She hated the thought of it. And there's Mr. Bedford
all set up and modernized in the farmhouse . . ."

"Waiting for the overspill. There's some that will know how
to profit by it."

"And now Vic and Muriel Baldry will have their chandelier
up—you've heard about it?"

"It's no use when they're going to Australia," Lex said indignantly.

"They'll have it up, you'll see. A lot of people are going to
Australia—I believe."

"I'm happier in my own home. If I'd had the cottage left
me."

"The television producer's wife was on last week. She was
wearing pearls."

"The dog . . ."

"The Maudes' baby's due. Alwyn was home, but he's gone
back to Spain."

"A bad lot."

"Your mother liked him, Lex. He seemed to understand her."

"But this dog here now, Dot, it's got canker in the ear," Lex said with emphasis. "It'll have to be got rid of."

"Perhaps you're right," Dot said calmly. "Your mother would understand that we can't keep Nelly, diseased and old as she is, in a modern house, and not with the overspill coming. Nelly would die of fright in the crowds."

Dot was about to say "Those Londoners!" but a feeling of loyalty made her restrain herself. Instead she said, "They're not always the best type chosen for an overspill. Look what happened at Embley New Town."

For a few moments they considered what had happened at Embley New Town. Then they had supper, watched the television (a Western, *Gunsmoke City;* a battle between two fish filmed under the sea; and a musical, *The Curly Miriam Show,* Curly Miriam being the latest "pop" discovery). After that they went to bed. Both felt, but did not say it, that the coming of electricity to Murston Lane, in defiance of all old Mrs. Unwin's fears and threats, had somehow dealt Mrs. Unwin such a blow that she could no longer be thought of as "away there, buried alone in Stamford," but at last as actually "dead, buried in Stamford." They arranged, without disagreement, to take Nelly within the next few days to the vet to be "put down."

42

We think we know the seasons by heart; perhaps we do; we've had them near and within us for long enough; we know the indignation of surprise when, entering the tropics, we find two seasons only which we've read about but have never entirely believed to exist. We enter people, too, and are indignant because they are not submitted to the divisions of our own rhythm of time, because they've found other laws that, dismaying to us, are part of their successful pattern of survival. It's as hard to be as people-minded as it is to be world-minded, to find, say, two seasons "filling the measure" of a man's environment and life, when Shakespeare has told us, and we have believed him, that there are four. And now the ice at the North Pole is melting, drifting south, we face a new Ice Age that confounds the prophecies of those who ever had time to talk, dream, write of inward and outward weather. Millions of years from now the Tree of Man may be found complete with its leaves to have been surprised within a world of ice.

The truly Adaptable Man is not only time-minded like Aisley, Alwyn, Russell, Greta, who believe that they have chosen their ideal climate of time; he is also place-minded, and may range the world—earth and space—to find the environment that he needs to grow and blossom in. Behind Vic's plan to go back to live in Australia, does there lie the reasoning of a man who is moving toward world-mindedness and who, being in this age white, not a criminal or a lunatic, is lucky enough to be able to choose his place? Why does he want to go there in the wilderness, in that terrible Down Under? the people of Little Burgelstatham keep asking. Then they tell one another of the English family who, equipping themselves for a weekend ramble from village to village in their summer-populated Lake District, set out from Darwin to walk south through the desert. Everyone knew what had become of them; the facts had been headlined in all the newspapers, including the *East Anglian*. One of the cuttings that

Bert carried about with him, though there was no Mrs. Unwin to show it to, told the story with photographs of the fateful expedition. It was clear to the villagers that once you emigrated to another land or hemisphere (even to another county or city, like London), the protective layers provided for you by the place of your birth and experience were torn away, you were exposed to dangers you had read about only in the newspapers; it was a ninety-to-one chance that you would be killed by disease or violence. They cited once more what had happend to Botti Julio coming so far from his own country merely to pick black currants: when could he not have picked black currants—or grapes, or tobacco—in his own country without running the risk of death? It was true that the Baldrys were not natives of Little Burgelstatham, but they had set up their home in the village, and Vic Baldry and his first wife had owned the White House long enough for him to have earned some of the protective privileges of natives. And now they were to leave, to go on a foolhardy expedition Down Under, to live and farm there—if they survived the snakes and the sharks and the desert.

Others said, Perhaps it was wiser to leave before the overspill came; now that the overspill was planned, there might be more chance of being killed in your own village.

The overspill. The overspill. It became a bogey more threatening than any medieval ghost; even the Reverend Pillow, who had exorcised many local ghosts, had to smile at the suggestion that he exorcise the overspill.

It was "progress," he said, the words coming strangely from an old man whose only Harvest congregation had been vegetables, three people, one dog, who slept side by side with his wife ignoring the dream of God, suffering the nightmare of twenty-three rooms accumulating dust. Progress. More factories, schools, work, money. Tydd New Town, its narrow muddy lanes widened into safe roads, its old damp cottages demolished. A wonderful plan, if there had been no people in Little Burgelstatham, Tydd, Lakenthorpe, Withigford, Murston.

People are often the last items to be included in Plans.

And now the children, too, played the new game of overspill.

"Here it comes!" they would cry, and in attitudes of defense, machine guns (*Gunsmoke City*) thrust against their bodies, they would face the imaginary pursuer, their guns describing a semi-circle in front of them, the bullet-noise *tt-t-t-t-t-tt rat-t-t-ttat—t* spluttering from between their teeth, while the overspill advanced unharmed.

"Can't touch me. I'm bullet-proof. I'm the overspill."

Then the enemy either vanished or became a turncoat, and no surge forward to take part in an old-fashioned fist-fight in which the enemy was never clearly identified, so that in the end everyone was fighting everyone else until a distraction of more interest and importance brought peace; there would be a jet, an American jet; earth-moving or ditch-digging machinery on its way to the Sapleys' farm; or the ice-cream man who toured the lanes in summer and most of winter enticing with his jingling tune, "*The Bells of St. Mary's, I hear them a-calling . . .*"

Then the enemy either vanished or became a turncoat, and no one cared—except the dog, for there was always a dog.

Meeting such a group of children in the lane one day on her return from posting a letter to Alwyn (and Jenny), Greta, whose child was expected in three weeks, felt her skin prickling with distaste at the spectacle of completely formed and born children playing, shouting, scuffling.

They're the farm manager's, she thought, assigning them to context. The two boys will stay at school until the leaving age, then they'll join the number of dark, secretive, stunted boys (called "lads" in the advertisements) who work in the fields from early morning till late at night. Their conversation will be unintelligible to strangers overhearing them. Give an example of "Synecdoche," "metonymy," quote battle speeches from Shakespeare; all that will be buried in their unopened books, but it will come out without their knowing it, and on Saturday evenings they will stand in groups, as their fathers do, staring into the disused village well at the scum, packets, papers thrown and floating there. But perhaps the overspill will change all this.

When Alwyn was home, Greta thought, he never played with the village children; or I never saw him.

She saw their curiosity, their stares, as she walked toward them.

"Hello, Mrs. Maude," someone said shyly.

How polite! Yet each one, Greta saw, had eyes sharp as flints that would cut and make fire if the children wanted it. She began to wish she could return home without passing them. Her feet hurt. She had a strong desire to sleep, but if she fell asleep here in the lane, the children would surround her, bind her with invisible bonds, walking miles from her head to her feet, from one side to the other, as if she were a mountain.

An absurd fantasy, she thought. I'd rather have spent the past months treating the fruit trees with Winter Wash than preparing for another human being, a child like one of these living synecdoches, metonymies, uttering their universal battle-cries. At my age . . .

But why had it all seemed so much like the fairytale—the mother dead, the son in grief, the children covered with leaves like fruit being protected from the frost? Peach-leaf curl. Botrytis. Thrip. Thunder fly. In the Glasshouse. In the Dwelling-place.

Soon the first lettuces will poke their two tiny leaves like tongues out of the earth.

"Old Mother Maude! Old Mother Maude!"

No children had ever called out to her in that way, and never would, in the country, for the country had a courtesy not found in the town, learned from the patterned lawful behavior of plants; but when the overspill came bringing London children with experience of so much power over their surroundings . . .

Perhaps Russell will move to London, Greta thought, dismissing her dream as soon as it appeared: a white house in a wide, tree-lined street, the trees with their black winter boles like charcoal drawings on gray paper, beautiful, until one remembered that the black was soot; but London; dignity preserved; Russell living at last in a warm, peopled world where ideas enjoyed forced growth out of season, where tomorrow sheltered those who thought and discussed them with the prestige of tomorrow; the well-known dentist; his fashionable wife; two prosperous sons. (Greta had not the energy to face the battle for survival which a daughter's birth would bring.)

Impatiently, not returning the shy smile of one of the children, she walked past the group in the lane. It would have to be Old Mother Maude, Old Mother Maude.

Old Mother Maude, she thought, and a concrete garden that grazes my hands when I try to get to it.

"Please when summer comes can we bag the nuts in your hedge?"

43 It was the night of the chandelier. The need for a party had diminished like a dying cyclone, and Muriel and Vic had invited the Maudes only (Russell, Greta, Aisley) for an evening meal. One by one the names on the guest list had been crossed out; the Sapleys were away on the Continent; the villagers would ask too many embarrassing questions about the trip to Australia.

"Isn't Australia a terrible place?" they would say. And Muriel would want so much to agree with them!

The television producer and his wife had not yet begun to spend weekends and holidays at their cottage. And what hope was there, Muriel thought, of going to the deserted cottage along the lane to surprise a real poet drinking claret on the lawn? Wherever the poets were living, it was not in Little Burgelstatham. As for Alwyn and Jenny Maude, they had deserted the district, they were living, aloofly romantic, in Spain. On the other hand, there were members of the W.I. who could have been invited to see the chandelier lit, but Muriel still found herself shy and awkward at the W.I. At times she was annoyed by the petty political emphasis; she enjoyed the craft classes (she had begun work on a tapestry of a hunting scene) and the competitions (many of which she won), but she could not follow the reasoning that baking a batch of date scones might put in power the local Conservative member who lived eleven months of the year in Hampstead.

The evening was cold enough for a fire. When the electricity had been installed at last, Vic had behaved for a time like a sulking child; he could not understand why the house should be as brightly lit as the pigsties; there was an absurd argument over the wattage of the bulbs, which Muriel had changed recklessly from dim forties to brilliant hundreds and hundred-and-fifties; in the end, however, Muriel won, for Vic remembered, showing the economical streak that almost became meanness, that they could use the bulbs when they went to Australia: the voltage would be the same. Muriel had so persuaded Vic that the lit chandelier would be one of the most wonderful sights they had known that he had engaged Olly Drew, Bert Whattling, and the only licensed builder who could be spared from seasonal work and overspill planning to make ready the ceiling of the living room to take the weight of the chandelier. And here was Vic this evening in sports clothes (bought in Australia) building a big log fire which, Muriel explained to him, would not only keep them and the guests warm but would cause the chandelier to make a pattern of dazzling light and shadow throughout the room.

The chandelier hung ready to be lit. Muriel had set the dining-room table beneath it, and as she moved around excitedly, nervously, putting dishes here, cutlery there, she felt that the house belonged to her at last, as if she had rid herself of all traces of memories of Anna as surely as if, in laying food upon the table for the celebration, she had laid also a special poison that memories would be attracted to and would feast on before they retired to their proper place, the past, to die. She knew that her problem in life now was Australia. Had she not been married before, had she and Vic surrounded their honeymoon with the usual expectations of intensity and bliss, forgetful of the balancing irritations and disagreeable discoveries, she might have been more concerned and unhappy at the thought that she was going with her husband on a life-long visit to his mistress. Vic had embraced a vast continent of mountain, desert, sea, gold (discovered or concealed)—Calgoorlie, Koolgardie, Calgoorlie, Koolgardie—had found satisfaction and riches in a piece of dead land where no matter how intently he listened he would never hear a heartbeat, nor would he be received by it as by a wife or a mistress. Oh, he might persuade himself that it warmed him, that people and trees growing in it were generated by his seed, that in time a few acres of it belonged to him; but it would be a land, not a woman, that cold, self-contained, would turn away from him in sleep, that would leave his house empty, dry, dark, that would be more ruthless in its plunder of his dreams than any wife with her permitted petty thefts.

If Vic had been a poet, Muriel thought, turning to her favorite memory, expecting it to give the usual comfort . . . This evening her trick of nostalgia did not seem to be working; instead of going there and back to a memorial lawn, she could stay in her own (her *own*) home, where the chandelier would be lit, where the room and the guests and she and Vic would receive part of the glorious dazzle of light. Perhaps, she thought, in my enthusiasm for the chandelier I have behaved like a woman who has taken a lover. Well, here was Vic, fetching and carrying for the fire, unselfishly providing the warmth, preparing, Godlike, to create the light. And now he was answering the knock at the door. Murmurs of disappointment. Oh. Hadn't he?

"Muriel!"

All pleasant and welcoming.

Greta and Aisley were the only guests. (Muriel remembered the time Greta and her clergyman brother-in-law came to look at the chandelier and found a rat's nest! And there was the time before when Greta gathered flowers in the lane, and Muriel drove her home. Muriel wished she had not confided in Greta about Vic and Australia.)

Greta explained that Russell had been working late. Confidentially, a new set of false teeth for a V.I.P. mayor? No. Councillor? No. Doctor? Well, who cared?

Greta saw Muriel's glance at her belly, the question in her eyes, the frown, momentary panic.

"It's all right, it's a fortnight yet, and I so much wanted to see the chandelier."

Muriel flushed with pleasure. "Did you?"

Her voice was soft and shy. I knew, she thought, that Greta Maude understood something, though we've never spoken of it. How small she is, even now! There's no bulk about her, only a tightness, a roundness, like leaf close to leaf on one of her well-loved cabbages. My forehead is smoother than hers. It doesn't seem quite nice for her husband to have chosen to make false teeth rather than to view my chandelier. I hope the Reverend Maude is not going to cough.

Aisley coughed, using the cough with the cunning of those

who realize the power of the body to speak more explicitly than words. The cough said, This is to remind you and me that I came to Little Burgelstatham to recover from quiescent tuberculosis, that I have stayed so long because it has taken so long to recover, that perhaps I am not yet ready to leave, that I still have this cough as an excuse to give to you and me, as the badge of an ailing clergyman.

"The nights are still cold," Muriel said sympathetically.

"You have to be careful," Vic said heartily, riding his sheep station.

Greta and Aisley took off their coats and followed Muriel into the dining room while Vic went outside for a moment, as a host will sometimes do, to scan the horizon (the Northern Territory) to seek reassurance from the primitive fear and desire that other guests will arrive—enemies, friends, strangers from a far country.

Vic came in, shutting the door carefully. His sense of adventure, unsatisfied in a way he could not explain, gave him a feeling of disappointment. He felt uneasy. He disliked more and more to be inside, he wanted to live in the wide-open spaces, he seemed to be finding it harder to breathe in England; something, not people, was using up the air and the space.

"I don't like it really," Muriel was saying, "but Vic says that when we get to Australia there'll be more space for them. I mean the calves and the poultry," she explained, as Vic came in.

"I was asking Mrs. Baldry about the methods of intensive farming," Aisley said. "I was talking to the Reverend Pillow on the bus; he tells me so many complaints have been received by the church. About the broiler houses, you know."

Not again, Vic thought.

"I'll see about the dinner," Muriel said, embarrassed, turning back to remind them, "When we sit down I'll switch on the chandelier."

"Oh, the chandelier!" Greta looked up at it, not knowing what to say. It was magnificent, of course, but she'd said that once before, and she could hardly keep saying it. When one was not of a literary turn of mind, one could not always find the words to comment on another's beloved chattels, whether they were jewels, washing machines, or Venini chandeliers. Looking at the chandelier, Greta felt a sense of peace and gratitude that someone in Little Burgelstatham *cared* about an object so beautiful and almost-useless, that would never kill thrip or thunder fly or peach-leaf curl, nor spin washing, dig drains, harvest wheat and barley, persuade hens that night was day and calves that there was no light. Greta could not explain her feeling of peace. The truth, perhaps, she thought, is that the chandelier does not belong to me, I have no desire to own it.

What fools they are, putting it up when they are emigrating soon. What expense, what wasteful expense. She frowned with an annoyance that she did not really feel.

She sighed. "It's beautiful," she said, immediately despising the naïve way in which Muriel seemed happy to be told that her chandelier was beautiful; she had not even expected an original or interesting remark.

"It reminds me," Aisley said, taking his place at the table and looking up at the ceiling, "of the great banquets in mead halls." He began to quote: " 'Whither has gone the giver of treasure? Whither has gone the place of feasting? Where are the joys of the hall? Alas, the bright cup! How that time has passed away, has grown dark under the shadow of night as if it had never been!' "

Greta allowed herself to smile a benevolent smile. Had Aisley lived in ancient times after all? It seemed as if, by returning to his Anglo-Saxon world, he might have achieved a victory that she, Russell, Vic, Muriel would never know in a battle they would never identify with weapons that were in part his personal re-sources and in part the shared army of Old English words that in camouflage still prowled the language and were recognized only by people like Aisley, who needed their help to struggle against their and his unfamiliar, hostile age.

Poor Aisley!

Greta smiled again to herself. Poor Aisley! So like Alwyn in his refusal to compromise with the times; with both it was all or nothing. She understood Alwyn's horror at having found himself trapped an afternoon within a fairytale, and his (and her) greater horror on learning that fairytales have consequences. Perhaps Aisley, living in his fairytale, would be set free to spend at least one afternoon in the age he had abandoned?

Muriel had been listening, enchanted, to Aisley's quotation. "Oh," she said, "do you really think so? A mead hall! A place of feasting. I've dreamed for so long about the chandelier and the time when there'd be enough light to do it full justice. Glass has a fascination. I've been reading . . . a little . . . Venice . . . gondolas and glass. I . . ."

Vic came in with the wine and began to pour it. Muriel had insisted on claret.

"I don't entirely disapprove," he said. "There's no room in this country to graze the amount of cattle or poultry that we need. We can't afford to have them free-running. This new boost of electricity, by the way, is going to do wonders for those who take over the White House Farm. People who are not farmers don't realize that we need light and power in the most unexpected places. Now, take Australia . . ."

Monotonously, persistently, he took Australia while Muriel served the food and the others listened to tales of a land that had so overwhelmed Vic that he could not yet separate its legend from its fact; he was in the mood for tall stories. Aided by the wine, his guests might have entered his mood had they not been, as Greta and Aisley were, so deeply concentrated within their own thoughts. Aisley was still in the Anglo-Saxon place of feasting; he was waiting for the chandelier to be lit. Had Muriel forgotten?

Dazed with mention of mead halls, of intensive farming, preoccupied with serving the food, Muriel had still not forgotten the chandelier; she had been waiting for the right moment, which had been delayed because, having no clear standard of "rightness," she let moment after moment pass.

She had begun her own meal. Suddenly she got up and switched off the wall lights, and when she, Vic, Greta, and Aisley had recovered from the blow of immediate darkness and could discern the outlines and mass of furniture and the rectangular window shape with the globes of trees like muscles of darkness beyond it, she went to the switch that would light the chandelier.

"I'm going to turn it on," she said.

Vic, determined to finish a remark that no one was listening to, said, "Anyone can see that the percentage there as compared to the percentage here . . ."

Someone laughed nervously. All sat with the relaxed expressions that come over people's faces in the dark, as if they were alone or asleep.

Muriel switched on the chandelier.

Aisley, still deep in his baronial feasting, showed his pleasure by looking up quickly at the myriad softly glowing bulbs and exclaiming with wonder. He had always thought of light as being red (ruby) or gold; he had not seen it, channeled into gray, like a stirred yet sparkling river flowing from the sun; it was as if the glass in each bulb had been ground from dust and mud, also from the gray of winter and its clouds, and the grayness that descended on human lives and their beliefs.

Aisley had no time for the habitual genuflection, prayer, apology. Greta, surprised, disappointed, Vic, with his practiced continent-commanding gaze, made their critical judgment of the chandelier, murmured their delight, then returned to their food and wine. Only Muriel, watching Aisley's face as he studied the chandelier, saw his expression change from delight to fear. This pleased her. Someone appreciates the awe-inspiring qualities. With an impulse of gratitude she leaned over the table to refill Aisley's glass, to remove his plate for a second helping, when she felt a blow on the back of her head, and as she lost consciousness she heard high-pitched screams, like cat-screams, she saw that the room was dark, and she felt Aisley's plate, full of broken glass, being wrenched from her hand.

44 "One can only conclude," the Tydd coroner remarked the following week, "that the weight of the chandelier, reputed to be that of a large car, was such that it was a miracle that anyone escaped death when the ceiling collapsed. We express our sympathy with the relatives and friends of the three dead, and we would ask the Society of Builders to be more careful in their supervision of those to whom they grant licenses."

Glancing around the courtroom, the coroner gave a slight, mournful smile that showed his new false teeth to advantage. He had chosen what he thought was a "lull" in local deaths to have his new teeth made; they had been finished just in time for what the newspapers were calling *The Chandelier Inquest*. It gave him an uncanny feeling to think that the local dentist whose wife and unborn child had died had worked late hours during the past week to finish the teeth of the man who would conduct the inquest, almost as if Russell Maude, by some ghoulish power, hoped to insert into the new teeth the words that would come from the coroner's mouth. Looking at Russell sitting alone in the back row, noting his placid face apparently unmarked by grief, the coroner felt his irrational fear and hate of dentists swell within him.

To spend his life with teeth! he thought contemptuously and unoriginally, for one or two members of the public were thinking similar thoughts. Russell Maude made the coroner's new teeth!

In Little Burgelstatham no part of anyone's body, however secret, was lost, broken, repaired, replaced, without someone gleaning the news, for the people of Little Burgelstatham were born and bred harvesters. When the overspill came and the sugar-beet fields were replaced by Council flats and the mounds of fresh dung by concrete excrescences, there would still be a harvest time, the growing, ripening, reaping, storing of people and their news . . .

272

Little Burgelstatham had been shocked by the tragedy, but had seemed to be equally shocked by the fact that the London newspapers reported it as they were in the habit of reporting disasters from Turkey or Persia—in small print at the bottom of the page, beside an advertisement for indigestion powder or petrol; though some of the villagers, hearing of this (for few read the London newspapers), understood that a chandelier tragedy in a village could not compete with the current ducal scandal. The older inhabitants linked the tragedy with the overspill, as if the overspill had been the instrument of it; others saw in it a warning of the perils of modernization (including electricity), of foreign merchandise and those who buy and try to display it; others read in it a sign of the imminence of universal doom. There was a silent feeling of sympathy for the bereaved, and special sympathy for Vic Baldry, who had had to put up with the whims of a chandelier-mad wife and who, it was said, would lie in the hospital or in bed unable to move for the rest of his life. He would need mirrors, they said, dwelling morbidly on the details, to see what went on around him, for he was completely paralyzed. They had taken him to a modern hospital in London, but later they would bring him back to the White House, and he would lie there in that big room, with a nurse caring for him day and night. There would be a huge mirror suspended above his face, and that would be his world, if he wanted a world after what had happened; but you were given the world whether or not you wanted it and in whatever shape or form it was presented to you, even if you had to live in it through a mirror, and in the very house where you had been struck down. It was said that the psychiatrists thought it better for Vic to come back home, to the scene of the crime, as it were; it would help him adapt, they said; other people had adapted to even worse conditions. Man was infinitely adaptable, they said, smiling, confident, encouraging.

As for those who had died—Greta Maude, Aisley Maude, Muriel Baldry—who had really known them? You need to know people to mourn for them. It is easier if they speak your language from the beginning and do not arrive in the dark from a foreign land.

Meanwhile, summer came with familiar ladywhite, briar rose, hogweed, harvest, summer tenants, and the unfamiliar overspill; and on the outskirts of Tydd the newly built bungalows and Council flats were prepared to receive their owners and tenants.

At first Russell stayed at home, pursuing his usual routine as if Greta were alive and Aisley still a guest in the house. Confronted with the burden of "things" that the dead make their chief legacy, Russell had not experienced the common bewilderment but had set about cataloguing, packing, and disposing of everything; he was surprised how easily he gained control of Greta's clothes and personal possessions once he had reduced them to a concentrated space. Before, when they had lain here and there (though not untidily, for Greta was always a tidy person), each possession had taken control of the space surrounding it, had beamed forth a power that was not limited by its shape and size—like a cat's eyes lighting and taking charge of the dark. Now, enclosed in suitcases, boxes, trunks, everything lay subdued, submissive, waiting to be sent to charities or relatives or to be put aside as memories. Russell knew that the village gossips were enjoying their feast with him and his family as the specialty of the time. The fascination of death and how the bereaved should be and are affected was endlessly interesting. Where are Russell Maude's son and daughter-in-law? the villagers were saying. Isn't it strange to go away like that to a foreign place, and no word, as if they've no roots anywhere, as if their loyalties were centered on new things, on things beyond ordinary comprehension and habit, not any more on home and family and village and country? What was happening to the world and its people? And here was Russell Maude making appointments for extractions and fillings, even with the new overspill people; and here he was getting the morning paper, coming home on the bus, as if nothing had happened; and there was no sign in his face, none that could be read by the most weather-wise gossip, that anything had happened to his wife and unborn child.

There seemed to be special indignation that Russell should still get the morning paper and ride home on the bus. Though they did not know what they expected him to do, they were alarmed by this pursuit of daily routine. You can't plow a field in thunder and lightning; you wait till the storm is over. You don't reap your harvest in winter. But what was the use of this argument? You did reap out of season now, and you sowed out of season. Why, even the hens had the lights in their houses burning day and night, like chandeliers, to deceive them into thinking they lived in perpetual daylight; and in the end it was no deceit at all, for it *was* perpetual daylight; so why shouldn't men work and play and smile and weep out of their season and time?

But—who decided the seasons? Who was the fixer and decider? You could tell that even old Reverend Pillow was bewildered by this problem, when surely he, of all people, should have known?

Russell catalogued and imprisoned the possessions of Greta and Aisley, but he could not control the influence of their death. For weeks he lived, borne along by their death, as if he were in an open boat in the middle of the sea. The force of their death had the effect of a gentle tide which made it seem to Russell, without oars, compass, destination, as if he controlled his own going; but that was not so, for his boat was no more seaworthy than other small boats, and after a few weeks of exposure to wind and weather and salt, the hull began to fall apart, and the sea—this sea of death that people had marveled to find so untroubling to Russell—swamped the boat with its breaking and entering. And then it was known that Russell Maude had moved house, had gone to live in a new bungalow in Tydd New Town (the competition to name the new town had not been successful; few entries were received, none, the judges thought, up to standard; only two or three names received the consolation prizes of a year's supply of frozen beans, peas, and fish-cakes, respectively).

Rumor said that Russell Maude became slightly unbalanced, that he made regular trips to London to visit the airport to look at the jets, and why should he do that if he was not crazy? He was never known to fly in one; he merely looked at them and returned to Tydd New Town. His methods remained out of

date, but he kept his skill and interest. Some said that, in a strange
way, he had grown to resemble his brother Aisley, as if at
Aisley's death, Russell had taken on the burden of being Aisley,
of solving Aisley's problems. He never talked of Aisley, nor of
Greta, but he had Bert Whattling plant and tend a fine garden in
the grounds of the bungalow. His few friends, his interests, were
the same, except that when Vic Baldry was brought back to the
White House and made comfortable by the London-trained
nurse (who reminded Russell of Greta when she was young),
Russell began to visit regularly, and it was Unity Foreman, still
writing in Cornstalk her "Letter from the Countryside, the
Charming Village of Burgelstatham," who made the remark
about the dentist and the paralyzed farmer, the two men with
mirrors, one with a tiny mirror to explore the hidden caves of the
human mouth, the other with a huge mirror in which he watched
the world go by, lying in an area of desert as vast as that which
he might have lived in had he returned to Australia.

Vic Baldry's view of the world was as perfect and smooth as
any view would ever be, although there was a star-shaped crack
on the right of the mirror (Vic's left) where the carriers had
damaged it. It was agreed that the flaw was too inconspicuous for
the mirror to be returned to the manufacturer, therefore it
stayed, and as Vic Baldry lay watching the world, everyone who
walked in the road outside the White House (beyond the roses)
had turns at occupying the break in the mirror: spattered, splin-
tered, starred with opaque glass, Bert Whattling cycled by; Lex
Unwin went to his work in the broiler factory (the milk-round
had been "centralized"; delivery was controlled from Tydd New
Town with a team of roundsmen from London—a special effort
was being made to help the people of the New Town to adapt to
their new way of life by finding them "country" jobs); the
mothers of Tydd New Town wheeled their new babies; and the
concrete mixers, bulldozers, arrived to prepare the foundations
for the supermarket. On a day when few people appeared in the
mirror, Vic Baldry, who could have strode alone across the unin-
habited desert of Central Australia, sank into depression; then,

even the sight of a little dog trotting along made him happy; and then he would hate the dog for its power to make him happy. And people who stopped to think about Vic and his appalling new life in Tydd New Town pronounced their judgment, as people like to do over the life and death of others: "He would be better if he were dead. No man can get used to such a life."

The marvel was, everyone said, that Vic Baldry had adapted himself to a smooth, weatherless world that he could not reach or touch—to living his life in a mirror.

But, imposing our own weather, our own limits of reach and touch, our own star-shaped irreparable flaw, don't we all live in mirrors, forever?